WILLPOWER

★

ANNA DURAND

*To Angela —
Congratulations!
Enjoy your prize.
Anna Durand*

Jacobsville Books

Lake Linden, Michigan
Toll-Free: 1-866-341-3705

Willpower
Copyright © 2013 by Lisa A. Shiel
First paperback edition 2014.
All rights reserved.

Cover photos copyright © iStockPhoto/StylePix/Lalo85
Used by permission.
Cover design by Lisa A. Shiel.

The characters and events in this book are fictional. No portion of this book may be copied, reproduced, or transmitted in any form or by any means, electronic or otherwise, including recording, photocopying, or inclusion in any information storage and retrieval system, without the express written permission of the publisher and author, except for brief exerpts quoted in published reviews.

ISBN: 978-1-934631-57-7 (pbk.)
ISBN: 978-1-934631-70-6 (e-book)
LCCN: 2014931743

Manufactured in the United States.

Jacobsville Books
www.JacobsvilleBooks.com
1-866-341-3705

Publisher's Cataloging-in-Publication Data

Durand, Anna.
   Willpower / Anna Durand.
     pages cm
   ISBN: 978-1-934631-57-7 (pbk.)
   ISBN: 978-1-934631-70-6 (e-book)
    1. Psychic ability—Fiction. 2. Amnesia—Fiction. 3. Family secrets—Fiction. 4. Love stories.   I. Title.
PS3604.U724 W85 2014
813—dc23

                                                    2014931743

Chapter One

The last tendrils of sunset spread out across the sky as the ten-year-old Pontiac Sunbird swerved into the driveway. The car's front bumper sideswiped a bush, spraying greenery over the hood.

Grace Powell gritted her teeth, her pale knuckles clamped around the steering wheel. She stared straight ahead, as if a taut string connected her eyes to the garage door. The glow of the headlights reflected off the big metal door. She squinted at the light. It pierced her vision like needles shoved straight through her eyeballs into her brain.

The car jerked to a stop inches from the garage. Grace uncurled her fingers from the steering wheel. Her head throbbed. Pains in her neck stabbed upward into the base of her skull. Christ. The migraine was getting worse. She shut off the engine. The headlights extinguished, bringing a blessed relief from the glare. She unhooked the seat belt. Her fingers slipped, and the retractor sucked the belt back into its housing with a *thwack* that made her wince. She eased the door open, dragged herself out and onto her feet, and then shut the door gently.

The garage stood attached to her home, a two-bedroom brick number with dirt-brown trim that matched the dirt-brown garage. A single light burned on the porch, next to the front door. Stains dotted the cracked strip of concrete that led from the driveway to the front door. The house squatted in the center of a one-acre lot, on the southern outskirts of Lassiter Falls, one of many Texas towns that hovered on the brink of becoming a city. A chain-link fence delineated the property.

Not that the property was hers. She rented the dump—okay, maybe dump was an exaggeration, though only slightly—because she couldn't afford anything else. Even apartments in this town cost more than her inconstant stream of income could handle.

Grace leaned against the car for a moment, enjoying the ever-deepening twilight, a respite from the knife-sharp headlights of other cars on the freeway and the sterile bulbs in the doctor's office. Her body ached from the hour-long drive back from Fort Worth. The trip had proved fruitless, netting her nothing but a burgeoning migraine and another visit to a specialist who could offer no explanation for her headaches—and no relief from them either. Doctors invariably asked questions she couldn't answer, then eyed her with a mixture of curiosity and pity as they offered excuses couched as possible explanations. Sure, the doctor today wrote her a prescription for some pills. She didn't bother to fill the prescription, though, because she knew the medication wouldn't work. Nothing worked.

The doctor had called her a "strange case." Comforting.

She rubbed the back of her neck, but the pain refused to relinquish its hold on her. With a heavy sigh, she pushed away from the car and trudged around its front bumper toward the concrete path.

The nape of her neck tingled. A current of frigid electricity rippled through her body. She froze mid step and listened for…something.

Someone is watching.

For months now, at odd moments, she'd felt a gaze fixated on her, trailing her movements, always hidden in shadows, hovering just beyond her comprehension. Of course, she dismissed the sensation as paranoia. Stress induced. Temporary.

The hairs all over her body stiffened.

A claw scratched at her shoulder from behind. She swung around, hands raised in defense, a shout lodged at the back of her throat.

A skinny, hunched man outstretched one bony hand. His fingers clawed at the spot her shoulder had occupied a second earlier. His brown eyes, wide and dilated, darted back and forth. A sheen of sweat glistened on his skin. His hair must've been trimmed with a chain saw, considering the way it stuck out in matted clumps. He looked as if he hadn't seen a shower in weeks, maybe months.

Grace scuffled backward.

The man stumbled forward.

"P-please," he said, the word punctuated with a burst of spittle. "Don't run. I need to talk. To you."

"You've got the wrong person."

"Grace Powell."

She ought to run inside, lock the door, and call the police. Instead, inching backward toward the front door, she asked, "What do you want?"

"Talk. To you. Please." He glanced over his shoulder and bit his lower lip, drawing a bead of blood. He dropped his voice to a hoarse whisper. "Inside. Hurry. They're coming."

"Who?"

"Inside. *Now.*"

She stared at the little scarecrow of a man as she edged closer to the door—and to escape. The scarecrow man was probably a druggie who got hold of some bad crack or crank or whatever people called it these days. With those pupils, dilated beyond the effect of darkness, he must've been high on something.

Think, Grace. What do you do when a drugged-out scarecrow wants to talk to you?

Damned if she knew.

Grace slipped a hand inside her purse and clasped her keys. Drawing them out behind her back with one hand, with the other hand she felt behind her for the door knob . The serrated ends of the keys poked out between her fingers. If forced to, she might use the keys as a weapon.

The scarecrow whimpered. "Please. They're getting closer. *In my brain.*"

His eyes bulged, as if they might pop loose from their sockets at any second. He panted and glanced around with jerky motions of his head.

"You wait here," Grace said. She closed her hand around the door knob. "I'll go inside and make sure they're not in the house."

She twisted the knob and shoved the door inward.

"No!" he screeched. "No!"

He rushed at her, his arms flailing. Spittle sprayed from his mouth as he sputtered objections at her, nonsensical phrases peppered with the words "no" and "please." She slashed at him with the keys and felt the metal catch on his cheeks. Blood oozed from the cuts, dribbling down his cheek into his mouth.

He clutched her elbow.

Wrenching her arm free, she threw herself backward through the doorway. Her shoelace snagged on the jamb. Her legs flipped out from under her. When her tailbone smacked into the floor, a lacework of pain fanned out through her hips and legs.

The scarecrow lunged at her.

She kicked at the door. Just as it banged shut, the scarecrow hit it with his full weight. The wood trembled. His cry, muted by the door, sounded more like the wail of a dying animal than the ranting of a madman.

Grace sprang to her feet. She flung herself at the door. Her fingers closed around the dead bolt and, fumbling to move it, she finally shoved the lock into place.

Aftershocks shook her entire body. Her tailbone smarted. Her heart pounded fast and hard, in syncopation with her gasps. Outside, the scarecrow wailed.

"They want your mind!"

Despite the thick wood separating them, his cry vibrated her eardrums with an intensity that rattled her brain.

Abruptly, silence descended.

She stood immobile, the keys still clenched between her fingers, the metal digging into her skin. The door knob jiggled. Fingernails scraped at bricks. An image flashed in her mind's eye—the dead, risen from their graves, scrabbling to get inside the mortuary. In the vision, the mortuary bore an uncanny resemblance to her house.

Scratch-scratch. Jiggle-jiggle. Scratch. Jiggle.

Silence. The dead had returned to their graves.

Her heart knocked against her rib cage, wanting out of her chest as badly as the scarecrow had wanted to get inside the house. She took a slow, deep breath. For a long moment, she stood there propped against the door, her entire body shaking. She was afraid to move, to make a sound, to think about what had happened.

Maybe the scarecrow had left.

She needed to know for sure.

Cautiously, she settled her forehead against the door, above the peephole. Her eye lined up with the hole. The scarecrow's face, distorted by the lens, filled her view. His eyes glimmered green.

Weren't his eyes brown before?

In the half cone of light created by the porch bulb, she might've mistaken brown for green. Hell, she might've mistaken up for down when the scarecrow jumped her.

He leaned forward, his green eye staring back at her through the hole as if he saw her. She swallowed against the tightness in her throat. The shimmering of his eyes was...preternatural.

His body convulsed. He squinted and chewed his lip, oblivious of the blood trickling down his chin. His eyes glistened.

Was he crying?

His body convulsed again. In the wake of the tremor, he stilled and tensed his body. All expression vacated his face. Maybe the drugs had worn off.

Without a sound, seemingly in slow motion, he hurled himself at the door. The concussion slammed her forehead into the wood. She stumbled backward and lost her balance. For the second time tonight, her buttocks hit the floor hard.

She shouted a wordless cry of pain.

Footsteps clapped outside, fading as the scarecrow fled the vicinity.

And just like that, it was over.

Chapter Two

She sat on the floor, stunned. Though her tailbone smarted, the pain began to lessen. At first her body seemed to have turned to stone, and she couldn't make her muscles move, but soon that sensation also diminished. Her pulse calmed, beat by beat, as she took slow breaths. With every second that ticked past, her body eased back into its usual state. Now if the rest of her would follow, she could pretend to feel like a normal person.

Hauling herself onto her feet, shuffling to the door, Grace peeked through the peephole. The scarecrow was gone. What he wanted, why he picked her—those questions would remain unanswered, unless the lunatic returned later to explain himself.

Right before he ripped her heart out barehanded and tossed it onto a barbecue grill.

Leaning against the door, she closed her eyes. It was over. She relaxed against the door. Whatever the scarecrow man wanted, he'd given up on getting it, at least for the moment. He wouldn't come back.

She hoped.

Every hair on her body prickled. She felt something nearby, like a magnet pulling at the atoms of her body. Her chest tightened. The air seemed to push against her, simultaneously compressing her chest and trapping the breath inside her. She willed her eyelids to part.

A man stood across the room from her, near the kitchen doorway. He held his arms at his sides, his head tilted to the left. This man was not the crazy scarecrow. No, this man watched her with a steady gaze, his blue eyes studying her face and then examining her body. His gaze felt neither sexual nor threatening, more curious than alarming. The irises of his eyes glowed like sapphires lit from behind. A breeze ruffled his blonde hair. Somehow, she knew he meant her no harm.

Crazy. He must've broken into the house. She ought to scream for help. She blurted out, "What do you want?"

His gaze settled on her face. Standing there as still as a boulder, he scrutinized her with unblinking eyes. Grace heard a car speed past on the street and peripherally saw its headlights slash through the interior of the house. Her focus stayed locked on the strange man, who kept on watching her. His blue eyes seemed to catch fire in the flare of headlights.

"Who are you?" she asked.

He ducked around the corner into the kitchen.

A gale tore through the house. Her hair whipped against her face. The gust whisked a newspaper off the coffee table and fluttered it in the air before releasing it to settle onto the floor.

Grace rushed into the kitchen. If the man came in through a window, it would explain both the wind and how he got inside the house. No one was in the kitchen. The window above the sink was shut. She spotted the window's lock, which was engaged. Moving to the back door, she twisted the knob. The lock resisted.

She searched the house room by room. Every closet, every nook, and every dark hole became a threat, a possible hideaway for the intruder, even the foot-high space under her bed. All windows were shut and locked, from the inside. Since the back and front doors were also locked, with dead bolts, the man could not have slipped in through any window or door. How did he enter the house?

Grace spun around. Behind her, the door to her bedroom hung open. In front of her, the hallway stretched into darkness. She hadn't dared turn on any lights during her search. Now the shadows loomed all around, grasping at her with claws of darkness and spitting shadow flames from their nostrils.

Call the police.

Her inner voice virtually screamed at her. But the man might still lurk in the house, perhaps trailing behind her to hide where she'd already looked. The idea sounded ridiculous. Yet the man broke into the house without cracking a window or jimmying a lock. Anything seemed possible. She needed to call for help.

The house had one phone. In the kitchen.

Between here and the kitchen lurked phantoms of every shape and size, plus one very real monster.

"Dammit," she muttered.

Grace bolted down the hallway.

In the kitchen, the overhead light vanquished the phantoms. No intruder awaited her. Nothing lurked there except air and light and the telephone. She snatched the cordless phone from its base and, fingers trembling, and 911.

When the operator answered, Grace's voice failed her. Yet when she did speak, her tone sounded calm, almost confident, despite the temblors in her limbs and the typhoon raging in her gut.

"Send the police," she said. "There's an intruder in my house."

The deputy aimed his best look of concern and pity at Grace, with a hint of irritation creasing the skin around his eyes. Grace slumped in the recliner across the coffee table from the sofa. With her foot, she rocked the chair in a ferocious rhythm.

The night had gotten worse. An intruder, she thought, must be the worst that could happen tonight. Then the deputy arrived and her day sank deeper into the cosmic toilet.

The sheriff's deputy, Reilly Skidmore, knew her. She had a vague recollection of him—of being ignored and taunted by him and his clique, the Super Nerds, guys too smart to speak to anyone who hadn't discovered a new protein by his fifteenth birthday. Back then, Reilly wore eyeglasses thicker than the arctic permafrost. Tonight he sported no glasses. And his skin had cleared up.

He did, however, retain that certain quality that made her want to deck him.

"About this intruder," Reilly said, "are you sure it wasn't the same guy who jumped you outside?"

"Positive."

"Maybe your eyes were playin' tricks on you," Reilly said. "Stress can affect a person in funny ways."

His Texas drawl oozed like molasses, slowing down some words and truncating others. Despite having lived in Texas since high school, Grace had never adopted the drawl and, thus, never quite fit in with the natives. Even if she'd consciously tried to sound Texan, she still would never fit in here. She didn't fit in anywhere, actually.

"I did not imagine it," she said, struggling to keep the anger out of her voice. "And there's nothing funny about confronting an intruder."

"Okay, okay. See, it's just that I didn't find any footprints other than yours and the first guy's. But those tracks don't prove anybody attacked you, only that someone was around. There's no sign of a break-in either."

She squinted at him. Tonight his Texas twang irked her for some reason, though it never had before. Every time Reilly spoke, his voice awakened a chorus of imaginary fingernails scraping across a blackboard in her mind. She found herself gritting her teeth and rocking the recliner even harder. The chair's base lifted off the floor slightly with each push backward, smacking down again with the forward motion.

"Maybe it was a black panther," Reilly said with a smirk. "Guy last week claimed one of them killed his cat. Turned out it was a black Rottweiler."

Grace huffed out a breath. "So I'm either crazy or stupid."

"That ain't it at all. I'm sayin' eyes can play tricks on us."

She glared at the wall. The conversation had spun in tornadic circles for twenty minutes. *You're crazy. No, I'm not. Yes, you are.* Reilly had searched the interior and exterior of the house, questioned neighbors on both sides of the street, interrogated Grace, and resolved nothing.

She was crazy. End of investigation.

"I'll keep an eye out for the guy who jumped you," Reilly said. "But I reckon he's long gone."

She wondered how Reilly became a cop. In high school, he bragged about winning a scholarship to Harvard, or maybe it was Stanford. Ivy Leaguers didn't generally wind up as sheriff's deputies. Of course, Reilly never boasted a perfect GPA, and didn't graduate at the top of their class. Neither did she, but her grades were solid throughout high school and college. Even after her parents moved away for their jobs, and Grace stayed behind alone to finish her degree, she still maintained a decent GPA.

Yet somehow she ended up barely scraping by as a book designer. Her dreams of becoming a teacher were dashed by budget crises at schools across the country, so her teaching certificate hung in the bathroom as a piece of abstract art. Thereafter, she retrained herself in book design and—after discovering no established firms would hire an inexperienced, unknown designer—she set out into the desert of self-employment. Oases were few and far between.

The point was, she understood how people wound up in jobs that bore no resemblance to their schoolyard dreams. So she ought not think less of Reilly because his plans didn't pan out either.

Reilly rose and clomped around the sofa to the front door. Grace followed, opening the door for him. As he pushed past her, Reilly shoved a business card into her palm.

"Anything happens," he said, "call me."

She noticed he didn't say if anything *else* happened. Clearly, the man assumed nothing really happened tonight. A weirdo accosted her. By Reilly's logic, the guy was probably a homeless man who meant no harm. Nothing worth fretting over. Although Reilly might not have said those precise words, Grace felt them bobbing just below the surface of their conversation tonight.

She took the business card. "Thanks."

With a curt nod, Reilly strode out the door. As Grace lingered in the doorway, watching him cross the lawn, a breeze kissed her face. The warmth of the breeze hinted at the summer heat that would set in shortly. This was April in Texas, after all.

Reilly climbed into his cruiser and drove away. The taillights of his cruiser receded until they vanished altogether. Grace shut the door, snapping the dead

bolt into place. She yawned. The action seemed to breach the dam that held back a deep reservoir of exhaustion. The fatigue flooded through her, carrying with it a chill that penetrated her to the core.

Today had really, really sucked. Strangely, though, the events of this evening served to extinguish her migraine. She couldn't recall exactly when the symptoms dissipated, but she thanked heaven they had. She could do without another brain-crushing, nausea-inducing headache.

On her way to the bedroom, she stopped off in the kitchen to double check that the overhead light was off and that the back door was locked. Once inside the bedroom, she eased the door shut and engaged the lock. Hiding behind a closed door alleviated the tension in her gut, though she had no idea what she was hiding from or how a door might protect her from an intruder who apparently wielded magical powers. Sometime between calling 911 and seeing Reilly's cruiser pull into the driveway, she realized that something important—and indeed magical—had happened to her. Not sweet, fairy-tale magical. Demonic, terrifying magical. The idea was ridiculous. Still, in her gut she felt the truth of her revelation.

She'd experienced a life-altering event. She glimpsed the Other World that existed within this reality, the world of ghosts and demons and supernatural forces.

Maybe she ascribed too much value to the incident. She might have, as Reilly suggested, suffered a stress-induced hallucination or a bizarre kind of mirage. The stranger she confronted inside the house never spoke or touched her. Maybe she did imagine it.

Sure, and maybe she suffered a narcoleptic seizure, dreaming the whole thing while remaining upright through some quirk of gravity.

Grace flopped onto the bed. All the windows were locked, the back door too. The intruder snuck into the house, and out of it again, without using doors or windows. Maybe he teleported himself, like in a science fiction movie. Maybe he was a ghost. She believed in neither ghosts nor teleportation.

Yet she believed the incident was magical. The intruder got inside somehow.

Unless she imagined him.

A chill shimmied up her spine. If she could imagine an event that seemed real, if she could give in to a hallucination so completely, she must have lost all sense of reality.

She must've gone insane.

Oh yeah. Today really, really, *really* sucked.

Chapter Three

Lying on her bed, Grace gazed up at the ceiling, not really seeing the ceiling, not really seeing anything. She replayed the events in her mind. Nothing made sense. A scarecrow accosted her. An intruder broke into the house, as if by magic. The scarecrow man she understood. The world hosted many psychos who needed no reason to torment another person. They did it for drug money. They did it for fun. They did it to satisfy the voices in their heads.

But she saw no rational explanation for the intruder.

Well, one explanation did fit. The last tether between her mind and reality might've snapped. She might've begun to hallucinate. Maybe the stress of her medical situation affected her more than she wanted to admit. Self-employment brought its own stresses, as she struggled to stay afloat in a sinking economy. Working as a freelance book designer gave her freedom, but it also meant she never knew how much money she'd make in a given month. Her inconstant stream of income meant she couldn't afford health insurance. She paid for her doctor visits and prescriptions out of her own pocket. Those doctor visits had become more frequent in the past few months. Three times in as many weeks, she found herself squirming in an uncomfortable chair waiting for a nurse to call her name.

Yeah, she had some stress.

In retrospect, calling the cops tonight was a bad idea. She had no one else to call. Her parents and grandfather, the only family she knew in her whole life, were gone. She'd lived away from them for six years, but to lose them completely, to have them ripped from her life forever…

She was alone.

So when a weirdo assaulted her and a shadow man invaded her home, she had no one to call but the authorities. It was still a bad idea. Now someone she sort of knew from years ago, someone who currently worked in law enforcement, thought she was a total whackjob. Other people's opinions meant little to her. The opinion of a sheriff's deputy might matter, however, if she ever needed real help. Worse, she recalled that back in high school Reilly liked to gossip. Thanks to her failure to think ahead, soon every cop in North Texas might know about the crazy girl in Lassiter Falls who imagined intruders. At least the footprints out front proved a real person assaulted her. Of course, as Reilly pointed out, the footprints didn't prove the man actually attacked her. They showed simply that a person other than Grace approached the house.

She was on her way to becoming the Lassiter Falls loon. One more check mark in the screw-up column.

Tears welled in her eyes. She touched the corner of one eye, feeling the warm tears dribble down her finger. Crying signified weakness, self-pity, all the things she loathed. Crying flashed her back to her school days—standing in front of the class, afraid to speak, the teacher ordering her to read aloud, tears spilling down her cheeks. Crying led swiftly to humiliation. Squeezing her eyes shut, she willed the tears away. Her eyes burned as the tears overflowed, faster now.

The curtains billowed. The door rattled against the jamb. A breeze tousled her hair. She glanced at the window. Closed. Locked. Down the hall, the air conditioner clicked off and silence pervaded the house.

The curtains rippled. The breeze whispered in her ear.

I'm not alone. The thought exploded in her mind. The tingling she'd experienced earlier resurfaced, stronger and sharper this time.

The air grew heavy and dense around her, as if she sat on the bottom of a deep swimming pool. She gulped in breaths, her chest aching from the effort. Air, she needed air. Leaning forward, she struggled to unlock the window. Her fingers slipped. The latch scraped her knuckles. She fought to breathe. The pressure of a hundred hands pressed against her chest, while the air congealed in her lungs. Darkness flickered at the edges of her vision.

The door burst inward.

Air rushed into the room. She collapsed on the bed, sucking in the air, her entire body shaking.

In an instant, the air felt normal again. She pushed up off the bed. Her muscles quivered as she scuffled to the door. The jamb had splintered where the lock fit into its slot. Fragments of wood littered the carpet. The door itself had warped inward at the center. She touched the distorted wood. The damage proved something happened in the bedroom. She didn't hallucinate this time.

Unless she was still in the grips of a delusion.

No, she could *not* be that far-gone.

When she tried to shut the door, it refused to latch. The bulge at the door's center distorted the whole thing so much that the door would not fit in its frame anymore. Replacing the door meant incurring another expense. Terrific.

Grace shambled to the bed and crawled under the sheets, rolling onto her side as she pulled the sheet up to her chin. Sleep wouldn't come, she accepted that fact. She thanked God for it actually. Sleep meant dreams, and so she prayed for insomnia.

Sleep came for her anyway.

A corridor. Beige walls. Twilight. Red pinpoints of light line the corridor at floor level. A bland voice speaks from nowhere and everywhere.

"Night mode on."

Further down the corridor, on her right, she spots a familiar door. Her heart skips a beat. Her stomach flutters. A force seems to draw her toward the door. One scuffling step at a time, she crosses the corridor.

Voices approach from somewhere beyond sight. Footsteps clap. She freezes. Her gaze lands on the shape reflected in the mirror-like floor. She stares at her own reflection, entranced by the shimmering image of her face, pale and indistinct.

Footfalls draw her attention to the corridor ahead of her. Two men are advancing toward her. She glances around for a place to hide, but she knows the doors are locked.

The men walk past, oblivious of her, chattering to each other.

"That's right, man, crazy."

"Think he'll do it?"

"No way."

"Escapees should get the harsh stuff."

"I agree, but..."

Their voices diminish as they disappear into the twilight of the corridor's depths.

She waits. Listens. He is calling to her, not with his voice, but rather with his soul. She inches closer to the familiar door. Why does she sneak when they can't see her? Shaking off the question, she settles her hand on the door knob.

The corridor vanishes. Now she floats in empty space, surrounded by stars. With one hand she reaches out to the stars, stretching a fingertip toward one in particular. The one that calls to her. His star.

The light explodes, engulfing her in blinding brightness and scorching heat.

Sand. Cold. Noises. Darkness blankets her. Nearby but out of sight, a snake hisses. Coyotes howl from far away. Dirt invades her mouth and nostrils. Grit burns in her eyes. She lies facedown on the ground.

Raising onto her knees, she gazes up at the sky. Stars glimmer there. The moon smiles down at her. She senses its presence drawing nearer and watches its mottled face swell. The light glows pure white, infusing her with a sense of familiarity.

The night spins around her. She grabs a bush, fighting to keep her balance. Thorns slice across her palm. She feels a warm liquid oozing across her flesh. Blood.

A figure rises out of the sand. A hand reaches out for her. Green eyes gleam.

"There you are," says the figure, though not in words, in thoughts.

Hot fingers clutch her arm. Sear skin. Tear at flesh.

Pain rips through her.

Grace woke with a jerk. For a minute, maybe longer, she held still and listened to the metronome of her heartbeat. Thump-thump. Thump-thump. Quick, but slowing with each exhalation. A powerful ache throbbed behind her temples. The darkness around her seemed alien. She squinted as she struggled to discern shades and contours. Where was she?

In bed. Of course.

Her left palm burned. She explored the flesh with one finger, gently prodding at the sore spot. A warm wetness coated her fingertip.

Blood.

She floundered for the lamp on the bedside table. Her finger bumped the switch and she twisted it. Light cascaded over her. She winced at the sudden brilliance, at the pain that stabbed through her eyes into her brain. The throbbing worsened into a pressure that spread from her temples to her forehead, into her jaw joints, and behind her eyes. Nausea welled up in her gut as a wave of dizziness overtook her.

She clutched at the sheets and stared at a small stain on the ceiling until the dizziness abated.

The migraine had returned, stronger than before. Though she let go of the sheets, she lay motionless for several minutes, until the nausea subsided too. Then, slowly, she pushed up onto her elbows. When that seemed all right, she dared to sit up. The light hurt her eyes, and she winced yet again. With her eyes half closed, she slid off the bed and stumbled across the room to her dresser. In the top drawer, she found a scarf made of thin fabric. Back at the bed, she draped the scarf over the lampshade to dim the light. Only then did she settle onto the bed again, flat on her back.

Even if she hadn't suffered a migraine earlier today, she would've experienced one now. Every time she had the dream about the strange twilight corridor, she woke up with a migraine. In the dream, a certain doorway always beckoned her to enter, or at least it felt that way. This time, her dream self left the corridor before entering the room. Most often, she did enter the room. After awakening, she never could recall what happened inside the room.

Occasionally when she had the dream, she sleepwalked. She might wake in the morning to find her lamp on when she knew she turned it off before going to sleep. Once, she awakened to find her handgun lying on her stomach. For a terrified moment, she imagined that in her sleepwalking state she'd killed someone. Quickly, though, she realized the illogic of that idea. If she killed someone, surely the police would've caught her. At least that was what she told herself. She kept the gun in her dresser, which meant she need not sleepwalk very far to retrieve it. The dream that night had been frightening, though the details of it quickly blurred upon waking.

She lifted her hand to study her palm in the muted lamplight. Dried blood outlined a cut two inches long.

A cut. Like in the dream.

Ridiculous.

She made her way to the bathroom, homing in on the glow of the nightlight plugged into an outlet above the sink. Leaving the overhead light off, she searched the medicine cabinet for a box of adhesive bandages. Once she found the box, she applied a dab of antibiotic ointment to the cut and covered it with a small bandage.

Back in the bedroom, she changed into a cotton nightshirt and crawled under the sheets. The haze of sleep clouded her mind. In the morning, she might find the cut had been a dream too, vivid as hell, but just a dream. Maybe she was still dreaming.

Her mind drifted into slumber.

Just a dream...

Chapter Four

When her clock radio buzzed at 7:45 the next morning, Grace hit the snooze button. Twice. Dreams, not exactly nightmares but disturbing anyhow, fractured her sleep. She fought to stay awake, yet always succumbed to slumber. And the dreams. They couldn't have been weirder or more disturbing if Salvador Dali designed them.

Her jaw felt tight, her eyes grainy. Post-nausea hunger growled in her gut. She'd forgotten about the migraine. By a miracle or a quirk of biology, she fell asleep again while the headache raged. She wanted to stay in bed, wrapped in her cocoon of blankets, free from thoughts of last night. If she could just escape the dreams. She had to get up, of course, and face life. Face the scarecrow man, and the ghost man, and the Vincent Price movie her life had become.

Her eyelids grew heavy. She drifted back into sleep.

A sharp knock at the door jolted her awake.

Grace rolled out of bed and onto her feet before she realized the knock came from the bedroom door, not the front door of the house. What the hell? As she blinked the sleep out of her eyes, she stumbled to the bedroom door which, warped from the previous night's weirdness, couldn't latch properly.

The door crept open a few inches.

Grace froze. Her pulse quickened. She glanced at the dresser, trying to gauge whether she might reach the gun in the top drawer before an attacker surged through the door at her.

Silence reigned, save for the thudding of her heart. The door did not move.

She leaned sideways to peer through the gap between the door and the jamb. The hallway looked empty. Grace tiptoed to the door, grasped the knob, and thrust the door wide open.

Empty space greeted her.

The warped door had probably drifted open on its own. She let paranoia get the best of her, a bad habit she seemed to have developed lately.

She retreated into the bedroom. After changing into jeans and a T-shirt, she wandered into the bathroom. Fatigue hung over her like a heavy cloak. When she examined herself in the bathroom mirror, her malaise mutated into disgust. Her hazel eyes were bloodshot. Her dark auburn hair, foregoing its usual curls, hung in greasy strands around her face. She slid her hands through her hair but the action served only to exacerbate the problem. A shower would help with the hair, but as for the rest of her body and mind, it would take bathing in bleach to cleanse the mildew.

She had transmuted into walking mold. Algae with a skeleton. So long had she languished in financial and emotional limbo that her soul moldered and became encrusted with gook. Now the yuck inside was showing on the surface—in the tangles her hair had woven itself into, in the pallor of her skin, in the frown that nestled into a permanent home on her lips. She looked like hell, which seemed appropriate, since she felt like she'd moved into a basement apartment in the nether regions.

Twisting the faucet on, she grabbed her toothbrush. Though she couldn't eradicate the spiritual mold in five minutes, she might at least look clean. Gazing into the sink drain, she scrubbed at her teeth.

A shape flashed in the mirror. She lifted her head to look.

He hovered behind her, silent, unmoving. The intruder who snuck into the house without breaking a window. The magical shadow man.

Their reflected gazes met. He stepped back, gesturing with one hand, confusion flickering on his face. She whirled to confront him.

The empty shower stall gaped back at her.

A gale swept through the bathroom. The roll of toilet paper flapped in its holder. Towels undulated on the rack beside the shower. Her hair lashed against her face.

She must've imagined seeing the intruder. The stress of everything triggered yet another hallucination. She needed to relax. No one had been there. The wind came from…the air conditioner, a window, or a freak indoor vortex. She was grasping at shadows, desperate to accept any answer, to grab hold of anything that might explain what she witnessed.

To hell with logic. A phantom man was not logical.

Out the corner of her eye, she glimpsed the closed window.

A coldness burrowed in her belly. Wind did not erupt in a closed room. Well, if she accidentally tripped a circuit in the universe that opened the

doorway to the beyond, anything could and would happen. Wind without source. Men who vanished. Air vacuumed out of a room.

If a huge rabbit bounded into the house and slapped a wet kiss on her, she'd commit herself to the nearest hospital. Until then, she would deal with her new reality. Make that *sur*reality.

Or plain old insanity.

She gave up on showering, settling for rinsing her hair in the sink. Two voices shouted inside her head—one warning of impending lunacy, the other urging her to give in to the new reality. The first voice grew louder, until she no longer heard the second. Its litany about the Other World became a memory, a paranoia to which she'd almost succumbed. Almost. There was no magic. No secret world. She hallucinated the intruder, both last night and this morning. The rest was remnants of nightmares. She suffered from an excess of stress, nothing more.

Yet the intruder was familiar to her. Oh sure, she knew him. He was *her* hallucination after all. Of course she recognized him, from her delusions and crazed dreams.

The dream.

She turned her hand upside-down, exposing the bandage that veiled her palm. Ripping off the bandage and tossing it onto the counter, she touched the skin. Not a scratch, not even a pinprick, scarred her palm. What did she expect, a gaping wound? From a dream? She remembered seeing a cut on her palm last night. That's why she bandaged her hand. This morning the cut was gone. She must've dreamed the injury too.

A spot of color on the counter drew her attention to the discarded bandage. A maroon blotch stained it. She reached out for the bandage. Her finger grazed it. She yanked her hand back and cradled it against her body.

Blood. The gauze was bloody.

Preserve the evidence, a voice in her urged. She jogged to the kitchen, where she retrieved a sandwich bag from the cupboard. Back in the bathroom, she tucked the blood-stained bandage into the bag, sealed the zipper lock, and stuffed the bag into the pocket of her jeans. Crazy, saving a bloody bandage. The blood had meaning, though, a significance she could not yet grasp.

Save the bandage, the inner voice urged.

So she did.

Chapter Five

Grace wandered into the kitchen. Normally, she'd pop a bowl of oatmeal into the microwave for breakfast. The post-nausea hunger still growled, but the idea of putting food in her mouth appealed to her about as much as swilling antifreeze.

A toaster pastry, stale and washed down with root beer, sufficed.

A rapping at the front door interrupted her last bite of pastry. Tossing the empty can of pop in the trash, she hurried to the door and squinted through the peephole. A man with gray-flecked chestnut hair stood on the porch, adjusting his navy tie which matched his navy suit. His white shirt looked crisp and unwrinkled. Reflective sunglasses shielded his eyes.

His tongue darted across his lips.

Grace opened the door a few inches, enough to poke her head into the gap. The man was of average height, with a trim physique fleshed out with muscles. He smelled of something stale and vaguely unpleasant, an odor she couldn't quite identify. A scar slashed across the right side of his neck, below the ear. His eyes, dark as coffee, locked on hers. His wide, thick lips parted into a smile. A subtle undercurrent in his presence unsettled her, like the flush of cold air when a ghost passed through a room.

"May I help you?" she asked.

"You must be Grace," he said. "Deputy Skidmore gave me your name."

She eyed him warily. No drawl colored his baritone voice, and he spoke in precisely articulated syllables. His jacket bulged under the left breast, a small lump that might indicate a cell phone or a day planner. Or a gun.

Christ, she'd gotten so paranoid.

He reaffirmed his smile. "Is everything all right?"

Trouble. The word echoed in her mind. Yet he looked harmless—a little too harmless.

"How may I help you?" she asked again, keeping the door wedged between the two of them.

"It's about the man who approached you last night." He lunged a hand through the doorway. "I'm Henry Winston, by the way."

She shook his hand. His skin was warm, almost feverish.

"What man?" she asked.

"The lost soul who approached you outside this house last night." Winston adopted a solemn expression. "It's a matter of some delicacy. May I come in?"

"No," she said, and guilt flushed her cheeks. If Reilly sent this man, then the matter he wished to discuss must bear some relation to her ordeal last night. This man might offer her a few answers. She ought to invite him inside, but that odd undercurrent within him set her nerves on edge.

Winston removed his sunglasses, tucking them in the inside pocket of his suit jacket. "I understand. A woman alone at home, a stranger at the door, and so forth."

She stared at the crown of his head. The hairs, short and thinning, poked up like fresh-cut grass, with Old Spice substituted for the aroma of turf. The cologne failed to mask the other, stale odor. She estimated his age as late forties.

Twice in their brief conversation Henry Winston had referred to "the man who approached" her, as if the incident involved nothing more sinister than a handshake. Winston's phrasing irritated her, but she supposed he was trying to be diplomatic. If he knew anything about the scarecrow man, the information might help her understand why the freak accosted her.

Ignoring the unsettled feeling in her gut, she swung the door open. "Come on in."

Winston strode past her, swerving left into the living room. He glanced at the sofa, and then opted to settle into the armchair across from it. He propped one ankle atop the other knee. Linking his hands over his abdomen, he gazed at Grace with a neutral expression.

She lowered herself onto the sofa, perched on its edge. Her hands she dropped to her sides, with the fingers tucked under her legs. Winston swept his gaze over her entire body, as if assessing a racehorse before making an offer to purchase the animal.

"What's this about?" Grace asked.

"The man you encountered last night. His name is Adam Hansen, and he escaped from a private clinic outside Dallas several days ago. I'm his psychiatrist." Winston stretched his arms out, one on each arm of the chair. "I need to find Mr. Hansen before he harms himself or someone else."

She waited for him to continue, but a long silence ensued. Finally, she asked, "What does this have to do with me?"

"I hoped you might be able to provide some clues as to his whereabouts."

"Sorry." She hunched her shoulders. "He babbled nonsense and then he left. I didn't ask for a forwarding address."

"What precisely did he say to you?"

Memories flashed through her mind. The creepy little man lunging at her. His claw-like fingers scratching at her. His voice, hoarse and fraught with anxiety.

They want your mind.

Her throat tightened. She swallowed against the constriction, focusing on Henry Winston. He watched her—and waited.

"Um..." She floundered for a believable lie, because she certainly would not tell Winston the truth. "I don't really remember what he said. None of it made sense."

Winston sat forward. "Deputy Skidmore mentioned that you claimed a second man broke into your home immediately after Mr. Hansen left."

She stared at him, unable to form a response. Reilly told this man, a complete stranger, the details of what happened to her last night. She understood Reilly sharing information about Adam Hansen's attack on her, because Winston did claim to be the scarecrow man's psychiatrist. But her encounter with the shadow man? Reilly had no business telling Winston about that.

So much for privacy.

"Tell me about this other man," Winston said.

Like hell, she thought, but said nothing. If Winston was a psychiatrist, after hearing about her encounter with the disappearing intruder he'd drag her off to his so-called private clinic and pump her full of enough drugs to put an elephant in a coma.

Next time she saw Reilly Skidmore, she'd slug him.

Which would get her arrested for sure. *Brilliant idea, Grace.*

"There's nothing to say," Grace told Winston. "I was mistaken."

Leaning back in the chair, Winston stared at her. She felt his attention focused on her like the hot glare of a high-wattage bulb aimed directly in her face. The urge to flee rushed through her, but she suppressed it. Her involuntary reaction to this man was ridiculous. Though he was rude and strange, those traits hardly qualified him for membership in Maniacs Anonymous.

"Perhaps you were mistaken," Winston said, drumming one finger on the chair. Then he broke eye contact and added, in a casual tone, "I understand your parents and grandfather passed away last year."

Grace went stone still. A cold pit hardened in her gut. Reilly couldn't have told Winston about the deaths of her parents and grandfather, because Reilly didn't know. No one knew.

Except for Grace.

"Your parents died in an auto accident," Winston said, "and your grandfather in a plane crash. Is that correct?"

"How could that possibly be any of your business?"

He shrugged. "It speaks to your emotional state at the time of your encounters last night."

The cold pit melted into boiling anger in her gut. She clenched her teeth. It spoke to her emotional state? His words sounded like code for *you're nuts, lady*.

Winston fixed his stare on her once more. "Do you sometimes wish you could join your loved ones?"

"Join them where?"

"In the hereafter," he said. "Do you ever wish you could die and be reunited with your family?"

She gaped at him, unable to respond. As if trapped in a bad dream, she listened from a detached viewpoint deep inside herself.

"Or perhaps," Winston continued, "you don't believe in the afterlife. In that case, you are completely alone and death offers the promise of oblivion. Freedom from life and struggles, from everything."

Grace snapped back to reality with a jolt that shook her body. This man either had a cruel sense of humor or he was the lunatic in this room.

"Tell me," Winston said, "how did you spend last summer?"

"None of your damn business."

He arched an eyebrow. "Are you unwilling to tell me—or unable to?"

She leaped to her feet. "I'd like you to leave now, Mr. Winston."

A smirk tightened his lips. Without a word, he rose and headed for the door. Grace followed close behind him. Winston swung open the door, stepped outside, and turned to face her. She stood with one hand on the door, ready to shut it in his face.

He leaned into the doorway. "It was lovely meeting you, Grace. Thank you for your hospitality."

She scowled at him.

The smirk widened. He pulled away from the threshold.

Grace slammed the door. She started to walk away, but then stopped. A shiver tingled down her spine. She swung back around to press her face to the door, aligning her eye with the peephole.

Henry Winston gazed at the door, expressionless, green highlights glowing in his dark brown eyes. He bent forward to peer through the peephole.

Grace jerked backward.

The dark circle of the peephole lightened.

Slowly, she leaned forward to look through the lens.

Henry Winston had backed away from the door. Patting the bulge in his jacket with one hand, he waved at her with his other hand. Was he letting her know he had a gun? Certainly, he wanted to intimidate her, though she had no clue why. She'd done nothing to him. They never met until today, as far as she remembered.

Which left plenty of room for doubt.

He turned and sauntered down the cement walkway.

She rushed to the living room window, adjacent to the door. Parting the curtains a couple inches to get a view of the walkway, she watched Winston amble across the lawn and down the sidewalk, out of sight.

A swarm of butterflies danced in her gut. She bit her lip and let the curtains drop closed. For a little while, she'd let herself believe things couldn't get more bizarre—but they just did. The motives of Henry Winston, and indeed his purpose in coming here, eluded her every attempt to comprehend them. Grace hugged herself, rubbing her arms. One thing she did know for certain.

Winston had been sizing her up.

But why? Who was he? What did he want? Was his name even Henry Winston?

More questions without answers.

Chapter Six

An hour later, after much wondering about Henry Winston's visit but without arriving at any conclusions, Grace gave up on the solving the mystery—at least for the moment. She changed into a beige pantsuit with a cream-colored blouse and flats that matched the suit. After a brief but futile attempt to improve her bedraggled appearance with makeup, she drove to Professional Personnel in downtown Lassiter Falls.

The head of the employment agency had expressed an interest in publishing his own book on the subject of job-seeking strategies. He wanted an estimate for book design, but insisted that Grace present her quote in person. The man apparently harbored a Luddite streak that ran deeper than the Grand Canyon. When she'd suggested that e-mailing the quote would save them both a great deal of time, he'd snorted.

"I don't trust e-mail," he'd said, in a tone that matched his derisive snort. "And I don't do business with somebody 'less I meet 'em in person first."

How quaint, Grace had thought, but kept the sentiment to herself. That was how she wound up traipsing all the way to downtown Lassiter Falls when she would much rather have stayed home to nurse the aftermath of this morning's migraine. She really needed this client.

Professional Personnel occupied a suite on the second floor of the newest structure in town, a two-story office building one block from the town square. Grace parked along the street. Several other cars occupied spaces along the curb. However, few vehicles traveled the street, which served as one of the main arteries in Lassiter Falls. The courthouse, a historic site dating to the late nineteenth century, loomed up ahead. Its clock tower jutted above the surrounding trees. At night, the clock glowed orange. On St. Patrick's Day it glowed green, and throughout December its face burned a festive red.

The courthouse reminded her of a Gothic castle. Its spires resembled turrets and its clock tower seemed perfectly suited for the purpose of imprisoning a deposed queen. The traffic circle surrounding the courthouse gave the illusion of a moat. Grace envisioned a dungeon hidden beneath the courthouse, knights dueling on the front lawn, a desperate lady waving a white hankie from the tower's apex.

Grace sighed. She wasn't destined for the tower, but for the office building in front of her. Tearing her gaze away from the majestic courthouse, she approached the modern, and to her mind, depressingly sterile structure known as Market Street Plaza. A pair of glass doors hissed open for her automatically. When she entered the building, cold air enveloped her as the doors hissed shut behind her. Goose bumps prickled her arms. Ahead, a wide staircase curved up toward the second floor. She followed the stairs to the second floor landing. Her loafers shooshed against the carpeting. She imagined herself gliding on a cloud, floating toward the gates of heaven—until the clickety-clack of someone typing in one of the office suites popped the bubble of her reverie.

At the landing, she turned left and trudged down the hallway to a composite-wood door emblazoned with the logo for Professional Personnel. A handwritten sign taped below the logo declared, "Come on in, ya'll." She pushed through the door.

The waiting room was vacant. The reception desk at the far end of the small room also stood unoccupied, the chair behind it turned to one side, a file lying open on the desktop. A light on the telephone blinked red.

Behind her, in the corridor outside, soft voices drew nearer.

Grace marched to the desk.

A woman emerged from a door to the right of the desk. She held a manila folder tucked under one arm. Plopping into the chair, she slapped the folder onto the desktop.

"Are you here to sign up?" she drawled.

"No," Grace said. "I have an appointment with Ron Petrovicz."

"Oh." The woman shuffled papers on her desk. "Ron was supposed to be here today, but I'm afraid he got called for jury duty. Would you like to reschedule?"

Grace felt a scowl creeping into her features. She forced a polite smile to cover it. "Why don't you just ask Mr. Petrovicz to call me when it's convenient for him. We can discuss rescheduling then."

"I'm real sorry about this."

Grace made a noncommittal sound. The receptionist wasn't to blame for her boss's rudeness. Petrovicz should've called Grace to cancel.

"I'll give Ron the message," the woman said.

"Thank you."

The woman reached for the phone. The conversation was evidently over.

Pressing the blinking button, the receptionist said, "You still there, Sally?"

Grace walked out of the office into the hall. This was just what she needed after the events of the last twenty-four hours. Wasting a good hour and half driving to and from the business district of Lassiter Falls swallowed up time she could've spent on paying projects. Besides, her irritation at Petrovicz's failure to cancel their appointment churned up the acid in her gut. She felt her migraine threatening to resurface too, as pangs erupted behind her eyes.

All her life she'd believed certain events occurred for a reason. Why she believed this, she couldn't explain. But whenever she tripped over a pothole in her life path, the notion of fate soothed her—mostly. Sometimes, like today, the notion also disturbed her. Why did fate want her to feel sick, delusional, severely aggravated, and utterly alone?

Lately, she'd realized fate was an illusion. So was control. She no more controlled her life than she controlled the programming on television. Just like networks would air drivel no matter what she wanted, her life would also bump and skip forward without her consent. Chaos governed the universe.

Still, she occasionally felt destiny's hand nudging her. Maybe she'd watched too many movies.

The carpet bounced under her feet as she tramped down the staircase. Maybe one look at Grace convinced the receptionist she wasn't their kind of book designer. "Sally" on the phone might've been Ron Petrovicz hiding in his office, awaiting a signal from his receptionist. Thumbs up, come on out. Thumbs down, lock the door. Grace's attire was professional, she thought, but her hair looked like straw laden with grease. She'd been too exhausted, and too harried, to take a shower.

Groaning, she shook her head at her own pessimism. Her looks, her clothes, none of that condemned her. Ron Petrovicz was at jury duty today. She had no reason to doubt the receptionist's veracity. Yet she did.

She doubted everyone.

Paranoia. It was the devil on her shoulder, whispering dark notions in her ear. She needed an angel to kick his ass off her shoulder.

She had good reason for a modicum of paranoia. Her brain had become a bit Swiss-cheesy in recent months.

Grace pushed through the doors and into the daylight. Halting on the sidewalk, she half closed her eyes as she let the sun melt the ice encrusting her soul. Birds chirped from the bushes. The heat still slumbered, though its eyes had begun to open, releasing a sticky breeze.

A man darted out from between parked cars, careening toward her. She jumped sideways. He brushed against her. His hand, warm and rough, clasped hers for an instant before he vanished around the corner of the building.

Grace felt an object in her hand, smooth with sharp edges. She uncurled her fingers. The man had shoved a piece of paper into her palm, a small sheet ripped off a notepad and folded into a square. The sheet's corners jabbed her skin. She unfolded the paper. Someone had scrawled a message on the sheet.

"Meet me at Ray's Country Café. Twenty minutes. Urgent. Your grandfather was murdered."

The brunch crowd haunted booths and tables throughout the old building that housed Ray's Country Café, an establishment that, despite it highfalutin name, was a traditional greasy spoon. The diner hunkered alongside the interstate on the outskirts of town, like any self-respecting greasy spoon would. The crowd hardly qualified as a throng of people, but it was large enough to quell the churning in Grace's gut. If the man who passed her the note attacked her inside this diner, she would scream. Surely, one of these people might rush to her aid.

Surely.

Grace chose a booth near the entrance, in the corner, a few feet from the picture window at the front of the diner. Hand-painted lettering on the glass announced today's special—chicken-fried steak with mashed potatoes, country gravy, and black-eyed peas. From the jukebox in the far corner, a country-western singer crooned a love song. Chatter from the back of the diner drifted forward on the breeze from the air-conditioning system. The smell of frying burgers tantalized her senses. She hadn't come to Ray's in years, since before her parents moved to California, yet she could still taste the burgers and curly fries, and the special sauce that made the diner famous locally.

The door chime jangled. A man stepped over the threshold.

The man who gave her the note? Maybe. Out on the street, he darted past her so quickly she didn't notice what he looked like, not even the color of his hair or the kind of clothes he wore.

The man surveyed the diner. When his gaze intersected hers, he hesitated. She returned his stare. He shifted his attention to the window. Apparently satisfied, he ambled toward her.

She stiffened. The guy might be crazy. He *must* be crazy. No one murdered her grandfather. Edward McLean died when the jet he'd chartered crashed over the Kansas prairie. Grace read the official reports in the papers, talked to the police, and watched TV news stories that played an amateur video of the crash over and over until the images burned themselves into her mind. A plane crash was an accident, not murder. Even if the pilot was drunk or the charter company got lazy with its maintenance, those actions didn't qualify as murder. Manslaughter, maybe. But not murder.

For the millionth time in the last two months, she replayed the crash video in her mind. A teenager had been filming his buddies doing donuts on their dirt bikes when the jet screamed into sight over their heads. The plane plummeted from the sky so fast that the video needed to be slowed down in order for the shape of the jet to be discernible, but what came next required no manipulation. Flames exploded. Smoke plumed upward. The horrendous crash of the impact drowned out the terrified voices of the teenagers.

The fire. The smoke. The anguish.

Her stomach churned. Her ears rang. She took an uneven breath. The fire and the smoke, she knew of those from the video footage. The anguish she'd imagined, in vivid and horrifying detail, for weeks afterward every time she closed her eyes. Footage of the crash site taken hours after the accident revealed debris scattered over farmland, smoke curling up from the twisted and shattered wreckage. According to the authorities, the plane depressurized for unknown reasons, leaving everyone on board unconscious or dead when the plane ran out of fuel and smashed into the earth. The bodies were burned beyond recognition.

Grandpa had worked as a neuroscientist, first at a university, and later for a private research foundation based in California. His later work formed part of a secret project, maybe for the government, though he wasn't allowed to tell her anything about it. His area of expertise had centered on consciousness research, the same topic his daughter, Grace's mother, studied as well. Christine Powell followed in her father's footsteps, to the point that she left her own university post to join the same secret project where Edward McLean worked. Grace's father, Mark, had been a computer scientist specializing in artificial intelligence. He too joined the mysterious project in California.

Grace knew nothing about the work her grandfather and parents did. She felt relatively secure, however, in her belief that no one murdered any of them. Why should anyone want to kill three scientists who shared a passion for neurology? The man walking toward her must be crazy. Edward McLean was not murdered.

She suspected the mystery man was nuts from the get-go, but she came to the meeting anyway. Maybe a tiny part of her needed to believe the plane crash and auto accident happened for a reason, more than bad karma or pilot error or a manufacturing defect. She needed a reason, a tangible shred of evidence, a crumb trail to guide her out of the woods and into the open space of clarity.

The man slid into the bench opposite her. He clasped his hands atop the table.

He must be nuts. But she wanted to believe his claim.

The conflict within set her stomach to roiling.

"I assume," she said, waving his note at him, "you're the one who gave me this. Would you care to explain?"

"You're Grace Powell?"

"Naturally. And you are?"

"Brian Kellogg," he said, examining his hands. "I worked with your grandfather."

"Did you know my parents?"

"No, they died before I joined the project."

Grandpa never mentioned a Brian Kellogg to her. He hadn't mentioned any of his colleagues. Whenever she asked him about his work, he snapped at her to mind her own business, or hung up on her after a curt brush-off. His odd behavior started after her parents deaths seven months ago, so at first she dismissed it as grief related, except it got worse rather than better as the months passed. She struggled to understand the change in him, to no avail. After her parents' deaths, he was the only person she could talk to, which made his withdrawal from her all the more painful. She needed a connection to life, through someone she trusted. Edward McLean had provided that link.

Until he cut her out of his life.

A month before his death, he cancelled a trip to visit her. She tried calling him to ask what happened, but got no answer at his home or office. She left messages that he never returned. His sole response came in the form of a terse message on her answering machine, left two days before his death. In the message, he warned her not to call him because he would be unavailable and he had nothing to say anyhow. Besides, he'd said in a rough voice, she needed to learn to get by without his support. At the time, she took the statement as an insult. After his death, however, she wondered if he knew he was about to die.

She had many questions. Brian Kellogg might hold the answers in his twitchy brain.

He looked to be in his mid thirties, although his brown hair and tanned skin made him appear younger. He was trim, not skinny. Thick eyebrows sheltered his caramel-colored eyes. He wore a heavy watch, the kind with two time zones and fifteen alarms, and he frequently checked its digital readout. He wore gray slacks and a white shirt with a gray tie loosened to accommodate his unbuttoned collar. Despite his one slip into the casual, his collar was starched to concrete. She looked under the table, pretending to drop her fork. His pants had sharp creases ironed into them and he'd double-tied his shoelaces.

Grace straightened in her seat. Shadows darkened the skin under Kellogg's eyes. His hair looked odd, as if he'd glued Barbie's fur coat on top of his head. Men. They just had to have something resembling hair on their heads or

they'd hide in a closet. She'd allocated all of two minutes to detangling her own locks and pinning them back with a barrette. Looks hardly seemed important when she was losing her mind.

Possibly losing her mind.

A crash echoed through the diner.

Kellogg jumped. As laughter erupted from the back of the diner, a waitress stuttered apologies for dropping a glass. Kellogg exhaled, massaging his hands.

"Mr. Kellogg," Grace said, "are you all right?"

"Sorry. I'm tired and…anxious. If they find out I've come here to see you, I'm dead."

His tone resounded with finality. She couldn't believe anyone would kill over her. She simply wasn't that important.

"They killed Edward," he said. "Dr. McLean. He was going to expose them."

"Expose who?"

"He found out they'd been lying to him. So they had him killed. The crash was a cover."

"*Who*, Mr. Kellogg?"

"Call me Brian."

She slammed her fist on the table. "Who are 'they'? I'm not psychic and I hate riddles."

An odd, almost confused look flashed across his face. He seemed to be waiting for her to say something, but when she didn't he cleared his throat and muttered, "This isn't easy for me."

"Not my problem."

"I'm sorry, I'm doing it again. Please forgive me."

She stood halfway.

He grabbed her wrist.

She glared at him. His face flushed as he released her arm.

"I don't know who they are," he said. "Edward never told me and I never asked. All I know is what I found out afterward."

She plopped onto the bench.

Afterward. After Grandpa died. She swallowed a glacial lump. She'd had two months to get used to the idea that she wouldn't see her grandfather again. She boxed it all up in the back of her mind, sealed with five layers of duct tape, blanketed in steel, chained to the farthest reaches of her psyche. Now Brian Kellogg tore through her security and ripped the box open. She felt naked.

"Edward was going to Washington," he said. "To talk to some senator he knew. He had evidence. He was determined to stop the experiments."

"What experiments?"

"It's hard to explain."

She fisted her hands, suppressing the urge to strangle him. He lured her here with a sensational statement that he had yet to explain or prove.

"Try," she said. "Or I'm walking out that door."

His gaze flitted across the diner, his head bobbing with a motion similar to a gazelle listening for lions. "Not here. It's too public."

A waitress, approaching the table, asked if they wanted to order. Kellogg threw a panicked expression at Grace, who batted it back to him with a roll of her eyes. The waitress tapped a pen on her order pad. Kellogg sat robot stiff, lips compressed. If they didn't order something, they might get kicked out of the diner. It wasn't a public meeting hall.

Grace ordered a chocolate malt and curly fries. The waitress scribbled the order on her pad and trotted away.

"Why did you want me here?" Grace asked. "If you're not going to tell me anything, I mean."

Kellogg leaned forward. Sweat rolled over his temples, down his cheeks. "Edward was murdered. I can prove it. I have evidence."

"Show me."

"It's at my motel room."

She blew her breath through her nose, certain that flames erupted from her nostrils.

He shifted in his seat. "He was dead before the plane hit the ground. Everybody on board was. They were murdered. The crash destroyed the physical evidence. The investigators identified pieces of all the bodies, except Edward's. Wasn't much to identify."

"Nobody knows if they were dead or unconscious."

"I know."

"You claim to have evidence."

"That's not the main reason I came. I have to warn you."

"About..."

"They want you."

Grace tapped her boot on the floor in a drum-roll cadence. She'd had enough of hearing about the nebulous "them." She should leave now, before Kellogg told her "they" were aliens from the planet Beta Zappa, come to Earth to kidnap humans for use as sex slaves.

"Nobody," she said, "would waste time coming after me."

"They think Edward gave you something."

"Unless you count DNA, he gave me nothing."

With a sigh, Kellogg launched into a stammering, unspecific monologue about an "item" Grandpa left her—something vital, something worth killing for, something "destined to change humanity forever." Those words, Kellogg claimed, came from Edward McLean himself, uttered when he told Kellogg about the item. Whatever the "item" was. Kellogg offered no answer, of course.

If she believed him, which she did not, she had to wonder why Grandpa chose her to bear his secret. She didn't deserve the honor of dying to save the world. Or to save a cockroach. According to everyone else on the planet, she was delusional, not heroic.

This was insane. No one murdered Grandpa.

She checked her watch. She'd wasted fifteen minutes listening to this garbage.

The scarecrow man.

No, that incident had no connection to Kellogg. One nut accosting her did not signify a conspiracy. Besides, Kellogg's assertion of murder was too much. If she accepted it, her notions about life and justice and security would vanish like shooting stars.

"Sorry," she said. "I don't buy any of this."

Kellogg reached into his pocket.

She tensed. An image of him withdrawing a gun and firing a round into her head flashed in her mind.

He pulled out a pen. She almost laughed.

Grabbing a napkin, he scribbled on it. Then he said, "This is where I'm staying. If you decide to believe, come by. I'll be waiting."

Kellogg handed her the napkin.

And then he got up and hurried out of the diner.

Chapter Seven

After leaving the diner, Grace headed for the Oak Hills Mall, the one concession Lassiter Falls had made to consumerism. Five years old, the mall housed the usual novelty shops, department stores, and jewelers.

She needed time to think. The encounter with Kellogg renewed her sense that her life operated by someone else's design—whether that someone was a human being or the force of fate—and infused her with a new sensation of foreboding. She needed people around her, without the obligation of talking to anyone or pretending to care about their problems while they yammered at her as if she were a therapist at a free clinic. She needed anonymity in a crowd.

College kids milled in the corridors, chatting loudly, listening to music through headphones. Older people speed-walked amid the throngs.

As Grace meandered past the novelty stores and jewelry chains, she remained aware of the noise around her even while tuning it out. The cacophony calmed her. It blocked her thoughts and drowned out the anxiety. No worries about her loss of sanity. Just a background of laughter, talking, and the ka-chunk of vending machines dispensing their wares.

She almost felt alive.

A pack of kids slammed into her. Nodding in response to their apologies, she veered toward the escalators. Part of her envied those kids. They had vitality, innocence, possibilities. She was no more than seven years their senior, yet she felt much older. Ancient. Half buried. Suffocating.

As she stepped onto the down escalator, out the corner of her eye she noticed a man stepping onto the track behind her. He moved onto the step directly above her. Great, a tailgater. She hopped down two steps to get a little distance from the creep.

He moved down two steps.

She hopped four steps, taking them two at a time.

He hesitated, then closed the gap and stopped one step behind her.

Grace glanced back at the creep. Her heart thudded.

Him. The shadow man.

No, it couldn't be.

She checked again. Him. Definitely.

"Don't look at me," he said.

His voice was deep, soft, and…familiar. Ridiculous. This entire situation was ridiculous. Men could not appear out of and disappear into thin air. Either she was insane or at this moment she was lying in a coma at a hospital somewhere, suffering bizarre and disturbing dreams.

"Why are you acting this way?" he demanded, though his tone stayed calm.

Her instincts urged silence. Never knew what might set off a stalker. "Hello" might be the word that triggered a killing spree that started with her. She had no desire to get her throat slashed today. Tomorrow, maybe.

He let out a sharp sigh. "I know you can see me."

Of course she could see him. Everyone could.

Right?

"Say something, dammit," he hissed, the nonchalance vaporizing.

Now her hallucinations cursed at her. Jeez, her mental state must've deteriorated at lightning speed for her mind to create visions that swore at her. Or perhaps this was her mind's way of dealing with anger at herself. She could take a little verbal abuse from her own psyche. Except this didn't feel like a hallucination.

Well, did hallucinations ever *feel* like hallucinations?

She fixed her gaze on the bottom of the escalator. Almost there.

"Fine, don't talk," the man said. He leaned over her shoulder to murmur in her ear. "Just listen. You have to be careful. They're after you."

"Leave me alone or I'll scream," she said in an equally soft voice, and instantly regretted speaking.

But she couldn't help it. The guy was ticking her off. Hallucination or not, he needed a serious dressing-down.

"Someone has to warn you," he said.

"That's novel. A stalker warning his victim."

Each time he spoke, with his lips so close to her ear, his breath whispered across her skin and sent a shiver rippling down her spine—an oddly stimulating shiver that didn't feel like fear.

She ought to move down another step. Her muscles refused to obey.

He sighed. The warmth of his exhalation set off a flurry of goose bumps.

"I'm not a stalker," he said.

She laughed. The tone echoed hollow and stark in her ears.

"They're coming for you," he said. "Be careful."

She twisted her torso to face him. "If I hear the word 'them' one more time—"

"Sh." He tilted his head, apparently concentrating on a sound only he heard. "I have to go."

"Wait."

He vanished.

A blast of air tossed her hair into her face. She brushed the locks aside. He had disappeared, like a light winking off, gone faster than the speed of a spinning atom.

During the course of their conversation, something inside her had changed inexplicably. The notion of a shadow man no longer bothered her, she realized. He disappeared at will. Couldn't everybody? Maybe not everybody vanished, but in a bizarre way she accepted that this man, whoever he was, possessed that ability. It seemed perfectly natural.

Shit.

The notion did make sense if he was, after all, nothing but a hallucination. A part of her believed that, but another part believed he existed as a real person, made of flesh and blood and bone. The split in her psyche gave her a stomachache.

And the start of another migraine.

She stepped off the escalator. People meandered through the concourse, chatting back and forth, window-shopping, oblivious of the supernatural happenings around them. No one had seen the man on the escalator. No one else *could* see him. Her mystery man acted unsurprised that she could see him even when no one else could. She avoided wondering why.

But she'd felt his breath on her. Warm. Tantalizing.

If no one else could see him, how in blazes could she feel him?

The concourse split around a fountain, dividing into three walkways. Grace chose one at random and picked up her pace. She wanted to hide, anywhere, get out of sight where no one would find her. When she was little, she used to hide up in the branches of an old oak tree in the backyard of her family's home. She found safety in that tree. Camouflaged by the leaves, alone with her thoughts, she sat cocooned in a blanket of greenery. The perfume of the flowering bushes below calmed her nerves.

In a mall, she was hardly likely to find an oak tree.

Ahead, a department store entrance gaped wide as a dragon's mouth. She hurried through the entrance, past rows of sofas and dining room sets, through the electronics department, up the escalator to the second floor. She pushed through aisles of clothing. A saleswoman thrust a bottle of makeup in her face while blathering on about its benefits for her skin. Shaking her head, Grace rushed past the woman.

A row of fitting rooms lined the far wall. A retail version of caves. Better than a tree. She veered toward the fitting rooms.

A cashier observed her. The girl canted her head in a cat-like expression of curiosity.

Grace halted. She couldn't jump into a fitting room to hide. The cashier would get suspicious, and probably assume Grace was shoplifting. She needed an excuse.

Her hands trembled. Her face tingled. *Calm down*, she admonished herself. Squeezing her hands into fists, she took a deep breath.

The cashier stared at her. The curious expression tightened into concern.

Grace relaxed her hands. With as much composure as she could muster, she strolled between two racks of blouses. She pretended to examine the seam on one blouse. Glancing sideways, she watched the cashier turn away to pick up a stack of jeans. The girl carried the garments to a group of display shelves, where she began to refold and stack the garments.

Grace snatched two blouses off the rack. She took them into the first fitting room. After pulling the curtain closed, she hung the blouses on the provided hooks and collapsed onto the bench. She drew her knees up, wrapping her arms around them.

Her life had flipped upside-down and rolled sideways. She might believe she'd lost her mind, except for a few pieces of evidence to the contrary. First, there was the sincerity of Brian Kellogg. He said someone murdered her grandfather and swore that he had proof, which he would give her when she contacted him at his motel. Her main reason for thinking she might've cracked up was the shadow man. Yet a real, physical force warped her bedroom door. She didn't imagine that event. The cut on her hand had been real too, as evidenced by the blood on the bandage.

Something was happening. She must find out what.

She ought to see Brian Kellogg. Find out what he knew. If the whole thing was a trick to lure her into his motel room for a Rohypnol cocktail, she'd castrate him. She'd had enough lies and evasion.

As she rested her forehead on her knees, the smell of clean denim filled her nostrils. She would interrogate Kellogg tomorrow. Right now, she needed a rest. Oh lord. She really, really needed a rest.

Her eyelids fluttered shut. One by one, her muscles slackened. The murmur of the ventilation system lulled her into a kind of trance, where all thoughts and worries slipped from her mind. A glorious peace settled over her.

The curtain fluttered.

She raised her head.

He stood before her, inside the tiny booth, his body inches from hers.

She sprang to her feet.

The toes of her shoes bumped into the toes of his. Her bosom grazed his chest. She found herself literally face to face with the man, though she was several inches shorter than he was. Her nose brushed across his chin as she wobbled on her feet. He bent his head to look down at her. She tilted her head back to meet his gaze.

He looked like an angel. A tall, muscular angel.

She couldn't move. His eyes, with those dark pupils ringed in shimmering sapphire, mesmerized her. The irises glowed like nothing she'd ever seen before. Without meaning to, but unable to stop herself, she leaned against him. The heat of his body radiated into her. His gaze held hers as he lifted his arms to cradle her in them. Everything inside her tensed. The sensation was not entirely unpleasant, but tinged with a need she didn't understand. A desire to stay close to him. To take comfort from his presence.

He spoke softly. "I'm not leaving until you hear me out."

"I'm listening," she said, unsure of how she managed to speak.

"You're in danger. Very nasty people want something they think you have."

"I have nothing. Unless they want my bad credit."

"They want a flash drive."

She furrowed her brow. "What?"

"A flash drive, a kind of external memory card that plugs into a computer. Edward left it for you."

Brian Kellogg had mentioned an unspecified thing that her grandfather supposedly left for her. Now this man, whoever he was, mentioned a flash drive.

She pushed away from him. The spell had broken. That delicious tension evaporated the instant she severed their physical contact. She felt a pang of disappointment, as if she'd just given up something that she wanted very badly. But what?

He reached for her, trying to wrap her in his arms once again. The tension rose inside her.

Oh hell no. She did not want this. Whatever this was.

She slapped both hands on his chest and shoved him backward. He stumbled, bumped into the wall, and then righted himself. His mouth quirked with what looked like annoyance.

He was annoyed? Screw that.

She folded her arms over her chest. "I know what a flash drive is, but I don't have one. My grandfather left me nothing."

Except a cryptic phone message that sounded like a warning. Of what, she didn't know. Maybe he knew this man would come for her.

"He must've hidden it," her stalker said. "Someplace where only you would find it. Whatever you do, don't give it to anyone. Destroy it."

"Yes, *sir*. Any other orders, commander?"

The hint of a smile flickered on his face. He raised a hand to touch her cheek with one finger.

She jerked backward. Her legs hit the bench, buckling her knees. She threw her arms back to catch herself but her hands slipped.

He grasped her arms, steadying her. "Careful."

His hands felt warm, the skin surprisingly soft. He was too close again. Much too close. She felt the heat of him on her skin, smelled his masculine scent—

She shook off his hands. "Who are you?"

"Listen to me," he said, pulling her closer. "Don't trust anyone. You have no idea how badly these people want that flash drive."

Her heart pounded. Indefinable feelings coursed through her body like electrical currents.

"Destroy the flash drive," he said. "It's the only way."

He held still for a moment. His fingers encircled her arms in a firm-yet-gentle grasp. His eyes locked on hers. She sensed a familiarity in his gaze, akin to a half-remembered dream. Her lips parted as her brain fumbled for words.

Without a word, he released her.

And then he vanished.

The old Pontiac got her home, that much Grace knew, though the details of the drive blurred into one big slab of missing time. They called it highway hypnosis. She remembered reading the term in a magazine or newspaper. Her mind shifted into automatic pilot, operating her muscles without her awareness of the actions. That was how she arrived home with no memory of the trip.

It was creepy.

She wanted to hide. She needed answers. No one vanished at will. No one vanished, period. She took physics in college and understood the laws of nature. A mass didn't go poof without releasing some kind of energy.

The gusts of wind.

Was a gust of wind enough to account for the energy of a vanishing human being? Damned if she knew. And she'd bet even the top scientists in the world would be damned if they knew.

They'd call her nuts anyway.

Slamming the car door behind her, she scuffled across the driveway and down the concrete path to the front door. As she slipped inside the house, easing the door shut after her, the old weariness seeped into her body once more. She wanted to sleep until everyone and everything she knew crumbled into dust and a fresh, sane world sprouted from the remains.

A new world without inexplicable phenomena. A place where she might actually feel normal and competent, both in mind and in real life. As she turned the corner into the hallway, she avoided glancing into the kitchen. If the shadow man awaited her there, she did not want to know about it. Her brain needed rest, not vague warnings of impending peril delivered to her by an anonymous stranger.

An attractive anonymous stranger.

The memory of his scent filled her nostrils. Her skin tingled as if his warmth still kissed her flesh. From deep inside her soul arose a sense of familiarity, of memories long forgotten, of things she ought to recall but that stayed buried inside her. Each time she saw the shadow man, she experienced this sensation of knowing but not remembering. She knew him. Yet he was a stranger.

She did not know him. Her life was an open book, of the boring variety that no one wanted to read unless they were stuck in a dentist's office and her life was the only reading material available in the waiting room. The tale of her life, at least thus far, excluded all adventure and risk-taking—and certainly all romance. She never met a man like her possibly hallucinatory stalker.

Except she might have. Her Swiss-cheese brain left big enough holes to fit even a tall, muscular man.

Down the hallway she trotted, ducking through the open bedroom door. Without thinking about it, she kicked the door shut behind her. The latch refused to engage, thanks to its warped center, the aftereffect of the inexplicable change in air pressure last night. The door creaked inward.

Grace grabbed the chair that sat by the window and dragged it toward the door. She jammed the chair under the knob to brace the door shut. No barricade would keep out the shadow man. She knew that. He appeared anytime he liked, wherever he liked, regardless of privacy or courtesy. Perhaps the barricade might keep out "them," whoever they might be, or at least slow them down to give her time for a prayer before they sliced-and-diced her.

Tired. She was so tired.

Crawling into bed, she settled onto her side with her knees drawn up close to her belly. Within minutes, sleep overwhelmed her. She dreamed of the faceless man. In a voice both inhuman and intimate, he urged her to stop fighting, to give in, to let him have what he wanted. She had no clue what that thing was, but she knew he wanted it. His need infected her, hot and dark and cloying.

Give in, give up.

More than anything, she wanted to obey the command. She wanted to give herself over to him, because that would be so much easier. So much simpler. Sink into the depths of his need, and lose herself in the scalding darkness.

Give in.

Grace twitched awake. Her heart hammered against her rib cage. She glanced around the room, certain she was not alone. Yet she was. It had been a dream, nothing more. Dreams could seem so real, but they weren't. She couldn't keep fighting the shadows in her dreams. She lacked both the time and the energy for it. She needed all her strength to battle the real shadows that lurked outside. She must insulate herself from them.

She sat up. Them. Who? Her head ached from thinking about it.

The bedside clock gave the time as four in the morning. She flopped back onto the bed.

For the next three hours, she slept in fits and starts. The dream returned each time she dozed, the same as before, like a movie played over and over and over. The man's voice echoed through her mind, low and distant.

Give up. You want to.

Like hell.

If they wanted her to give up and give in, they'd get a serious shock. She would not abandon herself to insanity or collapse on the floor in a shivering, weeping lump. She would fight—until the invisible forces were defeated.

Or until she was defeated.

One way or another, this craziness would end.

Chapter Eight

Her boots made a soft clopping sound on the pavement as Grace marched down the sidewalk. Yesterday, she'd walked with slumped shoulders and bowed head. Today, she held herself straight and tall, or at least as tall as she could get, being of average height. Something inside her had shifted. Doubts still niggled at her, but much less insistently than before.

At four o'clock this morning, she experienced a revelation. She was not insane.

Despite sleeping less than well, she felt energized. She had a mission. Find Brian Kellogg, see the evidence he claimed to have, and evaluate his claims about her grandfather's death. If the claim proved credible, she'd follow wherever the evidence led her.

Okay, so she had a mission but no plan. A mission was a starting point. Which was far more than she had yesterday.

As for the shadow man who cornered her in a fitting room yesterday…well, she'd sort that out later. At least today she had a destination.

The Bed & Bath Inn.

It was the cheapest motel in the vicinity of Lassiter Falls, situated along the interstate to take advantage of exhausted motorists. Though Grace had never patronized the establishment, from the outside it looked like a dingy, beat-up building divided into tiny rooms.

A chill shimmied down her spine.

Grace stopped. The sensation of being watched lingered, though the chill had dissipated. She twisted her head around to glance over her shoulder.

No one there.

She had wanted to drive to the motel. Then she realized she'd forgotten to gas up the car yesterday and it probably didn't have the juice to make it

the ten miles or so to the interstate. The migraine had impaired her thinking, or maybe her encounter with the shadow man left her dazed. She intended to stop at a gas station on the way home. She forgot.

So this morning she found herself walking to the nearest bus stop.

Someone is watching.

The thought burst into her mind. She stood there for a moment, facing forward again, and let the thought sink in as she listened and waited. Nothing happened. No stalkers leaped out from behind bushes. No footfalls clapped behind her. She found no logical reason to believe she was being tracked. Still, she patted her purse to feel the hard outline of her .357 Magnum revolver inside, snug in the holster sewn into the purse.

Yet as she started off down the sidewalk again, the uneasy feeling stayed with her. It haunted the recesses of her mind even after she boarded the bus. By the time the bus turned onto Main Street a few minutes later, the sensation had lessened but not disappeared.

The bus conveyed Grace into town amid a cloud of oily smoke and a throng of people who looked as hopeless and helpless as she'd felt for the past two months, until her pre-dawn epiphany. Maybe she would sink back into the malaise later, when Brian Kellogg turned out to be delusional and her shadow man proved to be a hallucination.

No. She was not crazy. If it took every ounce of strength she possessed to keep her head above the morass, she would never again allow herself to drown in a quagmire of self-doubt.

Never.

At least not today. At least not until lack of a decent night's sleep caught up with her.

Stop it.

The bus deposited her in front of the truck stop that hunkered at the base of the freeway on-ramp. The two-block trek from the truck stop to the motel, along the edge of the on-ramp, gave her time to organize her thoughts. She tried to organize her thoughts anyway. What could she say to Kellogg? What *should* she say? *Gimme the damn evidence right now, you scumbag* seemed inappropriate, thought it suited her mood. She was sick of feeling helpless and hopeless. She wanted to prolong the empowered feeling she'd woken up with this morning. Yet the closer she got to the motel, the less empowered and invigorated she felt.

Damn.

Just as she veered off the sidewalk and into the motel parking lot, she glimpsed a shape darting out of the ditch on the other side of the on-ramp.

Grace spun around to face the road.

The scarecrow man rushed across the single lane, heading straight for her.

She tore open the purse's main compartment, seized the revolver, and whipped it out of the purse. Leveling the gun at the scarecrow man, she shouted for him to stop.

He jerked as if she'd shot him. She hadn't. Her finger wasn't even over the trigger, but resting on the barrel above it.

His face contorted into a frightened expression. He mumbled to himself, the words indistinct. When his gaze fell on the gun, his eyes bulged.

The poor little loon seemed more scared than she was.

To hell with this. She lowered the gun to her side, aimed at the ground, and waved her free hand in a casual greeting. "Hi, it's me. Still want to talk?"

His lips worked soundlessly.

"Well?" she asked.

"Not here," he said. "They see. They know."

"Here or nowhere."

He hesitated. "All right."

Dragging his feet, he moved off the road and halted a half dozen feet from her, to her left and slightly in front of her. He cringed and flitted his gaze back and forth as if watching for demons from the fiftieth dimension to suddenly appear and suck him into their hell-world. He paced along the road's periphery, but maintained a couple yards distance between the two of them. Fine with her. She wanted to stay clear of him too.

"I'm only trying to warn you," he said. "Someone has to."

Someone has to warn you. The shadow man had said that to her yesterday.

The scarecrow took a step toward her. "He tries to stop me. But I push him out. Free. For awhile."

"Who tries to stop you?"

His lips curled. He spat one word. "Them."

"Who is 'them'?"

"The—ones. Who want me. And you. He tries to make me do things for them. Bad things. I don't want to. I want to help. Not hurt. Never hurt." He choked back a sob. "Please don't let him take me. Please, please, please."

His voice rose to a crescendo as he repeated the word please a dozen more times, faster and faster with each iteration. His cheeks flushed. His body trembled.

She must calm him down before he lashed out, enmeshed as he had become in a frenzy of syllables. She had no desire to become the object of his terror. Fear could easily shift into violence, especially in someone as deranged as this little man.

"I know you want to help," she said in a soothing tone. "I believe you."

He choked, coughed, choked again. His breaths came shallow and fast.

"I believe you," she repeated. "I understand."

"Understand? You do?"

"Yes. What's your name?"

He looked at the ground. "Andrew."

Henry Winston told her this man's name was Adam Hansen. Yeah, she really needed to fight hard to control her shock at realizing Winston lied to her.

"You wanted to warn me," she said. "What about?"

"They're after you now. The man with evil eyes. Darkness inside. His name..." Andrew thumped the heel of his hand on his forehead. "Can't remember. All fuzzy."

She waited, unable to think of a thing to say.

Andrew clasped his hands to his temples. Squeezing his eyes shut, he rocked back and forth on his heels. "Fuzzy, so fuzzy. Must clear."

Grace took a step backward and tightened her grip on the gun. "Why are they after me?"

"What Dr. McLean gave you. They want it."

"Dr. McLean. My grandfather."

"Uh-huh."

This loony little man said the same things Brain Kellogg had said—that Grandpa gave her something, an object that strangers wanted to steal. The shadow man claimed it was a flash drive. If so, she had no clue what the drive might hold. Maybe she shouldn't assume this lunatic could piece together enough coherent thoughts to tell her the truth. She should mistrust him—and the shadow man.

Unless the three of them worked together, in a conspiracy to confuse and irritate her, she had to believe them. Three people told her Grandpa left her something.

Andrew thrashed his head side to side. "Don't give it to them. Don't."

If she ever found "it," she would give the thing to no one. She wouldn't destroy it either. Whether it was a flash drive or something else, the object must contain the answers she sought. She needed those answers, desperately.

Whether or not Andrew could help her, he most assuredly needed help himself. Maybe she could help him. Together they might shed light on the shadows.

How had he found her here? Did he follow her? That might explain why she'd felt like someone was watching her ever since she left the house. She supposed he could've snuck onto the bus after she climbed aboard. This cloak-and-dagger stuff was new to her, after all. She knew nothing about counterespionage, or whatever spies called it when they tried to evade other spies.

Checking the surroundings for strangers with "evil eyes," she slipped the gun inside her purse, tucking it inside the holster. She had to trust someone. Since she would no way trust Henry Winston, that left her with a choice between the shadow man and this twitchy nutball.

She'd take the nutball.

"Andrew," she said, "will you come with me to meet someone?"

He wrapped his arms around his torso like a self-made straitjacket. "I don't know."

"Do you trust me?"

"Yes."

"Then come with me, Andrew. Maybe I can help you."

"Go. With you. Yes."

Turning away from him, she marched across the parking lot. The sound of footsteps behind her made Grace look back. Andrew had fallen into step behind her. He clutched his arms, head bent down, shoulders hunched.

She slipped her hand into her purse until her fingers grazed the gun. Safe. Maybe.

As she approached the door to Kellogg's room, her stomach twisted into a pretzel knot. A pang erupted behind her eyes. When she raised a hand to knock on the door, the pang stabbed deeper into her brain. God no, she could not handle another migraine. Not now.

Andrew shuffled up behind her, staying an arm's length away.

Hand hovering in midair, she hesitated. Took a deep breath. Let it out slowly. Repeated the deep breathing twice more. The pang faded. Her stomach still burned with acid, but at least she'd headed off the potential migraine.

She rapped on the door twice.

Grace had never gone inside one of these rooms before. She had noticed the Bed & Bath Inn many times as she drove past and read the sign advertising "a cheap, clean place to sleep." The sign made no mention of cable TV, room service, or other amenities. The bulbs inside the motel's sign flickered at night. In the daytime, the sign looked cracked and faded. Graffiti slashed across some of the room doors.

Icy worms slithered inside her gut. Behind her, Andrew sniffled. What a pair they made.

She rapped on the door again.

Kellogg's voice came through the scarred metal. "Yes?"

"It's Grace Powell."

The lock clicked. Kellogg swung the door inward. He motioned her inside. When she stepped into the room, Andrew started after her.

Kellogg's mouth dropped open.

Grace said, "This is—"

"Andrew Haley." Kellogg ushered the pitiful scarecrow into the room and shut the door. To Andrew, he said, "What are you doing here?"

Andrew's lower lip quivered.

"You know him?" Grace asked.

Kellogg nodded. "We both worked with Edward."

"What?" Grace felt a jolt of dizziness, as if the earth beneath her feet had tilted. "Andrew worked with my grandfather?"

"Uh, yeah." Kellogg guided the other man to the bed. "Why don't you watch TV, Andrew?"

"TV," Andrew said, perching on the bed's edge. "He's not in the TV. Good."

Kellogg walked to the TV and punched the power button. A talk show appeared on the screen. Two women were screaming and pulling each other's hair, their profanity bleeped out while the host nodded and gestured, his expression laden with contained glee.

"Couldn't you put on something calmer?" Grace asked.

Kellogg switched the channel. Mickey Mouse cavorted with Donald Duck. Andrew giggled.

Crossing the room in two steps, Kellogg opened the door and shoved Grace outside. He followed, shutting the door but not latching it. Traffic on the interstate rumbled in the background.

"Where did you find him?" Kellogg asked.

"He found me."

He stared at her.

She stared back at him.

"That's not possible," he said. "Andrew's been locked up in a mental ward for almost a year. He couldn't escape."

"Obviously, he could."

"He doesn't have the capacity to plan ahead. He can't remember things. Not anymore."

Through her teeth, she said, "I don't have to justify myself to you, Mr. Kellogg. *You* contacted *me*."

He averted his gaze to the pavement. "Sorry. I'm nervous."

Scared to death, she would've said. But if he wanted to play down his fear, she couldn't blame him. After all the strange things she'd seen in the past two days, she liked the notion of chopping the fear into bite-size bits too. She'd had enough riddles and evasion, though. She wanted answers. Now.

"You said my grandfather was murdered," she said. "Prove it."

"It's hard to explain."

A groan escaped her throat. She clenched her teeth and bit the inside of her lip. The tang of blood coated the tip of her tongue. Her jaw ached. Massaging the joint, she tried to relax the muscles. Though she sympathized with Kellogg, she'd slug him if he didn't produce evidence that supported his claims. Soon. Like in the next five seconds.

She forced a less-than-pleasant smile. "Please try."

"I've made you angry." He slumped his shoulders. "I apologize. But I...I know you won't believe me. Sometimes I can't believe it."

"Try me."

"We—Edward, me, Andrew, and others—worked in a research facility in California. A pharmaceutical company funded the project, or so I was told. Publicly, we were studying how the brain works so the company could develop new and better drugs to treat mental disorders."

"Publicly?"

"Only a tiny part of the facility was devoted to that research."

"And the rest of you were studying…"

"Parapsychology." The wind gusted, and he paused to adjust his hairpiece. "Psychic phenomena. You know, telepathy and the like."

"Why would a pharmaceutical company care about that?"

"I'm a subordinate. They tell me what I need to know, nothing more. The area I worked in wasn't strictly related to parapsychology, but it had relevant applications. I studied hypnosis as a means of manipulating a person's thoughts and self-hypnosis as a means of inducing certain psychic phenomena."

He spoke quickly. Her brain whirred at high speed, yet failed to interpret the meaning of each word before Kellogg launched into the next. "What does that mean?"

"Oh God." His mouth dropped opened once more. His body tensed. His eyes focused on something beyond her face.

She looked around but saw nothing. "Is something wrong?"

"Get away," he hissed at her. "Go!"

She shook her head.

With both hands, he shoved her backward. She stumbled, nearly landed on her butt, then found her balance. Kellogg choked, his eyes widening. He pawed at his throat. His tongue lolled out of his mouth as he gasped and clawed at the air in front of his face. His knees buckled.

Grace rushed forward to grab his arms.

In the instant her fingers brushed his sleeve, his feet were hoisted off the ground, seemingly by an invisible force. He dangled in midair as if hanging by a noose. Saliva gurgled from his lips. He thrashed his legs, clutched at his throat.

Grabbing his abdomen, she yanked him down. Despite an effort that choked the breath out of her, his body refused to move. He hung there, stiff and flailing, sputtering and grunting.

His body went limp.

He crumpled onto the concrete walkway. She collapsed with him, entangled in his limbs. For a moment she just lay there on top of him, too stunned to think and too out of breath to move. The second her strength returned, she extricated herself from his arms and legs.

She felt for a pulse in his neck. Nothing. She bent over him, pressing her ear to his chest. No sign of breathing or a heartbeat.

Brian Kellogg was dead.

He couldn't be dead. She jammed her finger into his neck again. Nothing. She slumped against the wall of the motel. Though it was the last thing she wanted to do, she raked her gaze over Kellogg's corpse. A person did not spontaneously choke to death. Something on his body must offer a clue to the real cause of his death. Of course, she was no medical examiner. What did she know about determining cause of death?

Then she saw it. A series of bruises had formed on his neck. Two big bruises discolored his throat near the larynx. Smaller bruises dotted the sides of his neck. The bruises looked the size and contour of fingertips.

Someone strangled him.

Impossible.

The man had levitated half a foot off the ground. He'd grasped at his throat and wheezed, clearly struggling to breathe. Now bruises had formed. Exactly like someone had strangled him.

Kellogg studied psychic phenomena. Could someone have used some type of mental ability to kill him? The idea sounded ludicrous, but so did the idea of a man vanishing into thin air. She could believe almost anything now—or at least consider almost anything.

Frozen wide open, Kellogg's eyes stared outward with the blankness of death. With the tips of two fingers, she eased the lids down over his eyes.

Strands of hair stuck out from beneath his hairpiece. Hair under a toupee? No, the hairpiece must've shifted position. A man wouldn't wear a toupee if he had natural hair. She tugged on the hairpiece. It slipped off in her hand.

Thick hair covered Brian Kellogg's head.

The hairpiece lay stiff in her palm. She flipped it over. A key was taped to the underside. Prying the tape off, she removed the key and held it close to her face. A number was engraved into the metal. The key might unlock a post office box, a locker at a bus station, anything.

She shoved the key in her jeans pocket.

Sirens ululated on the interstate. Two police cars, tires squealing as they swerved from the freeway onto an off-ramp, sped toward the motel. Within half a minute, they would careen into the parking lot. Brian Kellogg's body rested at her feet, his neck bearing the signs of strangulation. Another tenant of the inn must've seen her with Kellogg, witnessed his death, and called the police. The police were coming for her. She knew. Even if the witness remained anonymous, the cops would find her standing over Kellogg's body with no evidence that anyone besides her and the dead man had been in the area.

Shit.

She threw open the door to Kellogg's room. Andrew was gone. No, he couldn't have left. He would've walked right past her and, despite the chaos of Kellogg's attack, she would've noticed.

Someone whimpered.

Andrew. The sound came from the other side of the room—if eight feet away counted as the other side. She trotted around the end of the narrow bed, into the two-foot gap between the bed and the wall. Andrew huddled on the floor, mashed up against the wall in the corner. Tears streaming down his cheeks, he held his hands clamped over his ears. Tremors shook his body.

The sirens howled outside, louder, closer. Seconds away now.

Seizing Andrew's hands, she yanked him to his feet. He gasped in a breath and fought her pull.

"Come on," she said. "We've got to go."

"No, no, no. He's out there. It was him."

"The cops are coming. We have to go, Andrew. *Now.*"

"No! He'll get us too. Please."

The whine in his voice grated on her eardrums. She hauled him toward the door, but he planted both feet on the carpet and leaned back with all his weight. Despite his scrawny build, the change in momentum knocked her off balance. Her feet skidded across the carpet. Andrew keened. His wrists slipped from her grasp.

The sirens wailed. Voices shouted outside.

Andrew crumpled to the floor and curled up in a ball.

She couldn't carry him out of here. She couldn't stay either. The police would want to know who strangled Brian Kellogg. She could tell them an invisible man did it, or maybe the ghost of Jack the Ripper, but somehow she doubted the police would buy either explanation. Without another suspect, they would level their sights on her.

And pull the trigger.

She poked her head out the door. The police cars had parked at the far end of the building. Two officers were talking with a man in a bathrobe. The man waved his arms in her direction.

Andrew sobbed.

She couldn't leave him here alone.

No choice. She tiptoed out the door, hopped over Kellogg's body, and slunk past two more rooms to the end of the building. A field sloped down the hill away from the motel, into the woods half a mile distant. Rounding the corner, she continued up the opposite side of the building. Another row of rooms filled this side, identical to the others except in the numbers on the door. Three cars occupied spaces in front of the rooms.

She stopped. The police might search this side of building. She couldn't just mosey past them. The man in the bathrobe must've seen her. Even if he hadn't, the police would likely stop anyone who attempted to leave the motel.

The air felt sticky and warm, yet her teeth chattered. Dammit.

She angled off into the field.

He returned to blackness. They shut off the lights when he traveled. He gave up asking why a long time ago. They would only refuse to answer. *That's classified,* they'd say, as if they were secret agents. They liked pretending they worked for the CIA or the military, spouting terms that meant nothing in the private sector, treating him like a prisoner.

No, they viewed him more as a slave than a prisoner, someone who obeyed their commands without questioning, without thinking, like a robot made of flesh and blood.

"I'm back," David announced.

The electrode wires tickled his arms. The chair felt cold, hard. When he shifted position, the straps around his ankles, wrists, and forehead chafed his skin.

The lights came on in a burst of white. He blinked in the sudden glare.

One of the technicians jiggled the door knob from the other side. It had become a ritual. They jiggled the knob before entering the room to insure that he hadn't pulled a Houdini, unlocking the door and escaping without triggering any alarms. Next, they'd peek through the tiny window set into the metal door, in case he'd somehow manipulated the surveillance cameras into displaying an image of him seated in the chair while in reality he hid near the door waiting to ambush them. Never mind that he knew nothing about cameras or alarms and had no clue how he might manipulate those devices.

Finally, with reasonable assurance of their safety, they would enter the room accompanied by two armed guards. Never know, he might spontaneously acquire superhuman strength that allowed him to break the leather restraints, leap the fifteen feet from his chair to the door, and butcher them all with his bare hands.

They thought he was an animal.

In some respects, they overestimated his abilities. Yet in other ways, they underestimated him. They had no conception of what he could really do, if he chose to. If they knew, they'd realize no precautions would protect them. They also lacked one piece of information that might ease their minds.

He had given up on escaping.

Satisfied that he hadn't tricked them, the technician unlocked the door and entered the sterile white room. Tesler, the lead technician, was a tall and wiry man in his sixties, with short-cropped gray hair and freckles that hinted red hair had once crowned his head. He wore a lab coat with a name badge pinned to the lapel. The lump in his pocket marked the location of his tablet computer. All the technicians at the facility carried tablets instead of pen and paper. Handwriting was passé.

No guards accompanied Tesler. Strange.

David arched an eyebrow. "Would you mind unstrapping me?"

Tesler approached him. The older man eyed David's restraints for a couple seconds, then reached out to unbuckle the forehead strap. Clasping David's chin in one hand, Tesler twisted his head from side to side, scrutinizing his subject's face. He released David's chin and seized his wrist, measuring the pulse with two fingers.

On a metal table positioned near David's chair, the heart rate monitor showed his pulse. They kept him hooked up to so much equipment, various kinds of monitors and meters, that he felt like he might physically meld with the machines one of these days. Still, Tesler always ignored the heart rate monitor and checked David's pulse himself.

"Normal," Tesler said. He sounded disappointed.

David glared at him.

As Tesler released the other straps, he asked in a faux-casual tone, "How was Seattle?"

"Dark and dreary. You'd love it."

Tesler ripped the electrodes from David's head. Hairs dangled from the sticky patches. His scalp burned where the hairs had torn loose.

A smile flickered on Tesler's face. "Reynolds will take you to the debriefing room."

"Don't make me go, I'll miss you too much."

Tesler unhooked the straps that bound David's wrists. He pulled handcuffs out of his pocket.

As he secured the cuffs on David's wrists, he said, "Where did you go today?"

"Seattle."

Tesler released the straps around David's ankles. "Where else?"

"Outer Mongolia. I heard it's nice this time of year."

Tesler leaned over him, placing a hand over each of David's forearms. Tesler's lip twitched. "David, don't lie to me. You were gone for five hours. Where else did you go?"

"I got lost."

Tesler pressed the weight of his body down on David's arms. The metal of the chair pinched his flesh. David stared into Tesler's eyes. The man's fingernails dug into his skin, while his thumbs pressed into nerves. David's arms throbbed from deep within the flesh. He wanted to belt Tesler. He wanted to repay the man for all the pain he'd caused. All the pain he would cause.

Get off me.

Tesler's eyes widened. He flew backward, limbs flailing, a cry choked off in his throat. His face flushed bright red.

With a thud and a gasp, he hit the concrete wall.

Tesler blinked. Though he opened his mouth, no sound came.

Well, that was a new one. Not that he believed the ability had come from him. It was borrowed power for sure—and he knew exactly where it had originated. He must never let Tesler figure it out.

David rose from the chair. Even he didn't know the full extent of his abilities. No one did.

"You tripped," he said, striding toward Tesler to offer his cuffed hands to the man. "Better be more careful."

Tesler ignored David's offer of help. He pushed himself up from the floor. Smoothing his lab coat, he straightened his spine and rolled his shoulders back.

When he spoke, a sharpness edged his voice. "Nice, David. Try that again and I'll put you in a coma."

David swallowed the smart retort that bubbled up inside him. He'd probably aggravated Tesler enough for one day. The bastard could do whatever he liked to David, so long as he got nowhere near Grace.

David moved toward the exit.

Tesler knocked on the door. It swung outward as a guard outside opened it. The guard and his partner, both armed with bulky semiautomatic handguns, stepped into the threshold.

Tesler glanced at David's handcuffs. "Maybe you need shackles on your feet."

The guards guided David out into the hallway. He paused and glanced over his shoulder at Tesler.

He smiled. "You can't shackle my mind, Tesler."

"Yes, I can," Tesler said. "With drugs. Test me and I'll prove it."

David's smile faltered. Drugs. They had given him drugs before, though not to suppress his abilities. He had no idea if drugs really could interfere with his powers, though Tesler seemed convinced. He might be lying. Of course, they might've tested drugs on their other subjects.

Dammit. If they had drugs to stop him…

Grace would die.

Chapter Nine

She was lost. Grace cursed herself. She had headed into the middle of the woods, where the trees formed a canopy overhead, blocking out the rays of the sun. An ambient radiance guided her through the woods. Underbrush choked the ground. Briars nipped at her arms and pant legs.

She'd avoided the roads in case the cops fanned out in search of her. She assumed they knew about her. Call it intuition. Or just common sense. Or paranoia.

Maybe a little of all three.

Either way, she sensed the danger. Someone had known Kellogg would confide in her and opted to frame her for his murder. The good citizen in her urged her to turn around, report to the police, tell them everything—how she met Kellogg, what little he had told her—and then explain to them how he died.

Gee, Mr. Policeman, it was a ghost that strangled him.

Right.

The police had no way of knowing her name. The person who called them couldn't know her. She was safe.

Unless Andrew talked.

God, she had to stop torturing herself. The sensible thing to do was to go home, think, and formulate some kind of a plan to save herself. A plan to fight off invisible killers? No problem. She'd whip one out in five minutes flat.

More than a plan, she needed rest. Her body cried out for a break. Her mind slogged through the facts, unable to siphon off the relevant data. Her eyes were gritty. She pushed through a clump of briars. The trees thinned, opening into a clearing. Twenty feet away, a deer paused in its grass munching and looked up at Grace. She took a step toward the deer. The animal darted into the woods. The white tuft of the deer's tail bobbed through the brush until the creature melded with the darkness of the deeper woods.

Across the clearing, Grace spotted a woven-wire fence, camouflaged by vines and briars. The fence spanned that side of the clearing and disappeared into the woods. She trotted across the clearing. The fence was chest high and corroded. A strand of barbed wire had been strung along the top. The barbs looked rusty. If one of them nicked her, she'd need a tetanus shot.

She wasn't up to testing the structural integrity of her fate. Not today. It might collapse under her.

The fence lured her into the trees again. The fence must lead somewhere, to a road or a stream, something she would recognize. From there, she'd find her way back to town.

Or she'd upset a hive of killer bees and die from hundreds of stings.

Way to think positive.

Christ, she had to stop visualizing the worst possible outcome of every situation. Start picturing the happy endings. Even if she never made it to the happily-ever-after, at least she could nourish her psyche with the fantasy.

Half an hour ticked by before the woods opened onto a dirt track. Not exactly a road, the track cleaved the earth where vehicles had driven through an opening in the woods. Grass, sparse as a balding man's hair, had cropped up between the tire tracks.

She glanced up and down the track. One direction led toward town, the other out into the hinterlands. If she could just tell which one led to town...

The sun had started its westward descent through the sky.

North led to town. Studying the sun's trajectory, she guessed that taking the road left would aim her back toward town. Either that or some rancher would find her desiccated body lying in the woods a decade or two from now.

She followed the road leftward.

Twenty minutes later, a stream blocked her passage.

The dirt track had vanished into the shallow waters, reappearing on the other shore. The water was cool and relatively clear. She coughed. Her throat burned and tickled with each inhalation. Her tongue was parched. She'd be in trouble if she didn't drink something, even partially muddy water, very soon.

Kneeling at the water's edge, she cupped her hands together, scooped water from the stream, and took a sip. The water tasted faintly of dirt, but it soothed her parched throat. She gulped in the liquid.

A twig popped behind her.

She froze. Water dribbled down her chin.

Another twig snapped.

Slowly, she rose to a crouch and slipped the gun out of her purse. She squinted into the trees, searching for the source of the noises. The cracks had sounded close, somewhere behind her, but she couldn't tell for certain. She'd been concentrating on quenching her thirst, not inspecting the woods for enemies. No one could've tracked her out here. She would've noticed another person clomping through the thickets.

A twig cracked. Closer now, a few yards from her, the sound so loud it echoed in her ears. The hairs on her neck prickled.

Gripping the gun in her hands, vise-tight, she whirled around.

The track was empty. In the trees to her right, a beast growled.

"Who's there?" she said.

Rustling. Soft growling.

"Come out or I'll shoot."

The weeds parted. A dark shape slunk out of the shadows into the road.

She swung the gun toward the shape. The black cougar halted in the middle of the dirt track, ears flattened back, upper lip curled, a growl reverberating in its chest.

She held still, the gun directed at the cat. Although she'd heard tales of black cats showing up in the area, she hadn't seen one herself. The stories always sounded like rural legends to her.

Now she crouched face-to-face with the reality of those tales.

The cougar watched her. She watched it. Maybe it wasn't a cougar, but some other kind of large cat, like a jaguar. It hardly mattered at the moment. Whether it selected her as its next meal mattered a hell of a lot more. Her heart hammered inside her chest.

She didn't dare move.

Suddenly, the cat dashed into the woods. Twigs splintered in its wake. The sounds faded into the distance.

Her heart still pounded, so she sat motionless for a minute or two, drawing in deep breaths, until the rushing of blood slowed to a more sedate pace. Then she hopped across the creek.

And stumbled to a halt.

He stood there. In the middle of the dirt track. Straddling the strip of grass that bisected the trail.

She blinked. Nope, he was still there.

His blonde hair glistened in the filtered sunlight. She frowned at him. After their encounter in the mall, she had hoped he might leave her alone. But then, she couldn't expect a hallucination to heed her wishes. Problem was, she no longer believed he was a figment of her screwed-up mind.

She raised the gun. "Get out of my way."

"You don't want to shoot me."

"Don't push me. I'm having a bad day."

He pointed up the road. "You're going the wrong way."

"I'm going north."

"Not anymore. The road turned."

Reluctantly, she took her gaze off him and glanced up at the sky. The sun had shifted. It now hovered behind and to the right of her. She was facing southeast—approximately.

Damn. She hated admitting he was right. The ache behind her eyes burgeoned anew.

She lowered the gun. "I would've figured that out. Eventually."

"When you got to Cuba?"

He stepped closer to her.

She raised the gun, finger on the trigger.

He shook his head.

"Thanks for the help," she said, "but I can take it from here."

"Have it your way."

She spun on her heels and marched down the track in the opposite direction.

He cleared his throat.

She paused mid step.

"You need to go through the woods," he said, "or you'll end up going south again."

She clenched her fist around the butt of the gun. Saying nothing, she veered off the track into the trees.

She sensed him trailing her. Though she neither saw nor heard him, she felt his presence in the air, like rain about to pour down from the heavens. Not that she equated her shadow man with rain. She loved rain, and the smell of damp earth afterward that permeated the air. No, she did not equate her stalker with rain.

That would mean she liked him.

Up ahead, a trail cut through the trees. Animals had worn this trail into the landscape—deer, cows, horses. Humans might've used the trail as well, though she saw no footprints to indicate it. The boughs of the trees curled over the trail. Although the sun's glow bathed the woods, the orb itself—her compass—stayed hidden above the canopy. The sun's heat nonetheless warmed her skin, drawing a sheen of sweat from her pores. She stopped and tilted her head backward, squinting at the treetops.

"This way."

His voice murmured behind her, too close behind. She sensed him move closer still until his body felt mere inches from hers, though she didn't dare look back to see if her estimation was correct.

"Go left," he said, his voice soft and deep.

And sexy. A shiver snaked down her spine. The shiver wasn't creepy, but rather…

Oh, she absolutely would not finish that thought.

He grasped her shoulders and gently turned her leftward. Now she could see him out the corner of her eye. Tall and handsome and so very close.

She shook off his hands and snapped, "I know left from right, thank you very much."

"Then move."

Good idea. She fully intended to move. Her muscles, however, seemed to have gone on strike.

He scrunched his eyebrows. "You really don't remember me, do you?"

"Sure, I remember. You cornered me in a department store fitting room yesterday."

She marched past him down the trail.

Fifteen minutes had passed since he first appeared, ostensibly to guide her, and she had yet to see any evidence that they traveled in the right direction. He might have a worse sense of direction than she did. Or he might have a reason for keeping her lost.

She continued down the trail. Not like she had a choice. Stand still and die of heat stroke, or follow the directions given by a shadow man and possibly die anyway. At least moving gave her a chance of finding civilization again.

Her stomach growled. Her throat went dry again. A stabbing pain behind her eyes exploded into a headache. The sun dipped behind the trees, shining between the branches, scorching her eyes. The temperature dropped a little, though not enough to make a difference.

The birds silenced. Crickets chirped in the underbrush.

She held the gun in one hand. The feel of metal against her skin did little to calm the creepy feeling building inside her. She disliked the idea of wandering through the woods, alone, after dark. She had no choice. The sun was setting, and she still had no clue where she was.

The sun slid below the horizon. Soon its glow would abandon the earth as well.

The ground collapsed.

Her right leg twisted sideways, wrenching her knee. She threw her hands out for balance and the gun flew from her grasp. She hit the dirt face-first.

Her knee throbbed, a charming accompaniment to her growing migraine. She rolled onto her back. Pain radiated out from her knee. She winced and gasped. In the twilight, she spotted the obstacle that had thwarted her—a pothole.

The air seared her right arm. She touched the skin above the elbow. It was raw and damp with blood. She had a feeling these injuries wouldn't heal themselves overnight. This was no dream, unfortunately.

She had no time for injuries. She was lost in the forest, something she thought only happened in Grimm Brothers stories. She'd explored the woods countless times as a teenager, without getting lost. Back then, she stayed in the areas she knew. She should never have sauntered off into unknown territory. How could she have been so stupid?

Bracing herself against a tree, she tried to stand. Pain ricocheted up her leg. Her knee buckled. Her buttocks hit the ground hard as the back of her head smacked into the tree.

She shouted a curse.

Night settled over the woods like a blanket.

She struggled onto her knees. All the muscles in her leg cramped at once. Her arm scraped against the tree. Pain screamed through her body. Tears welled in her eyes. She blinked them back. No, she would *not* cry. She would crawl if she must, but she would never concede to the pain.

Of course, now that she really needed a hand, her shadow man had vanished. Typical.

She avoided thinking about the insanity of using the word typical in reference to a man who appeared and disappeared at will, poof, like magic.

A breeze wafted over her. Goose bumps raised on her arms and neck.

She stood, gritting her teeth against the pain. She retrieved her key chain flashlight from her purse and flicked the power switch. A cone of wan yellow light illuminated the trail. The light glinted off the barrel of her gun. When she bent down to pick it up, pain jabbed her knee as if a thousand needles pierced her sinews. She bit back a yelp.

Gun in hand, she straightened. Her hand shook. She couldn't carry the gun. Holstering it inside her purse, she flung the bag over her neck and shoulder. The purse strap cut a diagonal across her torso.

She trudged along the trail, inch by inch, her knee screaming at every movement. The breeze irritated the abrasion on her arm.

The flashlight flickered.

She tapped it. The beam died. She smacked the thing against a tree. The light flashed once and died. Tossing the flashlight into her purse, she trudged onward, testing the ground ahead with her toes, feeling for obstacles with her hands.

After an eternity, she stumbled out of the woods onto a paved road. A double yellow line traced the road's center. It was a highway.

She shuffled to a halt on the shoulder.

Headlights popped into view in the distance as a vehicle topped a hill. As the lights drew near, she heard the grumble of an engine. Though she dreaded hitching a ride, she couldn't walk all the way to town.

The vehicle neared. She waved her arms.

The vehicle, a late-model BMW, pulled up beside her. The driver rolled down the window.

A man, his face obscured by shadows, said, "Need some help?"

The voice. She knew him. She bent over to peer inside the car. Pains shot through her leg in a web of agony. Through gritted teeth, she said, "Henry Winston."

"Imagine running into you out here." He clicked a switch and the door locks popped up with a thunk. "Hop in. I was on my way to your house."

She stepped back. Henry Winston happened to drive down this highway. On this night.

"I live down the road," he said. As his gaze traveled over her bloody sleeve, his expression darkened. "We'd better get you to a hospital."

He ignored the obvious questions—*How did you get out here? Why are you standing alongside the road in the dark? Why are you bleeding?*—that any normal person would've asked. He'd met her once. He should treat her with suspicion. Yet he studied her with a thoughtful expression that lacked any hint of skepticism, concern for her condition, or even curiosity about her situation.

Winston leaned across the passenger seat to push the door open. "Come on."

"I'm fine. Just getting some exercise."

He scrutinized her through half-closed eyes. "Get in, Grace."

His voice, deeper and calmer than the waters of the Atlantic Ocean, elicited shivers in her belly. She stumbled backward. Her heel caught on the edge of the pavement. She sailed down the slope of the shoulder, landed on her butt, and tumbled backward until her head hit the ground. Her feet flipped up, almost went over her head, but then flopped down again. Her knee screamed. Her head throbbed. Tears trickled from her eyes as she clamped her jaw tight against the pain.

Staring up the slope at the car, she watched Winston slide onto the passenger seat. He swung one leg, then the other, out the open door.

The gun. She reached for her purse. It was wedged under her hip. She pushed up onto her elbows. White-hot pain scorched the raw flesh on her arm. Biting back a cry, she fumbled for the purse's zipper. Her fingers felt big and clumsy. The zipper slipped out of her grasp.

Winston's shoes clapped on the pavement. "Come on, Grace. You need medical attention. Let me help you."

"You killed Edward McLean."

The thought had burst into her mind and so she spoke it. Before now, she'd overlooked Winston as a suspect. As she uttered the words, though, they made a kind of sense.

In one step, he reached her.

She scuttled crab-like away from him, ignoring the pain that ricocheted through her body. The purse. She had to get the purse open. Seizing the bag, she clawed at the zipper. The indirect glow of the headlights stung her eyes. Squinting, she spotted the zipper pull, took it between her thumb and forefinger, and yanked. The zipper opened with a *zzzt* sound.

Above her at the slope's pinnacle, Winston stood eerily still, backlit by the headlights. The faintly blue glow lent his eyes the luster of faceted onyx.

He thrust a hand toward her. "I won't hurt you."

Yeah right, she thought, and plunged her hand into the purse. Her fingers touched metal. She found the gun's grip, closing her fingers around it.

Winston's hand hovered two feet above and six inches in front of her head. He wiggled his fingers. Even in the moonlight, he was a shadow. A dark wraith. His eyes gleamed, though his face was obscured by the darkness that enveloped him from this side. The light that wreathed him from behind petered out before revealing his front.

A shiver as cold as liquid nitrogen raced through her body. She sat there, tears dribbling down her cheeks. Tears of pain, not defeat. She gripped the gun, keeping it inside her purse for now. He looked unarmed—except for that suggestive bulge under his suit jacket. Even in these lighting conditions, she made out the unnatural shape that snuggled in the hollow of his left shoulder.

Winston growled.

No, she must've imagined the sound. Probably the wind.

He yanked his hand back. "The hard way then."

He slipped a hand inside his jacket.

Gritting her teeth, Grace pulled out her gun and sprang to her feet. Her knee gave out. She crumpled to the ground, lost her balance, and tumbled sideways down the slope. Winston shouted at her. When she hit the base of the slope, she shoved herself up onto all fours. By some miracle, she still held the gun tight in her fist.

Winston loped down the hill after her with an oblong object clasped in one hand. He stumbled, cursed, and trotted toward her as fast as he could. In a minute, he'd be on her.

She leaped to her feet. Pain tore through the muscles from her knee straight up to her hip. White lights danced in her vision. Her ears rang. *Breathe, dammit.* She sucked in a breath and, teeth clamped over her bottom lip, she limped along the hill's base.

Winston bounded off the slope. He spun in her direction, breaking into a fast jog.

Thirty feet separated them. Not enough.

Her knee slowed her progress. She pushed harder, grimacing and panting from the pain as much as the exertion. Faster, faster, she must move faster. The road followed the curve of the hill, and she traced the hill's contour, pushing harder. A wave of dizziness crashed over her.

She listed right, then left. The night tilted around her. Nausea swelled inside her as she tripped and stopped.

Behind her, shoes clomped through the sandy loam. Breaths grunted. Clothes rustled.

The world spun.

No, no, no.

"Ack!"

Her limbs morphed into stone. Her heart switched rhythms with a skip and a hop. The strangled cry had come from over her shoulder.

She wanted to turn to look, but the spinning forced her to stay rooted in place. The sound of footfalls had ceased. She took slow, deliberate breaths, focusing on a single star in the sky. It gave her a center of focus, something for her massively screwed-up sense of balance to home in on. And then she waited.

Silence.

The spinning diminished into rocking.

Crickets chirped.

At last, the dizziness subsided. She turned in a half circle.

Henry Winston lay sprawled on the ground. One knee was bent, his arms askew, the oblong object still clutched in his hand. Just beyond Winston's head, a figure loomed in the moonlight. His pale hair glistened in the silvery glow. Her shadow man.

He must've attacked Winston. Knocked him out. Or killed him.

Her knees shuddered. Her tongue had turned to sandpaper. Her throat burned. The embers in her stomach ignited into a conflagration.

Her hero stepped over Winston and advanced on her. Just as Winston's eyes had glowed darkly in the moonlight, his shimmered with the blue of a Caribbean inlet. When he halted several paces from her, the weakness in her legs spread through her hips into her belly, up through her chest and into her heart. Stepping closer, he reached for her face. She flinched, but did not move away. He gently ran his thumb across her cheek to wipe away the tear stains. His skin warmed hers.

A vehicle passed by on the road above. In the flare of the headlights, she saw his face was ashen, his eyes bloodshot.

"You need a doctor," he said.

"No," she said, though her voice wavered. "I'm fine."

Her knee buckled. She dropped onto the dirt. A tear trickled down her cheek onto her lip, seeping into her mouth.

No. Enough crying.

Her ears rang. The twilight world dipped and twirled around her once again. She lay down on the earth, which felt cool against her back, and let her eyelids flutter shut. A pair of arms slipped under her, hoisting her body off the ground. She opened her eyes just enough to see, through the darkness encroaching on her vision, the unearthly blue fire in his irises.

He carried her past Winston. Her head flopped sideways. The object Winston had held in his hand, she spotted it now. It was a cell phone.

She passed out.

Chapter Ten

The light blinded her. She squinted. Voices whispered around her. Machines beeped and clicked.

While her eyes adjusted to the light, the scene shifted into focus. A young man in a green outfit—the kind worn by doctors and nurses—bent over her leg, scrutinizing her knee with his lips pressed together and his eyes half closed. Red hair spilled over his forehead in stringy locks. His skin was pale. His hands were thin and long with pronounced knuckles. He didn't notice her watching him, or didn't show his awareness if he did notice.

Hovering his hands just above her leg, he swirled his palms over the contours of her knee. A warmth spread through the joint. Not painful warmth. The soothing kind.

The young man jerked his hands away and looked at her. He was a kid, no more than seventeen by her estimation. But then, some people retained their youthful features even into middle age. In the movies and television, some actors who played teenagers were actually in their late twenties. This kid might be older than he looked, and more threatening too.

"Are you a doctor?" Grace asked.

He flattened his palm against her forehead. His skin felt warm. He closed his eyes as he inhaled long breaths and let each out slowly.

Opening his eyes, he withdrew his hand. "It's done."

Weariness descended on her. Her eyelids lowered partway without her permission. She did not want to sleep. Well, okay, she *wanted* to sleep. But she refused to give in to the urge.

The boy backed away from her, retreating behind the curtain that surrounded her bed. To her left, on the other side of the curtain, someone coughed. She must be in the emergency room.

She tried to speak in forceful tone, but her voice emerged as a slur. "Wait."

"Sleep," he said.

Her eyelids shut. She couldn't sleep, not now, not yet. She sensed something important had just happened and she must investigate, not take a nap. The pain was gone—the pain everywhere, she realized, even the migraine—and she had too much to do, too many questions that needed answering. She could not laze around in bed.

Can't sleep...

Something touched her wrist. With great effort, she parted her eyelids just enough to peek through her lashes.

A nurse stood beside her, taking her pulse. The woman released her wrist and scribbled on a clipboard.

Grace cleared her throat. "Don't you have machines for that?"

The nurse smiled and drawled, "I was double-checkin' the machine. Never hurts, ya know?"

Grace blinked several times, trying to clear her mind. It still felt enmeshed in cobwebs.

The nurse patted her arm. "Welcome back, hon. I was wondering when you'd rise and shine."

She didn't feel shiny. The nurse looked it, however, with her bright smile and rosy cheeks. Dark blonde hair, cut short, curled in ringlets around her face. She was probably a few years older than Grace.

"Where am I?" Grace asked, raising onto her elbows. "Who are you?"

"I'm Hannah Martin," the woman drawled, "but you can just call me Hannah. You're in Lassiter Falls Community Hospital. You had a little whoopsy."

"A what?"

Hannah giggled. "An accident, hon. You remember what happened?"

In her memory, the incident had taken on the haze of a dream. "Vaguely. I feel okay."

Hannah glanced at Grace's leg, looked away, and then glanced back. Her expression went blank. Moving only her eyes, she turned her gaze on Grace.

"Something wrong?" Grace asked.

Hannah tapped Grace's knee. "The wound. It's gone."

Grace leaned forward to touch her leg. Her knee no longer ached. The leg of her jeans had ripped and frayed around the knee, yet despite the flesh showing through the holes, she saw no wound. No blood.

Not even a scratch. She flexed her leg. No shooting pains. No stiffness. She could've executed a cartwheel off the bed if she wanted.

"How long was I asleep?" she asked.

"Couple hours."

From the grit in her eyes, the taste of sleep in her mouth, and the mud coating her brain, she would've guessed her slumber lasted days. No injuries healed themselves in two hours. She felt fine, though, like nothing had happened. Even the paranoia and anxiety that overtook her earlier had dissipated. Though deep down she knew the ordeal had happened hours ago, she could almost believe days or even weeks had elapsed.

What the hell had come over her?

"Tell me what happened, hon," Hannah said.

Winston coming at her, gun in hand. Certainty flushing through her in the form of one thought—*he killed Grandpa*. Then running. Winston on the ground, cell phone in hand. Phone? It had to be a gun. Hands lifting her. Darkness.

"How did I get here?" she asked.

"A nice young man brought you in," Hannah said. "Wouldn't give his name. Said he found you alongside the highway."

Her stomach fluttered. "What did he look like?"

"Blonde hair. Beautiful blue eyes. Cute as a button, but real serious."

Grace stared at the curtain. Blonde hair. Blue eyes. He saved her life. Events appeared to support that notion, yet she couldn't believe appearances anymore. Brian Kellogg appeared to have been strangled. Her leg appeared to have healed. Her shadow man must've killed Brian Kellogg and now he wanted her dead.

Then why did he carry her to the hospital?

He might need her alive, until she gave him the flash drive or he figured out where Grandpa had hidden it. But his concern for her seemed genuine and, in the darkest corners of her mind, she recognized that he meant no harm. He could help her. She should trust him. She knew him.

Ridiculous.

If he didn't kill Kellogg, then she had another invisible man to deal with, and no clue how to do that.

She flopped back onto the bed, nestling her head on the pillow. The bed was raised so that it held her in a semi-upright position.

"You know him?" Hannah asked.

"Who?"

"The man who brought you in."

"Not really."

Hannah fluffed the pillow behind Grace's head. "The doctor'll be in soon to take a look at you."

"Again?"

"He ain't seen ya yet, sweetie. You've been asleep."

"But I woke up and he was here. Looking at my leg. He told me to sleep."

"The doctor's been busy with a critical patient. You must've dreamed it."

Grace said nothing. No point in arguing, really.

The nurse eyed her with a curious expression. "You've been to the ER before, haven't you? With real bad migraines."

Grace's breath caught in her throat. How did the nurse know about her headaches? Oh, duh. She'd come to this emergency room and seen doctors whose offices were in this hospital. Of course they'd have her records.

"Still havin' those migraines?" Hannah asked.

Limited honesty seemed the best policy right now, so Grace told the woman, "Sometimes. I've got medicine for it."

"Good." Hannah turned to leave, then glanced over her shoulder at Grace. "You need anything, you be sure to let me know."

Grace tried to relax, but she hated hospitals. And doctors offices. And needles. And blood pressure cuffs. The one wrapped around her arm right now, taking her blood pressure at regular intervals, pumped itself up again for a new reading. The pressure on her arm pinched harder and harder.

She squirmed on the bed. A sharp object dug into her hip. She shoved a hand into her jeans pocket and felt the key tucked inside it. Kellogg's key. Tugging it out of her pocket, she turned it between her thumb and forefinger. Bits of lint stuck to the tape residue on the key, along with a tiny breath mint. Her pocket wasn't exactly a sterile environment. She flicked the mint off the key. It flew past the nurse's left eye.

Grace winced. "Sorry."

"Don't worry," Hannah said. "I've had worse things thrown at me. What was that anyway, a TicTac?"

"Uh…yeah." Grace fiddled with the key. "Wintergreen flavor."

Hannah grinned. "My favorite. You got any more?"

"No. Sorry."

As the blood pressure cuff deflated, releasing its grip on her arm, Grace let out a breath. She adjusted her position on the bed—and promptly dropped the key on the floor.

Hannah snatched it up, glancing at the key as she handed it back to Grace. With the key once again in her hand, Grace closed her fist around it.

"Don't worry about your mail," Hannah said. "Store's closed anyhow."

"What?"

The nurse patted her arm. "My hubby keeps a box at Mail 'N More too. He gets off work at five-thirty, so he always has to rush to make there before the store closes at six."

"Oh. Right." Grace tried to act nonchalant, though her heart was beating faster. The monitor nearby registered ninety-eight beats per minute. "I just realized I forgot to pick up my mail today, that's all."

"Store opens at eight in the mornin', sweetie."

"Thanks."

"Sure thing. Now y'all take it easy till the doctor comes."

The nurse winked at Grace, and then departed. The curtain settled back into place behind her.

Grace tucked the key into her pocket again. She knew what the key unlocked now. Tomorrow morning, she would go to the Mail 'N More franchise and find out what Kellogg had hidden there. He must've hidden something in the box, else why bother concealing the key? Maybe some of the answers she sought awaited her there.

The heart rate monitor read one-hundred-five beats per minute.

Grace ran her hands over her injured knee—her formerly injured knee. She had not dreamed the man, or boy, who examined her leg. He existed. Once in awhile, a person had to accept the truth no matter how impossible it sounded. She had witnessed the evidence, touched it, smelled it. Men existed who could appear and disappear whenever they chose, commit murders while remaining invisible, and heal injuries with their bare hands. Or their minds. She hadn't decided which made more sense, although trying to find sense in the chaos seemed futile. The truth no longer made sense, while sorcery became believable. In this bizarre new world, logic was extinct.

She must protect herself, or risk her own extinction.

Monitors beeped nearby. A patient snored next door.

Stay alive. That was her priority. Finding answers to the many questions bouncing around in her brain, that might prove the only way to keep herself alive.

At the foot of the bed, the curtain billowed as if someone had walked through it.

A draft chilled her skin. She rubbed her arms and scrutinized the empty air around the bed. No one was there, of course. At least, no one she could see.

Hardly comforting these days.

She relaxed against the pillow. Well, she tried to relax anyway.

Stay alive.

Leaning back against the bed, she closed her eyes and tried to relax. From past experience, she knew the doctor wouldn't let her leave the ER until her heart rate dropped below ninety. *Relax*, she commanded herself. She pictured the oak tree behind her house, her favorite place to sit and take it easy. Listening to the birds chirp, feeling the grass beneath her, those things eased the tension in her on a normal day. This day was far from normal. Still, she imagined the scene. Let her muscles go slack. Let her mind empty of all thoughts.

Sitting under the tree. Leaning against the trunk. Watching little cumulus clouds scud across the sky. Feeling a hand grasp hers, their fingers intertwining. She let herself imagine muscular arms sliding around her, drawing her into an embrace, surrounding her with human warmth. She knew who it was now, who she needed, though she didn't understand why. Just this once, she didn't worry about why. The sensation, even the imaginary version, imbued her with a kind of serenity she'd never felt before.

Grace opened her eyes a crack to check the heart rate monitor. It read eighty-four beats per minutes.

She closed her eyes and drifted back into the fantasy. His effect on her was uncanny—and totally illogical. Right at this moment, she didn't care.

Blue eyes. Blonde hair.

Who are you?

An hour later, Grace shuffled out of the hospital into the night. She needed a taxi or a bus to get home. Spotting a bus stop on the other side of the parking lot, she trudged toward it.

Despite the ordeal of the day, she wanted to do something. Had to do something. Waiting for truth to find her didn't work. Success stemmed from action, therefore she must take action. Right now. The night camouflaged shadows and shadow men. It also concealed humans. She could sneak somewhere and accomplish something.

Great plan. Sneak somewhere. Do something.

Reaching the bus stop, she dropped onto the bench. She had no idea when the next bus might arrive. It gave her time to think, she supposed, but no great thoughts occurred to her. Clasping her hands on her lap, she studied the lines on her palms.

A memory catapulted from the depths of her mind. Winston striding down the hillside. Urging her to go with him. The gun—no, the cell phone in his grasp. The memory mutated. Winston sprawled on the dirt.

He killed Grandpa.

The thought exploded in her mind. She'd accused Winston of murdering her grandfather back on that roadside, seconds before she ran—okay, limped—away from him. At the time, he said nothing in response. No denial, no angry retort, no confused look on his face, no shouted expletives. He simply took one monstrous step toward her.

She had thought, when he reached for his cell phone, that he would pull out a gun. Going for a phone made no sense. Unless he thought he'd whack her with the device, he couldn't stop her with a phone.

Maybe he was calling for backup.

What kind of backup? The cops? Men in white coats to drag her off to an asylum?

A shadow fell over her.

She jerked her head to look up. Henry Winston stood in front of her, an arm's length away. A nearby streetlight cast a sallow glow on his face and glinted darkly in his eyes.

"Need a ride?" he asked, as casually as if she bummed rides from him every day.

"I'll wait for the bus."

"My car is more comfortable."

She forced a bland smile. "I'm going green. Saving the planet one bus ride at a time."

They stared at each other in silence for three heartbeats. He broke the silence first.

"Come with me," he said, his tone sharpening into a dangerous edge. "I won't ask again."

She glanced at the suspicious bulge under his jacket. Too big for a cell phone.

Winston took a step closer. "We need to talk."

Right now his eyes reminded her of doll's eyes, rather than jewels. Reflective but lifeless.

She resisted the urge to shimmy sideways on the bench, away from him. Showing fear seemed like a bad idea at this particular moment. So instead, she asked, "Talk about what?"

"Everything." He hesitated, and she could almost hear the gears clicking in his brain. Finally he said, "I suppose it's time I came clean. I work for the FBI."

"And I'm the reincarnation of Cleopatra."

Winston looked straight at her. Like a covered pot, his face revealed nothing of what simmered beneath the lid. His expression was cold, or maybe her bias colored her perceptions. She trusted no one.

Especially not him.

What a dark and lonely place in which to find herself. No one to trust, no one to lean on for support or comfort, no one to counsel her. The isolation had once frightened her. No more. That was her advantage over people like Henry Winston. They believed they could squeeze her into a hole and she would beg for light. They were wrong. She'd found herself in this place before. She knew it well and recognized the contours of the walls, the texture of the bars, the depth of the shadows.

The dark no longer frightened her.

"May I explain?" Winston asked.

"Why not. I could use a good laugh."

From an inner pocket of his jacket, he extracted a thin wallet. Flipping it open, he handed it to her. An ID badge with the letters "FBI" on it. The badge could've been real or a good fake. She would hardly know the difference.

She returned the wallet to him. "Nice forgery."

A muscle in his jaw pulsed. "As I said, I work for the FBI. I'm investigating your grandfather's death."

"Uh-huh."

Grace searched Winston's expression and his body language for a clue to his veracity. Maybe she had attributed evil to him where none existed. She let paranoia take root in her psyche, braiding its limbs around her mind, blocking rationality with its dense foliage. The sensation of someone watching her, hidden in shadows or crowds of people, stayed with her even now. The feeling swept over her at intervals, like the beacon of a lighthouse. Sometimes she felt a presence right beside her and swore she felt a hand graze her skin. Other times, she sensed the presence coming closer, moving away, dissipating.

Paranoia had become her best friend.

She couldn't dismiss her gut feelings. They had served her well in the past.

If she trusted her gut, then she was wrong about one very important thing. She wasn't without allies. Deep inside, she knew she could trust one person. Her shadow man.

Returning her attention to Winston, she said, "My grandfather died in a plane crash."

"I'm afraid not."

"You have a theory."

He rubbed his chin. "He was murdered. By a co-worker."

She had zero reasons to buy his story or to believe any explanations he offered, yet she could reject nothing at this point. When options melted away, the ridiculous became reasonable.

"The killer broke into your house," Winston said.

"To borrow my lipstick, I suppose."

"He wants a flash drive. He thinks you have it."

A flash drive. She was damn sick of hearing about the thing. "He's mistaken."

"Doesn't matter. He'll kill you anyway."

An eighteen-wheeler rocketed down the road, far exceeding the speed limit. The air displaced by the truck blustered over Grace and flapped Winston's clothes. Pebbles kicked up by the big truck's wheels ticked on the sidewalk. The headlights splayed across them both for just long enough to temporarily blind Grace.

She listened to Winston's story. He provided her with a solid, rational explanation for almost everything. Part of her longed to accept the story. Most of her knew she could not. It was a lie.

He hoped to seduce her with his lies—not seduce her into bed, but rather into lowering the drawbridge and admitting him into her personal fortress.

Winston explained that Edward McLean had worked on a secret project for a pharmaceutical company, studying how the brain works to help design better drugs. Her grandfather had been on the cusp of a major breakthrough, according to Winston, until one of his assistants grew jealous of his accomplishments and killed him.

The scenario made sense. Kellogg had mentioned both the pharmaceutical company and the study. She might've accepted Winston's version. Asked no questions. Fretted no more.

She couldn't. Kellogg had insisted the study was a façade. He'd insisted—and now he was dead. He died because he knew the truth. Because he tried to tell her.

"So," Grace said, "why was my grandfather going to Washington?"

"To receive an award."

"Why wouldn't he tell me about it?"

"Maybe he wanted to surprise you. Drop by on his way home."

Clever. A bit too clever. Somehow, he knew Grandpa had liked surprising her with his visits. The statement sounded innocuous, but she had trouble seeing it as nothing. Everything Winston said struck her as contrived.

With every word, he nudged her toward the conclusion he preferred.

Both Brian Kellogg and her shadow man told her someone had to warn her. About what, they didn't say. Maybe about Henry Winston. Of course, they might both be crazy. She might be crazy. Winston might be the sane one.

Sure, he might be sane. But sane did not automatically equal honest or trustworthy.

Winston slipped a photograph out of his shirt pocket. Handing it to her, he said, "This is David Ransom. He's a sociopath, a master manipulator and a murderer. He killed your grandfather."

She took the photo. The paper was limp, the gloss degraded. The snapshot captured a young man standing on a beach, probably along the ocean. The sunset blazed behind him as he smiled at the camera, his blonde hair ruffled by a long-ago breeze, his blue eyes focused on the camera.

David Ransom. Her shadow man.

She shoved the photo at Winston.

He arched an eyebrow. "You recognize him?"

"Nope."

"He's extremely dangerous. Volatile, unpredictable." Winston stepped closer and knelt in front of her. In a voice that sounded a bit too earnest, he said, "If you see him, call me. Do not approach him or talk to him."

"Yes, sir."

The sarcasm in the statement eluded him, she thought, because he gave a satisfied half-smile and rose to his full height. He expected everyone should obey him. Most people probably did. They fell for his pseudo-concern, ignored the subtle signs of darkness beneath the surface, and trusted what they heard rather than what they saw.

Winston called David Ransom a master manipulator. Maybe he was really talking about himself.

Retrieving car keys from his pocket, Winston said, "I understand why you don't trust me yet. But I can't help you without your trust. That's the key."

The key.

She jammed a hand into her jeans pocket. Her fingers contacted metal. It was the key Brian Kellogg had taped to the inside of his unnecessary hairpiece. She now knew it led to a mailbox in the local Mail 'N More franchise. Kellogg's key might prove, well, key in more ways than one. It might be the vital clue that unlocked the entire mystery. Or not. She wouldn't know until morning.

Her pulse quickened. Winston must never find out about the key. Of that, she was certain. Why she was certain, she couldn't explain.

She pulled her hand out of her pocket but left the key safely inside.

"You must come with me," Winston said. "For your own protection."

"I appreciate the offer, but no. I'll manage on my own."

Winston hooked his thumb through the key ring and flipped his keys in a circle. Once. Twice. He let them dangle then, clinking against each other.

"Where do you live?" Grace said.

Winston frowned at her.

She arched her eyebrows. "You're the one who said you wanted to come clean and you want me to trust you. Answering a few questions might help with both."

The frown morphed into a tight line. "I live in Los Angeles, but I've been camped out here in Lassiter Falls for nearly six weeks."

Which meant he arrived shortly after Edward McLean's death. She tried to sound nonchalant as she said, "Why didn't you tell me all this when came to my house the other day?"

"Because I didn't."

"That's not an answer. Tell me who you really are."

She met his gaze. His eyes were narrowed to slits. His entire face had tightened into a mask of contained anger. Lines fanned out from his eyes and creased his forehead. He clutched his keys so tightly in his fist that his hand trembled slightly.

Her throat constricted. She swallowed, but it felt like trying to gulp down a rock.

The anger tightening Winston's features slackened into a smirk. "All right, if you want honesty then I will give it to you. Just remember you asked for it." He folded his arms over his chest, tilting head back to stare down at her through narrowed eyes. "My name is Xavier Waldron. I've come to retrieve something my employer wants, which we know Edward McLean gave to you."

"You're mistaken," Grace said.

Waldron chuckled, though it sounded in no way jovial. "You are coming with me this instant, Grace. Your only choice is whether you walk on your own or I carry your limp, unconscious body to the car."

He was three feet away from her. He lifted a foot to move toward her.

She threw herself sideways, sliding across the bench.

Waldron grabbed for her.

Grace leaped off the bench and bolted. As she fled down the sidewalk, she heard Waldron calling after her.

"You can't hide, Grace. I know your secrets."

Did he know? Maybe. Even she didn't know all her secrets. For all she knew, she'd met Xavier Waldron before. It was possible. Her screwy brain left a lot to the imagination these days. They might've met during the eight months of her life she couldn't remember.

She ran—and she didn't stop until she'd jumped onto a bus headed for her neighborhood.

Maybe Waldron did know her. Maybe David knew her too. Some part of her might actually know which of them to trust, if she could trust either man. The knowledge was buried deep in her unconscious, like a treasure trove in an undiscovered tomb.

Amnesia really sucked.

Chapter Eleven

Mail 'N More resided in the corner space of a building on the courthouse square, beside the smaller of the two movie theaters in town. The building, constructed in the 1920s as a theater and remodeled once in its entire history, had the reputation of being haunted. The movie theater boasted two small screens, dilapidated seats, stairs that creaked, and sticky floors. In stark contrast to the theater, Mail 'N More featured shiny floors, a stars-and-stripes color scheme, and neatly arranged aisles stacked with neatly arranged merchandise of the office supply variety.

At three minutes past eight in the morning, Grace walked through the store's glass-enclosed entryway and between the automatic doors that whooshed open before her. An electronic doorbell bonged, alerting everyone inside that a new customer had entered the premises. A smiling employee trotted to her. The girl looked barely old enough to vote.

"May I help you?" the girl asked, her tone a little too energetic for first thing in the morning. Her name tag identified her as Ashlee.

Nobody knew how to spell anymore.

Grace cleared her throat. "I'm interested in getting a mailbox. Do you have a pamphlet or something?"

"Sure." Ashlee trotted to a nearby display of informational brochures, nabbed one, and brought it back to Grace. "Our rates are listed on the back page."

"Thanks." Grace surveyed the store with one long glance but failed to spot the boxes. "Where are the mailboxes anyway?"

"Let me show you."

Ashlee hustled out the automatic doors, waving for Grace to follow. They turned left toward a door Grace hadn't noticed before, set back in the corner of the entryway. A modest sign above the door announced MAILBOXES

24-HR ACCESS, with a down arrow suggesting they lay inside this doorway. Ashlee pushed the door open and led Grace into short hallway that dead-ended at a longer hallway. Rows of mailboxes lined the longer corridor, which stretched rightward along the store's wall. The hallway was brick, rather than glass, with mailboxes of various sizes set into the wall. They looked just like post office boxes. A door set into the wall at the far end of the hallway was marked EMPLOYEES ONLY.

The other sign had said 24-HR ACCESS. She could've stopped by last night and avoided the hours of tossing and turning as she tried to sleep while simultaneously wondering what Kellogg's mailbox held and worrying Xavier Waldron might abduct her from her bed. She'd gotten a little sleep, but nowhere near enough.

Ashlee was reciting the benefits of the store's mailbox services.

Grace raised her hand, interrupting the girl's spiel. "Thanks, I think I've got all the information I need."

Along the wall opposite the mailboxes, a long table held pens—chained to the table, naturally—and free pads of paper. Grace marched to the table. She picked up a pen and began circling items in the brochure. She hoped it looked like she was considering her options. She also hoped Ashlee would take the hint and leave.

Fortunately, the girl had decent manners. She told Grace to "come and catch me" if she had any questions, and then she left.

Grace was alone. At last.

She fished Kellogg's key out of her pocket. The number engraved on it was 208. She wandered among the boxes and, finding 208 in the middle, unlocked the box. Her shoulders sagged. The box was empty, save for a small tin of breath mints.

Picking up the tin, she studied the image of mint leaves engraved on the lid. She popped off the lid but saw only mints hidden inside the tin. Damn. She'd hoped Kellogg stashed the flash drive inside his mailbox. The key had been her one and only lead. Either Kellogg kept the key as a decoy or he died before hiding the flash drive in the box. Maybe he'd never intended to hide the flash drive there. Maybe he had no evidence, no flash drive, nothing more important than a grocery list to give her.

Shoving the mints in her purse, she shut the box and headed out of the store.

On the sidewalk, she paused. A plan would help. A psychic flash would be great. She had neither. As she took in her surroundings, something caught her attention. To the right of the Mail 'N More entryway, nestled against the brick façade, stood a newspaper vending machine. Inside the machine, the headline on the front page of the Lassiter Falls Gazette declared "Tourist killed in botched mugging."

Grace edged closer to the machine. Below the headline was a photo of Andrew Haley, handcuffed, being shoved into a police cruiser by two stern-looking policemen. Andrew's eyes bulged. His mouth hung open. In the background, she could make out the Bed & Bath Inn.

She dug quarters out of her purse and fed the machine to retrieve a copy of the paper. Back in her car, doors locked and engine idling, she read the article.

The story claimed a mental patient had strangled a tourist who carried no identification. Andrew, they said, had escaped from a hospital in California. For unknown reasons, he hitchhiked two thousand miles to Lassiter Falls, where he lived in alleys and abandoned buildings. The attack on the tourist appeared unprovoked.

Where had the reporter gotten his information? Andrew couldn't carry on a conversation, much less dictate his biography. The police must've released the information. Where they got it remained a mystery.

Maybe Waldron told them.

She must know for sure. And she needed to know more about Waldron. Like, oh, why he wanted to abduct her and what "secrets" he knew about her.

David Ransom might know the answers to her questions.

She must find David. An invisible man could hide anywhere he wanted. He could've been watching her right then, sitting beside her, laughing at her confusion, plotting ways of killing her. No, she couldn't believe he would kill her. He had saved her life. Besides, last night she'd realized she trusted him. She had no clue why, but at this point she had to trust her instincts. They were all she had to go on.

Waldron maintained David was dangerous. She trusted Waldron about as much as she trusted a coyote not to kill a rabbit. She shouldn't trust David Ransom either. But she did. Which was crazy.

Maybe she really had lost her mind.

Five minutes later, she still sat hunched in the driver's seat of the Pontiac. This morning she'd remembered the gas can she kept in the garage, stuffed into the corner behind the leaf rake. A hike to the nearest gas station got her enough gas to drive the Pontiac back to the station and fill up its empty tank. She couldn't face another day of bus rides.

The mailbox had been empty. Where had Kellogg hidden his evidence? Where the hell was this flash drive everyone wanted?

Kellogg had concealed the mailbox key. Why would he bother hiding it if the box held nothing?

She dug the tin of mints out of her purse. Popping open the lid, she gazed down at the round mints inside the tin. She poked the mints with her fingertip. The tin's metal bottom shifted.

Crappy construction in a mint tin. What a shock.

Hold on. She poked the mints again. The shiny metal beneath them moved, but the tin itself remained intact.

The tin had a false bottom.

She tipped the tin until the mints tumbled out onto the passenger seat. The false bottom shifted but stayed inside the tin. She used her fingernail to pry up the slim metal sheet, which someone had cut to fit the box, as evidenced by the sheet's sharp edges.

Grace removed the false bottom, setting it on the passenger seat. In the space now revealed inside the tin lay a microcassette of the type designed for small recorders used in dictation. Most people nowadays used digital voice recorders instead. Microcassette recorders were going out of fashion.

Taking the microcassette between her thumb and forefinger, she examined it. If Kellogg had concealed it with such care, he must've deemed the microcassette important.

She needed a microcassette player. Since she didn't have one at home, she'd need to buy one.

Mail 'N More sold office supplies.

Jumping out of the car, she locked and shut the door—and then half walked, half jogged back to the store. The same sales associate pounced on her as soon as she crossed the threshold. Grace asked about microcassette recorders, and Ashlee escorted her to the correct aisle. Grace figured she must've looked annoyed, or at least harried, because Ashlee excused herself more quickly this time, with the excuse that she saw another customer in need of assistance.

Grace chose the cheapest microcassette recorder and grabbed a package of batteries. Two customers got to the checkout line ahead of her. Their purchases seemed to take an eternity to ring up, and then the credit card reader malfunctioned. Grace drummed the toe of her boot on the hard floor. Her pulse accelerated with every second she waited in this line. Christ, she had possible evidence in her purse and no way of listening to it. What did the tape contain?

If it was nothing more than Kellogg's favorite pop songs, she'd scream.

The cashier struggled with the credit card reader.

Grace gulped back a groan. If this line didn't progress soon, like in the next nanosecond, she'd scream right here and now.

At last, the machine consented to read the other customer's card. A quick signature completed the transaction and the customer moseyed out of the store. The next customer paid quickly—with cash, thank heavens. Grace did the same.

A minute later, she was back in the car. Shoving the key in the ignition, she started the car's engine. The temperature outside was rising, along with the humidity. She turned on the AC but refrained from cranking it up to maximum. The noise of the blower would make it difficult to hear much of anything. So instead, she aimed every vent directly at her.

Then she ripped open the packaging, freeing the microcassette recorder. Inserting the batteries took three tries. The damn icons showing how to insert them were so small she needed an electron microscope to read them properly. With the batteries finally inserted, she shoved the microcassette into the recorder, cranked up the volume, and hit the play button. The tape whirred.

On the recording, someone sighed. A crinkling noise followed, calling to mind pages being turned.

"Where should I start?" a voice said.

Grandpa's voice. The cassette must be his audio journal. He had kept a journal of his thoughts, recording them throughout the day whenever he felt the need. Though he kept the contents of his journal private, he had told her of its existence. She'd forgotten about it. He'd also preferred microcassettes over digital recorders, she recalled. He wasn't averse to the digital revolution, but neither did he rush to adopt new technologies.

The sound cut in and out.

"—the beginning," Edward McLean said. "This morning, I made a decision. I should've exposed them long before now. I—"

Bumping and rattling noises obscured his voice. She waited it out. After a couple seconds that felt like hours, Grandpa's voice resounded in the car once again.

"—ever realized it would go this far. I'm the only one who can stop this. Everyone else has an agenda, some connection, or else they've been frightened out of their minds by his thugs. I've talked to Senator Faulkner and he assures me he'll help stop this madness. I hope to God they haven't gotten him as well."

A bang. Muffled shouting.

The tape hissed. Had the recording ended, or was more noise?

A chill whispered over the back of her neck. *Someone's watching.*

She surveyed the area outside the car. No one on the sidewalk. Her Pontiac sat on a slight hill, parallel parked a fifty feet from Mail 'N More. No cars were parked behind her, and only a smattering of other vehicles occupied spots in front of her car or on the opposite side of the street. Every other car sat empty, however.

The chill spread down her body, raising goose bumps from head to toe.

Get out of here, a voice inside her urged. She grabbed the microcassette recorder, punched the stop button, and yanked the keys from the ignition.

Thunder grumbled.

Beyond the windshield, the sun burned in a clear sky.

She shoved the microcassette recorder into her purse and slung the bag's strap around her neck, over her shoulder. She grabbed the door handle.

Thunder rumbled. No, not thunder. Almost like a voice. Low and grumbling and speaking words she couldn't understand.

She pulled the handle and thrust the door outward.

A blast of cold smacked into her. The door slammed shut in her face. The lock thunked into place of its own volition. The air grew hot and thick around her. Each inhalation strained her chest. Her lungs wanted to expel the air, but the pressure somehow clogged her lungs too, until she couldn't breathe at all.

No, no, no, this was wrong. An instinct she couldn't explain warned her not to give in, to fight the pressure by breathing. Darkness speckled her vision. Her pulse thundered behind the ringing in her ears.

Breathe.

Clenching her teeth, she breathed. At first, her lungs refused to operate. She shut her eyes, struggling to block out the ringing in her ears and the burning in her chest. *Fight*, she willed herself.

The first breath came in ragged gasps. She hissed it out between clenched teeth, one molecule at a time. The second breath was easier, though not by much. The pressure inside her lungs eased a little more with each breath. The air around her cooled as the pressure let up.

The engine revved.

She held the keys in her hand—didn't she? Opening her eyes, she glanced down to spy the keys clenched in her fist, the metal glistening in the sunlight that streamed through the windows.

The door handle was frozen in place. The lock was engaged but, though she clawed at it with her fingernails and yanked the handle hard, the door stayed shut. Pulling the handle should've released the lock, yet it refused to disengage. She used a key as a lever to push the lock upward. Still nothing. The mechanism was jammed.

She shoved her finger on the rocker switch that activated the electric windows. The window rolled down a few inches.

The switch rocked upward under her finger. Though she depressed it so hard her finger ached, the switch stayed in the up position. The window slid closed.

She banged her fists into the glass.

A voice—close, almost inside her head—chuckled in that low, gravelly, inhuman tone.

Then the voice spoke. Each syllable was drawn out to a second or two in length, which made the sound that much creepier.

"You are mine, golden girl," the voice rasped.

The gear shift lever clicked. She turned her head. The lever had shifted into reverse.

In the rearview mirror, she saw several empty parking spaces and then...

A massive full-size pickup. It was the brick wall and she crouched inside a tin can—one that might rocket backward at any second.

She swung her feet around and on top of the steering column.

The engine revved again. The brake pedal, depressed as far as it would go, began to slowly lift.

She pulled her legs back, took a deep breath, and slammed her feet toward the windshield.

The accelerator sank to the floorboard. The car shot backward.

The force hurled her into the steering column. Her torso crushed her legs into the wheel. Lightning glanced inside her head. Hot threads of pain, sharp as razor wire, webbed through her. A cry burst out of her. She gritted her teeth and flung her body sideways onto the passenger seat.

In the rearview mirror, the image of the full-size pickup swelled larger and larger. She drew her knees to her chest and kicked at the windshield. The glass cracked. Pain ripped through her, as if something inside her were cracking too. She kicked again. The glass buckled outward, breaking free of the frame in gummy clumps. She rose into a crouch on the passenger seat and propelled herself through the window. The instant she cleared the window, she rolled off the hood.

Her hip struck the ground first, setting off a cascade of pain. She clenched her jaw as tears stung her eyes.

The Pontiac smashed into the pickup with an explosive crunch. The car's back end crumpled.

She winced, though not in pain this time. Her insurance had a high deductible because she couldn't afford higher payments. She rather doubted the insurance company would agree to go after the responsible party, since he was invisible and had apparently controlled her car through paranormal means. If she claimed a ghost caused the accident, they'd shoot her up with enough Thorazine to put Godzilla to sleep.

Shoes clapped on concrete. Pushing up into a sitting position, she glanced toward the Mail 'N More entrance.

Two security guards were trotting out of the building toward her.

She looked at the Pontiac. The car was totaled. If she had stayed inside it, she would've died.

Something tried to kill her.

The security guards reached her. They knelt beside her, expressions grave, both staring at her as if her head had torn loose of her shoulders. She pressed a hand into the nape of her neck. Strands of hair tickled her hand. With her fingertips, she probed the base of her skull. Nope, still attached.

"Are you hurt?" one of the security guards asked.

She managed to shake her head without grimacing. "I think I'm okay."

The men helped her stand.

"What happened?" the second guard asked.

The car tried to kill me. She kept that to herself and said, "I don't know."

"Did the gas pedal suddenly go down? Cuz I saw a story on CNN 'bout that."

"That's exactly what happened."

It wasn't a lie, not really. The gas pedal had gone down suddenly. She couldn't tell the officer that a demon had possessed her car and floored the accelerator. She sincerely doubted he would understand the invisible man defense.

Sometimes, a lie sounded more honest than the truth.

Stan Arnold, the CNN fan, drove Grace home an hour later. He and his partner had waited with her for the tow truck and the police to show up. The cops had questioned her politely but thoroughly about the accident and decided the gas pedal really had malfunctioned, like in the CNN story Arnold mentioned. Grace said little, letting the men reach their own conclusions. She had no desire to tell them the truth.

After Arnold parked at the curb outside Grace's house, he took a few moments to offer her advice on how to deal with her insurance company. She let him talk and nodded her head at the appropriate moments. He was being nice, which she appreciated, especially since everybody else seemed to want to abduct or murder her. No point in telling this nice man she couldn't afford her deductible, and therefore would be without a car for the foreseeable future.

Finally, Arnold bid her goodbye. She thanked him with genuine gratitude, but then forced a smile as she exited his car. The brave face pinched a little more than usual today.

She waved as Arnold drove away.

Breathing deeply, she winced as the bruises on her chest, abdomen, and thighs flexed. Maybe that somber young man would come back to fix her up again. Whatever he did to her had seemed to drain him, though, and she didn't want to hurt—albeit inadvertently—one of the few people who had tried to help her. So maybe he should stay away. Bruises weren't life threatening.

Sighing, she trudged into the house. After the security guards had summoned a tow truck, she'd sneaked into the Mail 'N More restroom. She hadn't needed to relieve herself. Rather, she needed to see what evidence the invisible attacker left behind. There, in the flicker of a crackling fluorescent bulb in a bathroom that no one had cleaned since President Truman left office, she'd surveyed her entire body.

Large, purple bruises had formed on the backs of her thighs. Matching bruises dotted her chest and abdomen. Blood caked at the edges of several fingernails. All of those injuries must've resulted from either her struggle with the door or the backward thrust of the car. None proved what she knew had happened.

Someone tried to kill her. An invisible someone who wielded paranormal powers.

It sounded insane. But it was true.

As she shuffled into the kitchen, each movement tweaked the muscles, irritated the bruises, and elicited a faint grimace accompanied by a half-suppressed groan. She moved without lifting her feet from the floor, for each step twanged her muscles. While breathing was no fun either, she relished it compared to walking.

In the bathroom, she found an old bottle of prescription anti-inflammatory pills and swallowed one, washing it down with water slurped straight from the bathroom tap. She applied antibiotic ointment and an adhesive bandage to a small cut on her arm. That was all she could do for now, so she headed into the bedroom.

A man sat on the bed.

Grace froze.

Waldron looked at her without expression.

She needed a second—but just a second—to gather her courage and her thoughts.

"What the hell do you want?" she asked.

His voice sounded calm, yet hard as concrete. "You know what I want."

"I'm not going anywhere with you. And if you try to force me, I'll kill you."

He laughed.

Not a chuckle. Not a derisive snort. A full-out guffaw.

Grace stared at him, feeling certain her face resembled that of a cartoon character emoting shock. Waldron laughed as if they were good buddies and she'd just told him a whopper of a joke. He even looked…happy.

A shiver swept through her, frigid and sharp.

As quickly as his laughter had erupted, it ended. The stoic, vaguely threatening expression returned.

Waldron stood and took two steps toward her. "Don't make this worse than it needs to be."

He was six feet from her. She scuffled backward into the doorway.

In one swift motion, Waldron whipped a semiautomatic handgun out of a holster inside his jacket and, with the other hand, pulled a pair of handcuffs out of his hip pocket.

She knew that bulge under his jacket was a gun, not a cell phone. Being right about it hardly seemed important at the moment, though.

"Last chance," Waldron said. "Come willingly or—"

She spun around and bolted down the hallway.

Waldron took off after her. She heard his footfalls but didn't dare look back.

As she ran, she unzipped her purse and curled her hand around her gun.

A hand seized her left wrist.

Waldron wrenched her backward into him. He wrapped his other arm around her torso, pinning her arms as they bounced to a halt.

His lips brushed her ear. Softly, he said, "Stop fighting. It's easier."

His fingernails pinched her skin. She struggled against his embrace. He cinched his arm tighter around her torso. She fought the urge to kick and flail, because she knew that wouldn't help. He was stronger and bigger and armed with both a gun and powerful muscles that felt as unyielding as steel wires. She couldn't wrench free of him. She refused to let him know she had given up, though. She refused to look as weak and helpless as she felt, because he would just love that.

Her right hand was still clamped around her gun.

Waldron's arm was clinched around her just above her right elbow. She looked down at her feet. Waldron's much-larger shoes straddled her feet. If she moved her hand a little bit to the right...

He released her left wrist to reach into his jacket pocket. Peripherally, she saw him withdraw a long, thin object from the pocket.

A syringe.

She pulled the trigger.

The shot boomed through the house.

Waldron jerked and bellowed. Even through the deafening effect of the gunshot, she heard his cry. His mouth was inches from her ear.

His grip loosened just enough. She rammed her elbow backward into his gut and he stumbled backward. She yanked the gun out of her purse, whirled on him, and fired another shot.

He dove sideways through the kitchen doorway.

She ran out of the house.

No car. Jesus, no car. She had to get away from him *fast*. She ran down the sidewalk as fast as her legs would carry her, gritting her teeth against the pain of too many bruises. If she made it to the bus stop, and if there just happened to be a bus waiting there, she might have a chance. No, dammit, she had a chance either way. *Think*.

She fled past a car parked along the curb. A car with a man inside it. A man watching her. Through the open passenger window. He must've heard the gunshot. He saw her fleeing. Yet he looked interested, perhaps even a little excited, rather than disturbed. No time to think about that.

Around the corner. Panting. Praying.

No bus. Just an empty bench.

She kept running.

Chapter Twelve

She lost track of how many blocks she ran before she finally caught up with a bus. She boarded along with two other people who paid zero attention to her. The driver glanced at the hole in her purse, arched an eyebrow, and said nothing. The gunshot had torn straight through the leather and her previous escapades had left the bag scuffed and stained. The combined effect lent her purse a postmodern apocalyptic chic.

The bus transported her to within a couple blocks of the Prairie Grass Motel. The establishment's name had always seemed odd to her. Sure, they had grass here in Lassiter Falls. But this was hill country, not prairie. Today, however, she really didn't give a damn what they called the place so long as they gave her a room and let her pay cash. The pleasant gray-haired man in the office granted her wish.

Inside the room, she locked the door and closed the drapes. By the window, two chairs bookended a small, round table. She hauled one of the chairs over to the door, bracing it under the doorknob for extra protection.

Then she tossed her purse onto the bedside table and collapsed onto the bed.

The mattress was blissfully soft. The quilt featured a patchwork of pastel colors. She rolled onto her side. Letting her muscles relax, at last, she absently ran her fingers over the quilt's pattern. Everyone wanted the flash drive. They all assumed she had it or knew where to find it. If she didn't find the flash drive soon, whoever killed her grandfather would kill her too. If the presence in her car had been the same someone, then he'd already tried to kill her once. No, he could've killed her any time if he really wanted to. He—based on the disembodied voice, she assumed it was a man—wanted to frighten her, probably hoping that would induce her to cough up the flash drive.

Andrew Haley had mentioned a particular him. What had he said? *The man with evil eyes. Darkness inside.* Unfortunately, Andrew had been unable to remember the man's name or offer a more detailed description. Xavier Waldron's eyes definitely qualified as evil and he most assuredly harbored a darkness inside him. But given the skimpy description, she shouldn't assume Waldron was the man Andrew mentioned. Surely if Waldron could attack her in absentia, he wouldn't bother harassing her in her home. Then again, she didn't understand the mind of a psychotic.

She rolled onto her back, gazing straight up at the ceiling.

A draft swirled through the room. The room looked nice but it clearly wasn't well insulated, she mused, but then her thoughts spiraled back to the flash drive. Goose bumps popped up on her arms. The draft had turned chilly.

Look at the door.

The back of her neck tingled. Overcome by a sensation that she was not alone, she moved only her eyes to look at the door. The chair stood braced under the door handle, two of its feet tilted up off the floor. She shook her head. No one there, of course.

She yelped when he materialized near the door.

He just sort of…blurred into sight. Within a half second, the blurriness gave way to high definition and he appeared as solid as any object in the room. If she touched him, he would feel solid and warm and alive. She knew that. She felt it. He focused his blue eyes on her and excitement tingle inside her.

His mouth twitched at the corners. He crossed half the distance between them and halted.

She sat up, folding her arms over her chest. "Are you trying to kill me?"

"No. Someone else."

"Who?"

"I don't know."

"Come on, David."

His expression remained stoic. Damn, she'd hoped to surprise him with the revelation that she knew his name, to somehow make him show a little emotion, if only for a second. She never knew what he was thinking, good or bad, and never could discern his intentions. His actions, like phrases heard out of context, gave her clues she struggled to decipher. So she longed for an emotional outburst to help her out, or even a flash of anything on his face. Instead, he looked her up and down as if assessing her physical state—not in a medical way, but rather in a concerned manner tinged with something else she couldn't quite identify. Something familiar and far more personal.

Familiar? Please. She knew nothing about him except his name.

As far as she remembered. That phrase left her feeling less than certain.

She scooted backward until her back met the headboard. Clasping her hands over her stomach, she eyed him with an expression she hoped conveyed dispassion. "You know the guy who visited me in the hospital, don't you? The redhead who looked barely old enough to vote."

"I don't know what—"

She gave him a don't-screw-with-me look.

He stared at her for a second, and then said, "Yes. I know him."

"Is he invisible too?"

David furrowed his brow. Finally, some emotion.

Grace rolled her eyes at him. "For pity's sake, would you please drop the strong-and-silent routine? It's getting old. I know who you are, David Ransom, so you might as well talk to me."

"My name isn't who I am."

She snorted. Not the most feminine sound, but it made the point.

Motionless, he watched her.

She watched him right back.

After a moment, he broke eye contact and cautiously settled onto the bed near her feet. He asked, "Do you have the flash drive?"

"Screw the flash drive."

They exchanged stares again. If they knew each other, she might've thought her rudeness surprised him. They did not know each other. He couldn't know she rarely spoke her mind with such bluntness, for fear of offending someone. Impolite behavior betrayed three things she avoided displaying—anger, fear, and weakness. Sure, she felt them sometimes. But nobody needed to know. Once people knew someone's weaknesses, they could exploit them.

So his look of confusion couldn't stem from shock at her rudeness. Her refusal to follow orders confused him, no doubt, because he expected to get his way. He confided as little as possible in her while demanding her complete trust. She never granted her complete and unconditional faith to people who refused to reciprocate.

"You told me to destroy the flash drive," she said. "Now you want it. Give me one good reason why I should trust you."

He laid a hand on her ankle. The gesture, like much of his behavior toward her, felt intimate and oddly familiar.

He sighed. "I thought destroying the flash drive would protect you. I was wrong."

She couldn't look away from his eyes. Blue as jewels. Backlit by a fire within. The cool hue ignited a warmth in her belly that spread outward to infuse her entire being.

"I'm trying to help you," he said. "Did you destroy the flash drive?"

"I don't have it." She hesitated, then asked, "Why do you want to help me? I could be a criminal or a devil worshiper or something."

He shook his head. "You're a good person. The best, actually."

About to speak, she froze with her mouth open. His voice, soft yet firm, divulged a deep and inexplicable belief in her basic goodness, a faith beyond what his words conveyed, beyond anything anyone had shown her in all her life. If he was acting, he deserved an Academy Award. Her instincts told her he wasn't lying. He meant exactly what he said.

Maybe she could trust him. A little.

"If you really want to help," she said, "then help me get the flash drive."

"I don't know where it is."

"Of course not."

She regretted the sarcasm in her voice the instant she spoke the words. David sat absolutely still, his head cocked to one side, those luminous eyes fixed on her. After a few seconds, he turned toward the door and stepped through it.

He actually stepped *through* the closed door. Through a solid object.

A chill sidled up her spine.

Before she could wonder where he'd gone, David stepped back through the door into the room. He seated himself on the bed again, this time much closer to her. His hip nearly brushed against hers as he sat down, and he could've reached out to touch her face. Another wave of warmth swept through her. When she spoke, her voice came out a little more breathless than she'd intended.

"You walked through the door," she said. "How did you do that?"

He shrugged. "I thought I sensed activity out there. It's all calm, though."

She straightened her spine and toughened her voice. "Don't ignore my questions. I want to know how you can walk through solid objects. What the hell are you?"

"Later."

"No, now."

He leaned toward her, so close that his breath wafted over her. It smelled like cinnamon. How odd that a ghost should have nice breath. Or any breath at all.

"Are you dead?" she asked.

"No." He took hold of her shoulders. "Listen to me. You are in danger. The people who want the flash drive will stop at to find it—and I mean nothing. Blackmail. Torture. Murder." He pulled her forward until their noses almost touched. "We must find the flash drive. *Now*. Maybe then we can find a way to stop our enemies."

We. He kept saying we, as if they worked together or…something.

His breath tickled her lips, and she had the strangest urge to kiss him.

Instead, she asked, "Who are our enemies?"

"I don't know. I've met their employees, but never the person or group in charge."

The man with evil eyes. Grace swallowed against a newly formed lump in her throat. "I don't know how to find the flash drive."

David released her shoulders. He dropped his hands and folded them over hers, which she still held on her lap. His skin felt hot on hers. She hadn't realized how cold her hands were.

"I'll help you," he said.

"Okay."

He squeezed her hands, then let go and pulled away from her. "Did your grandfather leave you anything when he died?"

"Um, no."

"You didn't receive any of his effects?"

She thought about that for a moment. "Just a box of clothes and stuff."

David raised his eyebrows. "What stuff?"

"Mementos."

He jumped up, sending a little earthquake through the bed. "We should check all of Edward's effects. He might've hidden something in them."

She saluted him. "Yes, sir."

A smile threatened to rupture his stoicism. He regained control just in time, however—which, in her opinion, was a shame.

She clambered off the bed and onto her feet.

David started for the door.

"Wait," she said. "Someone attacked me in my house. He might still be there."

"I'll check."

He vanished.

Grace stood there, feeling more perplexed than at any other moment in her life. People did not disappear like that. He must be a ghost, but he insisted he was not dead.

Suddenly, she wished she drank alcohol. Getting soused appealed to her right now.

David snapped back into view. She'd blinked and—poof—he was there again.

"The house is empty," he pronounced, and motioned for her to come. "Let's go."

She didn't move.

He gestured again. "I'll answer any questions you want later. For now, we have to go."

"Fine."

Grace slung her dilapidated purse around her neck to hang across her torso. David watched as she marched to the door, shoved the chair aside, unfastened the lock, and flung the door open. He followed her outside, as if he needed a doorway to get out of the room. She strode to the bus stop.

"Where's your car?" David asked.

She sat down on the bench. "My car is trashed."

"What now?"

"We wait for the bus."

Grace rode the bus alone, since David disappeared again fifteen minutes later, right before the bus pulled up to the stop. The trip seemed to take forever, probably

because she spent the entire ride thinking about Waldron and the flash drive and going back to the house where more than one someone had attacked her recently. Andrew Haley struck her as harmless. Waldron was far from it.

She wanted to go back to the house slightly more than she wanted to lie down in the middle of the interstate at rush hour. David was right, though, and it was annoying as hell. She needed to go back so she could search through her grandfather's effects. Everyone else believed he'd left her the flash drive. If so, then he must've hidden it in his belongings, among the things he knew she would receive upon his death.

Which meant he knew he would die. Or at least knew somebody wanted to kill him.

The bus pulled up to the stop in her neighborhood. She disembarked, heading down the sidewalk toward home. As she turned the corner onto her street, she slipped her hand inside her purse to grasp the gun. She had four bullets left, since she'd fired two at Waldron. God, she hoped he was in pain. Lots and lots of pain.

The car she'd seen earlier was nowhere in sight. Either it had nothing to do with Waldron, which seemed improbable, or Waldron and his buddy had left the vicinity. Maybe the other guy drove Waldron to the hospital. Maybe he'd be laid up for days, safely out of her orbit.

Or maybe he'd found a better place to park his car, where she couldn't see it.

Might as well be positive. He probably left, at least for awhile.

She kept her hand on the gun anyway.

When she reached the house, she hesitated with her hand on the knob of the front door. She'd left the door wide open, more concerned with escaping than locking up the house. Waldron must've closed the door. Creepy.

She twisted the knob. It turned in her hand. Waldron might've shut the door, but he didn't lock it. Well, given that she had invisible beings trying to kill her, worrying about the unlocked door seemed a tad pointless.

Shoving the door inward, she walked into the house.

Quiet. Still. Vacant.

Grace wandered into the kitchen, and then the hallway. Empty.

A memory flashed in her mind. Waldron's arms around her. Hauling her backward.

She blinked away the memory. Jeez, she couldn't remember eight months of her life—eight months she really needed to remember—but she recalled in vivid detail events she would've preferred to forget.

Down the hallway. Into the bedroom. No one there either.

She swung open the folding doors that concealed the closet. Behind her shoes, at the back of the closet, sat a cardboard box sealed with clear packing tape. She'd opened the box once, glanced at the contents, and sealed it up again. They weren't her belongings. She had no use for them and she didn't like looking at them. It reminded her of Grandpa. It reminded her of how much she'd lost. She just couldn't deal with those feelings on top of everything else.

At the time when the box arrived, "everything else" had meant amnesia and migraines. Now the term referred to a hell of a lot more. Too much more.

No choice. She had to suck it up and keep moving. Falling apart was not an option. It would get her killed.

Pushing her shoes out of the way, she reached for the box.

A hand grasped her shoulder.

She yelped and jumped. Glancing backward, she saw David crouched behind her.

"Let me do that," he said.

Well, she couldn't see the harm in letting him carry the box for her. He might disappear with it, she supposed, but she doubted it.

Why she doubted it, she couldn't explain. She just did.

She scuttled backward, out of the way. David picked up the box and carried it to the bed, where he set it down on the comforter. Grace met him at the bed, seating herself beside the box, on the edge of the mattress. The comforter felt soft and cushy under her. Even better than the motel mattress. She longed to stretch out on the bed and take a nap.

Not yet. Suck it up, girl, and keep moving.

David ripped the packing tape off the box. It made a zipping sound.

The box's flaps popped up a little. Grace folded them back, revealing the box's contents. A sweater her mom had knit for her grandfather lay on top. She lifted it out, setting the garment on the bed. No flash drive there. David lifted out three framed diplomas representing Edward McLean's degrees—bachelor's, master's, and doctorate. There was a scarf, also knit by Grace's mother, and a photo album filled with images of their family. Grace lifted out a Christmas tree ornament, one of three she'd made in the fourth grade. One was for her parents, the other two for her grandparents. The last item in the box was a trophy from her grandfather's high school days, when he'd won a swimming competition. Packing peanuts filled the rest of the box. Grace rifled through the peanuts but found nothing hidden within them.

She propped herself on one arm, surveying the Styrofoam peanuts that lay scattered over the bed and the floor at her feet.

David sat down on the bed, on the opposite side of the box. He returned the three framed diplomas to the box.

Grace stared at the frames. Something tickled her brain. Knowledge just beyond her reach.

She grabbed the frames and deposited them on her lap. Turning each over to examine both sides, she compared the three frames. One had a slight bulge on its backside where the cardboard backing had warped. The bulge was visible only when the light struck it a certain way. Maybe it was a manufacturing defect.

"What is it?" David asked.

She raised a hand to silence him. Setting aside the other two frames, she took hold of the third and carefully turned the little metal prongs that held the backing in place. The cardboard came free. She eased it out of the frame, laying it on the bed. In the space now revealed, she saw a small, thin black rectangle of plastic.

Grace picked up the little object. A smile broke across her face as triumph buoyed her spirits. The object in her hand was a flash drive.

She grinned at David, waving the flash drive in the air like a miniscule flag.

"You found it," he said, sounding surprised and impressed at the same time. Before she could respond, he announced, "I should go. I've been out too long."

"Out? What, are you a fugitive?"

"Something like that."

He rose from the bed and stepped backward. She knew that meant he was about to disappear again.

She lunged off the bed, grabbed the front of his shirt, and dragged him closer.

"Oh no you don't," she said. "You promised to answer my questions."

His face was inches from her own. She felt the warmth of his body through his shirt. A ghost couldn't feel warm, and anyway, he said he wasn't a ghost. If not a spirit, then what?

"Are you an alien?" she asked.

He smiled and chuckled softly. "No."

"Then what are you?"

"A messenger. Someone has—"

"To warn me." She let go of his shirt. "Yeah yeah, I've heard that already. I have no idea what I need to be warned about, but I sure as hell know I'm supposed to be warned."

"Take the flash drive to Senator Faulkner in Washington. He'll know what to do."

"Destroy it, keep it. Go away, do me a favor. Make up your mind."

He brushed a finger across her cheek. "If you don't do this, they'll kill you."

"Fine, I'll take it to Senator Falcon."

"Faulkner. Elias Faulkner."

"Whatever." She pushed away from him. "Just tell me one thing before you—"

He was gone. Wind gusted through the room, swirling toward the center. The damaged door rocked on its hinges.

People kept ordering her around, demanding information from her, trying to kill her. None of them bothered to tell her what the blazes was happening. They expected obedience without question.

Grace flopped down on the bed. It was mid afternoon, though it felt like at least two o'clock in the morning. Her body hurt all over, from bruises and weariness. She could no more fight villains right now than she could scale Mount Everest. An anthill might prove too much for her.

Sleep. She must get some sleep.

Not here. The house felt…tainted. Waldron might come back for a rematch, and this time he just might win.

She tucked the flash drive in her jeans pocket. Picking up the document frame, she slid the cardboard backing into place and locked it there with the metal prongs. The diploma inside the frame was her grandfather's doctorate degree. She returned the frame to the box, resealing the packing tape. In case Waldron did return to the house, she lugged the box back to closet and stowed it behind her shoes.

At her desk, she plugged the flash drive into the USB port on the front of her computer. A message popped up on screen: ENTER PASSWORD.

A secondary message below that one warned that she had three attempts before the drive would be permanently locked. Terrific. She was too tired to figure out the password. Maybe after a decent nap, her brain would function better.

She stashed the laptop in its carrying case and left the house, heading out the back door. An alleyway separated the houses on her street from those on the next street. She decided against going to the same bus stop as before. This time, she walked in the opposite direction, to a bus stop a little farther away. The wait seemed interminable, but finally the bus pulled up and she boarded.

This bus had a different route. The closest stop to the motel was three blocks away. She lost track of time as the bus chugged down the streets, pausing at stops along the way. Eventually, she made it back to the motel and into her room. Her purse she tossed onto the bedside table and set the laptop case on the other table, by the window. After bracing a chair under the door handle, she kicked off her boots and collapsed onto the bed without bothering to pull back the quilt.

Her mind plummeted into sleep.

Grace woke as a gasp exploded from her. The dream. For nearly a year, it had recurred nightly. Until a few days ago, she hadn't dreamed of the corridor in months. Certainly, she had *never* dreamed of a faceless man until recently. This time, the dream had changed again. She had seen the mystery man's face.

He was Xavier Waldron.

The corridor. The room. The *man*.

Waldron. Her mind could've inserted his face into the dream because of her encounter with him earlier. The creep had assaulted her and tried to drug her.

No, the truth was far more unsettling. She knew, by instinct and emotion, that the figure in the dream had always belonged to Xavier Waldron. Somehow, he hid his features from her until tonight when, through a process that bewildered her, she unmasked him. In a dream. With her thoughts. Three days ago, the notion would've made her laugh. Today, she believed it with absolute certainty.

Waldron had invaded her dreams. He was no FBI agent. He wasn't even human, because no human could torment her by invading her dreams. Yet he seemed human enough. Totally evil, but human.

Questions and suspicions. Riddles and mysteries.

If he wanted her dead, why didn't he just do it? She hated being the duck in the shooting gallery, hearing the shots, uncertain which bang would signify the bullet that shattered her head. Waldron could've killed her anytime he pleased—strangled her, shot her, pushed her in front of a bus. Instead, he tormented her and tried to abduct her. He wanted the flash drive.

David had said someone else was in charge of Operation Drive Grace Insane.

A headache pushed against her skull with the force of ten hammers pounding inside her head. Even the pale yellow glow from the bedside lamp pained her eyes. Another migraine. Why did the dream give her migraines? Why did everything have to be so hard?

She covered her face with her hands. Light seeped between her fingers. She rolled over onto her side, her back to the lamp. She really didn't want to turn off the lamp. Never knew when a psycho might break through the window to assault her. So instead, she draped her arm over her eyes. It worked a little better than her hands.

What awaited her in the future remained a mystery, a gift she preferred to leave wrapped, not that she had a choice. Tomorrow collided with today no matter what. The gift would open itself. Her life had turned into a nightmare.

And all because of a tiny plastic rectangle.

A memory of the dream whispered through her mind in the form of the man's inhuman voice. He didn't urge her to give in, like before. Instead, he murmured something far more disturbing and bewildering.

You are mine, golden girl.

Chapter Thirteen

Grace woke to the sound of an engine growling outside the window. She didn't remember falling asleep again. The sunlight no longer trickled in through the gaps between the drapes and the window frame. She glanced at the clock on the bedside table. It was nearly eight o'clock. She'd slept for…a long time. Since she couldn't recall what time she'd made it back to the motel, she really had no clue how long she'd slept.

Pushing off the bed, she stood. Her bruises were firmly set now, but they hurt less than before. She walked toward the window, tripped, and knocked into the table hip first. Pain lanced through her. A little grunt burst from her. Okay, the bruises hurt less *except* when she banged them.

At the window, she parted the drapes a crack and peered outside. The parking lot was quiet, save for a big old four-door sedan that sat idling in front of the third room down from hers. A middle-aged woman slumped in the passenger seat of the sedan holding a road map, which she studied with intense interest. No one else was in sight.

Not that seeing nothing meant nothing was there.

Grace let the drapes fall closed. She tossed her purse onto the bed and grabbed her laptop case. Once she'd settled into a comfortable position on the quilt, she unzipped her purse. The gun lay snug in its holster. She brought it out and set it on the quilt beside her. She hadn't wanted to turn off the bedside lamp for safety reasons, but she forgot to keep the gun with her. Her brain had been more exhausted than she realized, apparently.

Digging in her purse, she located the microcassette recorder. Before tackling the password problem on the flash drive, she needed to hear the entire recording. It must contain vital information, otherwise Brian Kellogg wouldn't have taken such pains to conceal the tape.

She pressed play.

The tape hissed. "What's going on in there?"

Grandpa's voice sounded distant, strained, as if he had laryngitis.

Thump. Another voice croaked, "No."

Knock-knock. It sounded like someone rapping on a door. Interference whined on the tape. *Creak.*

A gasp. "Holy mother of God..."

On the recording, thunder exploded. Wind howled. Grandpa screamed.

Grace's throat constricted. Tears stung her eyes, but she blinked them away. On the tape, interference whined again. Someone wheezed, probably her grandfather. She bit her lip, shut her eyes, sucked in a breath. She must listen. She must know.

Laughter grumbled close to the recorder. "Say good night, Edward."

Every molecule of liquid in Grace's body seemed to freeze. She opened her eyes, glancing around the room. Nothing had changed. The voice on the tape sounded exactly like the disembodied voice she'd heard in her car.

The tape continued, this time with her grandfather's voice. "Stop this, please. You want me, the others are innocent. Let them go, take me inst—"

He cried out, the shout choked off by hands that, though she could not see them, she felt around her own neck as she listened to the strangled gasps and gurgles emanating from the tape. He'd suffered. Some invisible bastard had murdered him and he had suffered.

She choked back a sob.

The inhuman voice growled, "I'm coming for Grace next. You can't protect her anymore. I will have my golden girl."

The recording ended with a click.

Grace massaged her throat. A tear trickled down her cheek. *He suffered.* She studied the cassette player, as if it might sprout a mouth and chomp off her hand. She could no longer call such an event impossible. Anything was possible. The universe had gone insane. Grandpa had been murdered by a ghost, a demon, something evil beyond comprehension.

And now it wanted her. It killed her grandfather to get to her.

Golden girl. The disembodied voice called her that. In her nightmare, Waldron called her the same thing. The evidence seemed to connect Waldron to the disembodied attacker. But if he had that kind of power, why assault her in such an old-fashioned physical way, as he had in her house earlier today? Maybe the person or thing behind all this madness wanted her to think Waldron was her top enemy—so she'd stop looking for another culprit. She couldn't know for sure.

She knew almost nothing for sure.

The tape whirred inside the player. She pressed the stop button.

Her throat was so dry it hurt. She trudged to the bathroom, where she found a shrink-wrapped plastic cup. After a brief battle with the shrink-wrap, she freed the cup and filled it from the tap. The water was lukewarm, but it quenched her thirst. She gulped down the cup's contents, refilled it, and took her beverage back to the bed. She booted up the laptop. Plugging in the flash drive, she waited for the password message to appear.

She understood why her grandfather had taken precautions. Still, she wished he hadn't made accessing the drive so difficult. How he expected her to know the password—and what he expected her to do once she accessed the drive's contents—she didn't know. He entrusted her with a secret that others would kill to possess. He believed she knew what to do about the mess, how to clean it up, where to seek help, who to trust.

He credited her with greater intelligence than she had. Her skills of deduction and logic couldn't solve the mystery and save the world. If she had those skills, she would've figured things out by now. Obviously, he overestimated her.

Forget the self-pity. Take command, girl. Grab the wheel and steer the damn car. So what if demons could take control of the car anytime. Don't make it easy for them to kill you. Claw. Scream. Fight.

Self-delivered pep talks weren't ideal. With nobody else around to bolster her flagging enthusiasm, however, she had to make do with the tools available to her. *Stop whining*, she chastised. Whatever must be done, she must do it. Whatever force kept foiling her, she must expose and neutralize it. Wherever she must go, she would get there somehow.

In front of her lay a precipice—behind, an army of demons. The time had come to jump.

The password. Grandpa must've programmed the drive with a password he felt certain she would know. How? Without any clues, she couldn't narrow down the possibilities. The password might be anything.

He would have left a clue.

She shut her eyes, thinking back to when she found the flash drive hidden inside the document frame. No clues there. The frame had looked normal, just glass and gold-colored metal. The diploma housed inside the frame was nothing special either. It held sentimental value, of course. Edward McLean had kept all three of his diplomas in his apartment, hung on the wall in the living room, right next a photograph of Stonehenge. She'd asked him once why he kept a picture of Stonehenge on his wall.

"It's simple," he'd said. "Stonehenge is a mystery that modern experts believe they've solved, but in reality they've misinterpreted much of the evidence to fit their preconceived ideas. It's the same with the human brain. Scientists believe they understand a great deal about how the mind works, yet they've misinterpreted or outright dismissed the most important evidence."

His answer still confused her. Comparing the brain to an ancient monument seemed like an apples-to-oranges issue. She'd told him as much.

He'd smiled and said, "The bluestone, Grace, the bluestone. It's the key to everything. People prattle on about the Rosetta Stone, but it's the bluestone that matters. Once we find the brain's bluestone, we'll have a real clue to work with."

"Bluestone?" she'd asked.

"Yes. Stonehenge contains a type of rock called bluestone, which the ancients quarried hundreds of miles from the Salisbury Plain, where Stonehenge was constructed. Those ancient people transported the stones from the mountains down to the plain, supposedly without the wheel or beasts of burden."

"What's that got to do with the brain?"

"We won't know until we find the neurological bluestone."

She never had figured out what he meant. He could be outrageously cryptic when he felt like it.

Bluestone.

She looked at the computer screen, and the ENTER PASSWORD prompt displayed on its screen. Could that be the answer? It seemed too arcane.

Exactly the kind of thing Grandpa loved. The arcane and mysterious.

She typed BLUESTONE into the password field and hit enter.

The password box disappeared. A new message popped up in its place. This one didn't ask for a password. It displayed a single paragraph of text.

"This flash drive is dangerous," the note said. "Get rid of it ASAP. Contact Senator Elias Faulkner and arrange to transfer the drive to his custody. He'll know what to do with it. Then GET OUT of it, Grace. Do not get involved any further—I mean it. I'm sorry I had to involve you, but I had no way of getting the flash drive to Senator Faulkner myself. Please forgive me."

The note was signed "Grandpa."

Get out of it. Why the vehemence? He'd died before anyone or anything came after her. If he knew demons would try to kill her, he would've suggested she grab a shotgun and blast them into itty-bitty pieces. He would've warned her. And why give her clues that helped her figure out the password for the flash drive if he didn't want her to read its contents?

The note ordered her to stay out of it. David had issued the same command. Like she would obey a stranger. One who refused to explain himself. One who disappeared at will. Yet the more time she spent with him, the less he felt like a stranger.

The note was outdated. Given her predicament, Grandpa would want her to continue. Probably. She thought. Either way, his wishes no longer mattered. The situation had escalated too far for her to back out now, and she doubted she could back out anyway. Waldron seemed unlikely to leave her alone simply because she promised to stay out of his way—especially if she failed to turn over the flash drive. Clearly, Edward McLean had more enemies than he'd realized.

At least now she had a plan, sort of. She'd call Senator Faulkner, tell him what had happened, and ask for his help. If he refused, if he demanded she relinquish the flash drive, she'd hang up on him. The drive was her bulletproof vest. Possession of it warded off her enemies, at least for the moment. If she gave up the flash drive, nothing stood between her and the forces that wanted her dead. She already had an invisible someone who wanted her dead. She didn't need more demons nipping at her soul.

She closed the little window that displayed the note. A new window opened, this one a list of files contained on the flash drive. The files looked like spreadsheets or databases of information, along with a handful of text documents. She double-clicked on a file called "test sites." The spreadsheet that opened listed locations all over the world, from Seattle to Singapore, with abbreviations beside the place names—RV, AP, TK, PC, GP. The letters meant nothing to her, and the spreadsheet offered no explanation. Each location also had been designated as "active" or "inactive," but she couldn't tell what that meant either. As she scanned the list again, she realized only one of the locations was labeled "active," and that one wasn't really a location anyway. It was simply called "primary facility."

Brian Kellogg had mentioned working at a research facility. Could this "primary facility" be the same one?

She closed the file and opened one of the text documents. Fifty pages of dense text documented, in scientist-speak, the "protocols" for initiating "test episodes." Grace skimmed the document, but the sentences made no sense to her. She closed the file and tried another.

This text looked like a report of some kind, written in technical jargon way outside her expertise. The text was peppered with Latin phrases and extremely long words supposedly drawn from the English language, though she couldn't figure out what they meant. She tried looking up some of the words in an online dictionary, but apparently the terms were so arcane they didn't appear in a normal dictionary. The document also liberally used the abbreviations found in the spreadsheet.

She closed the document and skimmed the rest of the files. More gobbledygook. The last file was a database called "Interim Results." She selected a portion of the database labeled "RV" and scrolled through the contents, watching table after table of data roll across the computer screen. She saw numbers, symbols, incomprehensible text. Graphs interspersed between the tables and text illustrated "Rates of Incidence," "Projected Accuracy vs. Real-Time Accuracy," "Levels of Impulse Strength Over a 24-Hour Period," and more data that sounded like nonsense.

Giving up on the database, she opened the second to last file. It contained two pages scanned from a *Time* magazine profile of a man named Jackson Tennant, founder of Digital Prognostics, a company that produced security software for corporate, government, and consumer use. The company claimed their software detected potential security problems before they happened, hence the company's name. Prognostic meant able to predict the future.

Behind the article text, a photo of Jackson Tennant spread across the page and spilled onto the adjacent page. The photo showed a young man, perhaps thirty-five, lounging on the beach with a laptop computer beside him. A wind displaced his dark hair. Sunglasses masked his eyes. The sunlight on his face brought out the golden tones of his skin. He was attractive, in a spoiled-rich-boy way. The smirk on his lips intimated a disdain for the camera mingled with a craving for the attention it bestowed on him. He wore torn jeans and a T-shirt emblazoned with the logo for his company.

Digital Prognostics. What did the company have to do with anything? Her grandfather wouldn't have included the article on the flash drive unless it had some relation to the mystery at hand. She read the article again, more closely this time. Nothing relevant, not that she could see anyhow. The journalist salivated over Tennant's wealth and charm while criticizing his company's domination of the security software market, although Tennant also owned a number of subsidiaries involved in everything from manufacturing to, of all things, a cruise ship line. The article elucidated the government's antitrust lawsuit against the company, which Tennant dismissed as "so completely lame." Charts illustrated the conglomerate's growth over the past five years, its current market share, and other information irrelevant to her problems.

She skimmed over a quote from Tennant, then doubled back to reread the statement.

"I want to change humanity forever," Tennant says. "My software is the tool I use to implement that change."

The statement struck her as odd and vaguely creepy, but she couldn't deduce a connection between the flash drive, her grandfather's research, and Digital Prognostics. Though Jackson Tennant might be a weirdo, that didn't make him a psychopath.

Something destined to change humanity forever.

Kellogg had spoken those words when describing the "something" her grandfather had left for her. A the time, she dismissed his words as the ramblings of a nutjob. Maybe she shouldn't have.

She double-clicked the last file on the drive.

Scrolling down. Tables. Data. Nonsense, all of it. She stopped at a table that listed names of "travelers," their "designations," and a number described as "accuracy." The list named two dozen people. Each name was a hot link to a page on a web site identified only by a string of numbers and dots that she recognized as an IP address. Scanning the names on the list, she froze. One was familiar.

Traveler: David Ransom. Designation: RV (Level 10). Accuracy: 97.9874.

She clicked the link. Even a cheap motel like this one offered free Wi-Fi, so her laptop had already detected the connection. The website loaded. A dialog box popped up requesting a username and password. Terrific. Another password.

A light flickered on her computer, indicating the hard drive was working. The username and password appeared in the dialog box. User name: Hermes. Password: Elysium.

The reference to Greek mythology baffled her. Hermes had been the messenger of the gods, Elysium a paradise akin to heaven. The password for the flash drive had been related to Stonehenge. What did any of it mean? Maybe nothing. Maybe her grandfather was just being arcane.

She hit enter. The password box disappeared, replaced by another dialog box. This one held a warning. "Access to this page requires fingerprint ID. Please place your thumb on the reader."

She doubted the word "reader" referenced a connoisseur of books. Damn, she'd left her fingerprint reader in her other purse, along with her retinal scanner and DNA tester.

Her laptop's hard drive whirred to life. The message on-screen changed. It now said, "Loading fingerprint file." A couple seconds ticked by, and then the dialog box closed. The web page loaded.

The page was titled "Status report." A subheading identified the "traveler" as David Ransom and repeated his designation. She read the next line.

The air in her lungs seemed to turn to cement. Her skin tingled as every hair on her body stiffened. No invisible assailant caused her symptoms this time around, though. Goose bumps raised on her arms because of what the next line of text said. It gave today's date, but what came next left her feeling cold and warm at the same time.

Status as of 0800 hours: In transit at main facility, Mojave Desert, California. Vital signs normal. Excursion ends 1200 hours.

Her vision blurred and refocused. The document claimed David was not a ghost, not a demon, not a hallucination. He was real. He lived and breathed somewhere in the Mojave Desert. He was "in transit at main facility," but the statement made no sense. How could he be "in transit" if he was at a facility? Maybe they got the wording wrong and meant he was in transit *from* the main facility.

She stared at the text on the web page. *Vital signs normal. Excursion ends 1200 hours.*

Excursion. Traveler. In transit. What in the hell had Grandpa gotten mixed up in? What had he gotten *her* mixed up in?

A chill curled around her neck. She wasn't alone. With her finger hovering over the laptop's touch pad, she looked at the door. No one there. The chill deepened, and she rubbed her arms through her jacket.

She whispered, "David?"

The cold slithered down her spine, around her chest. A breeze, like the breath of a ghost, touched her hand. She couldn't breathe, couldn't move. Her finger, poised over the touch pad, jerked.

She had not moved her finger. Not on purpose.

She felt downward pressure on her finger. Fighting the pressure didn't help. Her fingertip depressed the button on the touch pad. On-screen, the web browser closed.

She tried jerking her hand away. It ignored her commands and moved without her consent. Her finger clicked the touch pad button again. And again. The file window closed. The mouse pointer on-screen spun across the desktop and clicked an icon. A message announced that the media had been ejected successfully.

What the…

Her hand lifted off the touch pad and reached for the flash drive plugged into the USB port. She struggled against the force that had taken over her hand. Her arm froze, trembling. She gritted her teeth and concentrated her every thought on regaining control of her own hand. Her arm shook harder. The muscles cramped. Pain fired straight up her arm into her shoulder.

She gasped. Her breaths came shallow and fast, almost hyperventilating.

Her arm jerked.

She shivered from head to toe. Her teeth chattered. Her arm burned.

A voice cried out.

Her arm dropped onto her lap. She slumped against the headboard, panting, and looked around the room. No one was nearby.

A human had cried out. She'd heard the wail.

Maybe the voice had been her own. No. The voice had sounded male, young, and frightened—and eerily close.

The hairs on her neck stiffened.

A voice spoke inside her head. "I'm not supposed to let you look. I'm sorry."

The same voice that had cried out before.

He spoke in a soft, uneven tone. "I promised to watch over you. Not let bad things happen. That's why you can't look."

She glanced out the corners of her eyes. Maybe the kid was hiding in the bathroom. She leaped up to check the bathroom, but it was empty. No one lurked in the shadows. She knew he was nowhere in the building. Nowhere in the state of Texas. He probably lived at the "main facility" in the Mojave Desert with David. Didn't take a clairvoyant to conclude that much. The voice belonged to the young man who'd healed her back in the hospital.

Standing beside the bed now, she listened for the fragile voice.

"Understand?" he said.

He was pleading for her agreement. She opened her mouth to speak but stopped. The kid could talk to her in her mind. Maybe she could communicate with him the same way.

Sure, I'll just beam my thoughts to him like a goddamn radio transmitter. No problem.

Bullshit. She was no psychic. Her only option for communicating with other beings was to do it the old-fashioned way.

"Who are you?" she asked.

Silence.

Frustration boiled inside her, but she slammed a lid on it. "I'm Grace, but I think you already know that. Please tell me your name."

His voice echoed in her mind, as real as if he stood before her. "Sean Vandenbrook."

"Are you with David?"

"Not supposed to say. Said too much already."

He was gone.

She sensed his absence rather than his departure. Couldn't explain why. Couldn't explain anything. She had conversed with a boy named Sean, in her head, over a distance of more than a thousand miles.

Grace shivered.

Grabbing the flash drive, she tucked it inside her bra. No man would think to look there, or at least she hoped they wouldn't. Sean said he wasn't supposed to let her look. At what? The flash drive, she assumed, since Sean had forced her to eject it from the computer. The order had come from David, no doubt. But she couldn't figure out why he sent a kid to stop her from looking at the flash drive. Until now, he had watched over her. Annoyed her. Evaded her questions.

Saved her life.

Maybe he was in trouble. Not that she cared. Her concern didn't signify anything personal. She wanted no one to get hurt, not Sean, not David, not anyone.

Excluding the person who murdered Grandpa. She prayed he would suffer.

David sought to prevent her from looking at the flash drive. He wanted her uninvolved. To hell with what he wanted. She needed answers. She needed the truth. She needed to ensure the murderer paid for his crime. To accomplish that, she needed more information.

She must look. She had looked, a little, and none of the information she saw made sense.

How could she expect it to? Nothing added up anymore.

Thoughts spun in her brain with almost dizzying speed. Invisible assailants. Telepathy. Neuroscience. Digital Prognostics.

Something destined to change humanity.

Her grandfather, a neuroscientist, had studied something so earth-shattering that dangerous people would kill to possess it. For the first time in days—no, months—she understood the root of her problems. The data on the flash drive, combined with everything she'd experienced, added up to one thing.

Her grandfather, and her parents, had studied psychic phenomena.

And someone wanted their research. Someone who would kill to get it.

Chapter Fourteen

Grace rubbed her neck. Her eyes felt gritty, her mouth dry. She sipped water from the cup on the bedside table and then she returned her attention to the document on-screen. Though she'd unplugged the flash drive, her computer was still logged onto the mystery site. She scrolled down the list of names until she found the one she wanted.

Traveler: Sean Vandenbrook. Designation: TK (Level 9). Accuracy: 93.725.

Clicking the link, she waited for the web page to load. When it did, she read the status report that, like David's, consisted of one short paragraph.

Status as of 0800 hours: In transit at main facility, Mojave Desert, California. Vital signs normal. Excursion ends 0900 hours.

In transit. At the facility. David's status report had said the same thing. It made no more sense now than it had a few minutes ago.

She reached for the touch pad, intending to close the browser window. A line of text at the bottom of the screen flashed. She hesitated. The text, a link to another page, flashed again. *View current excursion data (real time).*

She clicked the link.

The page switched to a chat-room style window. As in a chat room, the text appeared line-by-line on the screen. But, rather than being attributed to the screen name of the person typing the text, each segment was attributed to an abbreviation. The text was apparently a real-time transcription of a conversation between someone designated TK24 and another person identified as LEAD.

"I can't do it," TK24 pleaded, "I want to sleep."

LEAD seemed unconcerned. "Time's not up. Keep going." After a pause, LEAD added, "You're restrained. You can't get up, so stop trying."

"I can't do this anymore. Please."

"Tears accomplish nothing." Another pause in the text, and then: "Give him the lorazepam. He's useless now."

"Please no," TK24 begged. Grace could imagine the fear in his voice, despite the sterility of the typed words.

Suddenly, LEAD asked, "Who's logged on?"

A third individual, TECH3, responded. "JT's monitoring."

"Who else?"

"Nobody."

"What's that?" LEAD demanded. "Someone else is logged on."

TK24 said, "I'll do it. I'm okay now."

"No, it's too late," LEAD told him. "Session terminated."

The page went blank. A message glowed on the screen in bold, red letters. "Unauthorized access. Tracking..."

The last word blinked.

The message changed: "Re-initializing real-time link."

The chat window reopened. A single line of text, sent by LEAD, glared at her from the screen: "Identify yourself."

The cursor blinked on the screen, below the text. They demanded a response. She hovered her fingers over the keyboard. This could be a trap. Refusing to respond communicated weakness, fear. Responding would let them know she had control, or at least that she wasn't cowering under the bed. Even if that's what she felt like doing right at this moment.

But they didn't need to know that.

She typed two words. They appeared on-screen identified as GUEST. They could, no doubt, track her IP address or something. Better keep this brief.

"You first."

"Did you really think you could sneak in here?" LEAD asked.

"Looks like I did."

"You don't understand what we can do to you."

"The ignorance is mutual."

"You're not as clever as you think. Give up. It will be much easier on you."

She punched keys one by one, mouthing the words as she typed. "Go to hell."

"Hello, Grace."

She stared at the letters on the screen. He was up to something. He used her name, as if he thought it might intimidate her—it did not—but she couldn't figure out why he waited until now to show that her knew her.

Why did she assume DIR was a man?

The person on the other end of the virtual conversation entered another phrase.

"We have you."

Tilting her head, she considered the words. He wanted her to think they'd located her. But had they really?

With everything that had happened lately, testing her fortune seemed unwise. She tried to close the browser window on-screen. Nothing happened. She tried again. Nothing.

In the chat room, another message appeared. "We have control of your computer. Stop fighting us."

To the screen, she muttered, "Screw you."

"We have you surrounded. Give up."

Although they might've been lying, she couldn't take the risk. She tried to shut down the computer. It ignored her commands. She held down the power button for five seconds, which should've turned off the computer no matter what. Nothing happened. For several panicked seconds, she didn't know what to do.

Then she tossed the computer onto the bed, grabbed her gun, leaped to her feet, and bolted out of the motel room. Her purse she nabbed on her way out, slinging it over her neck. The room door slammed shut behind her.

A car swerved into the parking lot. The headlights raked over her as the sedan braked hard and whirled toward her, tires screeching. The car rocked to a halt, angled across the two empty parking spaces in front of her.

She spun to the left and ran.

Footsteps pounded behind her, advancing with each thunderous clap. She pushed her legs to move faster, her muscles to strain harder, until her thighs burned and her breaths shortened into gasps. It wasn't enough. The footsteps echoed louder and closer.

Further away, tires squealed and an engine roared.

A powerful hand seized her hair. White-hot pain ripped through her scalp. The force of the action flipped her feet out from under her. Another hand, as big and powerful as the first, clamped around her upper arm, holding her up with bruising strength. Her feet hit the ground again.

The man holding her yanked her head backward. Pain shot out across her scalp and lanced into the backs of her eyes. She gritted her teeth. Darkness flitted at the edges of her vision. No, no, no, she would *not* pass out.

The man gripped her right arm. Her left arm was free.

She rammed her elbow backward into flesh hardened by taut muscles. The man grunted but held his grip on her. She raised her arm for another try.

He let go of her left arm. Just as she slammed her elbow down, he clamped his arm across her torso, pinning her against him. She recognized the feel of him, the unyielding hardness of his body, the steel-bar quality of his arm fastened over her.

"Waldron," she hissed through clenched teeth.

His voice growled so close to her ear that she felt his breath on her cheek. "Did you think I'd let you go that easily? Your lovely body has quite a bounty on it, you know."

Her scalp burned. Tears welled in her eyes, squeezed out by the pain rather than her emotions. Oh she felt plenty emotional right now, but she refused to let it show. She would not cry, even from the pain.

Blinking away the tears, she said, "Bounty? What the hell are you talking about?"

"My employer will pay me a great deal of money to bring you in."

The sedan pulled up in front of them. They stood at the end of the building, where the sidewalk dead-ended at the grassy strip that separated the motel property from the interstate on-ramp. The sedan had veered onto the grass to stop directly in front of, but sideways to, the pair of them. The jaundiced glow of the parking lot lights revealed the car's driver. It was the man she'd seen parked along her street, inside the same nondescript sedan he drove now.

A smattering of stars glittered overhead. Only the brightest ones could punch through the secondhand smog from Fort Worth and the radiance of Lassiter Falls.

She still held the gun. In her right hand. The one pinned tightly under Waldron's elbow.

The memory of their previous encounter flashed through her mind. Except for the setting, that incident was virtually identical to this one. For a couple seconds, she wondered if she'd slipped through a crack in time and emerged back in that very same moment. Apparently, she'd learned nothing from the first time Waldron attacked her.

Or maybe he hadn't learned. The bastard seemed to have a limited playbook when it came to assaulting women.

She couldn't shoot him in the foot this time. Her arm was too tightly pinned, and her own foot was in the way.

"Stop fighting," Waldron murmured, his tone almost seductive. "You can't keep running forever, and when you stop I'll be here to catch you."

If anyone else had said those words, she might've taken it as an offer of aid and comfort. Okay, if David had spoken those words she would've taken it that way. From Waldron, the words echoed as a threat rather than a promise.

The car door swung open. The dark-haired man climbed out of the sedan and trotted to them. The new guy held a syringe in one hand.

Grace's throat tightened. She swallowed hard.

Waldron jerked her hair, tilting her head sideways, exposing the tender flesh of her neck.

The new guy lifted the syringe and stepped closer.

She wriggled in Waldron's grasp.

He cinched his arm tighter around her and leaned close again to whisper in her ear. "Relax, dear child, soon you'll be with David again. Well, you'll be in the same facility—but you'll never actually see him again. You belong to someone else now, and he has great plans for you."

The man with evil eyes. Grace shuddered.

Waldron chuckled softly.

The night felt colder, despite the warm wind, thick with humidity.

"What about the flash drive?" the new guy asked.

"It's either in the room or on her person," Waldron said. He ran the back of his hand down her neck and across her shoulder. "We'll search every inch of both until we find it."

Nausea swelled inside her. She choked back the bile. No time for revulsion. She must find a way out of this. Right now.

First, she needed to ask a question. "Was that your boss on the website? The one who calls himself LEAD?"

"He detected your clumsy attempt at espionage." Waldron nodded to his cohort. "Now, Lopez."

The other man lifted the syringe to her neck.

Panic shot through her. She could not let them inject her. Even if the drug simply knocked her out, that would give them a chance to do anything they wanted to her. Anything. She would be defenseless.

The needle grazed her skin.

She kicked out, but sandwiched between the two men, she couldn't get enough leverage.

Lopez flinched. The needle scratched her but didn't penetrate her flesh.

Waldron snatched the syringe from Lopez.

Grace squeezed her eyes shut, wishing with every ounce of her willpower that the needle would break or Waldron would drop the syringe or—

Waldron jerked and gasped.

She opened her eyes.

Lopez stared, wide-eyed, past her shoulder.

Waldron's hold on her slackened. He stumbled backward, out of her peripheral vision.

Lopez shook his head, slowly at first, then faster and faster.

Thump.

Grace stood motionless, afraid to move. She wanted to look behind her, but at the same time, she did not want to see.

Lopez had stopped shaking his head. He choked back a whimper as he focused his gaze on her.

She opened her mouth to speak, only to realize she had no clue what to say.

Lopez whirled and ran for the car. He flung himself into the driver's seat, slamming the door.

As if in slow motion, Grace turned around to look at Waldron.

He lay crumpled on the concrete walkway, eyes closed. The syringe protruded from his neck. She knelt beside him. Her hand trembled as she reached out to feel for a pulse in his neck. The blood surged against her fingertips in a slow-but-steady rhythm.

She had wished for a miracle. And it happened.

David must've done it. Or Sean.

Yet if one of them had helped her, he would've shown himself. Wouldn't he?

Rising, Grace turned away from Waldron. Fifteen feet away, inside the sedan, Lopez stared at her from behind the glass of the driver's window.

She ran past the car, across the parking lot into a grassy expanse that separated the motel from a little strip mall. Lopez didn't pursue her. She kept running, aiming for the strip mall. The back of the building looked bleak and lifeless. The sickly glow of sodium vapor lights, mounted on tall poles surrounding the mall, guided her to her destination. What she would do once she got there, she hadn't a clue.

A small loading dock stuck out from the mall's backside. As her feet hit pavement, she veered toward the loading dock. No vehicles were parked back here. The place looked dead. She halted at a set of steps that led up the side of the loading dock. Breathing hard, she sat down on the second step.

What now?

"I don't know," she muttered.

Leaning her head against the metal railing, she stared at the pavement beneath her feet, without really seeing it. Her vision had drifted out of focus. Her nap earlier had done little to relieve the exhaustion that seeped into every cell of her body and left her feeling like a cotton ball floating on the ocean. Soaked through. Limp. Adrift.

"You don't know what?"

Grace jumped. She jerked her head up, rotating her head to the left, toward the voice that had startled her. She knew the speaker's identity without looking at him, though.

"David," she said, because her brain refused to cough up anything better. Her conversation skills were mediocre on a good day. This was not a good day.

"Are you hurt?" David asked.

"No..."

He walked toward her, stopping a couple feet in front of her. Even in the yellowish light from the sodium vapor bulbs, his eyes flared a bright sky blue. The color was unnatural, almost inhuman. Every time she saw his eyes like that, it set off a chain-reaction chill inside her.

As he crouched before her, the strange radiance in his eyes dwindled. The irises were blue now, bright blue, but they lacked the burning quality.

"Thank you," she said.

He scrunched his eyebrows. "For what?"

"Helping me escape. Waldron deserved to get a needle jammed into his own neck for a change."

David just looked at her, brow furrowed.

"What?" she demanded.

"I didn't help you. I only got here a minute ago."

"No." The world listed beneath her, and she clamped a hand around the railing. "You must have. He didn't stab himself with the needle and syringes don't move on their own. Maybe Sean…"

David shook his head. "Sean can't. Not without help."

The ground settled back onto the horizontal. She still felt a little lightheaded.

Leaning closer, David rested a hand on her knee. "It was you."

She blinked slowly. "Excuse me?"

"You must've moved the syringe."

"I never touched it."

He squeezed her knee. "Not with your hands maybe."

"What?" She shook her head with such violence that her hair lashed her face. "No, it's impossible. Even if I understood what you're saying, which I don't, it would be absolutely impossible."

He smiled just a little. "You wouldn't be so upset if you didn't understand what I mean. You have the power."

She didn't want to ask, but the words came out anyway. "What power?"

"Extrasensory mental powers."

"Huh?"

He patted her knee. "Psychic abilities."

"Psychic…" Her voice trailed off, along with her thoughts. Several seconds ticked by before she collected her normal sensory abilities enough to speak. Then, in a tone far more confident than she felt, she declared, "That's insane."

He laughed. The sound was low and masculine, devoid of mockery. In fact, if she had to describe the quality of his laughter, she would have to label it affectionately amused.

She pursed her lips. "Why are you laughing at me?"

"Because you know it's true. You used your telekinetic ability to save yourself." He smiled—not just a little this time, but a full smile that made his beautiful features even more attractive. "It's a good sign. If your powers are coming back, then maybe your memory will come back too."

He looked entirely too happy about the prospect. Something stirred inside her, a feeling akin to dread mixed with anticipation. Right now the dread was stronger, but she felt the anticipation blossoming.

David slid his hand over hers.

She swallowed against the lump in her throat. "Do we know each other? I mean, did we know each other before you showed up in my house the other day?"

"Yes."

"How well?"

"Very well."

His throaty tone set her stomach to fluttering. She tried to withdraw her hand, but found she couldn't move or breathe. Her heart raced. He caressed the back of her hand, igniting an ember of heat there. The warmth flooded through her entire body in the space of three very fast heartbeats. She felt her cheeks flush.

"What do you mean?" she asked.

Her voice sounded pathetically breathless. She couldn't summon the will to care. She could do nothing except gaze into those blue eyes.

He raised his hand to her cheek. "We were engaged."

His hand felt cool against her flushed cheek.

She forced herself to breathe. "Engaged?"

"To be married."

The fire inside snuffed out.

She leaped to her feet. Shoving past him, she stumbled a few steps and halted, then spun to face him. Her cheeks flushed again, this time heated by the anger erupting inside her.

"That's ridiculous," she spat. "I'd remember if I—if we—"

"You don't remember anything from last summer, do you?"

Eight months of her life she couldn't remember. She wanted to scream or kick something. Most of all, though, she wanted to remember. She wanted to know for certain he was lying.

Except a small part of her wanted it to be true. A small part that grew bigger every minute. The insane part of her.

The anger fizzled. Her shoulders slumped. When she spoke again, her voice was calm and even.

"I wouldn't do that," she said, feeling not at all certain. "Get engaged to someone I'd only known for eight months. I'm way too cautious for that."

He strode toward her, stopping a couple yards away. "You changed during those eight months. You learned things about yourself, things you couldn't believe at first, things that tore apart your sense of order and stability. What you thought the world was, you found out it was something entirely different."

"That makes no sense."

"Explanations won't convince you. Only experience will."

"I'm not psychic."

"Yes, you are."

She felt the anger bubbling up again, about to boil over if she let it. Fear lit the fire under the pot, she knew. Fear was supposed to be cold. Instead, it heated her insides. Common knowledge could be oh so wrong.

Maybe that was David's point.

Christ. She did not want to know any of this.

"What are you?" she asked, unable to stop the words. "You say you're not dead, but a living person can't appear and disappear like a ghost. Either I'm hallucinating or you're not human."

"You're not hallucinating."

"I know, which means you must be dead."

He surged forward, grasped her upper arms, and crushed her to him as he kissed her hard. The heat of anger ebbed into a tingling warmth. She felt herself relax against him. Just as she was starting to enjoy the kiss, he pushed away from her.

"Do I feel dead?" he asked.

No, he didn't. He felt very much alive. She bristled at the annoyed tone in his voice, but she had to admit the truth. He felt real and alive.

"Okay," she said, "if you're not dead, then how do you do it? The vanishing thing, I mean."

"Astral projection." He shrugged. "That's the common name for it. In practice, it's a combination of remote viewing, telekinesis, and thought projection."

She felt unsteady and disconnected, as if her body were melting as her head floated away into space.

"It's hard to explain," David said.

"No shit."

He raised a hand toward her.

She scuffled backward.

"I'm sorry," he said. "I wish I knew how to help you accept all of this."

"I won't accept things that cannot be true. Whatever your game is, I am not playing."

He exhaled a loud, drawn-out sigh. "You weren't nearly this stubborn the first time around."

"Leave," she said.

He stared at her as if she spoke an alien language.

"Get out of here," she said, squeezing the words out through clenched teeth. "Leave me alone."

"No—"

"Yes." The syllable came out as a hiss.

His mouth dropped open. He shook his head.

She shouted, "Go!"

A gust of wind swirled around them.

David raised his hands in a compliant gesture. "Calm down, Grace."

"Do not tell me what to do."

The wind intensified, snatching up paper scraps and dirt, twirling the debris inside a mini vortex that danced around them.

"Don't do this," David said.

She scowled at him. "Don't do what?"

"Push me out. Please, give me a chance to—"

Get out. In her mind, she screamed the words.

The vortex slammed into him.

He vanished.

The little tornado evaporated.

The silence felt unnatural, as if she'd just gone deaf. In the distance, though, a dog barked. Her knees quivered. Everything seemed to tilt and roll around her. Gasping, she dropped onto her knees.

David was gone.

She'd killed him.

Chapter Fifteen

David returned to blackness. His forehead smacked into the floor. Phantom lights flashed in the dark, a figment of his mind brought on by hitting the concrete face first. The bare floor chilled his skin through his clothes. He couldn't move.

Strangely, he felt no pain now. He remembered the agony from seconds ago. His mind ripping. His body screaming. Blinding light. Two words blasting through his head.

Get out.

Grace's inner voice had shouted at him so loud his ears actually hurt. His brain hurt worse. Yet as soon as he'd slammed back into his own mind, the pain dissipated. He still couldn't move, though, and he fought the instinct to panic. That never helped. At least he could breathe. And see. And hear.

His body twitched. Saliva dribbled from his lips. His heart beat fast. Like an invalid, he lay on the concrete with his face pressed into the hard surface, unable to control his own body. Nothing like this had happened before. He'd traveled thousands of miles and viewed hundreds of sites. No one had pushed him out before.

And she didn't even realize she'd done it.

Their conversation must've sounded quite normal, if not exactly cordial. She was angry with him—and scared, though not of him or because of him, he sensed. She wanted him to answer her questions. He'd intended to but, well, he was concerned about her reaction when he shared the full truth with her. The news about her own abilities shocked her more than he'd expected, which made telling her more seem like an unwise option. She didn't remember any of it. Hearing the facts from someone she considered a stranger might not convince her.

He must convince her. Fast.

She'd gotten so frustrated with him that she struck out at him, unwittingly, in a way even she failed to see. She'd tapped into the invisible streams of power that permeated the universe. He'd seen her do it before, but given her current memory problems, he hadn't been sure she could still do it.

Until he felt the pressure hit him. A wave of unseen energy as powerful as a tsunami.

Then he knew. Grace was forcing him out.

The twitching ceased. David held still, gasping for breaths. The air was cold yet soothing. He pushed up with his hands, raising his body off the floor. His arms trembled. Gritting his teeth, he struggled to hold himself up. His arms gave out and he collapsed back onto the floor. Dammit.

A throbbing erupted in his head, a pulsating kind of pressure, as if his head were a balloon inflated to near the breaking point. He marshaled enough energy to slide one arm across the floor so he could rub his temple. Even that small effort left him shaking.

Behind him, the door knob jiggled.

He must get up. *Now.* If they found him in this state...

He rolled onto his side. With both arms, he levered his torso off the floor until he was sitting. For a few horrible seconds he felt as if he might pass out. The sensation faded, though, and he shifted into a kneeling position. His strength grew with each passing moment. He prayed it returned fast enough.

His body canted sideways. He flung his hands out, seizing the metal chair he'd occupied during his excursion. Since it was bolted to the floor, the chair offered a secure handhold. With the chair as his crutch, he managed to rise from the floor into a hunched standing position. Electrode wires, their ends ripped free from the chair, dangled from his head.

The chair. He rubbed his eyes to clear the fuzziness. The electrode wires were attached to the chair, or at least they were supposed to be. He must've torn them free when he flew out of the chair. But something else bothered him far more than the electrode wires.

The leather restraints. Some force had rent them apart, scattering the buckles across the floor. He couldn't have done that. The same force that hurled him out of the chair must've severed the restraints as well.

Grace had forced him out with a hell of a lot of power. More than he'd ever seen before.

The lights clicked on with a buzz and a flicker. He squinted. The door was slammed inward. Shoes clapped on the concrete.

David twisted around to look at the doorway.

Tesler raced across the room to him. "What happened to you?"

No compassion filled Tesler's voice. Rather, he spoke in an irritated, accusing tone.

The room tilted. David gripped the chair harder. "I don't know. I did what you told me to."

"Your vitals were off the chart," Tesler said. "A routine excursion shouldn't kill you."

"I'm not dead."

Tesler harrumphed, shaking his head. "You look like walking death."

"Thanks." David suppressed a chuckle. "Guess that makes you the grim reaper."

Tesler grasped an electrode wire and yanked it. The electrode ripped away from his temple. He winced. Pale hairs clung to the sticky surface of the electrode.

Tesler gestured toward the chair. "How did you remove the restraints?"

David looked at the chair and shrugged.

"You know what happens," Tesler said, "when you don't cooperate."

"You still don't understand." David took a step toward Tesler. "Nothing you do can stop me. Not even the drugs. Eventually, I'll be free."

"One thing would stop you."

David didn't need to read Tesler's thoughts to know what the man was thinking. He had the ingenuity of a fungus.

"Go ahead," David said. "Kill me. See how far you get reconstructing eight years of your damn research without me. Your leader won't be pleased with you then."

Tesler tilted his head back. He examined David over the tip of his nose. They both knew he could reconstruct the data without David like he could exist without his heart pumping lifeblood through his veins.

Oh wait. That assumed he had a heart.

Tesler flicked his wrist.

Two guards trotted through the doorway and around Tesler. They grabbed David's arms, secured his hands behind his back with cuffs, and shackled his feet. As they hauled him past Tesler into the hallway, David twisted his torso to glance back at Tesler.

"I told you," he said, "that I won't kill for you."

"Then you will die for the research."

The guards dragged David down the corridor toward the elevator. He let his feet drag on the floor. Why make it easy for them? Cooperation had gotten him nowhere and nothing, except separated from Grace. No more easygoing lab rat. He would fight them with every step, every breath, every ounce of power within him—even if it drained the very life out of him.

One of the guards kicked him in the shin. Pain shot through his leg. He clamped his jaw shut and swallowed the pain. He already felt as if a tornado had sucked him into its vortex, shaken the life out of him, and spit him out again. Fighting took energy.

Well then he'd get some. All he needed was a little rest.

In the elevator, the guards relaxed their grips on him. The guard named Battaglia, a huge man with a thin mustache and the eyes of a Pekinese, chatted with his partner about the outdoors. The two men agreed that it "totally sucked" to be stuck inside the facility for weeks at a time. The shorter guard, a young man named Norris whose frame resembled a troll's, lamented the lack of large-breasted women in the facility.

David kept his gaze on the elevator doors.

Norris jabbed him in the ribs. "Hey, freak. You ever had a girl?"

David concentrated on the doors. He had learned long ago that interacting with the guards provoked them. They had the brains of rabbits and the tempers of killer bees.

Right now he had no strength to deal with them.

Norris jabbed him in the small of his back. Pain branched up his spine. His knees shook. He stumbled backward, bumped the elevator's rear wall, and slumped against it for support.

"Well, freak?" the guard said. "You like girls?"

David gritted his teeth.

Battaglia sniggered. "Maybe he likes you better, Norris."

The elevator eased to a stop. David pushed away from the wall.

A chime rang. Through speakers in the ceiling, a recorded female voice issued instructions in a neutral tone. "Access to this area requires handprint identification. Please place your palm on the reader."

A panel beside the doors slid open to reveal a cavity that housed a square of smooth plastic etched with the outline of hand.

Norris slapped his hand onto the reader.

The chime sounded. The voice intoned, "Thank you."

The panel lowered. The doors slid apart.

The guards dragged him into the corridor. The three of them moved past rows of closed doors. A number on each door represented the room's tenant—or more accurately, the room's inmate. David and his colleagues had no names here, just ID numbers to help the guards and technicians tell them apart. No one really cared who they were, how they felt, or what happened to them after the tests were completed.

Lights along the floor illuminated the corridor. Security cameras, hidden in every tenth light, observed their progress. David had discovered many of their "secret" security measures. Guards babbled about everything when they thought they were alone. Why on earth they felt safely alone inside a facility populated with psychics, David couldn't fathom.

Battaglia unlocked the door to David's room. Norris shoved him inside, then clomped through the door behind him. Battaglia followed them inside, shutting the door.

Norris removed the cuffs. "Get in bed."

David complied. His head throbbed again. His muscles felt weak and heavy. His throat was parched.

"Water," he croaked.

Battaglia observed as Norris shackled David's wrists and ankles to the bed rails. A single lamp burned in the far corner.

"Water," David repeated.

The guards left. The door lock clicked as they engaged it from the outside.

"Are you all right?"

Sean shuffled out of the shadows. His voice was soft, his face pinched. The glow of the lamp lent his red hair a liquid quality, like molten copper.

"I'm alive," David said. "Thirsty and tired, but alive."

"You were gone a long time."

"I know."

He had volunteered for extra tests, so he could use the time to help Grace. Edward had asked him to watch out for her, and though he'd promised not to interact with her, he'd also promised to do whatever he could to help her. He would keep that promise, despite Tesler's suspicions, despite the damage it inflicted on his body.

Despite how much it worried Sean.

The boy had no one else to trust. He'd come to the facility two years before but, despite amazing progress, he hadn't lived enough to know how to handle Tesler and his goons. He hadn't developed the willpower.

He was only sixteen.

These days, Sean looked much older. His cheeks were sunken. Worry lines creased his forehead.

Sean slouched beside the bed. "They're gonna kill you."

"They won't."

"They'll give you the stuff."

David met the boy's gaze. "It'll be all right."

Sean hunched his shoulders and looked at the floor.

"Need a favor," David said.

"Sure, anything."

"I need you to keep looking out for her."

"I'm not good at it, not like you."

"You can do it."

Sean contemplated the linoleum.

David knew he was pushing Sean to the limits of his abilities and beyond. Although Sean possessed an amazing talent for healing, he could travel only with assistance and interacting with the world was impossible for him—without an intense boost of power from someone skilled in that area. David knew Sean disliked traveling, but he hated manifesting. It was intrusive and unsettling, even for a veteran. Pushing Sean over a threshold he feared crossing troubled David. He had no choice.

Grace was alone out there.

"Okay," Sean said, sounding miserable. "But she won't see me this time."

This time. The phrase set off alarms in David's head. "What do you mean this time?"

Sean stuffed his hands in his pockets.

David shut his eyes. Sleep beckoned him with its siren song. He forced his eyes open.

"She saw me when I healed her," Sean said, the words tumbling out in a rush. "I don't know how, I swear, I can't do that without your help."

"Doesn't matter," David said. "Just watch out for her."

"Okay."

Sean left.

David sucked in a deep breath. He needed rest, but he sensed he must wait a little longer before giving in to sleep. He counted the panels in the ceiling instead. When that failed to banish the drowsiness, he focused on spotting patterns in the swirls and dots on the ceiling panels. One group looked like Abraham Lincoln.

A few minutes later, Tesler entered the room. He stopped beside the bed, looking down on David with a slight smile as he brandished a syringe in his right hand. The needle glistened in the twilight of the room.

Tesler leaned over the bed and murmured, "You never could follow directions. Tell me where you really went. Perhaps I can keep them from killing you."

"I viewed the target."

"And?"

"That's it."

"David," Tesler said, wagging the needle in his face. "We both know you went somewhere else. Tell me where."

"Hawaii. It's nice this time of year."

"Have it your way."

Tesler tapped the bubbles out of the syringe.

Let them drug him. He would never tell, never let them intimidate him the way they intimidated the others. Tesler should've known better. The drug might shackle his body, but never his spirit. He could wait. Grace had the flash drive but her enemies seemed unaware of that fact, so she would be safe for awhile longer. Once she found the flash drive, she might decide to come here, to confront them herself. She was far too determined to sit back and let events unfold around her. Too determined and too willful. She'd march into a nuclear reactor if she thought "the truth" awaited her inside its walls.

She thought she was meek. Lord, if only that were true.

No. He liked her willful and determined. Even if it made his self-appointed job next to impossible to complete. Most of the time she kept to herself and gave the world the impression she was…well, not exactly meek, but she certainly hid her true nature deep inside. He'd seen it. That intimate knowledge made it hard for him to reconcile the woman he knew with the suspicious, self-doubting persona she displayed now. Maybe if she remembered those eight months, she'd shed her insecure shell and reveal the powerhouse underneath.

Amnesia left her vulnerable, but she was safe—for now. He had time.

Tesler squirted a jet of liquid from the syringe. He jabbed the needle into David's arm and depressed the plunger.

Eventually, Tesler and his cronies would run out of options. Then they'd awaken him. And he'd have one more chance to save himself and Grace.

His eyelids fluttered shut.

Grace wandered the streets of Lassiter Falls in search of a telephone. She needed to call Senator Faulkner. Even if he couldn't help, she had an obligation to contact him. Her grandfather had asked one favor of her and she must do it. She owed him that much, after all he'd done for her.

Everyone wanted her to do things for them. Even her grandfather issued post-mortem orders. Andrew Haley wanted to babble at her. Waldron wanted her, though for what purpose, she couldn't say. She decided she probably didn't want to know anyway. The knowledge would just creep her out more than she already was.

Waldron could've killed her. He needed her alive. She possessed what he wanted. What everyone seemed to want.

The goddamn flash drive.

Gimme, gimme, gimme. Those seemed like the only syllables anyone knew how to speak anymore. That and "do what I say right now." Only one person behaved as if he cared about what happened to her.

David.

Her throat constricted. Oh God. She'd killed him. Hadn't she?

Everything whirled around her, as if the sidewalk had transformed into a carnival ride. Her stomach lurched. She staggered to the nearest tree and propped her shoulder against it until the dizziness faded. Pushing away from the tree, she stood there for a moment.

Was David dead? Could she kill someone with her thoughts?

She'd been so angry. Actually, she'd been terrified that everything he said was true, which made her angry. Her mind replayed the moment. David's pleading expression. The swirling wind.

Don't do this.
Don't do what?
Push me out.

At the time, she'd barely heard his words. One thought had ricocheted through her mind, drowning out everything else. *Get out.*

David claimed she had psychic abilities. But what had he meant when he begged her not to push him out? It made no sense. Push him out of what?

Her mind.

The truth hit her like a punch in the gut. He had been in her mind, or connected to her mind, through some kind of psychic channel. No, that was impossible.

Except...

It made a bizarre kind of sense. She'd pushed him out of her mind. Forced him to go away. Why shouldn't she? He had no right to invade her thoughts, to make her see him and speak to him whether she wanted to or not. It was rude.

A harsh bark of laughter burst out of her. She was criticizing a man for rudely invading her mind. It was utterly insane.

Her neck ached. She rubbed it, to no avail. The neck pain was only the precursor. Next would come the headache and the nausea and a new swell of dizziness. Soon she'd sink into the mire of a quicksand migraine, and no amount of struggling would pull her out of it. She needed to find a safe place to wait out the migraine. A relatively safe place. If one existed.

She still had time before the quicksand dragged her under, time she must use wisely.

Down the sidewalk she marched, squinting because she swore the streetlights had gotten brighter all of a sudden. It was just the migraine, of course, making light seem sharper and harder, as if it were composed of a thousand tiny knives that pierced her brain.

David was not dead. She knew it, she thought. Maybe she just hoped. For the moment, she must assume whatever she'd done to him had caused no permanent damage.

She halted in front of a pay phone. It was bolted to the brick wall of a convenience store. No privacy whatsoever. An inconstant but ever-present stream of people strolled into and out of the store, some clutching monstrously large fountain drinks, others twirling their car keys, and still more munching on fried foods that looked full of enough preservatives to outlast the mummies of the Egyptian pharaohs.

Someone might overhear her phone conversation.

Waldron's buddies might've bugged the phones.

They could not possibly have bugged every public phone in Lassiter Falls. No one could. The thought failed to comfort her. She couldn't know for certain, not anymore. Anything goes, that was the new order of the universe. If David and his network of psychic friends and enemies vanished, invaded her thoughts, and took control of her body, then surely Waldron's friends could tap the public phone system.

The phones were hooked up to computers, weren't they? Waldron's pals had tracked an Internet connection back to the motel and seized control of her laptop.

The pay phone was too risky. She'd endured enough danger to satiate an adrenaline junkie for a lifetime. Minimize the risk. She must adopt those words as her new motto.

Not that her enemies gave a fig about her wishes. Or her sanity.

As she continued down the street, the trees on either side thinned. The buildings segued from businesses to houses. Ahead, the street intersected the main highway. Cars on the highway roared across the intersection at full speed, their headlights slashing through the night. The traffic signal burned red. The eye of death glowering at her.

Get a grip, girl.

She paused at the corner to rest and think.

On the opposite side of the highway sat Mesquite Hill Center. The strip mall housed a health club, a restaurant, a dollar store, and an electronics outlet. The dollar store was closed for the day, but the other establishment stayed open late, as evidenced by their glaring open signs and interior lights. A poster taped to the window of Bronco Electronics announced "dirt-cheap rate plans" for mobile phones. Sign up today, the sign urged, and get a free phone. Another sign in the store's window advertised prepaid cell phones. "No contract, total freedom," the sign declared.

A prepaid phone. Unconnected to the local system. Unconnected with her.

She jogged across the highway into the parking lot of the shopping center. Five vehicles occupied parking spots. The center's restaurant, Ruth's Tex-Mex Grill, had curtained windows. Through the picture windows of the health club, she saw two elderly men lifting weights and a woman riding an exercise bicycle as if a rabid pit bull were pursuing her. She tromped down the sidewalk, past the restaurant and health club, to the doors of Bronco Electronics. A bell jangled as she pushed through the doors into the store.

A salesman in a Hawaiian shirt scurried out of a back room.

"May I help you, ma'am?" he asked in his Texas drawl.

She pointed toward the display of prepaid phones. "I want one of those. Please."

"You sure? We got some real fine deals on full-service plans—"

"Just the prepaid phone. Now please."

Fifteen minutes later, she departed the store with a prepaid flip phone in her hand. The device weighed a few ounces at most and, when folded shut, fit in the palm of her hand with room to spare. The casing was gray and nondescript, which suited her fine. She'd paid cash, and the phone required no contract or account sign-up, so she felt reasonably sure no one would know she had the phone. To know if the phone was really safe, however, she'd have to use it. The thought sent a chill up her spine.

Before she could use the phone, she needed a number to dial.

She chewed her lower lip for a minute, then shoved the phone in her jeans pocket. She turned around and strode back into the store.

The same salesman approached her. "There a problem, ma'am?"

He looked genuinely concerned. Maybe he'd get in trouble if a customer returned a phone five minutes after purchasing it.

She smiled and said, "No no, it's fine. But I was wondering if I could try out one of your computers. I'm thinking about replacing mine, and I'd like to see how good the newest models are."

It wasn't entirely a lie. She did need a new computer, but lacking any funds beyond the ten bucks and change in her wallet, she couldn't exactly pick up a new laptop today. A computer might come in handy, though. Maybe if she ran to the nearest ATM and withdrew—

No, ATMs had a limit of $200. Besides, if she accessed her bank account then Waldron and company might notice it.

"Sure thing," the salesman said, his expression brightening. "Let me show you the one we just got in this week."

He led her to a display table that housed a desktop computer with a huge wide-screen monitor attached. Using the mouse, he opened programs and chattered about the computer's built-in features.

"Um," Grace said, "could I just play around with it for a few minutes?"

"You bet."

He released the mouse and stepped back.

Grace walked up the computer. Glancing at the salesman, she asked, "Can this get online?"

"Oh yeah. We have broadband."

He stood there watching as she opened the web browser. She hesitated. The salesman folded his arms over his chest and kept on smiling and watching.

Grace plastered her best smile on her face and said, "I don't want to take up all your time. You must have other things to do and I can fiddle with this on my own."

"You sure?"

"Positive." She broadened her smile. "Thank you so much for all your help. It's nice to know chivalry isn't dead after all."

The salesman blushed.

Then the phone rang and he trotted to the sales counter to answer it.

Grace's smile evaporated. Jeez, being cheerful had turned into an endurance sport. It used to come so easily.

In the web browser, she navigated to a search engine, typed in Faulkner's name, and hit enter. The results popped up within seconds. Oh, she coveted the store's broadband connection. Her Internet was glacially slow in comparison. Not that it mattered much, since she'd probably get bumped off by an invisible villain without ever seeing her home again.

She glanced at the search results. And froze.

The first link was titled "Senator Dies in Auto Accident."

Below the title, the search results printed the first couple lines of the news article. "Senator Elias Faulkner," the text said, "was killed early this morning when a drunk driver struck his car in a head-on collision."

Dead. Another person involved in this mess was dead.

She'd intended to look up the phone number for Faulkner's office. No point in that now. Her grandfather said to contact Faulkner, and mentioned no one else as trustworthy. She wouldn't know who else, if anyone, she could trust at Faulkner's office.

Closing the web browser, she hurried out of the store, past the health club, toward the opposite end of the building from where she'd entered the property. On the corner, a newspaper vending machine squatted at the edge of the sidewalk. Its front side faced her. She stopped there, her gaze inexorably drawn to the words printed on the paper, which was pressed against the machine's clear door. The headlines meant nothing to her. Something about local politics followed by mention of a fund raiser at the hospital. The rest of the text was below the fold, out of sight.

Some instinct made her fish three quarters out of her purse, drop them into the slot, and extract a newspaper from the machine. She flipped it over to see the stories on the lower half of the front page. Her skimming ended when she spotted the one-paragraph story at the very bottom of the page.

"Inmate Dies in County Jail," the headline said. The story began, "Andrew Haley died overnight of self-inflicted wounds while being held in connection with the death of Brian Kellogg, a tourist who was found dead at the Bed & Bath Inn yesterday."

Self-inflicted wounds. Sure. Andrew was nuts, but given recent events, she doubted he'd offed himself. The same invisible villain who'd attacked her and strangled Brian Kellogg most likely took care of Andrew as well. And Senator Faulkner.

And her grandfather.

She let the newspaper slip out of her hands. It fluttered to the concrete at her feet.

So many deaths. All over what? The results of secret research into psychic phenomena? Anyone who would kill for that information must be either insane or evil or both.

David.

His face flashed in her mind. Would he be the next victim? Her chest tightened, as if an invisible hand squeezed her heart. She felt tears pooling in her eyes, hot and stinging. She did not want David to die. She didn't want anyone else to die, but especially not him.

Maybe he'd told her the truth. Maybe she felt this sickening dread at the thought of him falling prey to her enemies because they had known each other before. If she could remember those missing months, she might understand her own feelings better.

Her cell phone rang.

It wasn't the new phone she'd just bought. The old one warbled from deep inside her purse.

Digging out the phone, she answered the call on the fifth ring, one ring before her voice mail would've taken the call.

"Hello," she muttered.

"Grace."

That voice. She recognized it. One word provided all the evidence she needed, because she'd heard the same voice before, whispering in her ear, too close.

Waldron.

"You may have scared Lopez," Waldron said in a calm tone laced with a malice that triggered ice-cold tremors inside her. "I don't frighten so easily. You look rather upset, though."

The tremors stopped. Everything around her seemed to have frozen, as if time had paused. The sole evidence of life was the thudding of her own heart. He was watching her. She felt it, an inexplicable sensation of his gaze on her, as tangible as the feel of his hand around her neck. Waldron's voice murmured into her ear.

"Gotcha."

She dropped the phone and ran.

Chapter Sixteen

Grace ran as fast as her legs would move. Maybe Waldron didn't really know where she was, as his one-word message implied. He might've lied just to torment her. She couldn't risk it, so on and on she ran. She didn't stop moving until the shopping center was out of view behind her, over the rise of a hill, and she'd passed from the commercial zone into a region of town filled with vacant lots. Abandoned homes slouched on a few of the lots. They looked as bedraggled as she must look—as she felt.

When she realized no one was following her, she stumbled to a halt.

No car engines grumbled. No footsteps pounded behind her. The only sound was an owl hooting in a nearby tree. The mournful sound made the desolation around her feel even more desolate.

Rubbing her arms against a sudden chill, she turned in a circle to survey the area. Not a single human being was in sight. No animals either. Nothing but dying grass, a handful of trees, and empty shells that had once been homes. The streetlights washed the landscape in shades of jaundiced yellow.

She stood there for several minutes, her mind blank. A deep weariness settled over her. She fought the urge to lie down on the cracked sidewalk. The throbbing in her head had joined forces with the pain in her neck that stabbed up into the base of her skull. The combined misery left her weak and exhausted and nauseous. Her knees began to quiver. If she didn't find a safe place to collapse, and find it very soon, her body would make the decision for her. Waldron and company would find her here, a human puddle on the concrete.

She considered each of the abandoned houses in turn. One looked about ready to collapse itself. Two others had boarded-up windows. No way could she break down the doors or the window boards, not in her current condition. The last house looked relatively intact, though in need of a paint job. The windows weren't boarded.

Summoning the last of her strength, she crossed the street to the little stucco house. The chain link fence was falling down, the gate halfway off its hinges. She sidestepped the gate and shuffled up the concrete walkway toward the front door. Fault lines as deep as the San Andreas cleaved the concrete. She hopped over the gaps, and the knee-high weeds that jutted up through them, reaching the closed door. She grasped the knob and turned. Locked. Damn.

The window beside the door was cracked, but not broken. Under the window, bricks that had once formed a border for a flower bed lay jumbled and half swallowed by the weeds. She picked up one of the bricks and used it to smash out the glass. Once she'd knocked out the last shards, she swung one leg through the window, braced herself against the inside wall, and swung her other leg inside.

The room she found herself in was dark, except for the light coming through the window. She stepped away from the wall, crunching glass under her boots. She cursed herself for not keeping a small flashlight in her purse. The one in her car's glove compartment was of no use now.

The house smelled of mildew and dust. The floor creaked as she tiptoed further into the room. Slowly, her eyes adjusted to the darker environment and recognizable shapes emerged from the gloom. A ramshackle easy chair, tucked into the corner. A blanket or sheet mounded in the center of the room. She kicked at the fabric heap, just to make sure it didn't hide anything living. The front door was behind and to the right of her, while straight ahead two more windows offered a view of the lifeless backyard. She slunk across the room and through a doorway on the left side, into what looked like a combined kitchen and dining room. A couple of wooden chairs lay toppled on their sides, refugees from a dining room set. Another doorway took her into a large, empty room replete with shadows. An overgrown bush blocked the view from the only window. Even in the gloom, she could make out a pair of bifold doors at stood half open, revealing the pitch-darkness inside the closet.

Lightning burst in the sky, silhouetting the bush outside the window. In the same instant, a gust of wind swirled past the house, shaking the bush. The shadows inside the room undulated.

Grace dunked her hand into her purse and curled her fingers around the grip of her gun.

Another stroke of lightning lit the room. She saw the closet was empty, then the darkness reclaimed the space.

She scuffled to the corner farthest from the door, where she could still keep an eye on the doorway but maintain a buffer zone between herself and the opening. The window was at the opposite end of the wall. She leaned back against the wall and let her body slide down until she was sitting on the floor. Although the carpet had lost its bounce, it provided enough cushioning to ease some of the aches in her body. Each flash of lightning stabbed into her eyes like a large-bore needle. She turned her head into the corner, to shield her eyes as much as possible, which wasn't much at all. She shut her eyes and tried to relax. Though the muscles in her thighs and abdomen no longer twanged when she moved, the tightness lingered.

Thunder rumbled, distant but resonant. The window glass rattled.

Big, empty houses gave her the creeps. As a child, she had been convinced that monsters lived in the shadows. According to her childhood theory then, an abandoned house must harbor hordes of demons. Like the ones pursuing her now. Those childhood fears might not have been so silly after all.

The floor creaked.

Just the house settling. The thought failed to alleviate the churning in her stomach or the slight quickening of her pulse. She slid the gun out of her purse. She laid it on her lap, one hand resting on the grip with her index finger over the trigger guard.

Fatigue settled over her once again. Her muscles felt heavy and limp. Her eyelids refused to stay open. Her pulse slowed, her breathing grew shallower, and she sank into sleep.

Grace woke with a jerk that thumped her head against the wall. She grunted, massaging the back of her head. She felt…weird.

An odd sense of pressure made her feel as if a very heavy sack rested atop her head, sinking down around her, first pressing down on her shoulders and then over her chest. She resisted the panic welling inside her. Somehow she knew that staying calm was the only option that would leave her intact. She took a very slow, deep breath.

Intact? What the hell did that mean?

The sensation of pressure oozed down her body, over her hips and legs. Within a few seconds, the sensation passed through and out of her.

She swallowed, straightened her back, and glanced around the room.

Lightning flashed, dimmer than before. The storm must've slipped around to the south.

The room was still empty, except for her. The weird feeling of pressure was completely gone now. The dreams were nothing new, but it had been different this time. Never before had she remembered the dream so vividly after waking. Never before had she remembered what happened after entering the locked room. Never before had she woken to feel an invisible weight pressing down on her, almost as if she were being shoved back into her body. Normally during the dreams—if she could call the bizarre episodes normal—she felt as if she inhabited someone else's body or mind, as if she were merely an observer rather than a participant. This time, however, she had felt completely herself. Yet the most disturbing part had been the sense of...

Traveling.

She sat forward. Travelers. Excursions. She had read those words in the research data on the flash drive. According to the data, David was a traveler. He claimed to have psychic abilities, and he claimed she had them too. If the term traveler referred to a psychic, then she had just been on an excursion.

She'd been traveling for quite some time without knowing it. Traveling while she slept. Taking excursions to see David. And she could only think of one reason why she might do that.

Everything David said was true. They had been...involved.

She closed her eyes. The memory came back to her, unbidden and unwanted. David lying in that bed, unconscious. Still as death. The only sign of life had been the almost imperceptible rising and falling of his chest. She remembered feeling for his pulse, and being rewarded with the slow-but-insistent surging of blood through his veins. He was alive. Comatose, or at least unconscious, but alive.

He could do nothing to help her anymore. It was up to her now.

She must save *him* this time.

Everyone remotely connected with the flash drive had not only died, but had been murdered by unknown villains. Her grandfather, Andrew Haley, Brian Kellogg, Senator Faulkner. They were murdered. She needed no evidence to tell her that. Whoever pulled Waldron's strings also killed anyone who came near the secrets contained on the flash drive.

Anyone who came near her.

She knew this. Actually, she felt it—and she no longer questioned her instincts. Lately, she'd doubted her intuition, her motives, her feelings, afraid those instincts would lead her into oblivion. Maybe she was crazy. Maybe she was paranoid. Maybe she was narcissistic. Those doubts had governed her life.

No more.

Drawing her knees up to her chest, she rested her arms on her knees. The thunder had faded into silence, and lightning no longer pulsated in the sky outside the abandoned house. With her back pressed to the wall, she felt a little safer than she had out on the street. Yet she realized she couldn't stay cocooned here forever.

She needed answers. She could wait for one of her pursuers to hand her those answers, or she could dig them out of the ground herself. The answers lay deep. She'd need a backhoe to excavate them.

The answers awaited her in California. David and Sean were in California, somewhere in the Mojave Desert. Her grandfather had worked for a company in California. Her parents moved to California two years before their deaths.

In her mind, the dots connected, though the picture they formed remained unclear, because she couldn't see many of the dots. Revealing them demanded a trip to California. A trip from which she might not return.

She would return. She had to. Either way, she must go. David needed her.

Okay, so she didn't even remember the guy. That fact had made her leery of him before, but her latest dream—mental excursion—convinced her that he told the truth. The feelings stirring inside her, once frightening, now felt almost comforting. Someone cared about her. Someone needed her. She could not leave him to rot in a drug-induced coma inside a windowless facility hidden out in the desert.

What if the coma wasn't drug induced? What if she had caused it? She used her powers on him, to make him go away, though she'd had no concept of what she was doing at the time. What if she'd hurt him by doing so?

No. She was not to blame. It was *them*. And she needed to know who they were.

Grandpa had worked for a company called ALI, Advanced Laboratories Inc. He kept the details of his work, and the location of ALI's facility, a secret. Knowing the details hadn't mattered to her back then. Now, she cursed herself for accepting the secrecy, the evasion, the lies. Grandpa had lied to her—about more than his job. She understood the secrecy of his work, since ALI probably made him sign a confidentiality agreement, but lying to her about own life…

She didn't know if she could forgive him for that.

He must've known David. He must've known about her relationship with him. She could no longer deny the deception. Edward McLean insisted everything was fine and convinced her they both led normal lives, when obviously neither one of them did. How long had he known he was in trouble? Months, she'd guess. He should've confided in her. They might've solved his problems together. Instead, he slipped a bag over her head and plugged her ears.

Worst of all, he let her believe nothing of import happened during the eight months she'd lost to amnesia. Getting engaged was hardly nothing.

And what about her psychic abilities? How long had she had them? Since she remembered everything outside of those eight months last year, she knew she'd had no such powers at any other time in her life. They must've emerged during those eight months. How had it happened? Who wanted to capture her now? Grandpa must've known the answers to those questions and many more, yet he kept the information from her. Even at the end, when he must've known she was in danger too, he said nothing. Instead, he gave her a flash drive that every bad guy in the western hemisphere wanted to possess.

If she discovered her grandfather had a good reason for lying, her unease might lessen. But if peeling back the skin of lies revealed a tumor beneath, then it just might kill her.

Nothing could undo the past, not for her, not for anyone. She must live with the truth.

She grabbed the prepaid mobile phone and dialed directory assistance. Two minutes later, she scribbled the number for ALI's job hotline on a scrap of paper she'd found in her purse. The company listed no other numbers and no address. She punched in the digits.

The call was picked up. A recorded voice intoned, "The ALI employment hotline is available twenty-four hours a day for your convenience. To hear the latest job openings, press one. To hear all job openings, press two. To search by category, press three. To speak with an ALI human resources specialist, press four."

Grace pressed four.

The same recorded voice said, "We're sorry, ALI human resources specialists are available during normal business hours only, seven AM to seven PM Pacific time."

She punched the zero key, hoping to get an operator. The recorded voice began reading off the initial menu options again. She kept punching zero.

Silence. Then, the voice announced, "Thank you for calling ALI. Goodbye."

Click. The damn machine had hung up on her.

She'd have to call back in the morning—after nine AM, since Pacific time was two hours earlier. She checked her watch. It was 12:48 AM. More than eight hours to go before ALI's employees arrived at work. Too much time. Waldron seemed unlikely to allow her an eight-hour hiatus before he resumed hunting for her.

Though she hadn't expected to get all the answers she needed from a jobs hotline, she had hoped for a little more luck than this. Something had to go right once in awhile.

She might have to accept that she wouldn't find the facility. Accept defeat.

Never. There must be a way.

Sean might help her. He seemed like a good kid, kind of like an abused puppy who craved affection while fearing it at the same time. She might talk him into disclosing the location of the facility. Though the plan nibbled at her conscience and she had no experience in enticing information from people anyway, she had no other options left. She had to try.

If she knew how to contact him.

Sure, no problem. She'd just call him on the phone and ask him to pop in for a visit. Even better, she could stand on the roof and shout over the Rocky Mountains to him.

She had forced David out by thinking about it, by wishing for it with every iota of willpower she retained. By concentrating. Through psychic power. The tactic might work for conjuring Sean, or at least sending him an SOS.

Just yesterday, the notion would've made her laugh. Tonight, she prayed not only that psychic powers existed, but that she knew how to tap into them. Right now.

Strange that she'd stopped wondering how Sean and David materialized out of air and disintegrated into it again. The question, once vital, lingered in the recesses of her mind, but she now rated other questions above it. Questions like who wanted the disk, who tormented her, who murdered all those people. Another question held within it the power to reveal all the answers.

What did "they" protect and why?

At this particular moment, however, she needed the answer to another, more mundane question. Where was the Mojave Desert facility?

She closed her eyes, focusing her thoughts on Sean. His face filled her mind's eye.

Come on, kid. Come out and play. I need your help.

Squeezing her eyelids tightly shut, she took in a deep breath. As she released it one milliliter at a time, she let her muscles slacken and her mind open. She didn't really know how to do the last part, but she gave it her best shot.

Come on, damn it. This has to work. Please, Sean, I need you.

A chill washed over her. She opened her eyes.

"How'd you do that?" whispered a voice from the opposite corner of the room.

Sean huddled there, kneeling, hands on the stained carpet. He kept his back to the wall, his head turned toward the doorway.

He looked at her sideways. "Normal people aren't supposed to do that."

"I'm not normal."

"Are you like me?" He lowered gaze and picked at the carpeting with one fingernail.

She shrugged one shoulder. "Doesn't matter how I did it. I need to talk to you."

"I'm not supposed to. David'll get mad."

A knot cinched tight in her gut. The first sting of tears pricked the corners of her eyes, and she bit the inside of her lip to stave off the flow. No crying. Not now. Too much was at stake. David would be okay, because she would find him.

David had hidden the truth from her too, at first. When he finally shared the truth wither her, or at least part of the truth, she shoved him away with so much force it kicked up a small tornado. She could apologize to him later. When she rescued him. Then he would need to thank her.

Actually, she didn't care if he was grateful. She just wanted him alive and conscious. She just *wanted* him. Here. With her. Annoying the hell out of her as usual.

She scuttled across the carpet toward Sean.

His eyes bulged. "Don't touch me."

She froze. A couple yards separated them.

"I won't touch you," she said. "I didn't mean to scare you."

He hugged himself, biting his lower lip. His gaze he fixed on the carpet.

She sat down cross-legged and rested her hands on her knees. Sean wouldn't help her if she scared him. The kid had sore nerves.

"Listen," she said, her tone soft, "I need your help."

"Me?" He lifted his head to look at her.

"David's in trouble, isn't he?"

Sean shrugged one shoulder, averting his eyes again. "Can't talk about that stuff."

"I can help him. If I know where he is."

"Nobody can help us."

"I can."

A lock of hair drooped over his eyes. He sketched invisible lines on the carpet.

"I can help you," she said. "But you have to tell me where you are."

"Why would you wanna help us?"

"I know what it's like to be alone."

He turned away from her, facing the wall.

She needed his cooperation, but her stomach burned at the thought of tricking him into telling her the location. Deceptions would make her no better than the people who sought her. She preferred that he volunteer the information. That was why she hadn't lied to him. She did know how it felt to be alone, powerless, plummeting from a precipice without a parachute. The people with the power—the kind of power money granted—enjoyed watching others flail and clutch at any handhold, however narrow or weak. She had been that victim once. Not anymore. Since her days on that precipice, she had learned one basic truth.

Power could shift hands.

Besides, not all power came from money or privilege. Some power originated deep inside the mind. No one could take away that power. They might suppress it temporarily with drugs, as she somehow knew they'd done with David, but the power always surfaced again.

She had the power. In more ways than one.

Sean stood. "I didn't tell."

He vanished.

Her one chance had just disintegrated. Dammit, one break wouldn't upset the balance of the universe. One lousy break.

She thumped her fist on the carpet.

A shape on the wall drew her attention. She scuttled closer to the wall, examining the baseboard.

She smiled.

There, in the dust that coated the baseboard, Sean had scrawled a message.

50 miles NE of Reston on Dry Lake Rd. Dirt road to left. Eyes and ears everywhere.

He had given her the location without saying the words. He could assure David that he hadn't told her. Clever kid. He gave what she asked for, and the rest was up to her. For the first time in more days than she could keep track of, she knew exactly where she was headed.

Reston, California.

Chapter Seventeen

Sirens wailed in the distance, drawing closer. The shrill sound woke Grace in increments—first her ears awakened to the noise, then her mind surfaced into consciousness, and finally she eased her eyelids apart to take in her surroundings.

Dingy carpeting. Dusty, mold-stained walls. A window blocked by an overzealous shrub.

The memory of last night returned to her just as gradually as wakefulness had. Her stop at the electronics store. Waldron's phone call. Running.

She rubbed her eyes. At least the migraine had left. Her brief nap before Sean came had taken care of that problem. Her mouth felt cottony, her neck ached a bit, and she felt as if she'd slept on a gravel road, but otherwise she was just peachy.

Glancing at her watch, she saw the time was 6:42. The sun was up already, its light filtering through the bush's foliage to cast faint streamers of light into the room.

The sirens wailed closer.

She snatched up the gun and scrambled to her feet. At the window, she tried to peer through the branches to see beyond the foliage, but to no avail. She trotted through the house, unlocked the front door, and rushed outside. At the broken-down gate, she stopped.

The sirens had withdrawn into the distance again. Within fifteen or twenty seconds, the sound died out completely.

A mourning dove cooed in the treetops nearby. She listened to the song as she calmed herself with three long, slow breaths. The cops were not coming for her. Waldron might be searching for her at this very moment, but she seriously doubted he'd involve the authorities, despite his former ruse of pretending to work for the FBI.

She headed off down the sidewalk, back toward the center of town. She must've taken a different route from last night—not that she recalled much about her flight from the strip mall—because she wound up passing through a small park she'd never noticed before. Probably because she rarely ventured into this part of town. Not much out here except an elementary school and the industrial park. The park consisted of one city block covered with trees and manicured grass, plus a smattering of manicured bushes and flower beds. Two concrete paths led through the park. She chose one and walked at a brisk pace.

When she came upon a park bench situated alongside a drinking fountain, she realized just how parched she was. Bending over the fountain, she pressed the button. A thin stream of water jetted out of the nozzle. She guzzled the lukewarm, metallic liquid, quenching her thirst in an unbroken series of gulps. Despite its flavor, the water soothed her throat.

She dropped onto the park bench. A breeze cooled her face, ruffling her hair. Reston, California. She must get there. The answers awaited her there. She felt it.

David awaited her there.

Sean had given her directions to the facility, whatever the place was. Now she needed transportation.

An airplane would get her there quickest. Right. Fly and get killed like Grandpa. His death hadn't given her a fear of flying—until she heard the tape of his last moments. Though the idea of flying didn't scare her, the idea of locking herself in a tiny space, high in the atmosphere, did. Grandpa died because he couldn't escape. He underestimated his enemy. She must learn from his mistakes.

Ruling out air travel left cars, buses, trains, and feet. The invisible assailant had totaled her car. A bus would take days, as would a train. She needed a car.

Renting was out of the question. Rental agencies required a credit card and using her card announced her whereabouts as surely as painting the coordinates on a billboard. If her enemies could find her at the strip mall, probably using the GPS in her regular cell phone, they could definitely track her credit card purchases. Even if she told the rental agency she just wanted the car to drive in the local area, she had a feeling Waldron would guess her real destination. And he would know what kind of car she was driving. He'd know the license plate number too.

Waldron and his cabal had killed everyone who so much as considered helping her. They whittled down her options until she held nothing but a sliver in her hand. Her fate called to her from California.

Whatever she did, they would find out.

Hell.

She started off down the concrete path again. When it met the sidewalk along the street, she turned right toward the center of town. She passed by the elementary school, where children frolicked in a sandy playground. The scenery turned from vaguely industrial to residential as she made two turns in her route, hoping she was guessing correctly about which way to go. The houses looked old, but mostly well-kept. Cars were parked along the street here and there. As she passed a beige Ford Taurus, she noticed a sign, of the plastic kind bought in a store, taped to the inside of the windshield. It announced the car was for sale.

This might be her answer. If she paid cash for a used car, buying it from an individual rather than a dealership, the transaction might remain unknown to her enemies, at least for a time.

The sign on the window gave the price as four thousand dollars.

So much for that idea. Even if she emptied her bank account, she didn't have four thousand dollars. She rather doubted the seller would accept five hundred and some change. The car looked in good shape, which meant it was worth more than five hundred dollars. She needed a car. Most of all, though, she needed help.

She couldn't force Sean to help her again. The poor kid had looked seconds away from a nervous breakdown. David was...unavailable. She had to figure this out on her own.

A memory unreeled in her mind. The encounter with David last night, when she'd gotten so angry she pushed him away with the force of a tornado. A lump hardened in her throat. He wasn't dead. She believed it because she'd seen him, lying in a bed, limp and unresponsive. Oh no, he wasn't dead, just drugged into a coma.

She swallowed hard and focused on the memory of what happened before she pushed him away. He'd said something about how he managed to appear and disappear at will.

It's a combination of remote viewing, telekinesis, and thought projection.

What did that mean? Telekinesis meant moving things through the power of the mind, just by thinking about it. She didn't know what remote viewing meant. Thought projection, however, seemed self-evident. It must mean that a person could project their own thoughts into the mind of another person, to make the other believe the notion was their own. David used a combination of the three abilities to effect his disappearing acts, and he also said she was pushing him out—of her mind, she later realized. So he must've projected the thoughts into her mind that made her believe she could see him and talk to him, when in reality she was conversing with him through some kind of psychic ability.

It still made no sense. She'd done more than imagine him standing in front of her. She'd touched him. She'd laid her hands on a real, physical man.

Christ. She would never understand this psychic mumbo-jumbo.

Still, if thought projection was possible, then maybe she could use it to her advantage. After all, she had lured Sean to her merely by willing him to come.

An idea occurred to her. Her sense of common decency balked at the prospect, but at this moment she saw no alternatives. She'd atone for her sin later.

She marched to the door of the house and punched the doorbell button. The muted tones of an electronic bell sounded inside the home. A moment later, the lock clicked and the door swung inward just enough to reveal the wrinkled face and bleary eyes of a man in his seventies.

In a voice that sounded as sleepy as the gentleman looked, he asked, "May I help you?"

"I'm sorry to bother you, sir," she said, trying for a nonchalant tone, "but I saw the for-sale sign and I'd like to buy your car."

The man rubbed his eyes, yawned, and straightened. "What?"

"I want to buy your car. I'll pay the full asking price if you'll accept cash."

He perked up at the mention of cash. A faint smile brightened his face as he stepped aside and swung the door wide, gesturing for her to enter.

"Cash'll be fine, missy," he said.

Now came the awful part.

Grace strolled into the house. The man shut the door.

He proffered a hand to her. "I'm Leroy Bevins."

She took his hand and dived straight into the lies. "I'm J—Janet Austen."

The lump reemerged in her throat. She'd almost said Jane Austen, then caught herself just in time to avoid becoming the worst liar in the entire universe. Janet Austen sounded slightly less deceitful, or maybe she was rationalizing. Either way, her mind could come up with no better pseudonym on the fly.

Leroy squeezed her hand and let go.

Grace extracted her wallet from her purse. Flipping it open, she fingered the bills stashed inside the wallet. Two fives and a ten. Not exactly four thousand dollars.

Steeling herself against what she must do, she whipped out the bills and offered them to Leroy. He started to take them.

And then he noticed the denominations. His brow furrowed. His lips puckered.

She focused all her willpower on one thought that she repeated in her mind.

This is four thousand dollars. This is four thousand dollars.

Fixing her gaze on Leroy's she pictured the thought as a laser connecting her pupils to his. The imaginary beam shot directly into his brain, delivering the thought she needed him to believe.

This is four thousand dollars.

She concentrated with such force that her jaw trembled. Her eyes burned, because she no longer blinked. A drop of sweat beaded on her forehead, dribbling down the bridge of her nose. She envisioned the laser growing brighter and narrower, intensifying.

Leroy's brow smoothed out. His puckered lips relaxed into a loose smile.

Taking the bills, he said, "I sure appreciate this, Miss Austen. Cash is a might easier to handle than a check. I hate just hate goin' to the bank. Do you know they charge me if I wanna talk to a real, live person instead of a machine?"

Grace relaxed a bit. Though she felt a tad woozy, she didn't dare let up too much on whatever she was doing to this poor man, at least not until she drove away in her new used car. She had no clue how long the effect might linger after she stopped actively forcing the man to believe her lie.

A knot cinched tight in her gut. She hated herself right now. Really, really hated herself.

Leroy stuffed the twenty bucks in his pants pocket. He walked to a nearby table, opened a drawer, and plucked a key chain out of the tangle of objects inside the drawer. Approaching her again, he handed her the key chain. A tag emblazoned with the Ford logo dangled from the silver ring, along with a single key.

Grace took the key chain.

"I need to sign the title over to you," Leroy said, heading for the door.

As he opened the door open, Grace laid a hand on his arm to stop him from stepping outside. Leroy furrowed his brow once again.

You already signed it over.

She fired the thought into his brain through the imaginary laser. A headache was blossoming behind her eyes, but she ignored it and concentrated as hard as she could.

Leroy unfurrowed his brow and chuckled. "Guess I already did that, didn't I? Forgetfulness seems to come with gettin' older."

Oh God. She absolutely despised herself.

Holding out his hand to her, Leroy said, "Well, you enjoy the car, missy. I sure enjoyed meetin' such a pretty little thing as you."

She shook his hand and rushed out the door. When she heard the door click shut behind her, she risked a glance backward. Only the scummiest scum on earth would do what she had just done to that poor man. She had no choice, she told herself. There was no other way to get a car without alerting Waldron to her intentions.

When this was over, if she survived it, she would return the car to Leroy Bevins—with a big wad of cash stuffed into the glove compartment.

Never again would she use her powers to manipulate an innocent person. Never.

Unless she hit another roadblock on the way to California.

Inside the car, she jammed the key into the ignition and jerked it. The engine started up. She buckled the seat belt, released the parking brake, shifted the car into drive, and headed off down the street in her new ride. The car she'd tricked an old man into selling to her for twenty bucks.

Oh yeah. She was the scummiest scum on earth.

The interstate was deserted. Grace drove west at eighty miles an hour, seated comfortably in the Taurus with the air conditioning blowing a constant stream of cool air at her. The headache had faded as soon as she stopped concentrating on laser-beaming her thoughts into Leroy's mind. As for her speeding, if a cop pulled her over, she'd accept the ticket. For now, she concentrated on a single goal.

Get to California.

That single need branched out into others—stop whatever was happening, free David from his captors, help Sean if she could—but everything else depended on her achieving the topmost objective. She must find the Mojave Desert facility. Then and only then could she move on to the number two goal.

Stop *them*.

She still had no clue who they were. But she must stop them, her enemies, from doing whatever the hell they were trying to do. Although she didn't know their ultimate goal, she sensed nothing good would come of it. Anything that involved bad guys, of the visible and invisible variety, experimenting on people with psychic abilities could not result in a smiley, happy ending for the world at large.

Before leaving Lassiter Falls, she'd stopped at the bank to withdraw the entire balance of her checking account—about five hundred dollars. It should give her enough to make it to her final destination. She did not want to use her credit card to pay for gas or food, because that would leave a digital trail. Her enemies might've guessed her destination, but they didn't know her exact route or the timing of her arrival. Total surprise was impossible, she figured. Partial surprise was the best element available to her.

The scenery, revealed in the glare of headlights, became lonely stretches of wooded hills, not a house in sight, not a light to signal other life existed in the universe. She was alone. Really alone. She'd gotten used to the isolation of having no family, no friends, not another soul in her life who cared what became of her. But this new isolation—alone in the world and hunted like an animal, isolated in spirit and in reality—affected her like an injection of liquid nitrogen into her bloodstream. Every cell in her body had turned to ice, it seemed. The only part of her that felt anything other than icy fear was the metaphysical heart of her being, the unseeable place inside her where emotions and instinct overruled everything else.

The part of her that felt...something for David.

She drove for hours, stopping occasionally to stretch her legs or grab a bite to eat. Caffeine from pop coupled with the urgent sense of danger nipping at her heels kept her going through the miles. By nightfall, she'd crossed the border into New Mexico and passed by Las Cruces. During the hours of cruising down the mind-numbing interstate, weariness had seeped into her at an ever-increasing pace until she knew she must stop for the night, despite the looming threat. The act of using powers she hadn't realized she possessed sapped her energy more than seemed possible. It depleted her at a level so deep within that she wondered if she'd drained away her very soul.

Half an hour outside Las Cruces, she pulled off the interstate into the parking lot of an independent motel. She spotted three other cars in the parking lot. After paying cash in advance for a single room, she relocated her car to the slot directly in front of her assigned room. Thick curtains concealed the interiors of all the rooms, but around the edges of the curtains the light from a TV flickered inside one room, three doors down from hers. All the other rooms were dark.

Inside her tiny room, she found a small TV so ancient it belonged in a museum, a dated but clean bathroom, a small bedside table equipped with a lamp and a worn-out alarm clock, and a bed fitted with sheets that looked surprisingly fresh and clean. A floral pattern decorated the white sheets, while a plain brown bedspread covered the whole thing. The lamplight washed the room in a pinkish glow.

Peeling off the bedspread, she slumped down onto the bed in a pseudo-sitting position. She was too exhausted to hold herself upright. She untied her the laces of her boots and kicked them free of her feet, then stripped off her coat, which she tossed over the foot of the bed. It landed half on the bed, half hanging over the edge. She took the gun out of her purse before dumping the bag on the floor. The weapon she set on the bedside table.

Expending her last bit of energy, she laid down on her side with her head on the pillow and hugged herself. She was alone. Like an astronaut marooned in space. Cold. Hopeless.

Tears stung her eyes. She swiped them away with back of her hand. More tears welled in the corners of her eyes. They came faster and faster, as her eyes burned and her nose began to run. Her body trembled with half-suppressed sobs.

Crying. Like a wuss. She'd turned into a puddle of weakness and self-pity. She hated crying, but no matter how hard she fought it, she couldn't stem the flow of tears.

The air temperature plummeted. A draft ruffled her hair.

Goose bumps raised all over her body. She rubbed her arms for warmth. Her heartbeat quickened. She pushed up onto one elbow and scanned the shadows.

"David?" she said.

A figure detached from the shadows in the corner.

Sean halted by the TV. "It's me."

Slumping back onto the bed, she mumbled, "What are you doing here?"

"David said you needed help but he couldn't come. So he sent me. Are you mad?"

He gazed at her, forehead wrinkled, wringing his hands and chewing the inside of his cheek.

"I'm not mad," she said. "I was surprised to see you, that's all."

He shuffled closer to the bed.

Though her arms shook from the modest effort, she pushed up into a sitting position, with her back braced against the headboard. She patted the mattress. "Sit down. It's okay."

He perched on the end of the bed, touching the mattress as little as possible while still counting as sitting on it. He averted his gaze to the floor.

She wanted to hug him, which was strange because she had never been the hugging type. Sean looked in need of comfort, though, and she felt something akin to maternal instinct urging her to give him that comfort. She didn't dare touch him. The kid would probably scream.

"David told you I needed help?" she asked. "I thought he was drugged. How could he tell you anything?"

The kid shrugged. "He told me, ya know, in our heads. I think it took a whole lot of energy to do it, but somehow he broke through the drugs enough to tell me you needed help."

Of course. In their heads. They conversed psychically. Well, she no longer had the luxury of doubting such things were possible. She knew they were.

"Okay," she said. "Why does he think I need help?"

Not that she didn't need help—because she absolutely did, more than anyone could know and in ways she didn't know how to articulate—but she had to ask the question anyway.

"Don't know," Sean told her. "He said come, so I came."

"I'm on my way," she said. "To help you and David."

"I know. He'll be mad at you for that."

Yeah, she'd just bet he would. Do this, don't do that. David loved issuing orders without explaining why she ought to do what he said. Well, she was coming to save him whether he liked it or not.

A spark of annoyance flared inside her. "Tell him it's no use trying to stop me. I've made up my mind."

Sean's mouth twitched upward at the corners. Almost a smile. "I get it. But he won't."

To hell with him, she almost said. She kept her mouth shut, though, because she was talking to a kid—a sweet, scared kid. Decorum was a bitch.

She didn't actually want David to go to hell anyway. Sometimes she wanted to scream at him, or throw small objects at him, but consigning him to hell was no longer on her to-do list.

"I'm not helping," Sean said, "am I? You need him, not me, right?"

She wanted to blurt out an emphatic yes, complete with spraying spittle. Instead, she gathered the threads of her dignity and told him, in the most ladylike fashion she could muster, "David's an adult who knows what he's getting into. You're just a boy, Sean. I can't let you risk yourself for me."

"I get it."

He looked so dejected that she wanted to say something reassuring. Nothing sprang to mind. Her brain felt sluggish, just like her body.

"If you're really okay," Sean said, "I better go."

She gave him a weak smile. It was the best she could pull off at the moment. To her amazement, her voice sounded convincing when she said, "I'm really okay. You can go."

Without a word, he vanished.

She settled down onto the bed again, on her side, facing the curtained window. She closed her eyes. David's face filled her mind. The image zoomed out to reveal him lying on a bed, unconscious, a needle plugged into the back of his hand while an IV dripped unknown drugs into his veins.

Dammit, she needed rest. She must push those thoughts out of her mind. Time gave her no leeway. Her enemies raced after her, probably not far behind with her luck, and they would not pause to let her contemplate her feelings. Besides, self-pity was a quagmire she might never extricate herself from if she willingly traipsed into it. Later, she could mete out the blame, to herself and others. Tonight, she must sleep.

She willed the thoughts away. Her mind descended into slumber, drifting into the plane where dreams lived.

Share your golden light with me, or I'll take it from you any way I can—even if it kills you.

The voice, fraught with a dark intensity, shocked her out of the dream as her mind rocketed up from the depths of slumber. With a gasp, she slammed through the barrier into wakefulness. Her eyes flew open.

Seconds ticked by as she struggled to sort out where she was. In the motel room. Somewhere in New Mexico. Reality trickled into her mind as the scene around sharpened into focus. She lay on her side on the bed, her chest heaving with each ragged breath. Her right hand was wrapped around an object. She glanced down at it.

Her hand gripped the gun. The safety had been disengaged. Her index finger was curled around the trigger. The barrel was jammed into her mouth.

She flung the weapon onto the floor.

The man in her dream, the one whose face looked like Xavier Waldron's. He had done this to her. Through some kind of psychic manipulation, he made her put the gun in her mouth. If he could force her to that then...

Christ.

She no longer felt certain her revelation about the shadow man's identity had been genuine and not another psychic manipulation. Anyone who could convince her to put a gun in her mouth might trick her into believing anything he wanted. To truly unmask him, she must find him in the real world.

And she knew exactly where to look.

She must get to California. *Now.*

Chapter Eighteen

Grace bit the inside of her lower lip as she scrutinized the road atlas. Twenty minutes ago, she'd given up on sleeping anymore and jogged over to the gas station next door to the motel. After buying the road atlas, she returned to her motel room. Now she sat on the bed with one leg folded under her and the other dangling off the edge of the mattress. The road atlas lay on the bed in front of her, open to the two-page spread showing California.

The bedspread was lumped on the floor at the foot of the bed. Both the sheets and blanket were shoved aside, just as she'd left them after her second attempt to get some sleep. The first attempt ended when she woke to find a gun in her mouth. The second ended when she gave up after nearly an hour of tossing and turning, unable to get anywhere near slumber. It was hard to relax knowing that her enemy could manipulate her thoughts and actions.

But if he could make her do whatever he wanted, why hadn't he?

He probably wanted the flash drive, like everyone else. She also wanted her to give him—what had he called it?

Her golden light.

In previous dreams, he'd called her "golden girl." She had no idea what he meant by either term. The point was, he wanted something from her. Possibly more than one something. Although he threatened to kill her more than once, he hadn't actually done it or even come close to it. The incident in her car had terrified her at the time, and in the moment it had felt like attempted murder. When she thought back to the incident, however, the truth seemed far less obvious. He could've killed her. Yet he didn't. Instead, he frightened her into believing he wanted her dead.

Maybe he would kill her, eventually, after he got what he wanted. For now, he clearly needed her alive.

Which meant she had a chance. A slim one, but hell, she'd take any chance the universe offered her.

She tapped her pen on the map, on the spot where she'd drawn a big black circle around her destination. Reston, California, was a tiny dot on the map identified with tiny text.

A cool draft rushed over her.

He's here.

Her heart beat faster as she looked up from the map. David stood at the foot of the bed, hands in his pants pockets. He wore a gray T-shirt and blue jeans. His eyes were a crystalline blue, not the fiery azure she'd seen on other occasions. The drape of the T-shirt revealed hints of the muscles underneath.

An image flashed in her mind. David's bare chest. Her fingers tracing the contours of his muscles.

Oh for pete's sake. Very bad people wanted to capture or kill her and she was fantasizing about some guy's muscles.

Not just some guy. Her ex-fiancé.

Were they ex? He'd never mentioned a breakup.

"You pulled out the needle," David said. "Thank you."

Grace dropped the pen. It rolled into the little valley where the facing pages of the atlas met. "You're welcome. How are you feeling?"

"Better. Clearer."

"Glad to hear it." She glanced down at her left hand, then back up at him. "If we were engaged, where's the ring?"

He shrugged. "I don't know. Maybe Edward hid it when he realized you had amnesia. When he made the decision to keep the truth from you for your own protection."

"Yeah," she snorted, "I've sure been protected good."

Walking around the corner of the bed, he sat down directly in front of her. Only the road atlas separated them. She thought about squirming backward to get some more space from him, until she realized, with a suddenness that made her heart skip a beat, that she didn't want more space. She liked sitting near him, gazing into those crystalline eyes. She felt safe.

It was insane, of course. She had only his word that they knew each other at all, much less with the intimacy implied by their alleged engagement. Whenever he was around, two parts of her battled for control. Half of her needed to doubt what he said, while the other half believed without reservation. The contradiction left her feeling off-kilter. That was why she tried not to think about it.

She studied David. Maybe she had contradictory feelings about him because her instincts were trying to tell her he wasn't who he claimed to be. The figure in her dreams, the real shadow man, wielded the power to control her, to make her believe what he wished.

Apparently he wielded that power. She didn't understand this psychic stuff.

David lifted his eyebrows. "Are you all right?"

"Huh?" She blinked, realizing her gaze was aimed at his mouth. She raised her focus to his eyes. "How does all this psychic stuff work?"

"What do you mean?"

"How do you do this?" She waved a hand, palm out, in his general direction. "I mean, you're not really here. You're in California. But it looks like you're here—" She patted her palm on his chest. "—and it feels like you're here."

She let her palm linger on his chest. The warmth of his body filtered through the fabric of his T-shirt. He looked down at her hand, then back up at her face.

"When I asked you before," she said, "you told me it was a combination of telekinesis, remote viewing, and thought projection."

"Yes."

She let out a sharp sigh. "Please elaborate."

"You know as much about it as I do, if not more."

She yanked her hand away and glared at him. "I have amnesia, dammit. I don't have a clue what you're talking about and I need you to explain it to me."

His lips worked as if he were trying to remember how to form words. Then he said, "It might be best if you remember on your own."

"I don't have time for that. Very bad people are hunting me and some of them apparently have psychic abilities. I can't protect myself if I don't know how the hell this works."

"Fine." He settled a hand on the bed, leaning against it for support. "This is all theoretical, you understand. No one really knows how it works."

She rolled her eyes. "Just get on with it."

"Telekinesis is the ability to move objects without touching them. It seems to involve affecting matter at the molecular level—for instance, shifting air molecules to make an object move. Thought control is, well, influencing another person's mind in order to convince them to believe or see what you want them to." He paused, frowning. "Remote viewing is harder to explain. Essentially, it's the ability to visualize any location, object, or event anywhere in the world—past, present, or future—simply by thinking about it."

"Like looking at a photo?"

"Sometimes it's like that, but it can also be much more." Without looking down, he lowered his index finger onto the road atlas like a needle dropping onto a vinyl record. His fingertip traced the blue lines of interstates. "A powerful remote viewer can actually send his mind to the desired location. He can float around, like an invisible bird, to get a broad view of the area and even to listen in on conversations. That's why we nicknamed it traveling."

He closed his eyes. Grace watched his finger moving around on the map. Despite his apparent lack of vision, his finger continued to trace the road lines on the atlas.

"A traveler can sense things," he said, "without knowing where or when it is. RV is a type of ESP, similar to clairvoyance.

"Are you doing it now?" she asked. "Remote viewing, I mean."

"Sort of. I'm sensing the lines on the map, though I wasn't trying to. When you use psychic abilities on a regular basis, you start to do things without realizing it. The powers become second nature." His mouth twisted into a crooked smile as he met her gaze. "Convinced yet?"

"Hmm..." She folded her arms over her chest. "That's a nice party trick, but how do I know you're not peeking?"

"Here." He took her hands and lifted them to his face, placing one of her palms over each of his eyes. "Now I definitely can't see."

At first, his skin felt cool against her palms. Second by second, his warmth seeped into her palms, setting off a chain reaction inside her. He was close enough that if she leaned forward just a little her lips would brush against his.

"Satisfied?" he murmured.

Oh no. She wasn't satisfied at all, not that she would ever admit that to him.

His tone became irritated. "Well?"

She suddenly remembered the map and the point of this little exercise. With her hand still covering his eyes, she glanced down at the atlas. His fingertip was tracing the twisting, arching path of roads.

His breath tickled her wrists. Against her will, her gaze wandered back to his face. To his lips.

Her cheeks flushed. She yanked her hands away from his face.

He opened his eyes, looking straight at her. "What's wrong with you?"

"N-nothing."

Time to change the subject. Fast.

Clasping her hands on her lap, she cleared her throat. "I get the remote viewing thing—I think. But how do you make yourself a body? Or is that a trick? Influencing my thoughts to make me think you're a solid object when you're not even actually here."

"It's not a trick. Not the way you mean."

"Then what is it?"

"Remember what I said about telekinesis? It's the manipulation of matter. And remote viewing is kind of like an out-of-body experience or astral projection. The third element, thought projection, is pretty much what it sounds like."

"So you are screwing with my mind."

"No."

He spoke the word with such vehemence that she felt a need to apologize, until she remembered he was the one avoiding her questions.

His voice softened as he said, "I wouldn't do that to you even if I could. I can suggest that you see and hear me, and you decide subconsciously whether to let it happen. If you let me in, then I continue to project my thoughts into your mind, which you interpret as spoken words. It's a conversation, not an intrusion."

She opened her mouth to ask another question.

He raised a hand to silence her. "I'm getting there. Once I've knocked on the door, so to speak, and you've let me in, then I can affect matter in the environment to build a physical form."

"You make it sound like you're baking a cake."

"I've given you a simplistic explanation of an extremely complex and esoteric process that involves multiple psychic faculties and requires an enormous amount of energy. Even I don't fully understand how it works, and I do this all the time."

"Really? All the time?"

He shrugged one shoulder. "In the past few days, it's been all the time."

"Before the past few days, how often had you done this creating-a-body thing?"

"We call it manifesting." His finger, still on the map, began drawing invisible, random spirals on the paper. "I've done it a number of times before, but not since last summer."

She wanted to ask the question but feared the answer. At the same time, she craved the answer. Last summer fell squarely into the blank spot in her memory. If she really had known David during those eight months, then anything that happened to him during that time could involve her. She wanted to know, yet didn't want to know. She *needed* to know.

Oh what the hell.

She asked, "Why not since last summer?"

"That's when I learned how to manifest." He straightened, his gaze fixed on hers. "You taught me how to do it. I've never used the ability with anyone else."

A shiver rippled through her. A strangely warm shiver.

"Oh," she said, her throat suddenly tight. "That's…sweet. I guess."

He watched her, not saying a word.

She slapped her hands onto her knees and stared down at the atlas. Lines of different colors snaked across the page, intersecting and diverging, some dead-ending and others stretching onward toward the edge of the map. Human lives did the same thing. Her life's path had intersected David's, but would it dead-end or continue onward?

For now, she knew one thing. Her path would take her straight into the Mojave Desert. Where it went after that remained a mystery. *If* it went on after that.

She glanced up at David. "How do you find me?"

"Via remote viewing. Even if I don't know where you are, I can sense you. It's like there's an invisible string between us and, if I let it, the string will guide me to you." The crooked smile returned. "Or sometimes you drag me here."

She felt her own lips curving upward, just a touch. "I drag you here. Right. I'm so good at making you do anything I want."

"You're more powerful than you realize."

"Oh please."

"It's true." He lifted a hand to touch her cheek. "You were the strongest of us all."

The lovely sense of warmth and security evaporated in an instant. She thrust his hand away.

He scrunched his forehead.

She scowled at him. "What do you mean us all? What aren't you telling me, David?"

"You and I were part of a scientific project funded by a multinational corporation. The objective was to prove psychic abilities exist—and to figure out how they work."

She felt ice forming at the core of her and, as much as she did not want to, she asked, "For what purpose?"

"Originally, the goal was strictly to expand scientific knowledge."

"And now?"

"I don't know. After your parents died, everything changed."

"What do my parents have to do with anything?"

He shoved a hand through his hair and stared into the corner. "They founded the project."

Silence filled the room, as if the lack of sound exerted air pressure. David watched Grace's expression for some clue about how she'd handled the avalanche of information he'd dumped on her. The revelation about her parents must've hit her especially hard. It was a lot for anyone to take.

But she wasn't just anyone. She never had been. When he called her strong, he meant more than her psychic abilities. She could handle almost anything the world threw at her.

He still worried. She'd been through too much already.

Every time she treated him like a stranger, he wanted to smash the nearest breakable object. Anger had never been an issue for him before. Although he had his moments, like anyone else, in general he maintained his calm no matter the situation. When Tesler shot him up with a home-made drug cocktail, or when the guards manhandled him like a sack of grain, he kept his cool. Each time he visited Grace and butted up against the wall of her mistrust, he lost his temper. He hated it.

She trusted him, whether she realized it or not. Deep down in the place where her memories were sequestered, she knew the reasons why she trusted him. If only those memories would break free, everything would be fine.

Probably.

It would be fine. He had to believe that her memory would return and things would go back to normal, because he couldn't accept the alternative. That she might never remember. That she might push him away—physically, psychically, emotionally—for good this time.

The thought made his gut twist and his jaw clench.

He refused to accept the possibility. Whether she embraced him or tossed him out the door, she needed to reclaim her memories. Amnesia seemed to have stripped her of the power she innately possessed, or at least it had suppressed that power. Without it, she was far too vulnerable. And the next time she got herself into trouble, he couldn't guarantee he'd be around to protect her.

Not that he'd excelled at protecting her so far, as she'd helpfully pointed out to him a few minutes ago.

He would do better. He must.

Grace drummed her fingers on her knees. "You're lying. My parents would not hold people hostage in the desert."

"I know that. The darker side of the project emerged only after Christine and Mark died. That's when someone else took over the project."

"Who?"

"I don't know. He never shows himself because he prefers to control things through his minions."

"Like Xavier Waldron."

He shrugged. "I don't know all of them."

Grace stared at him for a moment. Her cheeks were faintly pink, her eyes a little red. Half-moon shadows darkened the skin under her eyes. Her lips looked a touch pale too. She was exhausted, physically and mentally. If she didn't get some rest—

Here came the hard part. Somehow he must convince her to believe the one thing she seemed utterly incapable of accepting right now.

"No," she said, as if she'd heard his thoughts. Then she shook her head so emphatically that her hair flopped around her face. "It makes no sense. Why would my parents study psychic stuff?"

"Because," he said, "they wanted to help you understand your powers."

"That's ridiculous. I never had any power until—"

Her expression went blank. Her mouth fell open as her eyes widened.

Ah-hah. The triumph flooding through him must've shown on his face, because she clamped her mouth shut. Her expression tightened into a scowl.

"You've used your powers," he said. "Recently."

She held still and silent. Her scowl melted into a look of distress, as if she'd just committed a terrible crime by accident. The triumphant feeling flooded out of him as quickly as it had arrived.

He laid his hand over hers. "What happened?"

She bit her lip, bowing her head.

He squeezed her hand. "You used your powers, didn't you?"

"Yes," she whispered. "I tricked a nice old man into selling me his car for twenty bucks." The words now tumbled out in a rush. "I needed a car but I couldn't risk using my credit card to rent one and I didn't have enough money to buy one so I practically stole one instead. From an old man."

"Maybe he was happy to sell his car to a beautiful woman for twenty dollars."

She shook her head and sniffled. "I made him believe it was five thousand dollars."

A drop of water fell onto his hand. No, it was a tear.

He hooked his finger under her chin and lifted her head until their eyes met. She averted her gaze.

"It's okay," he said, rubbing his thumb across her chin. "You had no choice."

"You're wrong," she said. "It's not okay. I used a psychic power—thought projection, I guess—to manipulate an innocent person. I'm evil."

He almost laughed, though he felt nothing close to mirth. Evil was the last word he would ever use to describe her.

"Look at me," he said.

She didn't.

He tapped his thumb on her chin. "Please."

Slowly, she turned her eyes to look at him. Tears overflowed her now-bloodshot eyes.

Releasing her chin, he wiped the tears from her cheeks with his thumb. No more spilled from her eyes, but she still looked stricken. It made his heart ache.

"If you were evil," he told her in a soft voice, "then you wouldn't have any qualms about bending others to your will. I'm sure when this is all over, you'll find a way to make it up to the old man."

She sniffled. "I thought I'd return the car, secretly, with a wad of cash in the glove compartment."

He snatched a tissue from the box on the bedside table and handed it to her. "That proves it. You are not evil."

She took the tissue, blew her nose, and tossed the wadded-up tissue into the nearby trash can. Leaning closer, he kissed her forehead.

"Are you sure about that?" she asked.

"Positive." He kissed the tip of her nose. "You're not evil."

Her cheeks were distinctly pink now. Her eyes were dry, though red.

She gave him a slight smile. "Neither are you. Evil, I mean."

The flush of triumph cascaded through him again, stronger this time, infused with a nearly overwhelming desire to pull her into his arms and never let go. Unlike the first time, the triumphant feeling stemmed not from smug satisfaction that he'd been right, but rather from an ecstatic relief that she had just told him, in her own way, that she trusted him.

Maybe she hadn't declared her undying devotion to him, but it was a start. More than that, though, it was...

Hope.

She gazed into his blue eyes, feeling a bit mesmerized. They didn't glow, as they often did when he first came to her. She wanted to ask him about the fiery-eyes thing, but her voice refused to work. Her body felt paralyzed and tense, though in a strangely pleasant way, infused with a tingling anticipation.

David flipped the atlas shut. He picked it up and tossed it onto the bedside table.

His gaze never wavered from hers.

She felt a tightening deep inside her, a yearning for something so close yet out of reach—until this moment. Right now, what she wanted sat inches away from her. From the first time she saw him, she had wanted to trust him, to take comfort from him, to touch him.

He stretched out a hand, laying his palm on her cheek. Still, she couldn't move. He slid his hand into her hair, around the back of her head, and drew her closer as he leaned forward. His lips met hers, softly at first, then harder.

Fire swept through her body. Her eyes closed.

He deepened the kiss, sliding his hand down her neck. His other arm wrapped around her, pulling her against him. She slipped her arms around his neck and abandoned herself to the kiss.

Time seemed to stop. She heard nothing except the thundering of her own pulse.

His lips pulled away from hers. His embrace loosened just a little.

She felt a little woozy, but somehow she managed to open her eyes.

He watched her, his brow slightly furrowed.

"What's wrong?" she asked. Her voice came out as a throaty whisper, but at least it worked this time.

"Doesn't it bother you," he said, "that I'm not actually here?"

Maybe it should have. It didn't, which probably should've bothered her even more. Right now, she felt nothing except warmth, anticipation, and total security.

Reaching down, she picked up the hem of his T-shirt and raised it to expose his abdomen. Muscular, just as she'd imagined, though not in a freaky bodybuilder way. As she lifted the shirt higher, she laid one hand on his chest. Then she met his gaze and said, "Feels to me like you're here."

He exhaled an uneven sigh.

She laid both hands on his chest, tracing circles with her palms

The worry vacated his face in an instant, replaced by a sensual smile. He stripped off his shirt and pulled her tight against him. Her shirt went next, fluttering to the floor. The remainder of their clothing followed suit quickly. They kissed again, and again, as their hands explored each other. The kisses grew more passionate, the touching more intimate, until their bodies melded. Pleasure swirled through her, intensifying with each passing moment, until it sent her soaring out of herself, into a vast field of stars. The sensation of flying pushed her over the edge, and she felt him go with her.

By the time she drifted back into herself, a barrier had broken inside her mind. Memories flooded through her on the final crest of pleasure.

She remembered him.

Her body felt languid, relaxed. Her mind sank into a light slumber.

The jostling of the bed roused her. She parted her eyelids just enough to see David sitting near the foot of the bed, already half clothed. He was pulling on his T-shirt. The lamplight dimmed as it neared the foot of the bed, leaving swathes of shadow where David sat.

The bedside clock told her she'd slept for about ten minutes. Her mind felt fuzzy, her mouth cottony. Yet her body still felt deliciously languid.

Sitting up, she drew the sheet up to cover her chest.

David, now fully clothed, turned to look at her. He smiled almost shyly.

For a moment, she'd remembered him—not in the sense of recalling how they'd met or when he'd proposed to her, but in the sense of knowing him on a visceral level. Everything he'd told her about their relationship was true. The luxury of doubt had evaporated along with, apparently, her self-control. A blush fired up in her cheeks. What they'd just done...

She pushed the memory aside and said, "Why bother getting dressed? I mean, can't you just will your clothes to be on you again?"

"It doesn't work that way. Manifested or not, it's still clothing." He tugged the hem of his shirt. "You have to handle it like real clothes."

"Damn. It would've been so convenient to able to create my own clothes like—" She swept her hand up through the air, ending the gesture with a flourish. "—like *whoosh*."

His smile broadened. He chuckled softly. "Sorry to disappoint you."

Oh no, she was not disappointed. Not in any way.

He slid across the bed toward her. The lamplight spilled across his features. Her chest tightened. Dark circles under his eyes. A pallor beneath his skin. Dropping the sheet, she grasped his face in both hands. "Are you all right?"

He shrugged. "Running out of energy, that's all."

She studied his eyes, which looked dull and tired.

"I'll be fine," he said, taking her hands in his. "But I have to go. I'm sorry."

She wanted him to stay. Forever. "I understand."

He kissed her right hand, then her left. "I love you."

Her entire body stiffened. "What?"

Her voice came out sounding hard. For a second, she thought it wasn't her voice at all. But it was. She tried to summon an emotion, any emotion. Nothing came to her. She felt cold and empty, like the void of space.

Soaring into a void. Stars all around.

I love you.

She yanked her hands free. "Don't say that."

He said nothing. His eyes had taken on a glassy quality. A single drop of sweat rolled down his temple.

"I'm sorry," he mumbled, his voice weak.

His body jerked.

"David?" she said.

He sat immobile, silent, deathly pale.

Oh God. He was dying.

A chill crashed over him, like a wave of arctic water. Everything he'd felt tonight—joy, passion, contentment, and finally regret—fizzled out in a heartbeat as soul-drenching weariness pervaded every molecule of his body.

No. Not yet.

The regret niggled at him, a remote and disconnected sensation. He didn't regret what had happened with Grace. He regretted blurting out the three words most likely to make her flee in the opposite direction as fast as she could. For a moment she'd trusted him. For a moment they'd connected. It had been perfect—until he screwed it all up by telling her the one truth she couldn't yet handle. What the devil had he been thinking?

Another chill inundated him. The call to return tugged at his essence. He could ignore it for a few minutes more, ten at most.

"I have to go," he said, unable to keep the weariness from infiltrating his voice.

She nodded, her expression unreadable. "You should go then."

He didn't want to go, but his wishes could not overcome a lack of energy. When he fell back into his body, the real one, he'd sleep whether he wanted to or not.

"Where will you go?" he asked.

She looked at the window, seemingly focused on the folds in the drapes.

A deep sense of foreboding crept into him. It cinched tight around his heart.

He couldn't say why, but he glanced at the bedside table. The road atlas lay there, its cover shut. She'd been studying the map when he first arrived. He picked up the atlas, dropped it onto the bed between them, and flipped it open to the page marked by a disposable pen.

Grace let out a soft grunt of surprise.

Gazing down at the atlas page, David felt the ominous sensation grow stronger. It was a map of California. A circle of black ink marked a spot in the desert. Reston, the text said.

Something deep inside him twisted into big, hard knots that burned him like fire.

"Where are you going?" he demanded.

She looked confused for a second, but then she said, "California."

The need to leave tugged harder. He fought the pull.

"Are you insane?" he said. "That's the last place on earth you should go. Get as far away from California as you can. Go to South America, I don't care, just *stay away from Reston.*"

She got that look on her face, the one he knew meant she would do the exact opposite of whatever he told her to do.

The tug strengthened. Soon, he wouldn't be able to ignore it anymore. Christ, he couldn't leave yet. He must convince her, and make certain she would stay the hell away from the facility.

Grace slapped a hand down on the map. "I will do whatever I please, without or without your permission."

"Please listen—"

"Go to hell."

He had just enough power left to do one thing, though given his swiftly depleting energy level, he couldn't be certain how long the effect would last. No other options were viable. He must try this, and pray that desperation imbued the effect with more punch.

"I thought you were leaving," Grace said. "Or do I have to push you out again?"

"No," he assured her. If she did that again, it just might kill him, but he'd keep that information to himself. "I'll go."

He grasped her shoulders and bent close to whisper in her ear. "I'm sorry for this, but it's all I can do."

Before she could respond, he did it. The last bit of energy pulsed out of him into her. She gasped. Her stunned expression lasted only a second, and then she passed out.

He caught her as she slumped backward and settled her limp body onto the mattress, placing her head on the pillow. Rising from the bed, he pulled the sheets up to cover her. Stray hairs had fallen across her face. He brushed them away. She looked peaceful, innocent, safe. Maybe the first two applied. The last one, however, was nothing but an illusion. When she woke up, she'd be angry with him. She might never speak to him again. If his actions kept her alive, he would gladly accept the blame.

The energy was gone. He felt himself melting as the molecules that gave him form lost their cohesion, scattering into the air.

No choice now. He must go.

His vision went black. The tether pulled him backward, through a field of star-like lights, down a tunnel of blackness, and back into his body.

In the instant before he plummeted into sleep, he had time for a single thought.

She's going to die.

Chapter Nineteen

The interstate stretched out ahead of her through miles of desolation. Tumbleweeds danced across the road like ghosts of the towns and people who'd once populated the countryside during the frontier days. Few humans lived out here these days. Aside from a coyote that dashed across the road in front of her, she saw no signs of life.

Grace had woken up in the motel room, alone and wearing nothing but a sheet. Six hours had elapsed while she slumbered in a state of rest she felt certain David had forced on her. How, she didn't have a clue. Why, she could guess. To keep her away from the facility.

As if she had a choice anymore. She must go there.

He'd made her so angry, ordering her to run off to South America or wherever. Running would do her no good anyway, since her invisible stalker could apparently find her anywhere. Why wasn't the creep here now to torment her when she was at her weakest?

David had run out of energy. It forced him to stop using his psychic abilities, at least temporarily. He mentioned that the things he did required an enormous amount of energy. After she projected her thoughts into the mind of Leroy Bevins, she'd experienced a crash too. Maybe her stalker dealt with the same downside. If so, their common weakness might give her an opening.

She needed every advantage available to her, especially after she'd lost six hours on a forced nap. Whatever David had done to her, it knocked her out good. When she first woke up, she was so angry with him she wanted to manifest right next to his hospital bed just so she could slug him. After a couple hours on the road, though, she'd lost the anger. Fear crept back in, inspiring morbid thoughts about what David's captors might be doing to him. If they found out his IV was disconnected, if they knew he'd visited her, they might get very, very upset.

Tears burned in her eyes. This time, they were tears of rage instead of despair. She needed anger to fuel her right now, and anger toward her enemies felt a whole lot better than anger at David. Not that she'd forgiven him. She simply had bigger problems.

Their last conversation had been an argument. She told him to go to hell. A void. Stars. David.

I love you.

His words kept replaying in her mind at the most inopportune moments. She'd almost run off the road once thanks to the automatic stereo replay. Recalling the words brought back the feelings, both physical and emotional, she'd experienced with him last night. She'd remembered him, or at least she'd remembered the feelings he inspired in her. The intense, wonderful feelings. The visceral memories of what they'd shared once—and again last night. She trusted him, in a way she'd never trusted anyone. So much still eluded her, though.

Eight months of her life still eluded her.

Maybe that explained why she'd lost it when he told her how he felt. Feeling the truth of it, knowing it on an instinctual level, that was far different from actually remembering. She needed more than gut feelings. She needed real memories too. Recalling the feelings had instilled in her a sense of certainty—at least, it had last night. The light of day had burned off the certainty, leaving her with a disquieting sensation of floating on the ocean without a compass. Nothing made sense. One solitary goal—more of a desperate need, actually—kept her going.

Answers. She must find them. In California.

She'd driven for three hours without stopping, her eyes locked on the road, both hands clamped on the wheel. By then she was beyond exhausted. Against her instincts, which urged her to get to California fast, she started making hourly pit stops. At each stop, she gassed up the car, got a snack and a beverage, and forced herself to lie on the backseat for ten minutes, eyes closed, not expecting or wanting to sleep but knowing she must rest. If she could teleport herself to California, like in *Star Trek*, that would solve one problem. Unfortunately, as far as she knew teleporting was not possible. Manifesting a pseudo-body would work too, except for the whole enormous-energy requirement. So no manifesting. She settled for speeding across Arizona in a car she'd virtually stolen from a nice old man. Fortunately, her current bout of fear and anger overwhelmed her guilt over that incident.

You're not evil.

David's reassurance had, strangely, made her feel much better. It didn't make up for what he'd done, with his little psychic sleeping pill. Yeah, she knew he probably thought he was protecting her, but she still wanted to throttle him for it. Admittedly, compared to eight lost months, six hours wasted on sleeping hardly qualified as a tragedy—except for the minor issue of the bad guys on her tail and the creepy shadow figure in her dream who wanted her "golden light." Although she had no clue what that meant, she felt reasonably secure in assuming it was not good for her future well-being.

Weariness surged through her. She turned on the radio and hit the seek button. Finding only mariachi music, she shut off the radio. Her own thoughts would have to keep her awake. Problem was, her thoughts kept returning to the menacing figure in her dream. She focused on the road, but it stretched out ahead of her in a straight, hypnotic line. Her eyelids grew heavy. She turned on the air conditioner, full blast. The noise and cold air shocked her out of drowsiness, though she doubted the effect would last long. If a six-hour nap that ended ten hours ago could not sustain her through the trip, then a blast of cold air wouldn't last long either.

Think about something else. Anything else.

Okay, she could do that.

Since listening to the tape of her grandfather's last minutes, she'd shoved it out of her mind. The information the tape imparted induced fits of anger mixed with panic every time she thought about it. Someone murdered him, slowly, painfully. No mercy. No guilt. Edward McLean got in the way, and so he had to die—just like Andrew Haley, Brian Kellogg, and...

Her parents.

When Grandpa's plane had crashed two months ago, the authorities deemed it an accident. Something went wrong, the cabin depressurized, and the occupants died. No foul play, they said. She had demanded to know how the crash happened and exactly what sort of accident could cause the plane to depressurize. They gave her a vague explanation that she knew was a cover story, though the reason for the cover-up remained a mystery. With no recourse, she'd accepted the findings. She almost managed to convince herself Edward McLean's death had been an accident.

She knew he'd worked for a company called Advanced Laboratories Inc., or ALI, and that her parents had relocated to California two years ago to work for the same company. Why then had the flash drive included a scan of a magazine article about a different company, Digital Prognostics? That company created computer software. ALI was a privately funded scientific endeavor that revolved around the study of the human brain. On the surface, the two companies shared nothing in common.

Her grandfather would not have included the article for no reason.

She needed to take a closer look at the information on the flash drive. The last time she'd accessed it—the only time she'd accessed it—her enemies used it to track her down at the motel. It had seemed, though, as if they could only track her once she logged into their website. If she stayed off the Internet, they might not be able to zero in on her.

Right now, she felt like she was driving straight into danger while blindfolded. The flash drive might give her the information she needed to gain an advantage. She must risk it.

Seven months ago, her parents had died in a car accident. Two months ago, her grandfather died in an apparent plane crash, though she now knew it had been no accident. Could her parents have been murdered too? Already, she felt as if everything she'd known, or thought she'd known, was an illusion.

David claimed her parents not only ran, but founded the project in which he had participated. She sensed his involvement had been voluntary in the beginning, and later turned into captivity. Why on earth would someone hold people hostage?

Control. The people she knew were being held prisoner, David and Sean, both had psychic abilities. The unknown person or persons now in charge of the research project must view those abilities as a commodity worth killing for, but why? What did they hope to gain from imprisoning and drugging their subjects?

Give me your golden light.

Her stalker spoke those words in her dream. It had been far more than merely a dream, she knew. It had been some kind of psychic experience. The stalker invaded her mind, though he seemed oddly limited in what he could do to her. Lack of energy perhaps. Or lack of power. It would make sense that each individual with psychic powers had different aptitudes, or at least different skill levels. If David were here, she could ask him.

She was alone.

What if he never came back? Her resolve to find the Mojave Desert facility had ticked him off so much that he knocked her unconscious. No, his reaction had stemmed from another emotion, not anger. He'd been scared. Of what?

That she might find the facility. That she might encounter the people who held him prisoner. The people who wanted her. The murderers who took away her family. He was afraid she would get hurt.

Or killed.

David was with them now. He might die first.

The thought of her own death sent a spike of fear through her chest. But the thought of David's death sent her spiraling down into the freezing cold depths of terror. She could not let him die.

She would save his life whether he liked it or not.

His eyelids wouldn't open. They felt like lead aprons over his eyes. David tried moving his arms, his legs, his toes, anything. Each responded to his instructions, though with a sluggishness that dismayed him. His last visit with Grace had drained him so thoroughly he wondered if he'd ever regain his full strength.

Fortunately, he no longer needed to worry about the drugs inhibiting him. When he'd woken to find that someone unhooked the IV from his hand, he knew it must've been Grace. Even while unconscious, he'd been able to sense her presence in the room. She had left by the time he roused.

He'd realized immediately that he must conceal the fact that the IV was no longer pumping drugs into his bloodstream. The piece of tape that once held the needle in place was, by a miracle or sheer luck, still tacky enough to adhere to his skin. He'd broken off the needle's tip and taped the broken end to his skin so that it appeared as if the IV were still in his vein—provided no one looked too closely at it. The liquid medicine from the IV line dribbled over his skin and onto the blanket. By repositioning his arm and the blanket, he'd managed to direct the barely perceptible flow down the side of the mattress instead. He prayed all of his efforts would pay off, at least for a time. When he glanced down at his hand, he saw the needle remained in place, even all these hours later.

The room had no clock. His wardens didn't want him to know the time or the date. They liked keeping him drugged and confused, until they decided to perform another experiment with him as their guinea pig. Then and only then did they want him alert. The outside world had become a sort of dream to him.

Grace was out there. Alone. He sensed her drawing closer. Despite his warning that she must stay away, she was coming. Even before the amnesia, when she'd known him, she rarely listened to his warnings. When she set her mind to a task, her stubborn determination kicked in and only with great patience and his own stubborn determination could he dissuade her. These days, the problem was exacerbated because she still considered him a stranger. She bristled at everything he said, shutting him out before he could explain.

Back in the motel room, there had been a moment when he felt she trusted him. Several moments, in fact. It all ended the second he uttered those three words—followed by a command to stay away from the facility. It was his own fault and he knew it. Everything had been so easy before. Now he couldn't survive ten minutes alone with Grace without the conversation devolving into an argument. She mistrusted him. She mistrusted everyone—with good reason. Amnesia notwithstanding, the events of the past year and a half had changed her, he knew. Once he'd felt certain nothing could change her so much that he couldn't get through to her. He was wrong. She hid behind veils of anger, suspicion, and pain that he'd never seen before.

He wouldn't give up. He couldn't.

No place was completely safe, but the facility was the last place on the planet that she should attempt to infiltrate. The bastards in control here knew techniques Grace couldn't imagine, much less comprehend. Even if she regained her memory, she'd left before the project and the facility as a whole descended into the depths of hell. Once the bastards found her, they wouldn't ask her if she wanted to go home. They'd shackle her body and her mind, toss her into a dark room, and proceed to squeeze out of her every drop of psychic energy they could.

It would kill her.

He sensed her getting closer, nearing the point of no return. He must try again to convince her, if he could summon the energy for traveling. Remote viewing, though less energy intensive than manifesting, still drained him, albeit at a slower rate. Although the drugs no longer bound his powers and clouded his thoughts, he felt sluggish in every respect.

Pain sliced through his chest. He bolted upright in the bed.

Grace? No, she was too far away. The psychic call had come from close by.

A voice shrieked through his mind. "Please stop!"

Sean.

David sucked in a breath. Sean's agony and terror ripped through him with near-physical force. Wincing, he swung his legs over the edge of the bed. Shadows writhed in the corners.

His chest tightened. He gripped the edge of the bed.

Sean's voice echoed in his mind, the words half choked by sobs. "Please don't. I didn't do—"

A scream echoed down the corridor outside.

Jesus, no. Not Sean.

David leaped off the bed. Wires snapped free of the electrodes and sensors attached to him. He ran to the door and grasped the knob. It wouldn't turn. Locked.

Another scream reverberated down the corridor outside the door.

He yanked the knob but the lock held. He kicked the door and pounded his fists on it. He'd never get to Sean this way. Leaning against the wall, he let his eyelids flutter shut. However weak he might be, he had no choice.

Flying out of his body. Through the field of stars. Down a black tunnel. Into a pool of light.

An exam table stood in the center of the room. There, strapped to the table with leather restraints, lay Sean Vandenbrook. Tear tracks stained the boy's cheeks. Blood trickled from his nostrils. The flesh beneath his eyes had turned unnaturally dark, while the rest of his skin had taken on a frightening pallor. Sean's entire body trembled.

David watched, silent and unseen. He tried to think of what to do. There would be guards posted outside the doors to this room. They would rush inside if David tried anything, and Sean might be killed in the struggle. If David did nothing, Sean would die anyway. Tesler would make sure of that.

Clenching his hands into fists, David glared at the so-called scientist.

Tesler hunched over Sean, a syringe in his hand. "We know you visited her. Tell us what you told her or I'll have to pull it out of you."

Sean swallowed hard. His voice quavered. "I didn't s-see anybody. Just the site. That's all, I swear, the site. I did what you wanted."

"You're lying." Tesler pressed the tip of the needle to Sean's arm. "Liars must be punished."

"Please."

Tears flowed anew from Sean's eyes. He bit his lip, drawing blood.

Tesler plunged the needle into Sean's arm.

David lunged across the room toward Tesler. He seized the needle, ripping it from Sean's arm. Shouting for the guards, Tesler swung his arms up in self-defense, waving them around as if he were blind. Tesler couldn't see him, David realized.

He spun around and stabbed the needle into the Tesler's neck. He shoved the plunger downward.

Tesler's mouth gaped, the cry caught in his throat. His eyes went glassy. He crumpled to the floor.

The door lock chunked as one of the guards unlocked it.

David concentrated on the lock, visualizing it snapping into position. The lock chunked. Metal scraped as the guard struggled to turn the key. The lock held. David gritted his teeth. He didn't how long he could hold back the guards, which meant he had no time to waste.

Unfortunately, he had no clue what to do with Sean.

"Who's there?" Sean asked in a tremulous voice.

David leaned over the table so that the boy could see him. If Sean could see him. Tesler obviously could not.

"It's you," Sean said, his attention focusing on David's face.

Shawn could see him after all. He presumed that, in his weakened state, he lacked the power to project his thoughts into the mind of anyone except another individual gifted with psychic faculties.

"Did you see her?" David asked Sean.

"Yeah."

David unbuckled the restraints. "Did she see you?"

"Wasn't my fault."

"Dammit, I told you not to show yourself."

"Don't know how it happened. I didn't do it, I swear."

David's hold on the door shattered. He stumbled backward.

Sean slid off the table onto his feet.

The door exploded inward. Four guards rushed into the room. They halted a dozen feet inside the doorway. Jerking their guns back and forth, they surveyed the room as if searching for a ghost. Meanwhile, a technician hurried into the room and made a beeline for Tesler. The young man knelt beside his supervisor and felt for a pulse in Tesler's neck. Discovering one, the technician ordered two guards to help him carry Tesler out of the room.

While the others attended to Tesler, the remaining two guards grabbed Sean's arms. David recognized the men as his old friends, Norris and Battaglia. Norris pulled out a pair of handcuffs and moved to clamp them around Sean's wrists.

The technician and the two other guards carried Tesler out of the room.

David threw himself at Norris. He didn't need to hurl his astral body at the guard, since without manifesting, he didn't really have a body in the physical sense. His actions served as more of a focusing device. It still felt good as he knocked Norris to the floor. The man's hand popped open, sending the handcuffs skittering across the concrete.

Battaglia grabbed for Sean's arm.

David hurled himself at the muscular guard. Battaglia flew backward, smacking into the concrete wall. Dazed, he slumped sideways.

Norris started to get up.

David slammed his foot down on the man's chest, pinning him to the floor. Glancing back at Sean, David said, "I can't hold them for long and I can't help you escape. I'm sorry."

Sean nodded. "It's okay. I know a place to hide."

"You do?"

The boy managed a faint smile. "I kinda explored this place while they thought I was asleep. A lotta times."

An odd feeling of pride swelled inside David's chest. Sean wasn't as meek as their captors thought.

"Run," David said.

Sean ran.

David wanted to follow Sean, to make sure the boy reached his hiding place. He couldn't risk draining any more of his energy. So instead he issued a silent prayer and returned to his room.

His eyelids opened. He was standing in front of the door, just like before, with his hand resting on the knob.

Outside, footsteps resounded in the corridor.

He trotted to the bed and hopped onto it. After taping the broken IV needle to the back of his hand again, he reattached the wires to the electrodes on his head and the sensor clamped around his finger. The wires fed data to the machines that monitored his brain activity and heart rate. Plugged in again, he settled onto the mattress and pulled the sheets over his legs and hips. His heart was racing. He rested his head on the pillow and took several deep breaths to calm his heart rate. The staff seemed to have slacked off lately in their monitoring of their subjects, and he hoped that held true today.

Footsteps approached the door to his room and stopped.

Maybe his luck had run out.

He couldn't think like that. Unlike most people, he had the power to change his luck.

Willing his muscles to relax, he focused on the signals traveling down the wires into the monitoring equipment.

A key thunked in the lock. The hinge creaked as the door swung inward. Through his closed eyelids, he saw the room brighten thanks to the light spilling in from the corridor.

Someone tiptoed closer to the bed.

The man's breath wafted over David. It smelled of spearmint.

The visitor clucked his tongue. "Still napping, eh? I told Westcott you couldn't have been responsible for freeing the boy, and I was right. It must've been Grace."

David resisted the urge to reach out and grab the man by the throat. He recognized the voice. It belonged to Tesler.

The bastard laid a hand on David's arm. "And we'll have your girlfriend in custody by midday tomorrow."

His girlfriend. If Grace heard Tesler call her that, she'd shove a prickly pear cactus down his throat.

"I'm sure you're wondering," Tesler said, "how we know where she is. It wasn't hard to guess. She's coming for you, naturally."

It took every ounce of self-control David had not to lash out at Tesler. For the time being, however, he must convince everyone in this facility that he was still drugged. He had to just lie there and listen to Tesler's crowing—while simultaneously controlling the machines that monitored his vital signs.

Piece of cake.

"I doubt you can hear me," Tesler said, "judging by your EEG readings. But if you can hear me, listen closely. You can't save her, so don't even try." The bed creaked as Tesler leaned closer. "Even if you manage to fight off the drugs we've already given you, we have much stronger ones available to us. I have to warn you they have some nasty side effects. Cause any trouble and we can turn your brain to mush."

David struggled to keep his breathing regular. If he could've decked Tesler, he would've felt much more relaxed. As it was, he had trouble keeping his jaw from tensing. It took all his concentration and self-control to keep the monitors from alerting Tesler to his state of wakefulness.

Tesler leaned even closer. His breath washed over David's face. The man clucked his tongue.

"Your life would be so much easier," he said, "if you had done as we asked from the beginning. Deal with a few strangers. Why should that bother you? Too bad, you could've been the best on our team."

Tesler left. The door clicked shut. The lock thunked into place.

He'd hoped for more time. If they knew where Grace was headed, then he had hours at most, maybe just minutes, to reach her and warn her. If she would listen. If he could break through that wall of stubbornness. If he could make her trust him again. Tesler and his lackeys didn't know David had overcome the drugs, which gave him an advantage, however tenuous. Soon, they might realize he'd woken up. He shouldn't risk traveling right now.

Grace was alone. He had so little time.

To hell with it. He'd go to her. He'd convince her. And all the while, he would somehow maintain control of the monitoring devices attached to his body. No problem.

Grace might never understand how far he would travel to protect her, what obstacles he would surmount to find her, how many enemies he would battle to reach her when she needed help. Not that she would admit to needing help. But he knew she needed it today.

He must make her understand the danger.

Once her enemies located her, they'd bring her to the facility—and the unseen puppet master, the one who controlled Tesler and his goons, would take control of her. Once David had thought they intended to kill her. The truth he'd come to realize proved far worse. They wanted to keep her.

She couldn't grasp the implications of that. He knew all too well what it meant, and he would never let them get their hands on her. He must protect her, no matter the cost.

He would die for her.

Grace hurtled out of a dream, panting, clawing at the air. She was awake. Where? She rolled to the left, and nearly tumbled off the backseat onto the floor of the Taurus. Flinging her hands out, she braced herself against the back of the driver's seat, halting her fall. She rolled onto her back. The angle of the seat held her in place.

They're dead. Mom and Dad are dead.

Her throat constricted. Tears streamed down her cheeks. She took several deep breaths, fighting back the sobs that threatened to overtake her. She would not break down. Not now. Not with so much at stake. She didn't have the luxury.

The nightmare, a vision of the car accident that killed her parents, had felt like a memory. Yet she could not possibly remember the accident, because she had been in Texas at the time.

No accident.

A disembodied voice had murmured those words to her in the dream. What had the voice meant? Nothing, of course, because it had been a dream. A gut-wrenching nightmare, actually.

The voice that uttered the two words had sounded different from the voice of her invisible stalker. She didn't recognize the voice in her nightmare.

Sitting up, she examined her surroundings. The car was parked in front of an abandoned gas station along a desolate stretch of highway. Desert extended out around her on all sides.

Grace got out of the car, stretched, and strolled toward the edge of the road. A snake slithered across the two-lane highway—heading away from her, thank goodness. She watched the creature ooze off the pavement and onto the desert floor, where it swiftly vanished from sight.

The wind spit dust at her. She lifted a hand to shield her eyes. The sun was dipping low in the sky, a portent of the looming night. She would've preferred to make her foray into Hell in daylight, but she loathed waiting out another night. She wanted this over with.

The flash drive Grandpa had left her contained sixty gigabytes of data. A lot of information, though not an extraordinary amount these days. Edward McLean must've chosen the data carefully, copying only what he deemed most important. But what did it all mean? Why did strangers want the data so badly that they'd kill her for the flash drive? Why had Brian Kellogg said the data would change humanity forever? If David were here, she could ask him.

Butterflies awakened in her stomach. She wanted to see David and she wanted to avoid seeing him. Everything had changed between them last night. She didn't know exactly how or what it meant. Though she trusted him, she didn't know if she should. He'd knocked her out cold, simply because she refused to do what he wanted. Good intentions notwithstanding, his actions had cost her precious time.

She gazed across the desert. In the distance, a pair of vultures circled over a Joshua tree. An animal must've died there. Now its carcass would feed the coyotes and their leftovers would nourish the vultures. She felt a kindred bond with the deceased animal. Carnivores of another ilk were stalking her too. When she fell—*if* she fell—they'd pounce.

Back in the car, she started off down the road again. An hour later, she found a real gas station and pulled in to fill up the tank. The station was small, with just two pumps, but everything looked clean and well maintained. No option to pay at the pump, though. The pump was locked too. She waved at the attendant, who stood inside the tiny store holding a phone to his ear. The middle-aged man waved in response and then dropped his hand as if doing something below the counter. Grace tried the pump again, and gas flowed into the car's tank.

While she waited for the tank to fill, she surveyed the area. No other customers were in sight, but a van sat parked alongside the building. A little further down the road, a smattering of buildings clung to the two-lane artery. The tiny berg probably survived on the dribble of traffic that flowed down the highway—and the money from people buying gas, food, and lodging. No sign had announced the town's name. She did remember driving past a dilapidated billboard that advertised a motel located somewhere nearby. The establishment boasted free HBO and in-room microwaves.

Oh lord, a bed sounded wonderful. Sleep sounded heavenly.

No. She straightened, realizing she'd slumped against the car while entranced by her daydream about a passable mattress and a nice, long nap. No sleep. She must keep going. Her enemies would not declare a time-out so she could catch up on her sleep.

The pump stopped with a click. Grace replaced the handle and wandered into the store to pay her tab. Not feeling hungry, she grabbed a bottle of water and headed for the cash register.

Her cell phone warbled.

She jumped. From inside her purse, the phone warbled again.

The middle-aged attendant squinted at her. "You okay, lady?"

Swallowing the hard lump in her throat, she nodded.

The phone rang a third time. No one knew the number. The prepaid phone had no tie to her. Yet someone was calling.

Digging the phone out of her purse, she flipped it open and gingerly held it to her ear. She had the ridiculous thought that the phone might explode or send an electric shock into her brain. After everything she'd seen lately, nothing seemed impossible anymore.

"Hello?" she said into the phone.

"I've missed you."

The voice. The man who invaded her thoughts, who spoke to her in her dreams. The man who, she felt certain, had done his damndest to terrify her by ramming her car backward into a full-size pickup truck at top speed. It had worked too.

"What do you want?" she asked.

"I know where you are."

"How exciting for you." Through the window, she scanned the area around the gas pumps, the road in front of the station, and the empty desert beyond. "I'm not cringing."

"You will."

"No way."

In a surfer-dude voice, he said, "Way."

"What's your name?"

"God."

She rolled her eyes. "I'll assume you're dyslexic and you mean Dog."

"You can call me JT."

She mulled that for a half second, then said, "What do you want?"

His voice changed, deepening into an almost-supernatural timbre that made the hairs at the nape of her neck stand up. "Your golden light, of course. Give it to me now and I just might kill you quickly. Fight me and you'll suffer. A lot."

"I'm not afraid of you," she lied, injecting her voice with what she hoped sounded like confidence.

"David will suffer more. You'll watch him die in the slowest and most painful way I can imagine—and trust me, I've got a vivid imagination."

A wave of nausea crested inside her. She gulped against it. This man meant what he said. She knew it. She *felt* it. What he'd done to her so far had been nothing but a teaser.

Oh God. David.

She clenched her teeth and hissed, "If you know where I am, then come and get me, you coward. Stop hiding behind remote viewing and telekinesis."

He chuckled, and his voice changed back to surfer dude. "So you remember the lingo. Cool. Won't help you, though."

She fought the urge to spew a host of obscenities at him. He'd probably like it.

"Soon you'll be mine," he told her in a matter-of-fact tone. "And then we'll really play. Can't wait to see ya, babe."

Her lip curled. Babe? Was he kidding? This guy either had a split personality or he thought this was foreplay.

"I will stop you," she said.

"Come on, baby—"

She hung up and started to slide the phone into her purse.

He knew the number now. He might be able to track her through the phone. She couldn't risk it. She tossed the phone into a nearby wastebasket. If he wanted to torment her, he'd have to find another method of communication. She wouldn't stand here and absorb his crap through the airwaves. She had no time for it. Of course, he knew other ways to torment her, ways that required no phones or computers.

The attendant whistled to get her attention. "You paying cash or credit?"

She tried for a smile. It faltered, so she gave up and sighed, "Cash."

Wiping sweat from his face, the attendant accepted the bills she offered him. A patch sewn onto his shirt identified him as Earl. His cash register looked surprisingly modern. He punched buttons, eliciting beeps from the machine, and the cash drawer popped open.

"By the way," Grace said, "where am I?"

Without looking up, Earl replied, "Middle of nowhere."

"But which town is it?"

Earl pushed the cash drawer shut and met her gaze. "Welcome to Reston, California."

Chapter Twenty

Grace tried not to look stunned. She was within fifty miles of the facility, or at least the road that led into the facility. Her journey was almost over. The battle, she knew, was just about to begin.

How had JT found her? The prepaid phone should've been untraceable.

Waldron had tracked her to the shopping center, using the signal from her regular cell phone. He could've easily canvassed the businesses in the shopping center to inquire if anyone had seen a woman matching her description. If Waldron had put on his FBI airs, the guy in the electronics store probably would've answered any questions, just to avoid running afoul of the government. Waldron definitely knew how to intimidate people.

Even if JT didn't know exactly where she was, he had her number, literally. She didn't know if the prepaid phone had the same tracking capability as a regular cell phone, but she couldn't take the chance.

She tossed the phone into the wastebasket.

Handing over her change, Earl raised an eyebrow.

This time she managed a genuine, if strained, smile. "Do you have a computer I could borrow?"

His eyebrow lifted a little higher. His eyes darted sideways to glance at the wastebasket. He was wondering, no doubt, why she didn't use her cell phone to get on the Internet. Practically everybody did that these days. Her prepaid phone, however, lacked the bells and whistles.

Rather than try to explain that to Earl, she said, "My phone's dead and I really need to check my e-mail."

He just stared at her.

She bit the inside of her lip. Thought projection might work again. Oh hell, she might as well call it what it was—brainwashing. She was loath to employ the technique again, and not only because it made her feel like scum. It also left her exhausted. She needed every iota of energy.

Time to try the old-fashioned way.

"I'll pay you," she said. "To rent your computer for half an hour. How does a hundred bucks sound?"

"Um..." He eyed her with a narrowed gaze. "You look okay, I guess. But don't plug anything into the computer, like CDs or external hard drives. Stuff that might infect it with viruses or worms or what have you."

"Whatever you say."

"And don't download anything either."

She nodded. "Deal."

He waited until she handed over two fifty-dollar bills, then he trotted into a back room.

She hadn't lied...exactly. He said don't plug in CDs or external hard drives. The flash drive wasn't technically an external hard drive. At least, that's what she told herself. Besides, a white lie was far better than hijacking the guy's mind.

Earl returned a couple minutes later, carrying a laptop computer under one arm. As he held out the computer to her, he waved his free hand toward a table at the opposite side of the store, next to the self-service beverage dispenser.

"You can take it over there," Earl said.

Grace thanked him and took the laptop. She marched down the candy aisle, aiming for the table. Once there, she set the computer on the tabletop and settled into one of two plastic-and-metal chairs. When she flipped the computer's lid up, she discovered the laptop was already booted up and waiting for her commands.

Slipping a hand into her jeans pocket, she felt the flash drive.

Earl had left the counter. He was sweeping the floor in front of it, casting an occasional glance in her direction.

Damn. She needed privacy.

She refused to manipulate him psychically. Her conscience couldn't take it. But maybe she could manipulate the situation in another way.

Glancing around the store, she spotted a door marked restroom. It was located in the corner farthest from her. Hmm.

She closed her eyes and visualized a toilet. Water swirling inside it. Rising, rising. Spilling over the rim, pooling on the floor. She needed more. Something to attract Earl's attention to the restroom. She opened her eyes and stared at the restroom door, imagining a fist poised to rap on the wood. And then...

Bam.

Earl jumped. He twisted around to look at the restroom door. His expression turned befuddled. Dropping the broom, he trotted around the aisles to the doorway at the back of the store, which now hung ajar. His attention dropped to the floor.

"Crap," he blurted as he peeked into the restroom. "What in tarnation?"

Grace whipped the flash drive out of her pocket. She plugged it into a USB port on the side of the laptop just as Earl tiptoed into the restroom grumbling curses. If she had any luck at all, the toilet would keep him busy for a good while.

Turning back to the computer, she opened the list of files on the flash drive. Now that she knew something about the project, the files might make a little more sense to her. That was her hope anyway. She opened the "test sites" file that she'd looked at before. The spreadsheet contained the names of cities paired with abbreviations—RV, AP, TK, PC, GP. The first three abbreviations matched terms David had told her. Remote viewing was RV, astral projection would be AP, and telekinesis was TK. The letters PC and GP still meant nothing to her. Interestingly, GP was not paired with the name of a particular city, but rather with the designation "Universal." Unless it referred to the Universal Studios theme park, she had no idea what the designation meant.

She closed the test sites spreadsheet and opened a different one. This was the file that listed "travelers" and contained links to a password-protected website. She would not click the links this time, but she wanted to have another look at the list of so-called travelers. David and Sean were both on the list, which included about two dozen names. The first time she'd looked at the file, she had skimmed it and pretty much stopped when she got to David's name. None of the other names had meant anything to her. Now she scanned the list more carefully. At the bottom of the spreadsheet, she noticed two small tabs that had escaped her attention the first time around. One tab was labeled "Current," while the second was labeled "Former." The spreadsheet she was looking at now must include only travelers currently participating in the project, if participating was even the right word. They seemed more like prisoners. The second sheet must contain the names of travelers who had left the project, whether willingly or forcibly.

Her mouth went dry. She had a feeling forcibly meant one thing—dead.

Unscrewing the cap on her bottled water, she sipped the cool liquid and clicked the tab labeled "Former." Another list of names appeared on-screen.

Her heart thudded. The first name on the list was "Janet Austen."

When she told Leroy Bevins her name was Janet Austen, she'd thought the name popped into her head at random. Jane Austen, the name that had first come to mind, was a famous writer. Grace had read her books back in high school, so she assumed the name surfaced from the depths of her mind in the random way memories often did. The other day when she looked at this spreadsheet, she hadn't noticed the tabs at the bottom and, therefore, hadn't seen the second list of names. It seemed far too much of a coincidence that the name Janet Austen both appeared on the list of travelers and randomly occurred to her when she needed an alias. It must mean something.

She must've seen the list before. Months ago. During the period obscured by her amnesia.

Lifting a hand to touch the screen, she ran her finger tip under the entry in the spreadsheet.

Traveler: Janet Austen. Designation: Unknown, suspected GP (Level unknown). Accuracy: 99.99859.

She desperately wanted to click the website link. If she did, however, JT might track her as he or his minions had done before.

Hell, they knew she was coming anyway. And if she just took a quick look at the web page, maybe they wouldn't have time to pinpoint her location.

She clicked the link. The website loaded and, as before, software installed on the flash drive logged her into the password-protected page. It was a status report for the traveler called Janet Austen, similar to the status report she'd seen for David. But this one did not record the traveler as in transit.

Status unknown. Location unknown. Priority target, reacquisition in progress.

Her mouth went cottony again. She swigged water, but it didn't help. *Reacquisition in progress.* What the hell did that mean? And why did it bother her so much? She was not Janet Austen.

She went back to the list of files on the drive. Most of the files had unhelpful names that looked like random letters and numbers. She opened one. Gobbledygook. It was some kind of computer code, she guessed, or else an alien language. She opened two more files but found similar garbage. Well, it was garbage to her anyway. This was no help. She switched back to the spreadsheet of travelers' names.

Janet Austen was suspected to have GP, whatever that meant. Since Ms. Austen was a "former" traveler, did that mean Waldron or some other goon had killed the poor girl? No, they were reacquiring her, which sounded like she was still alive.

Raising her hand, she touched the letters on-screen that spelled out Janet Austen.

"It's you."

Grace jumped six inches off her seat, but managed to squelch the yelp that tried to burst out of her. The voice had come from behind her. She turned to see David standing there, gazing down at her with a noncommittal expression, as if he hadn't just scared the bejesus out of her.

"How long have you been there?" she asked, unable to suppress the annoyance in her voice. She got a little testy when every nerve in her body snapped simultaneously.

"A minute," he said, kneeling beside her chair. "You looked engrossed. I didn't want to intrude."

"Since when do you care about not intruding?"

He looked down at his hands. "Since last night."

Oh. Last night. She felt a blush rising in her cheeks.

A change of topic was in order. Immediately.

"What do you mean it's me?" she asked.

He met her gaze, his features tightened in confusion.

"A minute ago," she said, "when you surprised me, you said—"

"Oh." He pointed at the computer screen. "Janet Austen. That's you."

She frowned. "There may be a lot I don't remember, but I do know my own name."

"Janet Austen was a pseudonym."

"Why on earth would I use a pseudonym?"

As soon as the words left her mouth, she realized one awfully good reason why she might—to evade the monsters who were chasing her at this very moment. Yet those monsters ran the project.

No, at first her parents had run the project, at least that's what David said. She needed to know a lot more about the evolution, or devolution, of the research project begun by her parents.

She glanced over her shoulder toward the restroom. Though she couldn't see Earl, she heard banging and thumping, accompanied by muffled curses, emanating from the small room. Below the other sounds, the rushing of water continued.

David still hadn't answered her question. Turning to him, she said, "Explain to me about this project and why I used a pseudonym when I participated in it. Come to think of it, I don't have the slightest idea why I would've participated in the project either, so explain that too. Please."

He pursed his lips.

She folded her arms over her chest. "Tell me. I don't have time to remember on my own."

He stared at the computer screen for a second, then let out a sigh that seemed to deflate him. When he spoke, his tone was resigned. "I've only been trying to protect you. As you've pointed out, I've done a terrific job of it."

The bitterness in his voice made her want to hug him. Instead, she reached out a hand to touch his arm. Her fingers went through him like he wasn't even there. Which, technically, he wasn't. Every other time he'd visited her, he manifested a body.

She tried to touch him again, with the same result. Fingers through air.

Seeing her efforts, David released another sigh. "I didn't manifest. It takes a great deal of energy, and I don't want to waste any. I might need it very soon."

She clasped her hands on her lap. He might need all his energy very soon because she insisted on breaching a super-secret facility run by a psychopath and his merry band of homicidal puppets. The fact that David had tried to protect her and achieved something less than resounding victory was hardly his fault. It was hers.

Stop it. The blame lay not with her or David. It lay squarely on the shoulders of JT, whoever the psychopathic punk was. He must be stopped.

"Project Outreach," David said, snapping her attention back to him. "That's what it was called in the beginning. Christine and Mark—your parents—founded the project after they started working for ALI. Edward had brought them into the company. It was a legitimate enterprise with noble goals, and the three of them did a lot of good work there. Outreach was designed to explore the limits of psychic abilities."

Grace watched his face as he spoke. The tension had dissipated, replaced by a look of...fond remembrance seemed the best description. He must've liked the project back then, back when her parents and grandfather held the reins. He had clearly liked *them* anyway.

"You see," David continued, "other scientists had conducted studies that resulted in compelling evidence for the existence of psychic abilities. Humans could influence computers, for instance by changing a random sequence of numbers so that it was no longer random. Christine and Mark wanted to expand on the existing research, rather than conducting another study trying to prove psychic faculties are real. They spent a year searching for test subjects, screening and rescreening them until they felt certain the group they'd assembled had genuine extrasensory faculties."

His lips curved into a faint, almost wistful smile. "Everything was good at first. Thirty of us participated, voluntarily, as test subjects. The scientists—Christine, Mark, Edward, and half a dozen others—treated us with respect. It was like a family." He glanced at her sideways. "Then you came."

She squirmed in her chair. Despite what had happened between them last night, she still wasn't sure she wanted to hear about their previous relationship. It was too weird. But she must hear about it. She must know everything.

"You came for a visit at first," he continued, "but your parents got permission to show you the facility. It was out in the desert, underground, to limit interference from radio waves, human thoughts, and basically anything that might affect psychic abilities." He shifted position, as if an incorporeal man could get muscle cramps. "Anyway, you thought it would be fun to take one of the basic screening tests, just to see how it worked. Christine and Mark indulged you. No one expected the results to be positive—but they weren't just positive, they were off the charts."

Grace tucked one ankle under the opposite knee. A feeling of tightness started in her chest. If she didn't get a grip on it soon, the tightness would escalate into panic. She knew how this story ended.

A road. A deer. Blood.

Swallowing her discomfort, she said, "And then…"

"We got to know each other. You joined the project, as a test subject, against your family's objections. You wanted to understand your own power. And so did they, really, though the thought of experimenting on their own daughter was a little discomfiting. But you insisted." He smiled at her, that sweet and sexy smile that made her insides turn to Jell-O. "You were always stubborn."

She couldn't help smiling back at him. "Like you're not."

They just looked at each other, their gazes fused. The memory of last night flowed through her as a warm river of emotion and sensory recall. Though his expression stayed the same, she sensed that he was experiencing the same memory. She wanted to kiss him, but they were in a gas station and he had no physical form.

"What happened next?" she asked. "I mean, things went bad at some point."

David's smile disintegrated. "A year and a half ago, ALI was bought out by a multinational corporation called—"

"Digital Prognostics."

"Yes. How did you know?"

The scanned articles on the flash drive had told her. A man named Jackson Tennant ran Digital Prognostics. The truth hit her like a brick to the head. Duh. How could she have overlooked it before? Her telephone tormenter, JT, must be Jackson Tennant. A psycho owned and operated Digital Prognostics, the company that ran the Mojave Desert facility.

"How did you know?" David repeated.

She shrugged. "Grandpa told me. I take it things changed after the owners took over."

He nodded, his expression darkening. "Most of the scientists were fired and replaced with wonderful fellows who saw no ethical dilemma in using drugs to control us, the test subjects. Sessions that had lasted an hour at most were lengthened to several hours. We were pushed to our limits and beyond, no matter the physical or mental consequences. Some died. Some went insane. A group of eight tried to escape from the facility." His jaw tightened, and the muscle jumped. "They were gunned down in the desert. Another benefit of a remote, secret facility is that there are no witnesses."

Grace felt sick. She took a sip of water, which didn't help. Eight people murdered—and that had been only the beginning.

A man's face flashed in her mind and she asked, "Did you know Andrew Haley?"

"Yes. He was one of the subjects who went mad."

"He escaped. I met him."

David shook his head. "Nobody escapes. Edward managed to smuggle Andrew out of the facility and to a mental hospital. Our masters didn't know where and Edward refused to say. It made them extremely angry."

"Why just Andrew? Why didn't Grandpa help anyone else?"

"There wasn't anyone else, except for me and Sean. The eight were the first to die, but not the last."

He looked straight into her eyes, and the blue fire in them burned as intensely as it had on the first night she saw him—the first night she remembered seeing him. Every time he focused on her like this, she felt a connection to him, an intimacy beyond the physical. He knew her. She knew him. Maybe she couldn't recite his favorite foods or pick his favorite movie out of a lineup, but she knew him.

"Sean and I were okay," David said, "so Edward left us behind to keep an eye on things. He was already afraid for your safety."

"Why did I use a pseudonym? My parents ran the project."

David lifted a hand as if to touch her and then pulled back, apparently remembering he hadn't manifested. "From the start, Christine was worried that their research could be used for unsavory purposes. Mark thought she was paranoid, but he agreed to keep your name out of all records."

"What about the rest of you?"

"We knew the risks. Well, we thought we knew them anyway. No one could've predicted what would happen after the new management took control."

She felt a little weak from the dread swelling within her. She pressed on anyway, because she had no choice anymore. "How did my parents die?"

"We have to go back a bit further for you to understand." He stood and began pacing between the front windows and the table. "The trouble really started two months before they died."

Nine months ago

Christine Powell strolled down the corridor, the heels of her penny loafers slapping on the floor. Under her right arm, she held a clipboard tucked against her body. In her left hand, she twirled a silver-colored metal pen. The corridor lights reflected off the pen, shooting slivers of brilliance onto the walls and floor. Amid the twirls of light, her reflection shimmered on the smooth flooring like a spectral mirror image.

She kept her chin raised as she focused on the doorway ten feet in front of her on the right side of the corridor. The door hung open, the lights inside throwing a rectangle of yellowish light onto the corridor floor. Voices murmured within the room.

At the doorway, she hesitated. Her gut fluttered. Her fingers slipped, letting the pen clatter to the floor. As she bent to retrieve the pen, she whispered a mantra under her breath. "You can do this, you can do this."

Straightening, she stuffed the pen into the breast pocket of her lab coat. She could do this. It was a meeting, nothing sinister, simply a meeting to introduce the new head of security.

Then why did she feel as though she'd swallowed a lead weight?

A familiar voice from within the room called to her. "Come in, Christine. We've been waiting for you."

Edward McLean's voice bolstered her resolve, and she strode into the conference room. Her father sat in a leather chair positioned at the far end of a long table that stretched the length of the room. He motioned for her to take a seat. Though he tried to smile, the expression faltered, which only served to deepen the lines around his mouth and eyes. Christine marched down the table to lower herself into the chair nearest him. He had saved the seat for her. He always did.

At her left, Mark slumped in his chair. Worry lines wrinkled his forehead as he squinted into vacant space. With his elbow propped on one arm of the chair, he tapped his index finger against his lips.

Behind her father, a serious-looking young woman hunched in a folding chair. Her hands hovered over the keys of the notebook computer that balanced on her knees. Her name was Vanessa or Theresa, or something like that. Christine shrugged inwardly. The girl had worked at the facility for less two weeks and Christine was terrible at recalling names. After a few more weeks, maybe she would remember the girl's name.

It was Vanessa, she decided, because she needed to attach some name to the efficient-but-stoic secretary.

Across the table from Christine, a man with short gray hair sat straight as a column. His elbows rested on the table, while his hands were intertwined to support his chin. Freckles dotted his face. A smirk tugged at the corners of his mouth. Beside him sat another stranger. The second man had dark brown eyes, chestnut hair peppered with gray, and a muscular physique somewhat disguised by the loose-fitting suit he wore. His face, like a movie screen before the show started, displayed nothing yet held the prospect of coming attractions. Her throat tightened. She had the oddest feeling that whatever lay ahead, she must avoid it at all costs.

Mark fidgeted.

She leaned close to him. "Who are those men?"

"Don't know."

"What's this meeting about?"

Mark sat up, smoothing his shirt and lab coat. His tie was askew. "Must have to do with the buyout."

Yes, Christine supposed he was right. A much larger corporation had recently purchased ALI, in what her father had characterized as a hostile takeover.

Edward cleared his throat. "Now that we're all here, let's begin. We have some new colleagues to welcome."

As he ended the statement, his face pinched. He glared at the newcomers. Confused, Christine awaited the introductions. Perhaps then she would understand the tension electrifying the atmosphere.

Edward waved at the dark-eyed man. "This is Xavier Waldron. He has something to say."

Waldron rose. Strolling behind the chair in which the gray-haired man sat, he settled his hand atop the chair's back. The other man stiffened, though he tried to hide it under a pretense of adjusting his posture.

"Let's skip the pleasantries," Waldron said. "I know your names, I know what you do here. Now let me explain my function."

His gaze locked on Christine's. Her throat went as dry as the desert sand. Under the table, she clutched a handful of her skirt.

"This is no longer your playground," Waldron said. "I'm here to make this project profitable."

Mark stared at the tabletop and chewed the inside of his lip. Edward stared at the wall, face blank.

Someone had to speak, for heaven's sake.

Christine clasped her hands on the tabletop. Looking straight at Waldron, she said, "This is a research facility, not a McDonald's. We work for results, not profit, and what we do is for the good of humanity."

"Finding ways of controlling psychic impulses does not benefit humanity, Christine. It benefits you."

He'd used her first name. She puckered her lips, trying to avoid swearing at the cretin. She had a sick feeling she knew where the conversation would end up, and she didn't like it one bit.

"It benefits everyone," she said, rising to lean on the table with both hands. "We don't want to control these impulses, we seek to understand where they come from and how they can be managed so that the individual might function normally within society. I used to think psychic faculties were aberrations that drove the afflicted insane or turned them into monsters. Since founding the project, I've come to realize these people are gifted, not cursed." She locked gazes with Waldron. "The government would love to use them as spies or assassins but I *will not* let that happen. I will not let you use them to line your pockets either."

"Money is the last thing on my mind."

"But you said—"

"I said I'm going to make this facility profitable. I did not say *monetarily* profitable."

She bit her lip. What did he mean? She wanted to know but feared the answer.

"They are research subjects," Waldron said. "ALI owns them. Which means I, as director of operations, own them."

"You're not the director of operations."

Waldron gave her a vicious smile. He nodded toward Edward. "Ask your father."

She gave her father a questioning look. His shoulders drooped. He averted his gaze to his lap. She felt her mouth drop open as he slowly nodded.

Still slumped over his chair's arm, Mark slid one hand over his face to cover his eyes.

"This is Dr. Tesler," Waldron said, gesturing at the gray-haired, freckled man, "the new head of research and development."

Tesler smirked at her. She fisted her hands, sure she'd leap across the table and strangle both of them if she didn't control her anger somehow. What the hell was happening? Why was she the only one questioning the situation?

Waldron glanced toward the corner of the room adjacent to the doorway and flicked his hand. A man detached from the shadows behind the door and shut it with a sharp click. She hadn't noticed the man before. His black clothing melded with the shadows. He was Norris, one of the new guards brought in last week, but he wore a black outfit instead of his usual brown uniform. Black gloves covered his hands. He donned black combat boots as well. Under one arm, he held a black full-face helmet.

What the blazes?

She looked at her father. Edward had shut his eyes. The wrinkles on his face had deepened into canyons. He pressed his lips together. When he opened his eyes and met her gaze, a chill slithered down her spine.

Waldron spoke again, his voice dripping with arrogance. "After studying the security at this facility, I've come to one unpleasant conclusion." He settled his hands on the back of Tesler's chair. "It is a complete failure."

"We've done fine so far," Christine said. "No one knows we exist."

"Except everyone who works here and everyone they speak to outside the facility."

"They signed confidentiality agreements."

"Paper and ink." Waldron massaged the chair, flexing the sinews in his hands. "Every one of them is a potential breach and this is not a discussion. Measures have been taken. More will follow."

Christine looked at her father. He had closed his eyes again, his expression unreadable. When she glanced at Mark, he turned his head away to avoid her gaze.

Waldron pushed away from Tesler's chair. "From this moment forward, no one will enter or leave this facility without my express permission."

"We are not prisoners, Mr. Waldron."

"Correct. You are vassals and I am your lord."

Waldron flicked his wrist and Tesler hopped out of his chair. As Waldron sauntered around the table, Tesler trailed behind him like a loyal pet. As they moved past Norris, Waldron flicked his wrist once more and the guard fell in step behind Tesler. If they'd begun to goose-step, the fascist image would've been complete.

Christine swallowed against the tightness in her throat. She had no clue how things had changed so abruptly, and so terribly.

Oh yes she did. The takeover was far more hostile than anyone had realized.

At the door, Waldron paused. Without turning, he said, "Understand this. Anyone who challenges me, anyone who shows the slightest hint of disobeying me, will be silenced. Permanently."

The trio exited the conference room. The door clicked shut. The ventilation system whirred overhead. In the space of a few moments, they had become prisoners.

Mark cursed under his breath. Edward released a long, defeated sigh.

Christine flopped into her chair and stared at her father. "What's going on?"

"I've lost the war."

"What war? Who bought us out?"

Though she stared at him and waited for his response, he said nothing. His gaze was fixed on the far wall—or a sight beyond the wall. A sight inside his mind. A vision of what the facility would become, a slave regime focused on one goal.

Mining the human mind for profit.

Except Waldron claimed to have no interest in money. To him profit meant…what?

Control.

Mark rose from his chair and tugged her hand. He wanted to go. She didn't want to leave her father, but he wasn't there anyway, not mentally. She let Mark lead her out of the conference room, down the shadow-infested corridor, and to the offices that occupied the end of the corridor farthest from the elevator. Standing in the false twilight, holding hands, they exchanged tense looks. He appeared as numb as she felt.

After a moment, Mark entered his office through a door marked with his name and the title "Director, Information Systems."

She stumbled into her own office. Though she glanced at the lettering that spelled out her name and the designation "Assistant Director, Research & Development," her mind registered nothing. The words slipped through her brain unprocessed. Perhaps they had never meant anything. No, they had once held meaning. The title had signified her father's faith in her intelligence and dedication, the importance of the work she performed here. Now it signified nothing.

She sensed what would come. Her intuition warned her, like a tornado siren whooping as a twister headed toward the heart of town. This tornado struck in the darkest night. She couldn't see it coming. She couldn't stop it.

The phone on her desk rang. She jumped.

Snatching the phone from its cradle, she mumbled, "Christine Powell."

"Turn on your computer," a male voice instructed.

"Who is this?"

"Do it."

The voice. She recognized it. "What do you want, Waldron?"

"*Do it.*"

Her chest tightened as if a python had wrapped its body around her. Hands shaking, she wiggled the mouse to wake her computer from sleep mode. She drummed her fingernails on the desk. Through the phone, she heard Waldron breathing.

"It's on," she said.

"Watch."

A window opened on the screen, the video feed from the RV room. She recognized the pale blue walls, the bulbs that simulated natural light, the plush recliner positioned in the center of the room. Eggshell-colored carpeting covered the floor. Another chair, a new chair, sat beside the old one. It resembled a dentist's chair, minus the comforts. The secretary, Vanessa, reclined in the new chair.

No. Not reclined. Christine leaned closer. The girl was strapped to the chair with leather restraints that crossed her forehead, wrists, and ankles. The feed had sound too, which emanated from her computer speakers with a tinny quality.

The girl sniffled. "Please let me out."

An explosion thundered. The girl shrieked. Her body jerked, then sagged.

The camera zoomed in on her. Blood had begun to soak her blouse, in the center of her chest. Her eyes stared, vacant.

"This was a warning," Waldron said through the phone. "Don't expect another."

Click. The dial tone buzzed in her ear.

Christine dropped the phone.

Chapter Twenty-One

Present Day

Grace slumped against the chair. At the back of the store, inside the restroom, metal banged on metal as Earl struggled to repair what she had broken. A twinge of guilt rippled through her. She didn't know exactly what she'd done, so she had no idea how badly she might've screwed up the works. Later, she'd find a way to make it up to the poor guy.

If she survived to later.

She couldn't understand why her family, the people she had known and trusted her whole life, would let criminals take over their life's work. Why they let Waldron and Tesler bully them. Why they just accepted the situation.

"Why didn't they stop Waldron?" Grace asked.

"He assigned armed guards to watch them," David said. "They were prisoners, controlled in every aspect of their lives and work. They practically needed written permission to take a deep breath."

"But why? What was the goal? I don't get it."

"Waldron showed them what would happen if they rose up against him. The secretary was a stand-in."

"For what?"

"Not what. Who." He hesitated, his gaze intent on her. "You."

She closed her eyes. Waldron killed an innocent woman as a warning to her parents. If they resisted, he would do the same, or worse, to their daughter.

Grace opened her eyes. The threat must've worked. She now knew, however, that Waldron could not kill her. His boss wanted her alive.

"Why would my mother tell you all this?"

"She didn't have to. I followed her to that meeting, psychically. No one knew I was there."

"You like following women, hey? Or is it just the ones in my family?"

"No." He averted his gaze to the tabletop. "I heard Norris talking to another guard. He mentioned Waldron and said the facility was about to become a fun place. Coming from Norris, that's not a good thing. He was fresh out of maximum-security prison when he came here. I went to the meeting so I could find out what was going on."

"My grandfather would not hire dangerous criminals."

"He didn't know. ALI hired new guards after the buyout, and he had no say in it." David settled a hand over hers. "After that initial meeting, I followed Christine, Mark, or Edward as often as I could without being detected."

"Then tell me the rest."

Still kneeling beside her, he sat back on his heels. "This is where it gets really nasty."

Eight months earlier

Christine hesitated, one hand on the knob, her gaze focused on the sign that now adorned the door. The workmen had replaced the "Off limits—Under construction" sign with a new one that read "Isolation Chamber 1." How many more rooms had they converted into isolation chambers? And what precisely were these chambers for?

Three weeks ago, Waldron had ordered the RV room and all the other travelers' suites renovated. She'd argued that they remodeled the suites the previous year to create the kind of quiet, calming atmosphere the travelers needed to invoke their abilities. The suites needed no makeover. She still cringed when she recalled how Waldron had fixed his dark eyes on her and said, "No more coddling, Christine."

Never had she given him permission to call her Christine. Everyone except Mark and her father called her Dr. Powell. Of course, Waldron asked no permission before taking such liberties. She couldn't imagine him asking permission for anything. The man took whatever he desired, from liberties to lives. Still, she despised her name when it came from his lips.

The renovations had taken less than the month originally estimated. Now as she stood outside the "isolation chamber," the tremors in her hand jiggled the knob. She breathed deeply, struggling against the fear that clawed at her psyche. It was a room. Four walls, a floor, and a ceiling. A room couldn't hurt her—or anyone.

She twisted the knob. Locked.

Digging her keys out of her coat pocket, she inserted the one for the RV room. The key didn't fit. She tried all the others on her ring. None fit. Waldron couldn't lock her out. She had gold clearance, which gave her access to every room in the facility and every file on the computers.

She was a vassal now, not a scientist. Waldron let her retain the title of Assistant Director, but it meant nothing anymore. The facility belonged to Xavier Waldron.

The hell it did. She whisked her tablet computer out of another pocket and punched in a direct message to Waldron. "Please send me key to isolation room 1."

A locked door hinted at a secret. Waldron didn't want her to see the room. Why? What had his men done in there? She envisioned the possibilities, and her skin prickled.

At the end of the corridor, the elevator doors parted. She glanced sideways at the doors. Waldron stomped out of the elevator toward her.

Halting beside her, he said, "I was coming to see you when I received your message."

"You've changed the locks."

"How observant of you, Christine."

"Give me the key. I have access to all the rooms."

"Afraid not."

She clenched her jaw. "I have gold clearance."

He fingered the ID badge clipped onto her lapel. "I've reevaluated all clearances. Yours is now blue."

She bit the inside of her cheek. He had bumped her down two rungs on the clearance ladder. The act would lock her out of most of the labs and all of the traveler suites—or the isolation chambers, as they were now designated.

"What are you hiding?" she said.

"You're very pretty, Christine. Very desirable." He seized a clump of her hair and yanked her closer. "But much too curious for your own good."

She winced at the pain in her scalp. Her eye level fell at slightly above his nose. Their gazes locked as he flattened his other hand into the small of her back and crushed her against him until her nose smashed into his. His lips grazed hers.

Her stomach flip-flopped. She grimaced, struggling to push away from him. His arms were too strong, enveloping her like metal restraints.

He chuckled. "We could come to an agreement, Christine."

"I'd rather be gnawed to bits by piranhas, Xavier." She emphasized the name with a near snarl in her voice.

He mashed his mouth on hers.

She bit his lower lip.

Maintaining his grip on her hair, he touched the reddening spot on his lip. His voice grew rough as he said, "You want to see, Christine? You want to know? I'll show you."

He withdrew a set of keys from his pocket, and then jerked her head backward. She bit back a cry and spat at him. He unlocked the door, thrusting it inward. Darkness cloaked the interior.

He hurled her through the doorway.

She landed on her hip. Pain stabbed down her legs. A gasp exploded from her.

Stalking into the room, he flicked a switch and light flooded the interior. The floor, the walls, and the ceiling had been reduced to bare concrete. A single fluorescent panel had replaced the natural-light bulbs. In the center of the room, the austere metal chair sat where the recliner had once stood. The barest amount of cushioning softened the chair, and leather restraints dangled from it. A metal table occupied the nearest corner of the room, its surface home to devices she didn't recognize. In her soul, however, she perceived their purpose.

The concrete exuded a chill that infected her flesh. She rubbed her arms.

Waldron towered over her. His arms hung at his sides, hands clenched into fists. His lips he flattened together. The fluorescent lighting flickered off his eyes.

She avoided thinking about the shiver she'd gotten the first time she saw him. She avoided thinking about the violence with which he'd thrown her into this room. She avoided thinking about what might come next. Her thoughts concentrated on one image—the young girl, Vanessa, strapped into the chair that occupied this room, her face a blank oval, tears staining her cheeks, eyes red, skin white as a corpse's. She'd begged her captors for mercy, knowing they would grant death instead and praying it would come quickly, painlessly, but knowing it would not. When death came for her, it would rent her flesh, contorted her muscles, and wielded a pain beyond agony.

Christine swallowed, but the mass in her throat remained. Was she really thinking of Vanessa, or herself? Neither, she realized with a jolt. The face that replaced the secretary's in her mind's eye belonged to Grace.

Waldron slammed the door shut. "Let me demonstrate this room's function."

"I know what it's for."

"Get in the chair."

"Are you insane?"

In one step, he reached her. He grabbed both her wrists and hauled her off the floor, across the room, and to the chair. The concrete scraped her bare knees as her skirt rode up her thigh. She flailed her arms and legs but found no purchase, no advantage. She couldn't reach him.

He shoved her into the chair.

She lashed out at him. He smacked her so hard her head snapped back into the chair's headrest. Lights popped in her vision, phantoms of the pain ricocheting through her head. Waldron secured the restraints around her arms, legs, and forehead.

"If you kill me," she said, her voice a little slurred, "it will be the end of you."

"You think your husband will avenge you?" He straightened, studying her without expression. "Or your father? They've already given up."

She strained against the leather straps. They held tight.

"It's irrelevant," Waldron said, "whether they would or not. I've no intention of killing you."

He sauntered to the door. As he swung it inward, he clicked off the lights. In the light shining through the doorway, he looked back at her.

"No, I won't kill you," he said, and stepped into the corridor. "Not today."

He shut the door.

The light from the corridor shrank into nothing, consumed by the darkness within the room. The cold stung her skin. The dark caressed her. She felt the room tilt and sway. Her ears rang. Her stomach lurched. She gulped back her gorge, and digging her nails into the chair's arms, concentrated on breathing. In, out. In, out.

The dark. The cold. Buried alive.

Directly above her, layers of concrete. Beyond that, earth and rock and sand. The weight of cars and human bodies and wild animals all rested atop her head and shoulders. An image of the roof collapsing flashed through her mind.

Buried alive.

The room whirled around her.

The temperature plummeted. A wind gusted through the room.

"No," she mumbled. "Don't, they'll know…"

The restraints popped off her wrists and ankles. The forehead strap loosened and slipped free.

The room tilted. Her breaths came short and fast. She tried to stand, stumbled, and landed on all fours. The ringing in her ears got louder as her muscles grew weaker. Her arms trembled.

With great effort, she forced herself to breathe normally. In, out. In, out. The ringing lingered, though softer than before. Though she still felt weak, her muscles regained enough strength to push her up and onto her feet. She careened through the pitching, spiraling darkness toward the door—or where she thought the door was. She floundered into the wall. Concrete slapped her cheek.

Cold. Hard. A crypt.

She whimpered.

The door was flung inward. It crashed into the wall, bounced twice, and stopped.

A wedge of light shattered the blackness. Scuffling into the light, she collapsed onto the floor, panting. Sweat trickled over her lips into her mouth. The salty tang seeped over her tongue.

The room leveled. The ringing in her ears faded away.

She clambered to her feet and staggered into the corridor. Squinting, she palpated the back of her head. Her vision adjusted, and she spotted a figure across the corridor.

Waldron stood near the opposite wall. He folded his arms over his chest, sneering at her.

"You were trapped in a car trunk as a child," he said. "Suffered heat stroke before your aunt found you. Since then, you've had a paralyzing fear of dark, confined spaces."

"How could you know that?"

"Before you were cleared to work here, you underwent psychological testing."

The muscles in her neck and jaw cramped. She massaged her neck. Grunting, she said, "That was supposed to be confidential."

"Nothing is as it was supposed to be. Wouldn't you agree?" He strode across the corridor toward her. "I knew much about you before today. Now I know everything."

"You know nothing." She resisted the urge to take a step away from him. "What was the point of this little exercise?"

"To see if someone would rescue you." He took her chin in his hand. "And someone did. The test was not for you, Christine, but for our subjects."

He mashed his mouth to hers. She wriggled out of his grasp, hit the wall, and groaned as a torrent of nausea broke over her.

"You see," Waldron said, "they've been refusing to cooperate in our testing. I've read the reports written by you and your father. I know what these freaks can do. Since they weren't responding to Tesler's methods, I thought an experiment of my own design was in order."

Moments earlier, the darkness had ripped fear through her soul like a serrated knife. Now another kind of darkness exerted the same power over her. The memory of the isolation chamber would linger for awhile. But the memory of Waldron's dark, soulless eyes would stay with her forever.

She shivered.

"Which one was it?" Waldron asked. "I want the name. Was it Janet Austen?"

"Go to hell."

A drop of sweat trickled down her temple. Waldron touched it with his fingertip, letting the drop roll onto his skin. He ran the back of his hand down her cheek.

"I know," he whispered, "Janet Austen is a pseudonym. And she's been missing from the facility since I took control a month ago. None of the other subjects will reveal her true identity." He patted her cheek. "You, however, will."

She glowered at him but said nothing. He would not goad her into blurting out the information in a fit of anger.

His smile made her stomach twist. He growled, "You will tell me her name."

"You should've killed me."

"Locking you in that room." He shook his head slowly. "It's not the worst I could do to you."

He strolled down the corridor, entered the elevator, and was gone. Christine dropped onto her knees and cried.

Present Day

Grace stared at the computer screen without seeing the words displayed on it. The world around her had become a kind of dream, detached and blurry. The more she learned about her mother's ordeal, the deeper the numbness infiltrated her. Although she understood David's words, and recognized their meaning, she felt nothing in response. Nothing.

And that frightened her more than anything else.

Maybe she was too exhausted to feel anything. Maybe the truth overwhelmed her.

She had asked for the truth—no, demanded it—and now that David had told her, she wondered if she really wanted it. Her life might end today. What did the truth matter?

It did matter, though, a great deal. Despite the numbness, despite the ice spreading through her veins, she needed to understand.

"Was it you?" she asked. "Did you rescue my mother? And what took you so damn long? He was torturing her."

"I wasn't there. Tesler had me conducting RV sessions at the time and, well, I couldn't sense anything outside of the session parameters. Later, Christine told me what had happened because, like you, she assumed I was the one who helped her. But it wasn't me."

"Then who was it?"

"You."

She glanced at him sideways. "Me?"

He nodded. "Your parents had sent you back to Texas, but even from that distance, you felt your mother's anguish and couldn't keep from intervening." His lips twisted into a wry smile. "You always have been stubborn."

A warm feeling melted the ice inside her. It wasn't desire this time, but something gentler and more meaningful. Comfort. Familiarity. Affection.

"What else did you see?" she asked. "While you were spying on my mother, I mean."

"I wasn't spying."

"Yes, you were. It's not a criticism, it's just a statement of fact."

He made a face, one she'd learned to interpret. The one that conveyed exasperation and fondness simultaneously. The one he gave her quite often.

"Tell me what you saw," she said.

"A month after the scene with Waldron, I sensed a psychic disturbance—a big one—and I followed it." He hesitated. "Into Andrew Haley's room."

She swallowed, but the rock that had formed in her throat wouldn't budge.

"I watched them die," David murmured, "and I did nothing. I couldn't—"

He shifted sideways, turning away from her. She cleared her throat to regain his attention. He tensed but refused to look at her.

"I couldn't manifest," he said. "Without that, I can't affect the environment. To manifest, you need a connection between the host and the traveler. I didn't have that with Christine or Mark. I've only ever had that with you."

"But Sean manifested for me too. I don't feel very connected to him."

"He didn't manifest. At least, not on his own."

She opened her mouth. No sound came.

"You understand," he said, finally turning to face her again. "Don't you?"

Her throat was dry, her voice paralyzed.

"It was you," David said. "Without knowing it, you helped Sean manifest. You are the most powerful of us all."

She managed a weak "uh" before her voice choked off.

Snap out of it. The mental order yanked her back to reality, and she met David's gaze. He arched an eyebrow.

"Fine," she said, "I'm the queen of psychic crap. Doesn't help me much at the moment."

"Well—"

"Wait," she interrupted, as a realization hit her. "If manifesting requires a connection to the host, then this other traveler—the slimeball who attacked me in my car—has a connection to me? That's impossible. I don't know him and I don't want to."

"Sometimes when you follow someone around for awhile, you can develop a connection with them. It's rare, but it happens. And he's clearly obsessed with you, so I guess it's possible the intensity of his obsession somehow forced a connection between the two of you."

"You're saying he's been following me. Watching me. Stalking me."

"Maybe."

"Yuck." She froze. "Maybe?"

"There's another possibility. He might be so strong that he doesn't need a connection to manifest."

Her stomach churned at the idea. "Great, he can break into my head anytime he wants."

"I don't think so. To break into your mind like that, he must've needed a tool for picking the lock, so to speak."

"A connection."

"No, something else."

The creep and his "tool" could wait. She had other things on her mind right now.

Knowing the facts of her parents' deaths would give her a clue. To what, she didn't know. She simply knew she must hear the story, must understand the events, before she proceeded with whatever she would do next. Well, she knew she must find the facility. After that, her plan got a little fuzzy. Okay, a lot fuzzy.

"Finish the story," she said. "Tell me how they died."

Seven Months Earlier

Inside her pocket, the tablet beeped. Christine pulled out the device and brought up the message that awaited her perusal. "RV15 agitated," the message read. "Need your assistance—Tesler."

Andrew was acting up again. She stuffed the tablet in her pocket. Rubbing her neck, she thanked God the facility had gone into night mode an hour ago, plunging the corridors into twilight. Even that half-light, however, stung her eyes and she squinted. Her head throbbed and her neck ached. The day, which had begun at dawn, now dragged on past dusk. Ever since Waldron and his gang had taken over the facility, the term work day had ceased to mean "working in the daytime." These days it meant working whenever and for as long as Waldron commanded. He hadn't been exaggerating for effect when he called the facility's employees his vassals. They were more like indentured servants whose terms of service Waldron could extend for as long as he liked.

Christine scuffled down the corridor. At Andrew's room, she unlocked the door and entered. The lamp in the corner bathed a quarter of the room in milky light. On the bed, within the cone of illumination, Andrew lay still. No one else was in the room.

Tesler had sent the message. He'd summoned her here.

In that message, sent mere seconds earlier, Tesler called Andrew "agitated." She crossed the room, stopping at the bedside. Andrew's eyes jiggled beneath his closed lids. His chest rose and fell in a shallow rhythm.

Agitated? He was asleep.

As she reached into her pocket for the tablet, the door opened. Mark stumbled into the room, leaving the door open as he shuffled to the bedside. Shoulders slumped, eyes bloodshot, he stopped beside Christine.

"You called me?" he said.

"No, I got a message from Tesler to come right away."

"Message I got said it was from you."

She brushed a strand of greasy hair from his forehead. "Honey, you look tired. Go get some rest. I'll handle this."

"It's him."

"What?"

Mark stared at Andrew. He stood immobile and stiff, his unblinking gaze locked on the man who slumbered on the bed.

"Get out," Mark hissed. "Run."

"What?"

"Dammit, Christine, *run*." Mark lifted his gaze, eyes wide and staring into an empty, shadowed corner of the room. "He's coming."

She took a step backward. A voice inside urged her to heed his advice. She couldn't leave, though, couldn't abandon her husband with…what? Who was he talking about? Who was coming? *What* was coming?

Her gut twisted. Deep in her mind, she knew. Oh God, she knew.

Andrew's eyes opened. He turned his bleary gaze on her. His eyes shimmered green, as if lit from within. When travelers engaged their psychic abilities at a high level, it caused an eerie green or blue glow in the eyes—but only in the eyes of their astral bodies, not in their real eyes.

She wanted to back up to the doorway, turn, and run out of the room. Her body refused to obey her commands, though, staying frozen to the spot beside Andrew's bed.

"He comes for you," Andrew said, his voice rough and dry as sandpaper. He thrust a hand out to her, and she stumbled backward another step, out of his reach. Andrew's fingers worked as if trying to find her by touch. He said, "He wants the golden girl. Save her. The golden light is too bright. Save her."

Christine stared at Andrew. Her heart pounded so hard against her ribs that her chest ached. She felt light-headed, but oh dear heaven she could not pass out. Not here. Not now.

Andrew jerked. His eyes rolled back in his head. In a strangled voice, he shouted, "Go! Go!"

Then he collapsed onto the bed. His eyelids fluttered shut as his body went still.

Mark seized her arm and dragged her toward the doorway.

The door slammed shut in front of them.

A chilly wind gusted through the room. Goose bumps rose on Christine's arms. Mark grasped the doorknob and twisted. The knob refused to move. He yanked on it until his face turned red with the effort, but still the knob would not budge.

From behind them, an inhuman voice spoke. "I know your secret."

The hairs on the back of her neck stiffened. She turned sideways to search the shadows for a silhouette, but saw none. A traveler had entered the room, though not one of the travelers she knew. Only three remained at the facility, and of those only David could've managed to track her. But even if he had, he lacked the ability to manipulate the environment. This new traveler, she sensed, called upon more power than anyone except Grace.

"Give her to me," the voice demanded. "The golden girl is mine."

Christine hugged her arms to her chest. Golden girl. She had a horrible feeling she knew exactly what the traveler wanted. No way in hell would she grant it to him. Her own life didn't matter. She could not let this man, whoever he was, have what he wanted. She must stop him. He must never get his hands on her daughter.

Stop him how? He wasn't here. *Come on, Christine, think of something.*

Andrew's limp body lay crumpled on the bed. He'd tried to warn her.

"I won't help you," she said to the empty air.

Mark stopped fighting with the doorknob. "No, Christine, don't—"

"You came when I called," the voice said. "I am more powerful than you can imagine."

The message on her tablet. The traveler had sent it.

He knew how to control electronic devices and the environment, both of which indicated high-level abilities. And the green glow in Andrew's eyes...

Suddenly, she understood. This new traveler must've taken control of Andrew, and somehow that action triggered the paranormal glimmer in Andrew's eyes. But the new traveler seemed to have lost control of Andrew quickly, a fact that gave her a smidgen of hope. The new traveler couldn't read minds, she knew. No one could—or no one *would*, rather. She had one chance. Tracking her at the facility was easy, because it was a confined space. Most travelers, even the beginners, could track someone through a finite area like a building, especially a building well known to the traveler. Once a target got outside the traveler's familiar, confined areas, things got more complicated.

"All right," Christine said. "I'll tell you how to find her."

Mark stopped twisting the doorknob. He turned his wide eyes toward her.

She gave him a tight little smile. After twenty-nine years of marriage, he ought to know what the look meant. It was a request that he trust her and not interfere.

Narrowing his eyes, he frowned. Oh yes, he understood. But he wasn't happy about it.

"Who is she?" the traveler demanded.

Christine took a quick breath and said, "Her name is Allison Monroe and she's hiding out in the Salmon River Mountains in Idaho. That's all I know. For her own safety, I wouldn't let her tell me more. I knew you'd come after her eventually."

She hadn't known, and still didn't know, who he was. But she knew what he wanted from Grace.

Power.

And dear heaven, if he got it, the world was doomed. No living being should have the kind of power this traveler craved. She didn't even know for certain it was possible to achieve a state of such awesome power, much less survive it intact. The level of psychic energy required must be astronomical.

The feasibility hardly mattered right now. The traveler wanted Grace. He must never get anywhere near her.

"You lie," the traveler hissed.

Christine squared her shoulders. "If you want her, you'll have to search the Salmon River Mountains. That's where she is."

The air stilled. Silence descended over the room like a heavy curtain.

Her college roommate's family had owned a cabin in the Salmon River Mountains. She couldn't explain why that name had popped into her brain when she needed a location far from where Grace actually lived. She prayed only that the traveler would take the bait she'd dangled in front of him.

A draft tickled her skin.

"Tell me more," the traveler growled. "Where to find her. I need more."

Only four people knew the true identity of Janet Austen and where she lived now. She, Mark, her father, and David served as the sole guardians of the secret. From the beginning, they had concealed Grace's identity because Christine insisted on it. The others had thought her paranoid, but she heeded the soul-deep instinct that urged her to protect her daughter. Since the first time her father told her about Project Outreach, she'd seen the potential for good—and for evil.

A gust of wind tore through the room, nearly knocking her off her feet. Mark caught her, and they floundered into the door with a dull thud.

"Where is she?" the voice shouted.

"I told you all I know," Christine said. "Go there. You'll sense her."

Please go. Please, please, please.

A dark shape separated from the shadows in the far corner. The shape was vaguely humanoid, though far from human. When the being spoke, his voice burned with a quiet intensity that prickled every hair on her body.

"I will go," he said, "but if you lie…"

His voice trailed off, but she heard the silent threat that punctuated the statement.

And then he was gone.

The air changed, though not in any way she could quantify. The difference was intangible, inexplicable.

The door lock clicked.

Mark eased her away from him and reached for the knob. It turned in his hand. He yanked the door open and they fled through the opening, down the corridor. Mark grasped her hand so tightly it began to ache, but she clamped his just as tightly.

At the elevator, they halted. Mark pressed the button to summon the car.

"What are we doing?" Mark asked.

"Running." As she watched the numbers above the elevator door light up one after another, tracing the car's path up the shaft, she said, "What about Dad? He's on his way back from Washington."

"We'll call him once we're on the road."

She shook her head. "We can't take our cell phones or computers. They're trackable."

Mark sighed. "Then we'll find a pay phone along the way."

The elevator stopped with a soft thunk and the doors parted.

He led her into the car, pressing the button for the basement level, where the parking garage was located. The doors slid shut.

Christine watched the numbers count down the floors until the car eased to a stop and the doors opened again, granting them access to the basement level. An alarm bell clanged in the back of her mind, warning her that something was off. Where had all the guards gone? Why was nobody trying to stop them? They weren't allowed to leave the facility, yet so far they'd encountered no resistance.

The guard shack outside the elevator stood empty.

The alarm clanged louder in her mind.

She yanked Mark's hand, hauling them both to a stop.

"Where is everyone?" she said. "Even with the staff reductions, we should've run into guards. So why haven't we?"

"I don't know."

A figure stepped out from behind the guard shack.

Christine jumped—and then she recognized the man.

"David," she said, his name coming out as a heavy sigh. "What are you doing here?"

He stopped several yards away. "Something is wrong. You need to leave immediately."

"Yeah," Mark said, "that's what we're trying to do."

"You can't take your car. It's probably been outfitted with a tracking device."

Christine groaned. "Great. How do we get out of here then?"

David pointed toward an SUV parked three spaces down the row. "Take that one."

"Why?"

"It's Waldron's. He'd never let anyone track him."

"Keys?" she asked.

"Don't worry, I'll start it for you. Once you're far enough away, you'll need to switch cars. Don't use your credit cards or access your bank accounts—"

Mark held up a hand. "Thanks, we'll manage."

Christine scrunched her eyebrows, looking at David. "You can start a car?"

He shrugged. "Probably. It'll take a lot of energy, though, and I may not be able to help you anymore after this."

"We understand."

David looked at her, then at Mark. "Be careful."

With a curt nod to David, Mark seized her hand and dragged her toward the SUV. Once they were inside, with the doors locked, David strode in front of the vehicle. He raised his hands over the hood, hovering them in midair. He closed his eyes. His expression tightened into a grimace. She knew he wasn't actually touching the car, because he lacked the ability to manifest on his own, but David had always mimicked physical gestures as a means of focusing his power.

The tendons in his hands bulged as if he were lifting a heavy object.

It was too hard. He should stop. They could find another way.

She reached for the door handle, intending to fling the door open and shout for him to give up.

The car's engine sputtered, caught, and grumbled to life.

David opened his eyes, dropped his hands, and stumbled backward into the wall. He lifted one hand in a weak gesture for them to go.

Mark backed the vehicle out of the parking space. They sped out of the parking garage without seeing another person, dead or alive. Minute after minute ticked by as they raced down the dirt road that accessed the facility, passing through the invisible gateway. A network of infrared sensors and motion detectors, buried underground, formed an invisible fence around the facility. Trespassers would see nothing but open desert, yet their presence would be detected and any possible threat assessed long before they reached the facility itself.

No other vehicles intercepted them. The SUV jounced over the asphalt lip onto the highway, and Mark swerved the car into the right lane.

All seemed well. They were beyond the facility's perimeter. They could make it to safety.

Deep inside, though, Christine felt a primal instinct warning her that something was coming for them. Power. Darkness.

Death.

Chapter Twenty-Two

Present Day

"Where was everyone?" Grace asked. "How did they escape so easily? Did you follow them after they left the facility?"

"Slow down," David said, holding up a hand as if he could push back her questions. "The facility was empty. It was already at minimal staffing levels because it was the weekend. When I triggered the perimeter alarms, I made sure sensors went off on every side so that all the guards had to be deployed. It was the best chance I could give Christine and Mark."

"Why didn't you try to stop the traveler when he cornered them in Andrew's room?"

David's shoulders slumped as his head bowed slightly. "I couldn't. The traveler was too strong. If I'd expended all my energy on fighting him, I never would've been able to clear the facility. I made a conscious choice to leave them in that room while I set about triggering the perimeter alarms. I was fairly certain the traveler wouldn't kill them until he had you."

"Fairly certain?"

She regretted the edge in her voice the instant the words left her mouth. David lowered his head, eyes closing, and ran a hand through his hair. She noticed the tightness around his eyes, the furrowing of his brow and forehead, the darkening of the skin under his eyes, and the paleness of his lips. Christ, he must've burned a tanker load of energy on coming here and sticking around long enough to answer all her questions.

"I'm sorry," she said, reaching out to stroke his hair before realizing she couldn't. His appearance was an illusion. So instead she told him, "I know you would've done more if you could."

"I didn't save them." He spoke in a hushed voice, almost a whisper, keeping his eyes closed as he continued. "I followed them but I couldn't stop the—"

"Car crash," she finished for him. "Are you saying it was just an accident?"

He shook his head. "I don't know. Given the circumstances, I doubt it. But I can't know for sure. I had to whip up a localized windstorm to slow down the guards who were on their way back to the facility, to keep them from seeing which direction Christine and Mark went. By the time I got to them, the car was upside down on the side of the road. It was over."

They were already dead. That was what he meant. He got there too late to help them. She could see the guilt etched on his face and feel it rolling off him in psychic waves.

Maybe that was her own guilt spinning through the air around them. Her parents died because of her. Why had she hidden in Texas while a lunatic with supernatural powers hunted them? What kind of person was she?

"It's not your fault," he said, tilting his head to look at her. "You wanted to stay, but your parents insisted you leave and have no contact with them until the situation settled down. It never did."

She wanted to wrap her arms around him. She wanted to close her eyes, bury her face against his neck, and forget about everything. Unfortunately, thoughts kept bubbling up in her brain.

"If you left them alone in Andrew's room," she said, "how do you know what happened in there?"

"When I got to the site of the accident, Christine was still alive—barely. She had just enough time left to tell me what happened and to make me promise I'd watch out for you."

Another thought bubbled to the surface and she paused to consider it before speaking. "If my parents and grandfather were prisoners in the facility, how could Grandpa go on a trip to Washington?"

David shrugged. "I wasn't privy to everything."

"Hmm." She decided to let that go for the moment, considering that he was psychic, not omnipotent. "What's the deal with this golden girl and golden light stuff?"

"I'm not sure."

She resisted the urge to question him more. His face had gone pale, further darkening the shadows under his eyes.

He shut his eyes, sitting motionless and silent for so many seconds that she wondered if he'd gotten too weak to see or speak to her. When he finally opened his eyes, he did not look at her.

"There is a story," he said, "a myth really, about a power that trumps all others. It would make telepathy and manifesting seem like nothing—if it existed. Some of the older RVs, the ones who worked for the CIA back when they toyed with psychic espionage, talked about this power. They feared it." He tilted his head to head up to gaze at the computer screen, which still displayed the list of former participants in the facility's research. "They called it the Golden Power."

She leaned forward, resting one arm on the table. "Why did they fear it?"

"Two reasons." He paused, as if collecting his thoughts. "First, they were afraid it would turn out to have dire consequences for anyone who tried to use it. There is precedence for that fear. Reading minds sounded like a great idea, especially in espionage circles, but it turned out be so overwhelming for the mind reader that no one will even attempt it anymore."

"Why not?"

"Because it will drive you insane." He glanced at her. "And I'm talking completely, irretrievably, frothing-at-the-mouth insane."

"Oh." She gulped back the lump in her throat. "I won't try that then."

He returned his attention to the list on-screen. "The second reason the older RVs feared the Golden Power had to do with the old saying that absolute power corrupts absolutely." She opened her mouth to ask what he meant, but he held up a hand to silence her. "Patience, I'm getting there."

She pressed her lips together.

A faint smile flickered across his face, vanishing as he said, "First, you need to understand how our psychic abilities work. Our powers emanate from something we call the crossroads. It's where everything in the universe—thoughts, feelings, knowledge, memories—all come together, like roads intersecting. When we access the crossroads, we usually experience it as a field of stars."

Grace felt the blood drain out of her face. A field of stars. Last night, she'd soared out of herself and into a darkness peppered with stars. Floating there, she'd felt free and yet tethered to her body, alone and yet surrounded by…something. No fear. Just a sense of completeness.

"You've seen it," David said. "You remember."

"I saw it once, recently." The blood rushed back into her face, no doubt turning her cheeks a cherry red, as she remembered what they'd been doing at the time she experienced the crossroads. "Um, uh, I didn't realize what it was at the time."

He smiled as if he knew exactly when she'd spun out of her body and into the crossroads. Her blush grew hotter, until she wanted to splash water on her face.

Clearing her throat, she said, "If it looks like a star field, then why do you call it the crossroads?"

"Because when you're inside it, if you concentrate you can resolve the field of stars into a network of bright dots linked by multicolored strands. Sort of like a map."

She didn't know what to say to that, so she kept quiet.

"The crossroads is like a network of interconnecting highways," he continued, "but they're lined with chain-link fencing. You can see there's more out there, but you can't get to it. The story goes that only someone with the Golden Power can veer off the crossroads into the uncharted territory beyond, where everything that is known, was known, or will be known exists simultaneously."

She frowned. "What does that mean?"

"The Golden Power grants omniscience."

The thoughts had stopped bubbling in her mind. In fact, her brain had gone utterly blank.

"Anyone capable of accessing that power," David said, "would know everything—past, present, and future. Can you imagine what someone like our mystery traveler would do with that knowledge?"

"I'd rather not imagine it."

A door slammed shut.

Glancing backward, Grace saw Earl had closed the restroom door and was heading back toward the checkout counter. When she looked back at David, she noticed the redness in his eyes. Strange how an incorporeal man could look so physically drained.

"You should go," she told him. "Rest up."

He gave her a pained look. "Not yet."

David said nothing as she yanked the flash drive out of the computer, tucking the little stick into her jeans pocket. She carried the laptop back to the counter, handed it to Earl, and thanked him for letting her use the computer. Of course, she'd paid him for the privilege, so it wasn't like he'd loaned it to her out of sheer kindness. But she felt bad about the restroom debacle. An exuberant thank-you seemed only polite under the circumstances.

Earl looked wary as he shook her hand. Maybe she'd gone a little overboard with the exuberance. There was a fine line between atonement and overcompensation.

When she glanced back at the table where she'd sat a moment earlier, David was gone. Her exuberance, feigned as it was, deflated. She trudged out to the car and settled in for the fifty-mile drive to wherever. Sean's directions, scrawled in dust, had simply told her to find Dry Lake Road and look for a dirt road on the left. He'd also warned her about "eyes and ears everywhere." He must've meant the invisible perimeter, delineated with sensors, that David mentioned.

How she'd get past the sensors, she didn't know. David was far too weak to help her now.

"You want to get inside the facility."

She yelped at the sound of his voice. Gasping, struggling to regain her composure, she cast an annoyed look at him. "Must you always do that?"

"Apparently."

He still looked weak and tired, almost sick. She reached out for him but her hand passed right through his illusory form. Fearing the answer, she asked, "Can you die from using too much psychic energy?"

"Probably." He managed a wan smile. "But don't worry, I'm not there yet."

"That might be more convincing if you didn't look like—" Her throat constricted, choking off the words. Tears threatened to spill from her eyes. She swallowed hard, blinked away the moisture, and steeled her voice. "I need you alive, so don't go dying on me."

"I need you alive too, but I've given up on keeping you away from the facility."

"Good."

"I know I can't stop you. So listen."

She let silence be her response.

"Dry Lake Road," he said, "is fifty miles the other side of town. Turn left there, drive several more miles, and look for a black mailbox at the end of a dirt road. Follow that road to an arroyo. If you sit there for thirty seconds, the weight of your car will trigger a device that raises a keypad from a pole in the ground." He closed his eyes, slumping forward. "Punch in the number 43709. Wait five seconds *exactly*. Then type in 000."

"Then what happens?"

His image rippled and winked out. Cold air blasted through the car, lashing her hair across her face. The air burst out of her lungs in one explosive gasp. She tried inhaling but her muscles froze, and it felt like someone was sucking the air out of her body through a straw. She huddled in the driver's seat, her mouth open so far her jaw ached. Her ears rang. Darkness invaded her vision.

Her ears popped.

She gulped air. Her vision cleared and her ears stopped ringing. She pulled in breath after breath, until her breathing normalized. The same thing had happened to her when the mystery traveler attacked her in her old car, the one the traveler had totaled. It must've had something to do with the confined space.

Digging in her purse, she found a scrap of paper—an old gas receipt was all she could find—and a pen. She jotted down the numbers David had told her. These days, she didn't trust her memory.

Driving straight into town, she took a detour off the main highway to find the post office. A sign posted on the main road had alerted her to the post office's location, two blocks off the highway. She pulled into one of three angled parking spaces in front of the small, dilapidated wood building. A faded sign identified the structure as the United States Postal Service of Reston, California. Inside the little building, she found a table loaded up with postal supplies and pens chained to the tabletop. She chose a priority mail envelope, tucked the flash drive inside it, and sealed the adhesive flap. Next, she scrawled her name and address in the appropriate box on the envelope. A few minutes later, she'd bought postage for the slim package and sent it on its way.

The flash drive would be safe for a few days. By the time it arrived at her home in Texas, she'd either have dealt with her enemies or she'd be dead. The notion of her own demise no longer frightened her, which seemed bizarre and wrong and yet somehow necessary. She had no time to waste on pondering the implications of her newfound equanimity.

Back in the car, she found the highway again and headed out into the desert. When she spotted the sign for Dry Lake Road, she swung left onto the two-lane strip of blacktop. The paving soon transitioned into gravel. Twenty minutes passed before she saw the black, unmarked mailbox and veered left onto the nameless road. After a few more miles, the gravel segued into a two-track dirt path. The car jounced over potholes and rocks. Dust plumed up behind the car, obscuring her backward view. A tumbleweed rolled across the track in front of the car. In the fading daylight, she spotted Joshua trees dotting the barren landscape, and a humpbacked butte rose up in the distance, seeming farther away than the moon.

A person could get lost and die out here. Nobody would find the body for weeks or months, if ever. She pushed the thought out of her mind. No use dwelling on worst-case scenarios.

The car's headlights powered on automatically, detecting the waning daylight. Night seemed to fall swiftly as she drove at what felt like a snail's pace, hindered by the bumpy road and her fear of driving straight off the edge of the arroyo David had mentioned. Up ahead, a tall and narrow shape jutted up from the ground.

She stomped on the brake just as the headlights swept across the object. It was a sign. Mounted on a metal pole, the dusty white sign offered a warning in thick black letters.

"PRIVATE PROPERTY. Trespassers will be prosecuted. Deadly force authorized."

Oh yeah. This was the right road.

She hit the gas pedal and the car sprang forward, jolting over a series of potholes. The headlights revealed nothing except the narrow two-track ahead of the car and the vast, empty desert surrounding the road. Small eyes in the brush reflected the headlights. The darkness was complete now, oppressive and deep as outer space. To the right, far in the distance, a bluish-white light glimmered.

Despite the warm air flowing from the vents, goose bumps cropped up on her arms and neck.

Get a grip, she told herself. *It's just wildlife.* Christ, she'd gotten paranoid living in the city. She hadn't seen wildlife in so long she freaked out over it.

But that flash off to the right...

She gripped the steering wheel tighter. She'd sailed right past the point of no return a long time ago.

Ahead, the road fell away into blackness. A stream, she might have thought, if she weren't in the center of hell. In the desert, thunderstorms unleashed rivers in the form of flash floods, carving out channels that stood dry otherwise.

The dark patch loomed nearer.

Shadows.

She jammed her foot on the brake. The tires slid, fishtailed, and gripped the road once more. The car lurched to a stop, thrusting her hard against the seat belt. Dust erupted around the car. Unhooking the seat belt, she flung the door open and hopped out. Leaving the door ajar, she tiptoed toward the front bumper. The headlights illuminated the obstacle.

Inches from the front tires, the earth dropped away. An arroyo cleaved the desert, its walls steep and tall, its basin wide and littered with small cactuses. In the darkness, she could barely make out the other side of the arroyo. It stretched farther across than the headlight beams could penetrate.

Back in the car, she slammed the door shut. Had thirty seconds elapsed yet? Nothing had happened while she examined the arroyo. David's captors might've changed the protocol to stop her from getting into the facility this way.

She rolled down the window to peer down at the ground. Nothing. Retracting her head, she drummed her fingers on the window frame.

A noise erupted nearby, a cross between rustling leaves and mechanical humming.

She poked her head out the window, squinting down at the ground.

A patch of dirt shifted. Sand poured away as a pole emerged from the ground. The pole, metal and four inches wide, rose to a height that placed its top at her eye level. A panel slid open, revealing a cavity inside the pole. The opening housed a numbered keypad, just as David had told her. Above the keypad, an LCD screen stared at her.

A phrase blinked on the screen: "Enter access code."

Retrieving from her purse the receipt on which she had scribbled the numbers David dictated, she leaned out the window and punched in the code. Then she counted off the seconds—one-one-thousand, two-one-thousand, three-one-thousand. At the precise instant she got to five, she punched in the last three digits.

The pole retreated into the sand. The earth ahead of the car groaned. Metal clanged. The ground trembled. Two halves of a bridge rose up from the walls of the arroyo, joining at the center. Struts, unfolding beneath the bridge, braced the structure.

It must be a mirage. Any second the wind would blow away the illusion.

A gust buffeted the car. Clouds of dust curled up from the depths of the arroyo. The dust swirled around and over the bridge.

She glanced away. When she looked back, the bridge still spanned the arroyo.

All right then.

Easing her foot down on the gas pedal, she steered the car toward the arroyo. The rear tires cleared the bridge's lip with a thunk. She pressed the gas pedal harder and the car sprang forward, clearing the opposite side of the bridge with a smaller thunk.

She decelerated. Taking the bridge in one rush had robbed her of the time for fretting over its construction and the fact that it arose from the sand and God only knew how long it had lain there, unused, rusting, rotting.

A groaning sound drew her attention to the rearview mirror. She watched the reflected image of the bridge duck below the level of the road. Dust puffed up from the arroyo.

If she turned around, would the bridge rise up again to grant her passage out?

Didn't matter now. She was not turning back.

The road stretched out into the vast desert. Overhead, the first stars twinkled in the ever-deepening gloom of the night. Mountains hid behind a veil of haze, maybe fog or a far-away dust storm. If she followed this road until it ended, would her journey end in some magical kingdom of fairies and trolls and knights on white steeds?

She pictured David perched atop a white horse, clad in armor, wielding a gleaming sword.

The car hit a pothole. Her teeth snapped together and the vision left her.

Pow!

The car shimmied. The steering wheel trembled faintly. She gripped it tighter, glancing in all the mirrors to find the source of the explosive noise. It was too dark, though, and the headlights' glow couldn't illuminate the car's rear, where the sound had originated.

The steering wheel trembled harder. The vibrations bled into her hands, triggering pain in her wrist and forearm. She braked and eased the car to a stop.

A sick feeling settled over her as she swung the door open and stepped outside. Even in the gloom, she spotted the problem right away. The left rear tire had blown out. Oh great.

A chill washed through her. Blown out—or shot out?

Turning in a circle, she squinted into the night. The bluish-white light she'd seen before had divided into two parallel lights that bobbled in the distance, from the direction of the arroyo, coming closer with each second she stood there gaping at the shredded tire. A purring, faint and intermittent, escalated into grumbling.

She leaped back into the car, twisted the key in the ignition, and barely waited for the engine to catch before slamming her foot down on the accelerator. Damn the blown tire. She had bigger problems than the damage she might do to the wheel.

The car heaved forward. The steering wheel vibrated hard beneath her hands. She gripped it as tight as she could, fighting to keep the car aimed down the two-track.

Pow!

The right rear tire.

Christ, she couldn't hold the steering wheel. The car angled off the road, bounced over a small cactus, and bogged down in a conglomeration of brush. The engine sputtered and died.

Oh shit.

The vehicle jouncing down the road toward her enlarged until she recognized the shape as a Jeep Cherokee, black with tinted windows. She couldn't tell how many people hid inside the Jeep.

Or how many guns they carried.

If she ran, they'd catch her. If she crouched in the dirt, they would see her. They had spotted her already, or they wouldn't have raced straight for her.

The Jeep bounced over the pothole she'd hit a few minutes ago.

She grabbed her purse and leaped out of the car, fleeing down the two-track. Behind her, the Jeep swerved around the rear end of her car, which stuck out into the road. The Jeep's tires slipped in the sand. The vehicle shimmied. The tires gripped, and the Jeep rocketed after her.

Her legs cramped. The soles of her feet burned as if she ran barefoot across hot coals. She needed a hideaway. She needed a machine gun.

The Jeep, swerving off the track, sped across the rough desert to circle around in front of her. A cloud of dust enveloped her. She choked, coughed, blinked. Tears blurred her vision. Somewhere within the cloud, tires spun in the sand, whirring and kicking up bits of earth. A pebble smacked her in the cheek.

She froze. The dust cleared.

The Jeep had stopped twenty feet ahead, cross-wise on the track. The doors were flung open. Half a dozen men in black commando outfits, their faces covered by helmets, poured out of the Jeep. They toted guns of varying sizes. Their boots clomped on the dirt.

She thought about going for her gun, but every one of theirs dwarfed hers, and she suspected their weapons were automatics too. They could perforate her with a volley of bullets before she even got off one shot.

Her thoughts came fast and jumbled. She had no bright ideas, no plans, no goddamn talent for subterfuge. When the commandos stomped past the Jeep's fender, she bolted. A snake hissed, its head snapping up from the dirt. She leaped over the snake, tripped on brush, stumbled forward, and hit the sand face-first.

Footfalls pounded behind her. Men shouted.

Her cheek stung. She pushed up onto her hands. Her face had side-swiped a cactus. A few needles had embedded themselves in her cheek.

The snake rattled nearby. One of the men shouted a curse.

Tearing the needles from her cheek, she sprang to her feet and ran. Boots clomped in the sand behind her. Men shouted to each other. The voices issued from everywhere as they closed in on her from all sides.

She pulled the gun out of her purse.

A commando jumped from behind a Joshua tree. As his feet landed squarely in the sand, he leveled his gun at her. She swung the gun up and pulled the trigger. He ducked behind the tree. A branch exploded. She swerved left.

A shot exploded.

An object hit her from behind, too large for a bullet, knocking her legs out from under her. The commando wrenched her onto her feet. Twisting her arms behind her back, he clamped one hand around her wrists to pull her close against him. His helmet pressed against her face.

"Gotcha," he growled. Then to his buddies, he shouted, "Over here."

She could claw him, kick him, bite him, get away somehow. Then what? He had five well-armed buddies. They could call in reinforcements. She might run until her muscles gave out on her, thirst overcame her, or she passed out in the sand. They could wait inside their air-conditioned Jeep, sipping Perrier and playing bridge, until then. She would have no energy leftover for escape. Better to give up now.

Hell no, her instincts screamed. She must fight the bastards with every watt of energy inside her.

The commando twisted to face his buddies, dragging her with him. The others were still thirty yards away. Her gun had landed a few feet away, its muzzle buried in the sand.

She wriggled in his grip.

The commando's hand tightened into a steel clamp around her wrists. She bit her tongue and grunted. The tang of blood dispersed through her mouth. He tugged her wrists. Pain ricocheted between her shoulder blades. She'd had enough of strangers trying to kill her, chasing her across the country, demanding she give them things she didn't have and tell them things she didn't know, murdering anyone who helped her. They showed no remorse, no hesitation. Their cruelty knew no limits.

Enough.

She kicked at his legs. When her heel connected with his shin, he bellowed, his grip loosening. She wrenched her wrists from his grasp. Clenching her teeth against the pain in her shoulders, she whirled toward him and rammed her knee into his groin. His back arched as a grunt burst out of him, but he snatched at her anyway. She kneed him again, then slugged him in the gut.

Doubling over, he dropped onto his knees.

She grabbed her gun and bolted.

"Get her!" the commando roared.

More shouts erupted behind her. Gunfire detonated. Sand plumed upward like tiny volcanoes. Small cactuses exploded. Something buzzed past her head. Her legs pumped as fast as they could, but she knew she couldn't go much farther. Ducking into a stand of Joshua trees, she paused long enough to deduce she had no options, as usual. No houses nearby, no cars she could conveniently steal, as if she had a clue how to steal anything. Should've apprenticed with a master criminal instead of attending college.

The shots discharged closer, louder. Leaving the shelter of the Joshua trees, she sprinted across the wasteland, from nowhere to nowhere. No one to save her now. Nothing to do to save herself.

She kept running. Her leg muscles burned. Her chest ached. Her breaths came fast and hard.

The Jeep's engine revved.

Risking a glance backward, she saw the Jeep rocketing after her.

Then the ground dropped away beneath her, and she sailed into the void.

Chapter Twenty-Three

Her feet hit the bottom. Her legs crumpled, and she tumbled backward. Her head struck a hard surface—the arroyo wall, she realized, as phantom lights danced in her vision. She'd fallen into another arroyo, or maybe an offshoot of the one that blocked the road.

A figure leaped into the arroyo from above her head. The commando landed directly in front of her, spun around, and thrust his gun in her face. She lurched sideways to squeeze around him. A starburst of pain behind her eyes stopped her mid step. She fought back a retch.

The commando seized both her wrists in one massive hand. Threads of pain shot up her arms into her shoulders.

Not like this, they could not take her like this, so easily, so quickly. *Fight, dammit, give them hell.* She couldn't. Her body felt as limp as towels linked together with string. Her tongue was parched and bloody. She breathed hard, fast, unable to swallow enough oxygen. The first sharp pain of a migraine blossomed behind her eyes. A twinge in her neck stiffened into the sensation of a steel rod jammed up her neck and straight into her brain.

She needed help. God, she hated admitting it, but she could no longer deny the truth. She needed somebody somewhere to somehow help her. No one was around. Just a battalion of commandos operating on orders to capture her—dead or alive, she suspected.

Anybody. Anywhere. Somehow.

A bright light popped on, aimed straight at her face. A flashlight.

The pain behind her eyes burst into a full-fledged migraine. The light hit her with a physical force, driving the pain deep into her brain. The sound of her own breathing hurt. Her stomach heaved, and she gulped back her gorge.

The commando spoke. His words pierced her brain, sharp as needles, though she couldn't comprehend the meaning. She squeezed her eyes shut. *Please, anybody, help me.* No, not just anybody. His name wisped through her as a fleeting thought and she grabbed it, holding onto it like a mental life preserver.

David, help me. I need you.

The migraine bulldozed all thoughts from her mind. She pressed her hands against her temples. The commando yelled. Calling his friends, she realized between waves of dizziness.

David, please.

He came. She sensed his presence, though she couldn't open her eyes. The flashlight beam was too bright, the pain too intense. Despite bouncing on the waves of nausea and dizziness, struggling to stay afloat, she felt better. Safer.

The commando grunted. Feet scuffled. Sand sprayed her face.

Silence.

Voices shouted above and behind her. The other commandos.

Arms cradled her body and lifted her. She chanced opening an eyelid a sliver. David carried her down the arroyo, his face stern, his arms strong beneath her. He was holding something in his left hand, an object that bumped against her every so often. She shut her eyes as he broke into a trot. Rather than exacerbating her symptoms, the bobbing motion of his gait soothed her. The glow from the flashlight weakened and faded into blackness. A chilly breeze wafted over them, and she huddled closer against David, absorbing the warmth of his body. The pain in her head ebbed as a tide of weariness swept into her.

David halted.

Commandos shouted, their voices distant.

"Where is she?" one asked.

"I dunno," another answered. "Didn't you see?"

"She couldn't have disappeared."

"Look! Donaldson's down there."

"Check him out...we'll go this..."

The voices diminished until she could no longer distinguish the words. The grumbling of the Jeep's engine grew fainter.

The migraine was almost gone now, vanishing in record time. Yet even when she'd been engulfed in the pain, she'd felt safer than she should have, safer than logic allowed. Commandos hunted for her. They would find her and, when they did, they would kill her. If they didn't, then whoever had sent them would. It didn't bother her. The intense weariness, an aftereffect of the migraine, skewed her thoughts. She wasn't thinking clearly. She had trouble thinking at all.

David bent his head down beside hers. "You're safe."

Too exhausted to speak, she pressed her face against his chest, curling her fingers around the neck of his T-shirt.

No more shouting. No footsteps. No engine noises. The commandos were out of earshot, maybe even gone altogether, having given up the search. She harbored no illusions that they'd give up permanently. They would be back. Soon. With a lot more men.

David ducked his head out into the arroyo. Empty. Carrying Grace, he knew he could never outrun the guards. Carrying her while clutching the guard's helmet and trying not to trip in a hole or smack into a big rock was even harder. A crack in the arroyo wall, four feet deep and three feet wide, had offered refuge. Their concealment was aided by a large cactus growing at the apex of the arroyo wall, which shaded the fissure. Although the commandos had scanned the arroyo visually, the crack was not obvious, especially in the dark. The cactus cast a long shadow on the arroyo wall so that, in a quick glance, the crack looked like a part of the shadows, not a fracture in the wall.

He knew this landscape the way he knew his own mind. Months of exploring the vicinity of the facility, psychically, had given him an intimate knowledge of every slope and gully, every rock outcropping and copse of Joshua trees. He knew the locations of three abandoned homes, nothing more than shacks now, and the path of every arroyo within fifty square miles. His travels had acquainted him with the creatures that inhabited the desert, both human and animal. No one knew this area better.

Except, perhaps, the architects who had built the facility.

Grace clutched his shirt tighter and moaned.

The bastards had hurt her. He didn't know how, couldn't see a wound or a mark, but he knew they had done this to her. Pain had possessed her body like a parasite, eating away at her strength, and he had no idea what to do for her, if anything could alleviate the pain. She seemed unable to speak.

She needed a doctor. He couldn't trust anyone in Reston. He wasn't sure she'd make it to the next town, over a hundred miles away, even if he conjured a car and drove two-hundred miles an hour the whole way. Her face had paled. A bead of blood formed on her lip where she'd bitten it. Scratches drew red lines across her cheek.

Dammit, help her. Don't just stand here.

The arroyo snaked eastward about two hundred feet, then forked northeast and southwest. At the fork, the walls sloped at a more oblique angle and animals had worn a path up the slope at that spot. He could at least get them out of the arroyo there. After that, he knew exactly where to take them. The route ran through his mind, a series of lines on a mental map, leading toward the one safe place he knew.

He lunged out of the fissure.

Grace huddled in his arms, her body limp, as he traversed the arroyo and found the trail up the slope. Once he'd climbed out of the arroyo, he paused to check her pulse. It beat strong and steady against his finger. Her breathing was slow and shallow. She seemed to be sleeping, rather than unconscious. He relaxed a little. Rest would do her good.

While the sun dipped ever closer to the mountains, David strode across the desert toward a house he couldn't be sure still stood. He hadn't seen the place in six months.

His arms quivered. Sweat trickled down his brow. Even in a manifestation, he could exhaust himself, and he was no good to Grace if couldn't walk. Besides, he might grow so tired he'd snap back to the facility, back to a locked room miles from her. He would not abandon her.

Not after what she'd sacrificed to get him here.

He halted in an area populated by rocks. He dropped the helmet. Kicking aside some of the rocks, he cleared a spot and lowered Grace onto the sand. She didn't stir. God, she looked weak. Vulnerable. If they found her like this, she couldn't defend herself. Tesler might haul him back to the facility at any moment by administering drugs or an electric shock to break the connection. He must see her through whatever injury or illness had seized her, because she would never survive alone, not like this.

She opened her eyes partway. Red veins webbed the whites of her eyes. She sniffled as her gaze settled on his face. He wanted to hold her, but feared he'd cause her more pain. So instead, he smoothed the hair away from her face.

She spoke, her voice rough. "It's over."

She's dying. He bent over her, his gut wrenching into knots. "What happened?"

"Migraine. It's going away, though."

The tension flooded out of him in a long sigh. She had meant the migraine was over. He shook his head and almost laughed. She wasn't dying. Though the migraine had weakened her, she would recover. In fact, she looked much better already. Her cheeks showed a slight pinkness, rather than the frightening pallor he'd seen when he found her in the arroyo.

"I'm okay," she said.

Sitting down beside her, he managed a weak smile as he stroked her hair. "I was afraid they'd hurt you."

He slid his hand down to her cheek—the one without scratches on it.

She scrunched her face into a confused expression. "How are you here? I thought you were too weak to manifest."

"I was," he said, taking her hand in his. "You gave me some of your energy. That's probably what caused your migraine."

"What?"

"You wanted me here, and you made it happen." He squeezed her hand gently. "Now be quiet and rest. We still have a ways to go."

Grace shivered. The chill of night had settled over the desert.

In one motion, he scooped her into his arms and rose. As he started down the path outlined in his mind, she looped her arms around his neck. Whatever happened, they would deal with it together.

Whether she liked it or not.

Sizzle. Crackle. Grace opened her eyes. The migraine had ended. She was tired, weak, hungry, and thirsty, but no longer in pain. She lay on her side, on the floor, where David had set her down…how long ago? The memory seemed more like a half-remembered dream.

The wood felt rough and cold against her skin. A draft swirled over her and she shivered. Something thunked. A door closing, she thought, unable to muster the energy to lift her head and look. The draft ceased. Across the room, a fire burned inside an old fireplace. Two logs crackled. Flames licked upward from the logs.

A figure passed in front of her. She pushed up into a sitting position, supporting her body with her arms.

David kneeled by the fire. He held twigs and broken boards under one arm and, piece by piece, tossed them into the fire. She watched him stoke the blaze with a five-foot metal fence post. He had carried her here and started a fire. He was taking care of her. No one had done that for her in a long time.

He turned toward her and sat down, patting the floor beside him. "It's warmer over here."

She scuttled toward the fireplace. Sitting several feet from him, legs crossed under her, she studied the fire. Orange and yellow flames darted up from within the pile of wood, flickering and dancing.

David scooted closer to her and clasped her hand in both of his. She turned sideways to rest her head on his shoulder. He felt so solid, so real, that she had forgotten what he was—an illusion. Sure, he existed, in a building out there in the desert, but he was not really with her, not really touching her hand, not really giving her a look of earnest concern.

His face was haggard, his lips pale. As he exhaled, he let his shoulders sag. She shifted her attention to his hand, cupped over hers. It looked real. Everything looked the opposite of how it was these days. Her life looked normal. People looked like people, even the ones she now knew were not people, but instead humanoid mirages.

She nudged David's hand with one finger. His flesh gave under the pressure, until her fingertip bumped the bone. His skin felt warm and pliable, the bone firm, the muscles taut when flexed and soft when relaxed. Beneath her finger, she detected the coarseness of hair, the texture of skin, and upon pressing, the surge of blood flowing through veins. David's explanations did nothing to subdue her confusion or the surreality of the situation.

She scraped her fingernail lightly across his hand. "Can you feel this?"

"I feel everything." He reached up with his free hand to lift her chin, bringing their gazes into alignment. "You ought to know that after last night."

She felt like curling up in his arms again, feeling his warmth surround and infuse her.

His gaze was intent. She looked away, focusing on the fireplace, at the embers glowing beneath the half-consumed wood.

"When you left me in the car," she said, "there was wind and pressure. It made my ears pop. What was that?"

Releasing her hand, he slipped his arm around her shoulders. "Breaking the connection too abruptly can cause a sudden expulsion of energy. It's often experienced as a localized shift in air pressure. Inside a confined space, it's more noticeable. We call it backfire."

"Right." She'd pretend that made sense, because if he offered more details her head might implode. "You said I gave you energy."

"Yes."

"How?"

He shrugged and tried to laugh, but coughed instead. "I don't know how you do it. I can't do it, and neither can anyone else I've met."

The firelight no longer lit his face. Now, it seemed to draw the energy out of his body as fuel for its flames.

"Are you all right?" she asked.

"I will be. The shot of energy you gave me is almost gone, though."

"Maybe I could give you more."

"No." His expression hardened to match the tone of his voice. "It's too dangerous."

She said nothing. Her gut told her the same thing, but she didn't like seeing him weak and virtually defenseless.

"You should go," she said.

"I don't like leaving you alone."

"I'm used to it."

"They'll find you. One against a dozen, maybe more." He brushed his thumb across her cheek. "Not good odds."

"Odds can be beaten."

He didn't scowl, though she expected he would. Instead, he turned his head to study the fire, his expression not blank, but simply inscrutable as he said, "You're inside the perimeter now. If you try to leave, they'll find you. If you stay in this house too long, they'll find you. You might reach the facility, and I might be able to help you get inside it, but—" He looked at her, and this time he did scowl. "What do you hope to accomplish there?"

She lifted one shoulder in a lazy shrug. "Not sure. I'm trusting my instincts here, and they tell me the answers I need are inside that facility."

"We've already established I can't stop you." He stared down at the floor, tapping one fingernail on the scuffed wood. "I know the grounds around the facility. Sean knows the interior better than anyone except the engineers and architects who built it. He's hiding inside the facility now, but I can find him and get his help in sneaking you inside."

"Thank you."

Reaching into his back pocket, he brought out a yellowed and wrinkled piece of paper that was folded in quarters. As he unfolded the sheet, he held it out to her. "I found a pen in your purse and an ancient sheet of paper wadded up in the corner there." He pointed over his shoulder. "So I drew you a map."

She took the paper and ran a fingertip over the black ink lines drawn on it. One zigzagging line ducked between and around shapes and words he'd scrawled across the page. Landmarks, she realized, and explanatory phrases to guide her.

"It isn't the most direct route," he told her, "because the direct route is too exposed. This way will take a little longer, but it should get you there with the least risk of being spotted."

She noticed he didn't say zero risk, just less risk. Complete safety no longer existed for her.

"Your gun is in your purse," he said. "I picked it up back in the arroyo."

"Thanks."

Bending sideways and leaning backward, he retrieved an object from the shadows behind him. When he sat straight again, he offered her the object. It was a full-face helmet like the ones the commandos wore.

"Take this," he said, thrusting the helmet at her. "Traveling at night is difficult, and the facility's security force isn't the only danger out there. If you step on a rattlesnake or run into coyotes..." He grasped her right hand and folded her fingers around the helmet's bottom rim. "The helmets have built-in night vision capability."

She accepted the helmet. He gestured for her to put it on, and she did. Darkness swallowed her.

"In daylight, the visor acts as sunglasses," David said, his voice coming through clearly, if a bit softer. "This button turns on the night vision."

He guided her finger to a switch on the bottom rim. She flicked it.

The world transformed into shades of green. The fire was blinding on the night vision screen in front of her eyes, and she swiveled her head to look into the darker recesses of the room. She made out the individual boards that formed the walls, the outlines of the window frames, and even a Joshua tree that stood maybe twenty feet beyond the window.

Shutting off the night vision, she removed the helmet. "Thank you."

"Stop thanking me," he muttered. Then he pressed his lips to hers in a brief, tender kiss. "Just be careful."

And he was gone.

A breeze whistled through the old house. The floorboards creaked. The windows rattled. Inside the fireplace, flames whipped back and forth, dwindling until only the embers remained.

The storm ended in a flurry of dust. Flames burst up from the embers in the fireplace.

David had broken the connection more carefully this time, or else the room was big enough to dampen the backfire.

She was alone. Again.

"Move and I'll split your head open. Don't care if you are female."

The maw of a shotgun gaped at her, nearly kissing her nose. A man loomed above her, shadows masking his features. A faint grumbling issued from behind him, and a bright light from outside silhouetted him from behind. The front door hung wide open.

Still groggy from sleep, since she had woken up seconds earlier, Grace struggled to make sense of the images. Gun. Man. Light. She had fallen asleep in front of the fire, that she remembered.

The man gesticulated with the gun. "You're trespassing. Just 'cause I don't live here, don't mean you can break in. "

"I thought the house was abandoned."

"Yeah. But I still own it."

Grace yawned. She couldn't help it. Her brain needed oxygen. The landlord, however, took her action the wrong way.

He jammed the gun into her forehead. "I said don't move."

"It was a yawn, not an act of war." To hell with this. She slapped the gun away, pushing onto her knees. "My car broke down. I was lost, so I started walking and came to this place. Since it looked abandoned, I decided to sleep here. Sorry I offended you."

She hopped onto her feet.

He swung the gun toward her. The barrel bumped her chest. "How'd you find me?"

"I told you, I got lost."

"Carlos sent you, didn't he?"

"I don't know any Carlos. I got lost."

"Sure." He shuffled backward. "The stuff better be here. If it's not, your pretty little face is gonna wallpaper this room."

Drugs. The word popped into her mind as the man kneeled, keeping the shotgun sighted on her head, and pried one board loose from the floor, then another. He dragged an olive-green canvas bag out of the hole and plopped it on the floor. She waited for an opening to run, but he kept the gun pointed at her. Though his aim varied by a few inches, he wouldn't need a straight line at her head for the shot to kill her. If the blast hit her shoulder or her chest, she'd probably die all the same.

The commando helmet lay near her feet. Her gun was inside her purse, which also lay nearby. To grab either, she'd need to duck way too close to the shotgun's muzzle.

The man unzipped the olive-green bag. She glimpsed white bricks wrapped in plastic. Duct tape secured each package. Cocaine. Maybe heroine. She'd seen enough cop shows to recognize the stuff.

How did this creep get inside the facility's perimeter?

There were no fences. Anyone could walk across the perimeter, ignoring the warning signs. The sensors would detect the intrusion, however, and commandos would be dispatched.

Everything inside her went cold. The commandos had shown up quickly when she breached the perimeter.

Out the window, through the grime encrusting the glass, she saw a vehicle with its headlights blazing. The grumbling she'd heard was the engine idling. Her heartbeat quickened.

"Lucky for you," the man said, zipping the bag and dropping it into the hole, "it's still here."

"I told you, I just got lost."

"What were you doing out here in hell's back forty? You know this whole blasted desert is owned by some nasty corporate types."

"I—" She couldn't think of a good lie. She couldn't think of a *bad* one either.

With his foot, he maneuvered the floorboards back into place. They snapped into position.

She felt the earth liquefying beneath her, in a metaphorical sense, at least so far. If she moved too quickly, she'd plunge into the mire. If she waited too long, it would swallow her. Neither option appealed to her.

"It's silly," she said. "I was looking for UFOs. Took a wrong turn and got lost."

"That's the worst-smelling load of bat guano I ever heard. Carlos, you scumbag!"

The gun trembled in his hand. His trigger finger wobbled.

She dove sideways just as he jerked the trigger. The shot detonated with deafening force. Wood splintered and sprayed across the room. Bricks around the fireplace crumbled.

The man bellowed a wordless cry of rage and anguish.

Grace snatched up the helmet and her purse, scrambling for the door.

Another shot boomed behind her. The door frame exploded into projectile slivers.

She crawled out the door on all fours.

Footsteps crashed behind her. She yanked the gun out of her purse, rolled onto her back, and aimed the gun at the doorway.

The man stomped into the opening, shotgun leveled at her head.

She pulled the trigger.

As the shot resounded in the air, the man jerked, seemed to freeze for a split second, and then tumbled backward to hit the floor with a concussion that shook the cracked glass in the window.

Had she killed him?

The thought triggered a swell of nausea, and she rolled onto her side, afraid she might vomit. The nausea passed in a few seconds, though, leaving her trembling and sheathed in a cold sweat.

She had to make sure he was...not a threat anymore.

Still gripping her gun, she pushed onto her knees and finally clambered to her feet. The man lay motionless just inside the threshold. On tiptoes, she approached the doorway.

His eyes were open. Blank. Sightless. Dead.

She'd killed a man. He was a drug dealer. How many lives had he taken, through murder or from the drugs he peddled? He had tried to kill her, after all. She did nothing more than defend her life.

Whirling around, she sprinted for the vehicle, a black Land Rover. She flung the door open and jumped inside, tossing her purse and the helmet onto the passenger seat. Maybe she wouldn't need the helmet after all. Plucking David's map out of her purse, she set it on seat beside the bag. She slammed the gear shift lever into reverse.

Easing her foot down on the accelerator, she turned the Rover around to head in the direction indicated on David's map. Soon, the dark outline of the old house vanished from sight in the rearview mirror.

This was a little too easy.

The thought niggled at her as the Rover bounced over the terrain. She had to ignore the concern, because getting to the facility as quickly as possible was the top priority. The drug dealer had undoubtedly triggered the perimeter sensors, drawing a horde of commandos who were swarming the old house at this moment. The Rover left tire tracks, which the commandos could follow.

Hell.

She would drive the Rover to within easy walking distance of the facility, and then abandon it to finish her journey on foot. It seemed the best, and fastest, plan.

Less risk, not zero risk.

She relaxed into the seat. The supple leather cradled her body. The vents bathed her feet in warm air that leeched the chill out of her flesh. The radio, its volume turned down, murmured classical music. Between the front seats, a cell phone sat in its cradle. The fuel gage registered three-quarters of a tank. Attached to the dashboard, a GPS unit showed the car's position as a mobile dot superimposed over a satellite image of the desert.

Stopping the car, she took a couple minutes to compare David's map to the GPS display. As she set off again, she felt more confident in her ability to find her way. The universe had granted her a measure of good luck, at last. Angering a drug dealer and being forced to shoot him hardly counted as good luck, but his leaving the Rover idling did. Thank heavens. She needed a break almost as much as she needed dinner.

The Rover bumped over a rut. Her buttocks lifted off the seat, but she held onto the steering wheel, keeping the vehicle on course.

The phone rang.

Her grip on the steering wheel loosened, and the Rover swerved toward a Joshua tree. She jerked the wheel to avoid the tree, stomped on the brake, and gasped as the car skidded to a stop.

The cell phone, cupped in its cradle, rang a second time.

She picked up the phone but did not answer the call. The phone's LCD screen said "caller unknown." While the phone rang a third and fourth time, she debated answering the call. No way in hell, she decided. It might be Carlos, and she had a feeling she did not want to chat with him.

The phone rang once more and stopped.

Grace stared at the LCD screen. Her heart was beating so fast she could barely catch her breath.

The phone made a bloop-bloop sound. "New text message," it announced on the screen.

Biting her lip, she tapped the screen to open the message. It contained three words: "I see you."

Could he really see her?

The Rover's engine died. She twisted the key in the ignition. Nothing. The door locks clunked into position. She yanked on the handle. Locked. She pressed the button that lowered the windows. Nothing. The phone rang. She reached for it, but then hesitated with her hand resting on the device. It rang two, three, four times.

She answered.

On the other end of the call, a man snarled. "You're mine."

"Excuse me?"

"I wasn't dead. Did you see any blood, lady?"

She flashed back to the man lying flat on his back, eyes open but sightless.

At least, she'd thought they were sightless. Dead. Had she seen blood? In the murky conditions, she couldn't say for sure. The voice on the phone sure sounded like the same drug dealer.

Through the phone connection, the man snarled, "Think you can steal my car and get off scot-free? Think again." He paused. "Tell Carlos I'm onto him."

"I don't know any Carlos." The desperation in her voice surprised her, though she couldn't imagine why. She was desperate. "You can have your car. Just let me go."

"Uh-uh, lady. I'm comin' to punish you good."

"How? I've got your car."

"You ain't gone far and I've got a GPS app on my backup phone that lets me track the car from anywhere." He sniggered. "You can't do nothing except wait for me, missy. You're trapped."

He hung up.

You're trapped. Like hell. She scrambled into the backseat headfirst, dragging her body after her as glanced around in search of anything that might help her escape the vehicle. When she saw nothing, she scaled the backseat too, landing in the rear cargo area. Empty garbage bags. A gasoline can. A small tool kit. A jack. And a short-handled shovel.

She grabbed the shovel and climbed back into the driver's seat. There, summoning all the anger and frustration she had bottled up inside her, she slammed the shovel's tip into the windshield.

Cracks webbed through the safety glass, transforming it into a gummy sheet. She swung the shovel harder. It punched a hole in the sheet, admitting a breeze that chilled the sweat beading on her skin. She struck the glass again, widening the hole. Using the shovel's blade, she folded the glass out of the way. The opening was just large enough for her to squeeze through it.

First, she tossed her purse and the helmet out the hole. Stuffing the map under her waistband, she crawled over the dashboard and shimmied out the hole headfirst. Once on the hood, she turned around to slide off it, with her boots hitting the ground first.

A series of booms echoed across the desert floor.

She looked back in the direction she'd come from, back toward the old house. Bluish-white lights twinkled there, low to the ground. Headlights. The commandos must've arrived. The booms must've been gunshots.

The drug dealer probably was dead this time. She didn't know how she felt about that. Some comfort came from knowing that at least she hadn't killed him.

In the beams of the headlights, she consulted the map. Choosing the direction she thought was right, she started away from the Rover at a brisk pace. She'd find the facility or she'd die from exposure—or a snakebite.

Either way, her journey ended tonight.

Chapter Twenty-Four

Grace tilted her head back to stare up at the structure in front of her. The green hues of the night vision display in the helmet revealed a bulbous shape seated atop tall metal scaffolding. It was a water tower, seventy or eighty feet high.

Turning, she surveyed the desert one more time. She hadn't seen any headlights for awhile, but that fact didn't make her feel any better. The commandos had night vision helmets identical to the one she wore now. If they had opted for stealth, then she might never see them coming.

She detoured around the water tower. The landmark appeared on David's map, which told her to head straight for the humpbacked butte in the distance. She wouldn't reach the butte, according to the map, but its silhouette would guide her in the right direction. Thank heavens for David's remote viewing, because without it she'd have no chance of finding the facility. A few days ago, she would've dismissed the very concept of extrasensory abilities as bunk. Her life had changed so radically in such a short time that she marveled at the fact she held onto her sanity. Of course, her life hadn't really changed. The amnesia had tricked her into believing she was a normal, boring girl.

Now she knew better.

The ground sloped upward at an ever-steepening angle. Her thighs ached as she mounted the rise, halting at the crest. Ahead of her, the ground sloped downward in a gentle grade. She stood on the rim of a bowl-shaped depression that, when viewed from the lower terrain surrounding it, looked like yet another flat expanse of desert. Only from this vantage point could she see what the depression contained. There, perhaps a quarter-mile away, sat a dark shape that she recognized as a low, sprawling complex of interconnected buildings.

The facility.

She stifled a triumphant cry. At last, she had reached her destination.

The night vision display flickered. The words "low battery" flashed on the screen.

Terrific. Well, at this point, she probably didn't need the high-tech guidance anyway. If she walked straight down the slope, and straight across the depression, she would run into the facility.

Switching off the night vision, she removed the helmet. With it tucked under her arm, she lifted her foot to step off the summit.

"Hold it right there."

Her heart thudded at the sound of the male voice issuing from behind her. She lowered her hand to her unzipped purse, slipping her fingers inside to grasp the gun.

Something hard and cold rammed into her back, right between her shoulder blades.

"Don't," the man said in a stern voice, "or I'll blow a hole straight through you."

She froze.

"That's right," he said. "Now raise your hands and turn around, slow and easy."

She complied.

A helmet covered the man's head and face. Nothing on his black outfit identified him or his employers. The man towered at least eight inches above her, his physique packed with enough muscles to give him a threatening aura even if he hadn't been pointing a weapon at her. In both hands he gripped a bulky gun with a huge clip that contained enough bullets to rip her into confetti.

He clicked a button on the two-way radio clipped to his jacket and said, "I got her."

A gruff voice came through the radio. "Hold her there. We're on our way."

The other commando hadn't asked where this guy was. They must have some kind of tracking system, like GPS, to keep tabs on each other in the field.

She glanced down at the helmet tucked under her arm. Did it contain some kind of tracking device that had led this commando to her? It might've taken them awhile to realize she had one of their helmets. Either way, it didn't really matter anymore. She was caught.

The commando jabbed his gun into her ribs, just below the sternum.

She winced and scuffled backward half a step. Her right heel tipped over the sharp crest of the hill. She teetered but held onto her balance.

The commando jabbed her in the ribs again, harder this time.

She grimaced, clenching her teeth.

"You better hold real still," the man said, "my trigger finger's starting to itch."

"Your boss wants me alive."

The man snorted. "Accidents happen."

Wonderful, she got caught by a maverick with an itch to shoot her. With his gun's muzzle embedded in her abdomen, there wasn't much she could do.

She had psychic abilities, for pete's sake. Those abilities could surely help right now, if only she could remember how to use them. Amnesia really sucked.

Wait a minute. She'd visited the facility in her dreams countless times, traveling there psychically to visit David. She'd used her powers to push David away. Those incidents told her that, somewhere deep inside, she still knew how to access those abilities. Her conscious mind blocked the memories and convinced her she was powerless.

David showed her the truth. He gave her the information she needed to regain what she had lost. It was up to her to make use of the information.

Now or never.

She kept her eyes open, but let her vision drift out of focus. With an effort, she relaxed every muscle and banished all thoughts from her mind. The whisper of the breeze, the rustling of the commando's uniform, even the beating of her own heart—it all faded into silence. The blurry world around her melted into blackness. She felt her consciousness rising, floating, pulled toward something she could feel but not see.

A point of light shimmered. Then another. And another.

She surfaced into a field of cool white stars. Hovering. Weightless. Free.

David. He called to her. Not in voice or thought, but in spirit.

Though she wanted to go to him, wanted it so badly her soul ached from the need, she couldn't give in to it. For the moment, other matters needed her attention more urgently.

Turning away from his call, she sank downward out of the field of stars, back into the real world.

Floating above the desert, she gazed down at her own body and the commando standing in front of her. She must do something. Anything.

She focused her mind, gathering energy from…somewhere.

The gun flew out of the commando's hands. It sailed through the air, hitting the ground thirty feet away.

The commando shouted. He floundered backward, as if he'd been kicked in the chest.

She'd intended to fling him backward with as much force as she'd used to discard the gun. Her control was faltering. She felt it. Doubts niggled at her, barely noticeable at first, but growing louder and sharper as panic iced through her.

The commando tripped. He flopped onto his butt, dazed.

Grace slammed back into her body with a force that rocked her off balance. She teetered backward. Her right foot slipped off the precipice. Though the drop wasn't steep, she lost her footing and tumbled to the ground. The momentum sent her rolling down the slope sideways.

Automatic gunfire chattered overhead.

She rolled down, down, down. Vegetation scraped at her. Rocks bruised her flesh. Nothing slowed her descent until the ground leveled out and she lost momentum. Hitting the ground face first, she came to a halt sprawled on her belly.

Everything hurt. Her head felt like someone was sitting on it. She flailed her hands to push the weight away from her head, but found nothing there. Searing pain erupted behind her eyes. The flavor of dirt and blood tainted her mouth. She pushed up onto hands and knees. Nothing seemed broken. Opening her eyes, she ran her hands over her body in search of wounds. Nothing serious. Scrapes and cuts and sore spots that would mature into bruises. A cut near her mouth accounted for the tang of blood on her tongue.

Sitting back on her heels, she swept her gaze up the hillside.

The commando stood silhouetted against the night sky.

She didn't move. Maybe he couldn't see her. Yeah right. He had night vision, and she had crappy psychic abilities that only half worked and left her drained and saddled with a burgeoning migraine.

At least she had made it to the crossroads, on purpose this time. And she'd used her telekinesis with moderate effectiveness. Not bad for her first conscious attempt.

The commando leaped off the crest of the hill. She lost sight of him on the shadowed slope.

Crap.

Scrambling to her feet, she took off in the direction of the facility.

The door clicked shut. David opened his eyes to find the room empty, though he'd already known it would be. He both heard and sensed the departure of the tech, a nervous young woman sent by Tesler, who was probably busy plotting the horrors he would inflict on Grace once they captured her.

The young tech's mind was shockingly pliable. No wonder they hired her. She would accept any story, comply with any orders, simply to avoid confrontation. Maybe she'd been abused as a child. Maybe she lacked character. The reason made no difference. She'd helped Tesler conflict untold pain and torment on their test subjects. In spite of her crimes, however, David felt a twinge of guilt over influencing her mind so that she believed he was still in a drug-induced coma. He hated manipulating people.

When Grace had told him how desperation had forced her to trick a man into selling her a car for twenty dollars, he'd understood her anguish over what she'd done. He felt the same guilt every time he was forced to bend a pliant mind to his will. He should've told her that. Instead, he told her the one thing he should not have said—at least not yet.

He'd told her he loved her.

It had been a mistake. He meant it, but she wasn't ready to hear it. Confused by her amnesia, frightened by the current situation, she'd shut down at the very mention of a certain four-letter word. He couldn't take it back now. He wouldn't take it back.

Pushing back the sheets, he sat up and swung his legs off the bed. He didn't need to get dressed, because even in a coma he still wore his jeans, T-shirt, and socks. Tesler and his lackeys didn't care about their subjects' comfort. David bent down to pluck his sneakers from the floor, where they'd been tucked under the bedside table. He shoved the sneakers on his feet, tying the laces as fast as his fingers would move.

Grace was coming.

He must help her. He must find her. Despite receiving a gift of energy from Grace, he didn't have enough of a reserve leftover to reach her psychically. Not directly. Not in a way she would understand. If she remembered how this all worked, he might attempt to guide her obliquely. In her current state, she simply wouldn't get it.

Sean would. If it took his last ounce of energy, he must contact Sean and enlist the boy's help. Sean wasn't as drained as David. He ought to have enough energy to help Grace.

Sliding off the bed, David straightened and walked to the door. The knob felt cool when he laid his hand on it.

One chance. That might be all he had. All they had. Whatever happened, he and Grace would see this through together.

Twisting the knob, he eased the door open and stepped out into the corridor.

Running, running, running. She didn't look back. Focused on the terrain ahead of her, discerning faint outlines as her eyes adjusted to the darkness, she pumped her legs as fast as possible. Looking back would distract her, and she might trip. If the commando was closing in on her, she couldn't do much about it anyway. Shooting him in the dark, while running full speed, would be a waste of a bullet. Stopping to take aim and fire gave him a chance to catch up, and she still might miss the target. She was no sniper.

It was too dark. The commando blended into the night.

Ahead of her, the squat silhouette of the facility enlarged as she drew closer and closer. She saw no lights to give her a clue where there might be an entrance. A wild guess was her only option.

David had said Sean would help her. Neither of them had shown up yet.

What if they couldn't? What if, at this very moment, both David and Sean languished in a drug-induced slumber?

No. She felt David. The sensation made no sense, and it left her feeling a bit uneasy, but she knew that the slight pull she felt was him. Alive. Aware. Somewhere close by.

Not close enough.

Running, running, toward the facility. Her head throbbed. The ambient light seemed too bright, and the glow from the crescent moon rising directly in front of her struck her eyes like invisible needles. Though the cold wind generated by her motion felt good, her muscles screamed for a break that she couldn't give them. Not yet.

The building loomed nearer, larger, blocking out more and more of the sky. The moon vanished behind the hulking structure.

The darkness grew deeper. She wanted to draw on her powers, to see what her eyes couldn't. If she did that, her migraine might get exponentially worse. She could not risk it.

The crack of a gunshot echoed behind her. Too close.

Dirt erupted to her left. Way too close.

Twenty feet from the building, she realized there were no doors in front of her. She skidded to a stop, whipping her head left and right, searching for a door-shaped outline in the gloom.

Behind her, footfalls slapped on earth.

She spun around, the gun in her hand.

A shape darted toward her from less than fifty feet away.

She aimed for the humanoid blob and shouted, "Freeze or I'll shoot!"

The shadow hesitated, then straightened into a man-size outline. Thirty feet away. Maybe less. Dammit. Judging distances was next to impossible out here, with shadows swarming everywhere.

The commando sniggered. "I got mine sighted on you too, sweetheart."

He meant his gun, she realized. The big one filled with enough bullets to take out a herd of elephants.

Could she hit him with her first shot? Since she'd only fired on a human being once before, when she thought she killed the drug dealer, her confidence was a something less than inspiring.

So was her confidence that this creep wouldn't kill her for the thrill of it.

Accidents happen, he'd said before. And David told her the facility hired dangerous ex-cons as security guards.

"Drop the gun," he ordered. "Or I'll make sure you can't run away again."

"No."

"I said drop the gun."

"And I said no."

She could practically feel his disbelieving stare. It probably resembled the look David gave her every time she refused to do what he wanted, except without the underlying fondness. Men expected her to obey their orders, and she was sick and tired of it. Besides, without Sean or David to help her, she had no clue how to get inside the facility. The commando was her way in.

He wanted to kill her, if he could get away with it by framing it as an accident. Maybe she should put the gun down, so he couldn't claim he shot her in self-defense. If she dropped the gun, he could still shoot her and claim self-defense, by planting the gun in her lifeless hand. It seemed to her that keeping a loaded weapon trained on the commando gave her the best chance of survival.

"I've shot one man tonight," she said. "Do you really think I'll feel bad about shooting you?"

The commando made a dismissive sound. "You screwed that up, sweetheart. The loser was wearing a Kevlar vest under his shirt. Now if you'd shot him in the head…" He shrugged. "You don't have the killer instinct, honey."

She wanted to shoot him just for calling her sweetheart and honey.

The commando's radio crackled and a masculine voice shouted through the little speaker. "Battaglia, what's your status? There's no sign of the girl out here."

So the Neanderthal had a name after all.

She caught a flash of movement as Battaglia reached up to press a button on his radio. In a tone sharpened by arrogance and tinged with cruel amusement, Battaglia said, "I got a sign of the girl right here in front of me."

"You've got her?" the other voice asked.

"Affirmative."

"Take her inside. We'll meet you there." Static crackled. "And you'd better not lose her this time, Battaglia."

"She's going nowhere, sir."

The Neanderthal made a sweeping gesture with his left hand. "Let's go, sweetie."

"You first," she said.

"No." He shifted his right hand, giving her a glimpse of his weapon's outline. "You first, or I blast a hole in your shoulder. It won't kill you, but it will make you a lot more cooperative."

Well, she wanted inside the facility. He was giving her what she wanted.

So why did she have a cold lump in her stomach?

Turning to her right, she trudged along the wall of the building. Battaglia followed her, she knew, though she didn't glanced back to make sure. His footfalls clomped slightly out of sync with hers. The building seemed interminable, cloaked in darkness, without any windows or doors. After a few minutes that felt like hours, Battaglia ordered her to stop. A rectangular depression in the wall suggested a doorway.

Crossing in front of her, Battaglia found a keypad next to the doorway and punched in the code. A mechanism chunked. He reached for what she assumed was a door knob, twisted it, and thrust the door inward.

Muted yellow light poured out of the opening. It stung her eyes like the midday sun.

Squinting, she saw Battaglia remove his helmet. The light cast a flattering glow on his features, lending his skin a golden hue that complemented his dark brown hair. He had a thin mustache that softened the angular planes of his face, but his squinty eyes and heavy brow hinted at the caveman within. He smirked, like the Neanderthal she knew he was.

"Ladies first," he said, gesturing with his gun for her to enter the building. His other hand he slipped into his pocket.

Now that he'd opened the door for her, she didn't really need him anymore.

As if he'd read her mind, he lunged at her. Instead of grabbing for her gun, he threw his arms around her in a bear hug, crushing her to his chest. The gun was still in her hand, smashed between their bodies. She struggled, but his muscle-bound body contained her like a cage. She couldn't shake free of him, she couldn't move her arms, and she couldn't get leverage with her legs.

Trapped.

No. She had one chance.

Battaglia clenched her tighter. She couldn't catch her breath. Wriggling her fingers, she hooked one around the trigger of her gun.

"Time to say good night," he murmured.

At the corner of her eye, she saw his left hand slide up her shoulder, raising a syringe to her neck.

She pulled the trigger.

Battaglia jerked.

At first she wasn't sure which one of them she'd hit. Then Battaglia stumbled backward, releasing his hold on her. The gun tumbled from his grasp. She still held her gun. A quick glance at her own body revealed no blood or anything else to indicate a wound.

Battaglia just stood there, his body shaking, his face red.

She'd expected him to look pale and weak. Instead, he looked thoroughly enraged. "You shot my foot, you—"

Grace fired at the keypad beside the door. As the shot exploded, the keypad shattered into bits.

Battaglia roared.

She swiped his gun from the ground and bolted through the doorway. Spinning around, she slammed the door shut. The lock chunked. She didn't wait to find out if Battaglia could force the door open manually. Clutching both guns, she ran.

The corridor dead-ended at another. The new corridor went only left, so she skidded around the corner and took off in that direction. The new corridor intersected with another, giving her three options—left, right, or straight ahead. She chose straight ahead. Where she was going, she didn't know. On and on she ran, deeper and deeper into the facility, past dozens of doors. She didn't try to open any of them, because she knew what she needed did not wait inside any of those rooms. Instinct drove her onward, without reason but not without purpose.

To find him. That was her purpose. To track down JT, aka Jackson Tennant, and repay him for everything he'd done to her and her family—after she got the truth out of him.

David had asked her what she intended to do once she got inside the facility. At the time, she couldn't answer him. Finally, she knew what must be done. What she must do. Which villain she must confront. The destination was clear, if not the path. Something inside her knew where to go. She trusted that instinct.

She careened around a corner.

And smacked face first into another human being.

Chapter Twenty-Five

Her body slammed into his, her eyes level with the man's nose. She recognized that nose. She recognized the warm solidity of his body and the scent of him that filled her nostrils. Resting her hands on his chest, she felt the knit fabric of his gray T-shirt. Joy swelled inside her. As she tilted her head up to look at him, a single breathless word issued from her lips.

"David."

He bent his head to meet her gaze, his eyes wider than usual. Though his lips parted, no sound came out.

It seemed ridiculous given the circumstances, but she felt her mouth curve into a smile. She wanted to kiss him, hug him, giggle uncontrollably, kiss him again—

Instead, she just grinned at him like an idiot and said, "How did you find me?"

His eyes narrowed, his brow furrowed, and he said, "I didn't. I was looking for Sean, but I'm too weak to find him psychically so I have to search the old-fashioned way." He frowned. "It's incredibly frustrating."

"Yeah, being normal sucks, doesn't it?"

His frown melted into a slight smile as he slipped his arms around her. "You have never been normal."

She couldn't help it. She had to rise onto her tiptoes and kiss him. He reciprocated, pulling her snugly against him. She looped her arms around his neck. Her right hand clasped her gun, while her left gripped the strap of Battaglia's huge weapon.

When the kiss ended, Grace stepped away from David. Arms at his sides, he arched an eyebrow at her.

"I have to find JT," she said.

He flinched as if she'd slapped him in the face. "No."

"Yes. And you can either help me or get out of my way."

"He'll hurt you."

She noticed he didn't say JT would kill her. The lunatic probably wouldn't, at least not right away, not until he got from her whatever it was he wanted. Power, she assumed. What form that power might take, she hadn't figured out yet.

From down the corridor she'd just left, footfalls echoed. The noise drew nearer with each percussive step.

"Oh great," she said. "It must be Battaglia."

David's lip curled and his jaw tensed. "Battaglia is chasing you?"

She nodded. "You know him?"

Although David said nothing, she saw the answer in the tightening of his features. He knew, and clearly despised, the muscle-bound commando.

David snatched Battaglia's gun from her left hand. He seized her hand and took off down the corridor, dragging her with him. His longer legs moved him faster than her legs could propel her, forcing her to sprint at full speed. The footsteps behind them were drowned out by the clapping of their own shoes on the smooth flooring. In her dreams, the corridors were lit by small bulbs along the floor. Tonight, however, bright daytime lighting spilled out of bulbs recessed into the ceiling.

Battaglia was unarmed, which gave them an advantage—unless the Neanderthal had another gun hidden on his person. It could've been tucked inside his jacket or strapped to his ankle. She should've shot him again when she had the chance, but she didn't like shooting anyone unless it was unavoidable. Shutting the door on Battaglia had slowed him down, at least.

With no warning, David stopped. She barreled into his backside, knocking herself backward but hardly disturbing his balance. As she regained her footing, coming up beside him, he thrust an arm out to keep her back. His expression was intent, focused on the intersection twenty feet ahead of them. She heard nothing and saw nothing.

He tilted his head as if listening.

She wanted to ask what was going on, but the tension in his body and the intensity of his concentration made her hesitate.

The clomping of Battaglia's footfalls had ceased.

She glanced over her shoulder. No one there.

Damn, this was no good. No good at all.

David swung his head left and right, as if searching for something. An escape hatch maybe. A doorway. A window. Anything.

A cold finger trailed down her spine. She spun around, half expecting to see Battaglia right behind her with his hand stretched out to her. Nobody was there. She stared down the corridor, her back to David.

Battaglia strode out of the adjoining corridor. He raised a semiautomatic handgun, sighting it on her.

She held her own gun trained on him.

David cursed under his breath.

She chanced a look backward, leaning a little sideways to peer around David's shoulder.

Twenty feet away, standing at the junction of two corridors, stood Waldron and a pack of armed guards. The men wore their black outfits, sans helmets.

They could try shooting their way out of this quandary. Waldron's men wielded enough firepower to win the battle, however, and she or David or both of them might die or suffer a debilitating injury. She just couldn't risk David's life. Besides, she wanted to meet JT. She'd intended to burst into his office, or bedroom or whatever, unannounced and fully armed. The universe had other plans.

She tossed her gun onto the floor. The clack as it hit the shiny tiles reverberated through the corridor.

David jerked his head to look back at her. "What are you doing?"

Settling a hand on his arm, she exerted a gentle pressure. "Put the gun down. It's pointless."

His face contorted in a mixture of panic and anguish. She wanted to comfort him, but really, she had no comfort to give. Physically, she felt okay. Her psychic faculties, as David called it, still felt a little fuzzy and weak. David said he was experiencing a power outage of his own. Forced to rely on everyday means of defeating their foes, they had little chance of succeeding given the current situation.

Apparently reaching the same conclusion, David flung Battaglia's gun toward Waldron. The weapon smacked onto the floor ten feet from the man and skittered across the surface, coming to a stop inches from Waldron's shoes.

"Good dog," Waldron said.

He motioned to the guards and to Battaglia. Two of the guards with Waldron marched forward to grab David by the arms. One guard brought out a zip tie, one of those nylon strap thingies equipped with a ratcheting mechanism that both secured and tightened the tie. The guard gathered David's hands behind his back and strapped the zip tie around his wrists, ratcheting it until he couldn't separate his hands.

From the other direction, Battaglia strode up to Grace. He picked up her gun, tucking it inside his waistband, and took both her wrists in one of his huge, muscular hands. At least he'd immobilized her hands in front of her, not behind her back. With his free hand, he reached into his pocket to extract a zip tie. He wrapped the nylon strip around her wrists, cinching it tight. She winced as the tie dug into her flesh.

"Too tight?" Battaglia said in a tone of mock concern. He slipped a finger under the zip tie and yanked hard, spinning her around to face the others. She stumbled two steps forward, until she managed to rebalance herself.

Waldron locked his gaze on her. Smirking, he said, "I believe you're late for an appointment with the president of the company."

Giving a flick of his finger, Waldron turned on his heels and started down the corridor. The guards took his cue, herding their prisoners down the corridor behind Waldron.

They were going to see JT. She felt a disorienting combination of relief, anxiety, and numbness. Whatever the outcome of their encounter, she knew one thing for certain.

The nightmare would end tonight.

Their captors herded them through the complex, into an elevator that barely held the entire group, out into another network of corridors, and finally to a door at the end of the hallway. An engraved sign posted beside the door announced, "Jackson Tennant, CEO."

A shiver swept up her spine, prickling every hair on her body. Was it fear or anticipation? A lot of both, she decided. JT was inside that door. Before he tortured and killed her, she wanted some answers from the creep. Since he clearly needed something from her, that would give her leverage. She hoped.

Waldron approached the door. He slid a card through a reader attached to the door frame, and when the mechanism beeped its approval, he punched a series of numbers into the keypad mounted above the card reader. The door lock chunked. He twisted the knob, pushing the door inward.

Grace looked at David. His expression was unreadable. Back to stoic man, which she supposed was a good thing in these circumstances. She felt nothing close to stoic, though she prayed her demeanor gave away no hints about her inner turmoil.

Waldron entered the room first. David's guards urged him through the doorway next, followed by a couple more guards for good measure. Battaglia hauled Grace across the threshold after them.

The windowless room was smaller than she'd expected, maybe fifteen feet across and twenty feet long. A good size office, for sure, but not megalomaniac big. A wood desk the size of a small boat hunkered near the far wall, its surface gleaming. A floor lamp in one corner bathed the room in golden light. A huge, overstuffed leather chair squatted behind the desk. In that chair sat a man not much older than Grace. She recognized him without introductions.

Jackson Tennant reclined in the chair with one arm draped on each arm of the chair. His head rested lazily against the chair's back as he gazed at her with half-closed eyes. The image of him from the *Time* magazine article flashed through her mind. His dark brown hair was a little shaggier these days, and he wore a tan polo shirt with gray slacks rather than the jeans and T-shirt he'd donned for the magazine spread. He looked thinner too, verging on emaciated. The surfer-dude tan he'd shown off for the press had long since faded into a pallor that lent him a ghostly aura.

"Gracie," the man said, drawing out her name as if he were savoring a piece of chocolate.

The sound of his voice triggered another shiver. Steadying herself, she looked straight into his eyes and said, "Hello, Jackie."

His eyes flew open. He clenched his hands into fists. "My name is JT. Only my parents called me Jackie, and they're dead now."

Something about the tone of his voice when he told her his parents were dead made her wonder if he'd played a role in their demises. Coming from this man, no amount of cruelty would surprise her. At least now she knew one button to push to get him royally ticked off, though she still hadn't a clue just how she might use that information.

JT twisted his expression into a peevish look as he surveyed the mini army of guards congregating in his office. Glancing at Waldron, he waved a hand in a sloppy gesture.

"Get them out of here, Waldo," JT said. "You and Batman can stay, but make these other goons disappear already. I want some privacy."

Grace felt her eyebrows scrunch, an unconscious manifestation of her puzzlement. Waldo? Batman? Okay, she assumed Waldo meant Waldron, since JT was pouting in the direction of the older man. But who was Batman?

"The prisoners are dangerous," Waldron said. "We need the extra guards."

JT snorted a laugh. "They ain't going anywhere, man. They're tied up and locked inside a totally secure facility. They're way helpless."

A muscle ticked in Waldron's jaw. He remained silent for several seconds while JT eyed him with casual disdain. The younger man twirled a silver pen in the air with two fingers.

Waldron blinked first.

Hissing out a breath, he whirled to face his men. He issued quiet but stern orders to the guards, who filed out the door one by one. They shut the door behind themselves, leaving only Waldron and Battaglia inside the room.

Batman. Battaglia. Oh brother, the lunatic with psychic powers liked to make up nicknames for everybody. What was he, twelve years old?

Yeah, a twelve-year-old with the keys to a nuclear missile silo.

Still twirling the pen, JT fixed his gaze on her.

She squared her shoulders and asked, "Did you kill my parents?"

He laughed.

It wasn't the throaty laugh of a masculine CEO. It was the whispery snickering of a little boy who thought he'd squirreled away all the good candy without anybody realizing it.

Her entire body tensed. She resisted the urge to hurl herself across the desk and throttle the murderous twit. He thought what happened to her family was funny.

"What did you do?" she demanded.

He gave a careless shrug. "They lied to me. So I punished them."

In a voice almost too soft to hear, David said, "Easy."

At the sound of his voice, the knot inside her loosened a smidgen. She kept her gaze locked on JT, but she took a slow, calming breath. The creep wanted to make her squirm and thrash and claw at his eyes like a wild animal. She would not give him the satisfaction.

JT crossed his right leg over the left, tapping his right foot in the air.

Grace willed her body to relax. If he wanted her tense and angry, he'd be disappointed.

He sighed, shaking his head. "David thought he pulled one over on me, telling Chris-Chris and Mikey to steal Waldo's car. Everybody knows Waldo had it put in his contract that we would not under any circumstances plant tracking devices in his car or on his person." JT snickered. "On his person. I love that. It's so anal."

Grace kept her face impassive. The twerp would get no response from her.

JT waited only a heartbeat before continuing. "When I got back from the wild goose chase your mommy sent me on, I had Batman here review the surveillance tapes from the parking level. Then I activated the secret tracking device in Waldo's car and—ta-dah!—I had them."

The childish glee in his voice grated on her nerves. The anger boiled inside her, contained but not extinguished. No amount of meditation would quell the fury. She could hope for nothing more than to disguise her feelings.

JT's voice took on a mock-wistful tone. "It was so thoughtful of them to drive way out into the woods on a deserted road. Not a car in sight for miles. Not that it would've mattered if somebody had seen the crash, 'cause I made it look really authentic. Mikey lost control, nobody'll ever know why, and the car flipped. Over and over and over..." He smirked at her. "They were dead and rotting before anybody even knew they'd crashed."

The room twirled around her, like one of those tilting, spinning rides at a carnival. Snippets of memory rushed past her mind's eye. The car. The road. The deer. She fought back a tide of nausea as her knees buckled. The ringing in her ears drowned out JT's laughter. She collapsed onto hands and knees.

The memory hit her so hard she gasped.

And then the present vanished, and the past engulfed her.

The car. Her parents in the front, talking, their faces pinched with anxiety. She was in the backseat again, perched on the seat's edge, as if a wormhole had sucked her into its time-warping depths, depositing her in the past. Her past. Yet she could do nothing to change what she knew was coming. Her thoughts—the thoughts of the old her, the one who'd lived through this first time—echoed in her mind.

How did I get here? Oh lord, I did it again.

She'd traveled somewhere, without meaning to, without even knowing how she did it. A sense of impending danger had come over her and, wham, she knew her parents were in trouble. Knew it was her fault. Waldron must've found out about her and gone after her parents to get to her.

Gotta do something. Gotta warn them.

She pounded her fists on the glass but they passed right through it. Oh God, she had to manifest right now. Even in the best conditions, while safely contained in a laboratory with medical types keeping watch over her, traveling and manifesting took great concentration and energy. At this moment, with her heart pounding and adrenaline coursing through her body, she had no hope of accessing her higher level powers. Christ, she'd only begun to understand her powers at all when her parents made her run off to Texas.

David. She needed him. But she couldn't concentrate enough to even locate him, much less connect with him.

A breeze wafted through the car.

Her skin tingled. *Someone else is here.*

A deer galloped out into the road. It halted on the center line, eyes wide as it stared at the oncoming car. Her father slammed on the brakes. Her mother cried out in surprise as the tires squealed.

The deer bolted into the trees alongside the road.

Dad let out a heavy sigh and accelerated the car.

They thought the danger was past. She knew it wasn't.

The breeze inside the vehicle tickled Grace's cheeks. Strange that she could feel it when she had no body, except the one she imagined, the one that was an illusion only she could see.

The other traveler chose not to reveal his or her presence. The draft flowing through the sealed car, rustling her mother's hair, offered the sole evidence of another consciousness in the vicinity. She knew what the breeze meant. She sensed the other traveler nearby, like a storm cloud crouching at the horizon, about to unleash lightning and hail and torrential rains.

And she could do nothing to stop it.

Dammit, she must do something. If she couldn't manifest, then at least she could let her parents see her.

Deep breaths. In and out. She focused all her energy on one thought.

See me.

Christine Powell turned her head and gasped. "Grace?"

Their gaze met. Her mother saw her. That meant she could hear Grace too.

"Mom," she says, "there's someone else—"

A force hit her with the kinetic energy of a meteorite. The door behind her flew open an instant before she sailed backward out of the car. Falling, her body was falling through empty space. She smacked into the ground on her back, landing with a thud that would've hurt if she had a physical body. For a moment she couldn't breathe or move. The thunderous flow of blood through her veins obliterated all other sounds. A psychically imagined body could feel as real as a flesh-and-blood one.

Pow!

The sickening crunch snapped her out of her stupor. She scrambled to her knees on the asphalt. The road stretched out in front of her.

A hundred feet down the road, the car slalomed off the pavement into the ditch. It flipped into the air, hit the ground upside down, and rolled over and over, spinning toward the line of trees.

Grace screamed.

The car slammed into the trees on its side. The crunch-bang echoed through the still morning air. The silence that followed rang in her ears.

She staggered down the road, then broke into a full run. She should've been crying, should've been shaking, but all she felt was cold and numb. Thirty feet from the car, she skidded to a halt. Her muscles felt paralyzed. Her bile rose in her throat as she gaped at the bent, broken thing that had once been a car.

A gust of wind blustered over her.

It was him. She knew. Though he hid his identity, she recognized what he was. A sick man with too much power. He must be stopped.

She pulled all the energy she could muster from the crossroads and hurled it at him. The energy spun around him like an invisible spider web. Though he struggled against her, she used the energy to force him to appear.

He was a shadow figure. Dark, swirling, not quite human. His face was obscured.

In raspy voice, he said, "You are mine."

The energy disintegrated, and the world went black.

Chapter Twenty-Six

On her hands and knees, shaking all over, Grace fought to catch her breath. She remembered waking up in her house on that day, lying on the kitchen floor, with no memory of what had happened—no memory of the previous eight months. The amnesia had set in on that day seven months ago. Ever since then, she'd been oblivious of the truth about her family, herself, and the dangers that lurked just out of sight.

She had dreamed about the accident, but the dream had misled her. Faced with gaps in the story, her mind replaced what she couldn't recall with whatever seemed appropriate, but appropriate wasn't always correct. What she'd experienced a moment earlier had been a genuine memory, as real and vivid and accurate as the event itself. She knew it was right. She felt the truth of it.

The shaking had subsided. She pushed up onto her knees, and finally, rose to her feet. Glaring at JT, she said, "You killed them. I was there, I saw it."

He rolled his eyes.

Since he'd already admitted, obliquely, to killing her parents, she hadn't expected much of a reaction. He felt no remorse. To him, their deaths were an inconvenience at worst.

"What do you want from me?" she asked.

He glanced down at his desktop, then back up at her.

She took a few steps closer to the desk. Waldron shifted, as if considering stopping her, but JT gave a single shake of his head that halted Waldron where he stood. Grace bent forward to examine the desktop. A laptop computer occupied one corner, but another object had caught JT's attention. A mat calendar covered a rectangular section of the desktop, directly in front of JT, and atop that calendar sat a scrap of gauze stained with a dark red substance.

Blood.

A sick feeling started in her belly. She recognized that blood-stained gauze. Sure, gauze all looked the same and blood tended to look the same too. Nevertheless, she felt certain the gauze lying on JT's desk belonged to her. The blood stain had come from her. The dream she'd had days ago, the one where she got cut and woke up with a cut on her hand that vanished later. She'd saved the bloody gauze, feeling she might need or want proof that the dream had been, in some sense, real.

"You stole that from my house," she said.

"Actually," JT said, looking almost proud of himself, "Waldo got it for me. He didn't see its value, but I knew."

Straightening, she gulped down the lump that had formed in her throat. "You knew what?"

He smiled at her, and a chill spread through her veins. Planting his elbows on the desktop, he steepled his fingers to rest his chin on them. "I needed a link to you. A connection to help me find you, since your folks did such a bang-up job of hiding you from me. It was so rude, ya know?"

"What do you mean a link?"

"Blood is the essence of life. We can't live without it." Glancing down at the gauze, he sighed. "Your blood linked me to you."

"How?"

He picked up the gauze, lifted it to his mouth, and licked the blood stain.

Waldron made a disgusted noise. Grace managed to restrain her own revulsion.

JT dropped the gauze. "That's how."

She said nothing, did nothing, keeping her eyes focused on him. If he wanted a knee-jerk response, he'd have to try harder. Licking her dried blood was gross, but not enough to break her composure. The little creep seemed to relish goading people into lashing out at him—or maybe it was only her he enjoyed goading. Either way, she would not give him what he wanted. Ever.

"This amount of blood," JT said, "helped me find you, but it didn't have enough oomph to give me a real, blood-and-guts connection to you. I want more. I need more. And you will give it to me."

"I don't think so."

He chuckled. "You have no choice, Gracie. I want your power. I will have it."

She wanted to shuffle backward, get away from him, huddle next to David, anything except stand here face to face with the craziest loon she'd ever met. Her hands trembled a little. She clasped them to hide the tremors. And she did not move. Did not break eye contact. An instinct warned her that doing either would escalate the situation.

Pulling out a desk drawer, JT procured from its depths a large rubber band and a needle attached to a blood collection tube. He intended to draw blood from her. And do what with it? She prayed he wouldn't drink it, because that would be entirely too disgusting.

He set the needle and rubber band on the desktop. Then he said, "You see, I need a more intimate transfer of life energy. I need your blood in my veins."

She glanced over her shoulder at David. He looked alternately perplexed and annoyed. Beside him, Waldron grimaced as if sickened by the very thought of what JT proposed. Yeah, it was pretty icky. Not as icky as licking her dried blood, though.

"If our blood types don't match," she said to JT, "you could die from injecting my blood into your veins."

"I've already checked that. We're good to go."

Terrific. She could only hope that he'd checked wrong, and her blood would kill him after all.

Or she could end this farce right now.

But how? Three against two sounded like iffy odds. Well, she had goddamn psychic powers, didn't she? Using them tended to leave her exhausted beyond description, and often suffering from a massive headache. If David had recovered enough to use his powers, then the odds would tip in their favor. They might escape before depleting their energy, psychically or physically.

It was the only chance they had.

Now, if she could let David know her plan…

He said mind reading was dangerous, and she had no desire to turn into a frothing-at-the-mouth lunatic. Maybe, though, she could transmit an idea to him. No mind reading. Just thought projection. She had manipulated a man into practically giving her a car, but she didn't want to influence David's mind. She wanted simply to let him know what she intended to do and what she wanted him to do in return.

Worth a shot.

She closed her eyes.

"Uh-uh-uh," JT said in a scolding tone. "Use your powers in any way and David gets splattered on the walls. Not really the décor I had in mind, but it'll work."

She looked back at David. Waldron held his gun to David's temple, his finger over the trigger.

Could she act faster than he could pull the trigger? She couldn't risk it. After all, she wasn't exactly an expert at this psychic stuff. Dammit.

Maybe she could do something, without JT noticing.

He hunched over his desk, fingering the rubber band. The pallor in his face had deepened, and his lips looked drained of color as well. From this angle, she saw that his cheeks were sunken.

"You look half dead already," she said.

Head bowed, he rolled his eyes up to stare at her. "I'm fine. I'll be fantastic once I have the Golden Power."

"I don't have it. You won't get anything useful from my blood."

He picked up the needle and walked around the desk, halting a couple yards from her.

Now or never.

Without closing her eyes, she pictured Sean in her mind and stretched out tendrils of energy to search for him. She'd never tried this before, as far as she remembered. The tendrils snaked out in several directions, invisible to everyone but her—she hoped.

JT said, "You better hold her, Batman."

Grace ignored the clomping of Battaglia's boots as he came up beside her. She concentrated on the tendrils of energy, feeling for a hint of Sean's presence.

Battaglia grasped her bound hands and yanked her toward him. His other arm he looped around her shoulders, squeezing her tight against him. She tried not to react, but even distracted as she was by her search for Sean, she couldn't help flinching at Battaglia's embrace. He jerked her hands up, stretching her arms out to expose her inner arm.

JT rolled up her shirt sleeve. He tied the rubber band around her upper arm.

Sean. There, she felt him. He wasn't far away, actually. David had said neither he nor Sean could manifest, or affect the physical world, without her assistance. Since she felt less than able to offer such help right now, she'd have to go with another plan. Instead of drawing him to her, she sent a message down the tendril that led to Sean—and she prayed whatever she was doing would work. Hard to feel confident when she didn't understand how her own powers worked.

JT found a vein inside her elbow. He lowered the needle toward her skin.

She gathered every particle of energy inside her, compacted them into a stream of thought, and beamed it straight into the brain of one man.

"Wait," Waldron said.

JT frowned like a child who'd just been told not to eat that delicious cake sitting right in front of him.

Waldron cleared his throat and nodded toward David. "I, uh, think I should take this one outside. He's probably considering trying something while we're all distracted by your phlebotomy experiment."

Waving the needle at Grace, JT said, "He's our insurance against *her* trying something."

"I'll keep my weapon aimed at his head. But let me take him into the corridor. If she tries anything, I can still shoot him, but he won't be able to see what's happening in here or do anything to help her."

JT's expression turned contemplative for a moment, then he shrugged and said, "Whatever. Do it your way, Waldo."

Though she couldn't turn to look back at them, what with Battaglia holding her in a snugly threatening embrace, she heard two sets of footfalls move away toward the corridor. The door opened and shut behind Waldron and David. She felt David's absence, like the sunlight disappearing behind a cloud.

Sean was almost here. Time to let Waldo go.

She released him with a snap of power that surged back into her, melting into a faint sensation of static electricity. Neither JT nor Battaglia seemed to notice it.

She needed more power. Way more power.

David had explained that psychic abilities stemmed from a place, or maybe a state of mind, known as the crossroads. His explanation had left many questions unanswered. Still, if she could reach the crossroads again—as she'd done twice now, once accidentally and once on purpose—she might draw in enough power to really do something.

JT ran a finger over her skin. "Where'd that stupid vein go?"

Keeping her eyes open, hoping she looked scared rather than absent from her own mind, she let go of the invisible tether that bound her to the world around her. Her mind soared out of her body, up through a dark tunnel, and shot out into the vast blackness of open space. Star-like pinpoints of light winked into existence. They surrounded yet never touched her. She imagined throwing her arms open wide, welcoming in the power that burned everywhere in the void. It flowed into her, warm and soft and natural as a her own blood. It belonged to her, and she to it. Ribbons of light unfurled from the darkness between the stars to draw variegated lines connecting them.

Networks of power.

One line glowed brighter than the others. When she focused on it, the white strip pulsed green and then blue. At one end, the line broke free of the star anchoring it and writhed across empty space, stretching out into nothingness. A new light coursed down the line, turning it a shimmering gold.

It wanted her to follow it. She wanted to obey. The need almost overwhelmed her as she sensed the raw and unfathomable power the line promised her.

No. She couldn't go anywhere except back to the facility. Everything that mattered to her in the world depended on it.

The golden line beckoned her.

She turned away from it. The loss flooded through her like grief, but faded as quickly as it had come. The power she'd gathered from the crossroads burned inside her, a welcome fire to chase away the cold. She sank down, out of the void, falling faster and faster the closer she got to the real world. This time, though, she softened the reentry in a way she couldn't understand but knew how to accomplish. Rather than slamming back into herself, she settled in gently.

"Ah," JT said, tapping her arm along the inside of her elbow. "There it is."

He'd located the vein again. Adjusting his grip on the needle, he prepared to pierce her skin.

"Experiment's over," she said.

He scrunched his lips as he squinted up at her. "Not hardly."

Without even tensing a muscle, she flung JT and Battaglia away from her simultaneously. The billionaire crashed into his desk and tumbled backward over it, end over end. Battaglia hit the wall so hard the door rattled in its frame. His eyes bulged, then fluttered shut as his body slid down the wall to crumple on the floor.

A crashing sound erupted outside the door, muffled by the barrier.

That wasn't her. Sean must've arrived at last.

Grace whirled toward the doorway.

"Hang on," a voice croaked from behind her.

She hesitated. A scrabbling noise made her twist around to glance at the desk.

JT clung to it like a castaway to a life preserver. His hair was tousled, his mouth open as he gasped for breaths. The redness of exertion, and perhaps pain, colored his pale cheeks.

Why was she waiting? Not because he'd told her. No, surely not. An intuition encouraged her to hear him out. She could always hurl him into the wall in a minute or two.

The notion struck her as exceedingly odd, yet true. At least for the moment. The power burning inside her had dimmed a teeny bit. How much longer she could retain it, she didn't know.

JT pushed up onto his feet, dragged his chair closer, and plopped down onto it.

Grace nabbed Battaglia's weapon from the floor near the unconscious guard and yanked her gun out of his waistband. Striding to the desk, she trained her gun on JT He looked terribly annoyed, but also very weak.

"I need to show you something," he said, pointing at the laptop computer that sat on one corner of the desktop.

She marched around the desk to stand beside his chair, careful to keep her gun aimed at his head. Nodding toward the computer, she said, "Go ahead."

He dragged the laptop computer across his desk toward him. Flipping up the computer's lid, he tapped keys. A window opened on-screen. It looked like a video feed, though the room it showed was cloaked in shadows. He tapped more keys, and on the other end of the feed, lights powered on inside the room. He was remotely controlling the lights and who knew what else.

"What are you doing?" she demanded, jamming the gun into his skull.

He paused in his typing. "Turning on the lights so you can see. Don't worry, Gracie, I can't kill you with my computer." He threw her a sidelong glance. "Which doesn't mean I can't kill you at all."

"Shut up and get on with your show and tell."

He punched keys. The camera panned left and stopped, then zoomed in on a lump on the floor. Though a blanket covered the lump, a rounded shape stuck out from under it.

A human head. The lump was a person.

Grace swallowed. Her jaw tightened.

"Watch this," JT said, pointing at the screen.

Above the blanket-covered human lump, a newspaper was taped to the wall. JT zoomed in on the paper, until she could read the date printed below the masthead. Today's date.

As he zoomed out again, JT told her, "I have the guards change out the paper every day. I knew this time would come, and you wouldn't believe it without proof."

"Believe what?"

He waved his finger at the screen. "About time the old fart woke up."

On the screen, the person swaddled in the blanket stirred, shoved the blanket off, and pushed up into a sitting position. The man scratched his bald head and yawned, deepening the wrinkles on his face.

Oh God. It was her grandfather.

"This is a trick," she hissed. "My grandfather died in a plane crash."

JT smirked. "I made it look that way. But I needed to know what he knew, so I held onto Edward. No matter how much I hurt him, though, he wouldn't tell me anything. It was really annoying."

She couldn't speak. If her grandfather was alive...

"Oh," JT said, studying her expression, "I'm afraid your folks are dead, dead, dead. I lost my head when Chris-cross lied to me. She shouldn't have done that." He leaned back in the chair, folding his hands over his abdomen. "When I found out Edward was lying to me, that he wasn't in Washington lobbying for grants for the project but was plotting with a senator to shut me down...well, I reined in my anger and came up with a better plan for him."

She thrust the gun in JT's face. "Where is he?"

The scumbag smiled at her. *Smiled.*

"Where?" she demanded.

"I'm not telling." His lips worked as if he were trying not to giggle. "Until you give me what I want."

"My blood."

"Mm-hm."

She bumped the gun's muzzle into his forehead. "No way."

"Can't kill me, Gracie. Not if you want to find Gramps."

She stared at him, anger boiling inside her. Killing him sounded like a great idea. Though she was no murderer, and had never wanted to kill anyone before, right now she wanted to pull the trigger more than she wanted to breathe.

But she couldn't. Not yet.

JT propped his left ankle atop his right knee. "I can tell from your cute little frustrated expression that you're finally catching on. You have no choice."

He emphasized the last two words, as if she needed a reminder. She did not.

"You can't find him without me," JT said.

Acid churned in her stomach, and she felt a surge of queasy desperation. Until a realization flooded over, cold and sudden as a bucket of ice water dumped on her head. He was wrong. She didn't need him to tell her where to find her grandfather. She could do it alone—psychically.

David had said a traveler needed a connection to the other person in order to track them. Everything he'd done, everything she'd felt from and for him, told her that she already had the best connection of all.

Love.

It linked her to David, and to her grandfather. She could find Edward McLean without any help from anyone, especially not Jackson Tennant.

She took a step back, snaked her left arm under her right to reach the desktop, and slammed the computer's lid shut.

The look of self-satisfaction on JT's face crumbled. His eyes widened as his mouth dropped open just enough to prove he understood that his advantage had snuffed out in the space of one second. He knew she'd figured out she didn't need him, though he still needed her. Almost in slow motion, his expression morphed through childish irritation and into seething anger. Lips squeezed into a pout, he huffed out a breath through his nose.

"It won't work," he said, sounding less than convinced himself. "You're not strong enough to find him with your powers. Amnesia makes you weak. You don't remember how to do that stuff, which means you totally suck at it."

His tone had shifted into childish territory again, lending him the air of a little boy holding his breath until he got his way. He wouldn't get his way this time.

She stood there looking at him, her gun pointed at his head. A moment ago, she'd wanted to kill him. Now, she didn't know. Maybe she ought to kill him, because he sure as hell wouldn't give up stalking and tormenting her until he got his way. But shooting an unarmed man, it made her gut twist.

The door burst open.

Grace didn't jump. Didn't even flinch. Somehow, in the back of her mind, she'd known the door would be thrust inward—and she'd known who would walk through the opening.

David stomped across the office to the desk. He paused for only a split second to glance at the unconscious guard slumped against the wall. Battaglia showed no signs of rousing anytime soon. Sean hovered outside the doorway in the corridor, clutching a handgun. Waldron lay sprawled on the floor at Sean's feet, in the direct path of the handgun's muzzle.

Her guys had disabled Waldron and commandeered the man's gun. Sean must've received her message after all. She really hadn't been sure that had worked until right this moment.

Across the desk from her, David glowered at JT. Wow, he looked as ready to kill the murderous twit as she had felt moments earlier.

She tossed Battaglia's gun to him. David caught it in one hand.

"Keep an eye on him," she said, nodding toward JT. "While I plan our road trip."

He arched his eyebrows, but leveled the big gun at JT.

She wondered why the creep hadn't tried to attack her. Given his pallid skin and sunken cheeks, he probably lacked the strength to challenge her physically. Crazy though he was, he must've known his current limitations. That's why he had Waldron and Battaglia, his devoted minions.

Well, maybe not that devoted. She got the feeling Waldron disliked JT with an intensity that bordered on the murderous. Battaglia seemed to care mostly about his own wants, which revolved around violence mostly.

A sickly mastermind. Minions with shaky allegiances. Perhaps the situation wasn't as hopeless as she'd thought.

An alarm buzzed.

The sound echoed down the corridor. Red lights along the floorboards began to pulse outside the office door. Inside the room, everything stayed the same. A recorded voice issued from speakers hidden somewhere in the room and the corridor.

"Emergency," the female voice declared. "All personnel should make their way to an approved evacuation route in a calm and orderly fashion. Emergency—"

The message repeated, then fell silent as the alarm continued to buzz in rhythm with the pulsing red lights.

JT chuckled. "Guess you didn't know about the cameras. They're everywhere. Plus, Waldo would've called for backup."

Eyes and ears everywhere, Sean had told her. And she'd completely forgotten. Why hadn't Sean reminded her?

She glanced at the kid in the hallway, holding a gun on the much-bigger Waldron. Sean looked up at her, as if he'd sensed her attention on him. His cheeks flushed and he shrugged one shoulder.

No, she couldn't be mad at him. He'd done what she asked, without question and without hesitation. If she remembered knowing him before, maybe she'd understand why he trusted her that much. Sean was too polite to toss her an I-told-you-so.

Not that any of them could've done much about the security cameras.

Grace squinted at JT. "What's with the emergency declaration? You that afraid of me?"

"Not hardly. I don't need help anymore, but I don't want any witnesses either."

She almost asked witnesses to what, but then decided the answer would only unnerve her. And she needed all the nerve she had.

"Give up," JT said, spreading hands wide. "You can't win."

She marched around the desk, heading straight for Sean.

The boy looked up in surprise. She reached out to pat his arm.

"You warned me," she said, "and I screwed up. I need your help again."

Sean bit his lip. "Okay."

"You know this facility inside and out, right?" When Sean gave a weak nod, she whispered, "Good, I need your expertise right now. Want to help me save the world?"

The boy's eyes bulged. He blinked and glanced down the corridor. As his eyes returned to normal, his face took on an expression she'd never seen on him before—at least so far as she recalled. He looked not quite smug, but definitely full of mischievous confidence.

"Sure," he said.

Grace tapped her gun against her thigh. She had an idea. And she was positive David would hate it.

Oh well. He'd get over it.

Stepping over Waldron, she sidled up close to Sean and ducked her head to whisper to him. "I need you to tell me how to do something."

David refused to look back at the doorway. He wanted to see what Grace was doing, wanted to hear what she and Sean were talking about, but he knew if he averted his attention from JT for one second, the bastard would take advantage of the lapse.

From somewhere out of sight, down an adjoining corridor, boots pounded out a cacophonous beat. Soon a battalion of guards would arrive.

Whatever Grace was up to, it couldn't be good.

Boots pounded closer.

JT leaned his head back against the chair, eyes half closed. He looked far too comfortable with his situation.

Turning sideways to the desk, keeping the gun aimed at JT, David called out to Grace, "Get in here, both of you."

Grace pointed at Waldron. "What about him?"

"Forget Waldron. Get in here and shut the door. Lock it manually if you can."

At Grace's urging, Sean hustled into the office first. Grace followed close behind him and closed the solid metal door. She found the lock, engaging it with a faint click.

"What now?" she asked, walking up beside David.

"Not sure yet."

Though her expression betrayed nothing, he sensed her unease. Not psychically, not really. He felt it in the way two people who knew each other intimately, in the emotional sense, could discern the other person's feelings. Unease was warranted. Once the guards arrived, they'd find a way through the locked door. Ram it down. Blast a hole through it. Anything.

JT lounged in his big leather executive chair, hands dangling off the chair's arms, a relaxed half smile curving his pale lips. Despite his deathly complexion, he seemed fully at ease and confident. He believed they had no way out of the office and that his lackeys would rescue him in short order.

David ground his teeth. He'd had enough of JT.

Grace settled a hand on his arm. "It's not worth it."

"Yes," he said, striding around the desk to JT, "actually, I think it is."

He smacked the gun into JT's head. The bastard grunted. As his eyes drifted shut, he slumped in the chair.

"Feel better?" Grace asked.

He crossed around in front of the desk again. To Sean, he said, "Do you know another way out of this room?"

The boy nodded. He pointed a finger toward the left rear corner of the office. "Hidden door over there. I've seen him use it, when he doesn't want anybody to know what he's doing. There aren't any cameras in here. He sneaks out to a secret control room where he can spy on everybody in the facility."

Grace made a disgusted noise. "Of course he does."

Sean led David toward the secret door, which was well concealed, given the fact that David saw nothing but blank wall in that spot. Peripherally, he saw Grace snag the blood-stained gauze from JT's desk before hurrying toward David. Knowing Grace, she couldn't stand the idea of the lunatic billionaire licking her blood off the gauze. When she got home, she'd probably burn the damn thing. Hell, he'd light the fire for her.

Stuffing the gauze in her pocket, she halted beside Sean. David stood on Sean's opposite side. Close up like this, David noticed a slender crack in the wall that was practically invisible unless a person knew to look for it.

"Oh," Sean said. "Forgot about the code."

Before David could ask what code, Sean darted over to the desk. He flipped open the laptop computer. Fingers hovering over the keyboard, he stared at the screen. His expression went blank.

"The video feed," Grace said in a voice so quiet he strained to make out the words. What video feed, he wanted to ask, but the question could wait.

The door knob rattled. Voices murmured on the other side of the door.

David said, "The code, Sean."

The boy kept staring at the screen.

A fist, or a similar blunt object, banged on the door. A hard male voice said, "Sir, are you in there?"

Bang. Another fist thump.

Sean blinked several times in quick succession. He switched his focus to the keyboard as he punched keys for letters and numbers.

JT had clearly taken no precautions against travelers spying on him in his own office. Overconfident as he appeared to be, he likely thought he had all of the travelers under control, drugged into near-comatose states or so beaten down by the experiments that they lacked the energy for extrasensory spying.

Mostly, JT was right. David clenched his hands into fists. Even he and Sean had trouble pushing through the drug-induced stupor.

Sean tapped one final key.

Inside the wall, a mechanism thunked. A door-size panel separated from the wall with a faint hiss, opening away from them on silent hinges. Lights came on automatically to dispel the blackness beyond the portal. The doorway revealed a passage that extended for perhaps thirty feet, then made a ninety-degree turn to the left.

David motioned for Sean and Grace to enter the passage. They crossed the threshold single file, Sean leading the way.

Half turning, David looked at the laptop computer on JT's desk.

"Coming?" Grace asked.

"Yes." David raised the gun and fired three rounds into the laptop. Splinters of plastic and metal spewed from the computer. "I'm coming now."

He walked through the doorway toward Grace.

A swishing sound drew his attention back to the doorway. He paused to look back.

The door shut with a dull thunk. David hoped destroying the laptop would at least slow down JT's efforts to track them. He had a hunch the jackass kept the program that controlled the secret door on his computer and no other. David had bought the three of them time, though how much, he couldn't say.

"Where are we going?" he asked Grace.

"JT's private control room."

"To…"

She looked straight into his eyes and said, in a matter-of-fact tone, "To destroy the facility."

Chapter Twenty-Seven

"Are you insane?" David seized her arm, dragging her to a stop. He gaped at her, eyes wide and locked on hers. "Say that again, in case I was having a stroke and didn't hear you correctly."

"You heard me," she said. "I'm going to destroy this facility."

Between gritted teeth, he said, "I repeat, are you insane?"

"Possibly."

"Destroy it," Sean said in a quiet, almost reverent tone. "Get rid of all their research, so maybe nobody can do to anyone else what they did to us."

"Exactly," Grace agreed.

She'd considered the possibility that a computer wiz like Jackson Tennant might've backed up the data off-site, but then she realized if he'd done that he wouldn't need the flash drive her grandfather left for her. Maybe he viewed the facility's research as too explosive to risk letting it outside the facility's computer system, even for backup purposes. JT clearly didn't like to share.

It made no difference either way. She must destroy this place, even if it proved to be but one head of the hydra. They could chop off the other heads later, one by one. Destroying this facility was, she felt certain, vital to tearing apart JT's clandestine empire.

"We can't do this," David said. "There are human beings inside this facility."

"They're evacuating," Sean pointed out, "so we won't be hurting anybody."

"We have to be sure everyone's out."

Grace studied David's expression. He looked tired, harried, and vaguely annoyed, but no longer in shock over her plan. She laid a hand on his cheek and said, "We will be sure."

His skin felt different. She couldn't quite describe the difference. He felt more...real.

Sean led them through the network of corridors with a confidence she'd never seen him in before. He knew exactly where he was going. And he knew freedom was no longer out of his grasp. She had an idea of what that felt like because, though she hadn't been physically held prisoner, her amnesia had boxed her in like a cage. Now she felt the bars weakening.

No doors opened off the corridors. The emergency lights cast a pulsating red glow on the blank gray walls. They rounded another corner and there, at the end of a short corridor, stood a metal door that bore no markings and had no knob. A keypad affixed to the wall beside the door restricted access. Shawn trotted up to the doorway, hesitating with his hand raised over the keypad.

Grace and David came up behind Sean. Just as she started to wonder whether he knew the password, Sean tapped a series of keys on the pad. A blooping sound heralded success, and the door swung inward with a thunk and a hiss.

They walked into a room measuring ten feet wide by ten feet long. A huge flat-screen TV occupied one wall, its screen divided into eight square sections that displayed rotating, full-color views from the security camera feeds. Beneath the TV screen sat a surprisingly modest metal desk equipped with a new-looking desktop computer, complete with a wide-screen monitor and a wireless mouse and keyboard. A nondescript office chair completed the room's furnishings.

Sean sat down on the office chair and began typing on the keyboard.

"What are you doing?" Grace asked.

"Checking the thermal sensors." His fingers tapped out a fast, irregular rhythm on the keyboard. "If anybody's left in the facility, we'll see them here."

An image appeared on the computer screen—shades of blue, red, green, and yellow.

David, standing beside her, pointed at the colorful blobs on the screen. "These are heat signatures given off by human bodies. The facility is equipped with infrared sensors that can detect them." David bent down to squint at the screen. "Where is this, Sean?"

"JT's office, and the corridor outside it."

"Is there anyone else left inside the facility?"

Sean shook his head. "Just us and the nine people at JT's office."

"Six guards plus JT, Waldron, and Battaglia."

Grace knelt beside Sean, her eyes focused on the screen. "Can you bring up the camera feed from JT's office?"

"Told you, there isn't one." Sean hunched his shoulders. "JT likes his privacy."

"Of course he does." She gnawed the inside of her lip, staring at the colored blobs on the thermal sensor. "What about the cameras in the corridor? If the door to JT's office is open, maybe one of the outside cameras can see inside."

"Maybe," Sean said, as he set about punching keys and tapping the mouse button. The images on the big-screen TV changed. All but three of the feeds disappeared from the screen, and the remainder expanded to fill the space. The feeds offered three slightly different views of the corridor. The closest camera was posted above the door to JT's office, aimed out at the corridor. The next camera out pointed toward the office at an angle. The third was at the end of the corridor furthest from the office, aimed straight at the office door. It was too far away to see much, though.

"Can you zoom in?" she asked. "With the camera at the end of the corridor."

Sean fiddled with the mouse and the feed from the camera furthest from the office expanded to fill the entire TV screen. The guards milled around outside the office, but between their bodies she spied the interior of the room. Battaglia was out of sight, probably to one side of the doorway. Waldron stood at the desk, his hands on the wooden surface, bent over as if conversing with JT. The billionaire lounged in his executive chair, gesticulating with his hands. Although she couldn't see their faces, their body language hinted at an intense and not entirely cordial discussion.

Waldron threw up his hands and spun away from the desk. He stalked out of the office, past the guards, and out of sight. At his desk, JT retrieved something from a drawer.

"Can you zoom in more?" she asked Sean.

Sean tapped a button on the keyboard.

The image pulled in tighter. It had enough resolution to show JT's face with only a little fuzziness. In his hand he clasped a syringe filled with light blue liquid.

"What is that?" she said, not really expecting a response.

David, bent over the desk, turned his head to look at her. "It looks like the drug cocktail they used to give some of their test subjects, back when they were trying to find ways to enhance psychic abilities. They stopped using the concoction because it had nasty side effects. Several people died."

Her chest tightened as if a phantom hand clenched her heart. "Did they give you the cocktail?"

"Once." He straightened, stepping away from the desk. "I survived."

She almost made a sarcastic comment about stating the obvious. Something in the tone of his voice stopped her. Later, she might ask him what the drugs had done to him. She might ask a lot of questions about his time in the facility. For now, she asked a different question. "What is JT doing with those drugs?"

"I remember," David said, "there was some discussion about using the drug cocktail to trigger latent abilities. The scientists had a theory that everyone has the potential for extrasensory faculties buried deep inside them. They theorized that if the drugs could enhance existing abilities, then perhaps a higher dosage could also bring out latent abilities."

"A higher dosage? More than what killed people?"

"Not everyone died. Andrew survived multiple injections."

"Who would be willing to risk that?" She glanced at the TV screen, which showed JT lowering the needle to his arm. A lunatic would risk it, naturally, for the chance to gain untold power. She rose from her crouch and said, "JT's been injecting himself. That's why he can only use his abilities to harass me sometimes, and that must be why he looks like a man who's not just knocking at death's door, but standing in the threshold. The drugs are killing him."

"Not fast enough."

The anger in his voice snapped her attention to his face. He looked tense, though not vengeful.

"He's killing himself," she said. "We don't have to do it for him."

David remained silent for a few seconds, then he took in a long breath and, as he let it out, turned to face her. He said, "How do you intend to destroy the facility?"

"The armory." At his puzzled expression, she explained, "It's full of ammunition, which is essentially explosives. I'm going to find a way to set it off."

He practically shouted, "Set off an explosion?"

"Keep it down, will you?"

In a calmer voice, he said, "And how do you plan on detonating the ammunition?"

"Not sure yet."

"Well, as long as you have a plan."

Sean had switched back to displaying three camera feeds on the TV screen. The guards were jogging down the corridor away from JT's office.

"They're coming for us," David said. "We have to get out of this facility while we still can."

"I agree," Grace told him.

His mouth dropped open as he stared at her. "You're abandoning your plan that easily? I was prepared to argue my case—" his expression went blank, and then he closed his mouth, clenching his jaw so tightly he probably could've squeezed charcoal into diamonds between his teeth. "You're not abandoning anything, are you? The plan is to remote view the armory, spot a way to set off an explosion, and manifest in order to accomplish the task."

Oh, she wished he didn't know her quite so well. Everything would've gone much smoother if he hadn't figured it all out.

"Yes," she said, "that's the plan."

He motioned toward the door. "Let's go. You can do that from outside the facility."

"In a minute." Looking at Sean, she pointed at the big TV screen. "Show me the armory."

The boy complied, tapping keys until another feed replaced the images from the corridor outside JT's office. This feed showed a dimly lit room packed with metal boxes, racks of guns of all sizes, and shelves of Kevlar vests. She let the image burn into her mind, until she felt certain she could recall it later.

Then she let David usher her out of the room. Sean pushed past them to take the lead, guiding them around corner after corner. Minutes passed as they wended their way through the network of passages, but finally they reached a sturdy door identical to the one Battaglia had led her to after he captured her outside the facility.

Sean entered the code on the keypad, waited a few seconds, and entered a second code. The locking mechanism chunked. The door swung outward several inches.

David shoved the door open all the way. He tiptoed across the threshold into the blackness outside the doorway. Fluorescent lights flickered on, illuminating a narrow passage carved out of the bedrock.

Grace followed David into the passage, with Sean trailing behind her. The kid paused long enough to shove the door closed again.

Eyeing Sean, she asked, "If you knew the way out, why didn't you escape before now?"

"Couldn't get into JT's office. Anybody who wants in has to swipe their ID card and enter a passcode, but that's just for show. See, what nobody knows is that JT looks through the security camera to see who's there. Then he decides whether to let you in."

It made sense. JT was paranoid, secretive, and possibly the biggest control freak the world had ever seen. And he loved messing with people's heads.

They started off down the passageway. It was narrow, so they half walked, half jogged single file through the rough-hewn tunnel. The air grew stuffy and thick. She felt cramped, like she couldn't get enough room or breathe enough oxygen. The sweat evaporating from her skin did nothing to cool her. David and Sean appeared unaffected by the conditions. She watched them pull farther and farther ahead of her, and though she tried to call out to them, her vocal cords emitted no sound. Her head felt heavy, her thoughts fuzzy. This was wrong, all wrong.

Pain stabbed through her head. She cried out. As the sharp pain dissipated, a crackling sensation erupted inside her brain. She fell to her knees on the floor, clutching her head in her hands, willing the crackling pain to end. It kept going, like an electrical storm in her brain.

The pain vanished. She sobbed with relief. But something was still off inside her, something that felt dark and alien and intrusive.

She dropped her hands to rest them on her thighs. Her mind felt numb and disconnected from her body. Had she traveled without realizing it? Was she really here? Where was she?

A hard object pressed against her right palm. She looked down at her hand, where it rested on her thigh. She was gripping a knife. A shiny, curved blade. Long and wickedly sharp. The wooden handle pressed into her palm.

David ran up to her, dropping to his knees in front of her.

Kill him, do it now, you want to, so go ahead and do it.

She rammed the knife into his gut.

"No!"

The word burst out of her as an anguished howl. She tried to yank the knife out, but it refused to budge. Tears streamed down her cheeks, blurring her vision. She shouted wordless cries of rage and grief.

Hands grasped her shoulders, drawing her into an embrace that felt warm and strong and familiar.

"David?" she asked, though she knew it couldn't be him. *But oh God, please let it be him.*

"I'm here," he murmured in her ear. "What's wrong? What happened?"

He stroked her hair and rocked her gently in his arms. Her face was tucked against his neck, and the scent of him filled her nostrils. The feel of his body, so warm and real and alive, broke the spell. It had been a vision, terrifying and vivid, yet not real. The thoughts had come from her own mind, yet not her own mind. Different. Colder. She could feel the other mind, the invader, touching her psyche. Grasping for a handhold. A way to control her. She'd almost given it to him.

"Grace?" David said, his voice tight with worry.

Sniffling, wiping the tears from her eyes, she said, "It was JT. He got into my head and made me see things. Maybe the physical proximity gave him more power, or maybe he injected himself with even more of that drug cocktail." She lifted her head to meet his gaze. "However he did it, it was much worse than the other times."

So many deaths, all my fault, I could have saved them all. But I didn't want to, I wanted them dead.

No. Those thoughts originated from JT, the creep who wanted her sanity for a keepsake. He'd have to fight for it. He'd have to kill her for it.

She looked down at her hands.

Her nails. Crusted with blood. Red liquid dribbling from her fingertips.

Do it, do it, DO IT!

The voice screamed inside her head, the voice that was not her own. She fought back with everything she had. The presence ripped free of her, like claws tearing flesh. White-hot pain sliced through her body from head to toe. Her stomach heaved. She choked back the gorge. Coughing, clutching her abdomen, she bent forward.

David grasped her face, one hand on each cheek, and tilted her head up to face him. He locked his gaze on hers, his forehead wrinkled, a frown gouging deep lines across his face. Her pulse beat like a bass drum in her head. Though his lips moved, she heard nothing but the drumbeat.

Look at me, he mouthed. Or maybe he'd spoken the words. The drumbeat inside her drowned out everything else. With an effort that almost hurt, she forced her eyes to focus on his.

A gentle warmth washed over her, into her, chasing away the chill left behind by JT's attack. The false images and alien thoughts faded away until they became wisps of memory. The drumbeat silenced as her heart rate normalized. Sweat trickled over her scalp, down her neck.

"I'm okay now," she said.

She felt David relax and watched the lines on his face smooth out as his frown melted into a more neutral expression. Brushing a lock of hair from her face, he asked, "Is he gone?"

"Yeah. I pushed him out."

A ghost of a smile flickered on his face. "I know how that feels."

"I pushed him a little harder than I pushed you. He really did not want to go."

"I hope he's in so much pain he's curled up in the fetal position under his desk."

The dark thread of anger in his voice was unmistakable. She didn't like hearing it. If David gave in to his anger, JT would win. She could never let that happen.

She slid a hand through his hair, kissed him softly, and whispered, "He can't hurt me again. I won't let him."

He looked less than convinced in the half second before he brushed his lips over hers and stood up, lifting her to her feet with him. He clasped her hand. "Let's put as much distance between you and that bastard as we can."

Then he led her down the tunnel.

Chapter Twenty-Eight

Grace hurried down the corridor in Sean's wake, propelled onward by David's arm around her waist. Though she felt stronger with each step away from the facility, the aftereffects of JT's attack proved longer lasting than ever before. Evicting JT from her mind had drained her, for sure, yet the attack also left her with a curious side effect. Along with her physical strength, she felt something else building.

Her powers.

She might've thought she'd tapped into the Golden Power, unintentionally, except that she didn't feel omniscient. Far from it. She felt like a dinghy out on the open ocean, where land is out of sight. Still, she sensed an unknown source replenishing her psychic energy, boosting her powers. It made no sense. Then again, since when had anything about her extrasensory abilities made sense?

Other questions seemed more pressing at the moment. While concentrating on the ground ahead of her, afraid she might trip if she glanced away, she asked David, "Why do things that happen in my mind feel so real? I really thought I'd killed you. I could see and feel the blood on my hands." She thought of the bloody gauze, the sole physical evidence of the cut that had once slashed across her palm. "I dreamed once that I cut my hand and, when I woke up, my hand was bleeding. Then later, the cut was gone. It's crazy."

"Whatever happens to your metaphysical body," David said, "also happens to your physical body. It's because of your mind that your body functions. The two can never be fully separated. If your mind thinks your hand is injured, then your hand is injured. It's that simple."

Ahead of them, Sean halted. The tunnel had dead-ended at a door identical to the one that granted access to the escape route. This door, however, had no keypad or card reader. Instead, a large metal lever opened the door.

Sean tried to move the lever, with little success.

David released Grace and strode up to the door to help Sean. Together, the pair heaved the lever up to unlock the door. The mechanism groaned. Sean and David panted with the effort, their faces contorted, their arm muscles flexing. When the lever finally clicked into its open position, the mechanism let out one final groan of metal on metal. The men adjusted their holds onto the lever and pulled on it. The door swung inward inch by inch, its bottom edge scraping across the dirt floor.

They opened the door a couple feet and, sweat dripping from their faces, gave up the battle. The gap offered just enough space for one person to squeeze through, into whatever lay beyond.

Darkness, she saw as she leaned sideways to peek out the doorway. A breeze wafted through the opening, carrying with it the indefinable yet distinct smell of the outdoors. The dry, chilly air tickled her skin.

David motioned for Sean to step aside. When the boy did, David sidled out the door. He vanished into the darkness outside. The soft crunching of his footfalls provided the sole evidence of his presence.

Seconds later, his footsteps drew nearer again. His silhouette filled the gap between the door and its frame. Light from inside the tunnel revealed his face.

"It's clear," he said, "for now. Let's go."

Sean exited next. Grace shuffled to the door, turned sideways, and slipped through the gap. The night air enveloped her in its chill. Tilting her head back, she saw the clear sky speckled with stars. To her left and right, she found earthen walls and, straight ahead, a steep grade inset with steps cut out of the ground itself. The steps led up to ground level.

David took her hand, helping her up the steps. Sean waited for them at the top, his body visible as a silhouette against the starry sky. Far in the distance, a coyote howled.

"Move," David said, his tone more gentle than his word choice.

She let him pull her away from the steps, out across the depression that cradled the facility. A statement he'd made minutes ago bubbled to the surface of her mind, and she had to ask, "Are you sure nothing can separate the mind from the body?"

"One thing can," he said. "Death."

"So whatever happens to your mind happens to your body."

"The mind *is* the body."

"Whatever." She tripped over a rock. David caught her, and they resumed their brisk walking pace. Shaking her head, she told him, "It's like I went to bed one night and woke up in a parallel universe."

"Same universe. But now your eyes have adjusted, letting you see the things that hide in shadows."

The shadows of what, she almost asked, then decided maybe she didn't want that much clarity. Understanding, truth—she had demanded them, damn the cost. She'd sacrificed everything for a truth that didn't ease her mind and that nobody else in the world would believe. In spite of what she'd lost, she knew with stark certainty that she would, without hesitation or regret, do it all again. Her parents and grandfather had given their lives willingly to protect her, to protect the world from enemies bent on attaining a kind of power no living thing should possess. If necessary, she would make the same sacrifice, because she hadn't quite given up everything yet. She had one gift left to give.

Her life.

JT had murdered her parents. He had faked her grandfather's death and now held him hostage. She must know why. She must understand.

The cut on her palm had faded. Soon it would vanish, taking with it the memory of the dream. Would everything that had happened lately dissipate into the void of yesterday? Would she someday think of it all as a bad dream?

No. Nothing could erase the memory.

Grace twisted around to look back. There, maybe a quarter mile away, stood the facility. It looked different than the first time she'd spied it in the darkness. Then she realized why. The tunnel had led them out on the opposite side of the facility from where she'd entered.

The plan. In the chaos following JT's attack, she'd forgotten about the plan to destroy the facility. Right now seemed like a good time to implement it.

She wrenched her hand free of David's and stopped dead.

He stopped too, and glanced back at her, though she couldn't see his face. She knew what expression he wore even without seeing it. Annoyed. Confused. Worried. She likely wore the same look.

"No," David said.

"Yes." She planted her hands on her hips. "I have to do it."

"Fine. Then I'm going with you."

He wanted to travel with her. The idea shot a spark of excitement through her. Had they traveled together before? What had it felt like, to share a psychic experience? She wanted to find out. Sharing such an experience with JT felt like the worst kind of torture. But sharing it with David...

His hand found hers in the darkness. He twined his fingers with hers.

Boom.

The ground shook. As the echoes of the first explosion died away, a second detonation rocked the earth. The booming ricocheted off the walls of the depression.

A third explosion went off at the nearest end of the facility. The ground shook so hard Grace lost her balance, stumbling into David's arms. They held each other up as the tremors subsided and the cacophony faded into a silence that felt unnatural.

David's mouth brushed against her ear. "Did you..."

"No. You?"

"Definitely not."

She stared into the darkness, which she would've sworn had gotten darker, but discerned nothing. A cloud of what she took for dust blocked out part of the sky. As the cloud thinned, flames emerged from where the facility's black shape had squatted.

"Who did it?" she wondered aloud. Then the answer struck her. "JT. It must've been."

"But why?" David asked.

"Because he's a spoiled brat who didn't get his way."

David tightened his hand around hers. Without a word, he turned and broke into a jog, hauling her with him. She had to run to keep up with him.

A sensation rippled through her. Indescribable. Unpleasant.

He's watching.

She froze. David nearly yanked her shoulder out of its socket before realizing she'd stopped. Halting, he half turned to look back at her. His fingers still grasped hers, though barely.

"We're not alone," she said.

"Damn straight you aren't."

The voice was not David's or Sean's. The words, and the tone of the voice, sent a shiver down her spine. Off to the left, a shape separated from the darkness. The shape drew closer, until it resolved into a human silhouette that stopped a dozen feet away. Although she couldn't make out any facial features, she knew who it was.

JT sniggered. "Gotcha."

David launched himself across the distance to JT, tackling the other man.

Except he didn't. He couldn't. David sailed right through JT—not past him, but actually through him—landing with a thud and grunt.

"Oh sorry," JT said, with mock chagrin. "Shoulda warned you. I'm not really here."

Grace couldn't speak or move. She watched as David levered his body up off the ground, hopped to his feet, and turned to face the apparition of JT.

For he was a ghost, essentially. Not the ghost of a dead man. The ghost of a living soul.

"One more thing," JT said, his tone a little too smug. "I may not be here, but my peeps are."

Her voice unfroze just enough to utter two words. "Your what?"

"My peeps. My guys." He waved an arm in an expansive gesture. "They've got you surrounded."

Lights flared on all around them. Grace flinched and squinted, throwing up an arm to shield her eyes. Her vision adjusted fast enough that she saw the beams emanated from lantern flashlights, of the multi-million-candlepower variety, and the lights were held by black-suited commandos. Six of them. The guards who'd stayed behind when the facility was evacuated.

Shit.

"Let's get down to business," JT said. "Where's my flash drive?"

Chapter Twenty-Nine

Grace stared at the illusion of JT, wishing it were nothing but a hallucination. She knew better. The mechanics of psychic phenomena still confused her, but she'd learned from firsthand experience that something unreal could exert very real forces and cause genuine damage.

As she tilted one hip to adjust her stance, a hard lump pressed into her belly. Her gun. She'd tucked it inside her waistband during their flight through the tunnel. Even if she managed to pull it out unnoticed, she had little confidence that she could cause enough damage to matter, at least not before several large and heavily armed men tackled her.

"Do you really think I'd bring the flash drive here?" she said. "I'm not that stupid."

Although she might not have been the smartest person on the planet, she'd at least had the brains to mail the flash drive to herself, at her Texas address. It was safe, relatively speaking, for the time being.

"Give me my flash drive," JT said, "or my guys will kill your guys. And they'll start with your boyfriend."

"Maybe you shouldn't have blown up your only other copy of your research."

"What makes you think it was my only other copy?"

"Because if you had another copy, you wouldn't be pestering me about the flash drive."

"Good point." The apparition of JT shrugged. "Might as well tell you. You won't live long enough to tell anyone else." He let out an annoyed sigh. "Edward didn't just make a copy of all the research, he also completely erased it from the facility's computers in the process. And he did such a good job we couldn't recover anything from the servers."

Well at least one part of the nightmare finally made sense. JT and his minions had gone to deadly lengths to obtain the flash drive because it contained the only copy of the facility's research. She doubted one little flash drive could hold the entirety of the facility's research, but it must contain the crucial bits needed to bring down JT, his cohorts, and possibly his whole empire. She'd had the key to his destruction in her pocket all this time.

Ideally, one of them needed to travel to wherever JT was hiding and stop this madness at the source. Unfortunately, that plan had two problems. First, David couldn't manifest without her help, and second, her strength had returned but not to the point where she felt capable of manifesting for any meaningful length of time. For those two reasons, she'd ruled out stopping the physical JT. She must stop the astral JT instead. Luckily, despite the drugs, he clearly lacked the ability to manifest.

JT apparently had no powers, or extremely weak powers, without the drugs. That might mean they had a chance. She needed no drugs to access her powers, and yet using them drained her quicker than slashing her wrists. From her past experiences with JT, she suspected his drug-induced powers drained him even faster. On top of that, he was dying. She knew what she had to do. She just wasn't sure how to do it.

Though David had gotten up off the ground after his spill, he lingered behind JT, twenty feet from Grace and Sean. She stared intently at David until he turned his eyes toward her.

As if he could read her thoughts, David mouthed, "No."

She didn't dare make any response. If JT decided she and David were conspiring against him, she couldn't predict the mad man's response.

"Give me the flash drive," JT said. His voice had taken on a petulant tone. "I'll count to ten and if you haven't given it to me by then, your boyfriend dies."

The commandos had spread out to form a circle around them. Because there were only six of them, that meant they stood widely spaced around the three prisoners and the apparition of JT. Two of the commandos held their weapons trained on David. One kept his eye on Sean, while a full three commandos had Grace in their sights.

In a different situation, attracting the attention of three brawny men might boost her ego. Right now it made her entire body tense.

She pulled her attention away from the three big weapons aimed at her and locked her gaze on the apparition of JT. He was, naturally, smirking at her.

"I bet I can find you," she said.

The smirk melted into a pinched expression.

She pointed toward the heavens. "You know, through the crossroads."

His eyes widened for an instant, but then the pinched look evaporated. "You wouldn't. Not with sweet David's life on the line."

He made the word sweet sound like a hideous insult. To him, it probably was.

She closed her eyes and let her mind float up, hovering a dozen feet above her body. As she looked down at her body, a feeling coursed through her, one she could only describe as a psychic shiver.

JT glared at her physical self as he clenched his hands into fists. "Come back or he dies. You have five seconds. Four, three…"

She hurled out a blast of energy that manifested as a hurricane-force wind. The gust spiraled out from her position, flipping the commandos off their feet one by one and flinging them backward through the air. By the time the spiraling gust hit David and Sean, they were flat on the ground, facedown in the sand. The commandos were slower to react—too slow. They sailed a good fifty feet and hit the ground hard enough to knock the sense out of them, if not render them unconscious. After circling their prey, the commandos had set down their lantern flashlights. Now, those lights sat on the ground unattended, forming a triangle around the three former prisoners and the mad man who wasn't there.

The apparition of JT roared with animalistic rage. "Waldron! Battaglia!"

A hundred feet away, just over the lip of the depression, a monster snarled.

No, not a monster. It was the mechanical snarling of a vehicle engine as it revved to scale an incline. A pair of headlights popped into view as the vehicle, still invisible in the darkness, hurtled over the summit and down the slope toward them.

She had her gun, but she couldn't shoot JT's apparition and shooting the approaching vehicle would do no good. She'd still have the men inside it to deal with.

She sank back into her body, opened her eyes, and shouted, "David, help me!"

As he sprang to his feet, David glanced at the vehicle and then at her. She nodded.

She felt him near her, though his body hadn't moved. His presence surrounded her and she opened herself up to him in a way she couldn't have imagined until last night. She let him into her mind. Their combined power surged through her, warm and sweet and crackling with energy. In unison, they switched their gazes to the onrushing vehicle.

The black SUV flipped into the air. It smacked into the ground upside down with a crunching thud. The windshield turned opaque as the safety glass cracked.

David's knees buckled but he didn't collapse. He hung there like a marionette, arms and legs limp, as if an unseen force clutched his neck. His face reddened as he struggled to breathe.

Ten feet away from David, the apparition of JT held up one arm with his fingers curled in a strangulation gesture. JT shook his hand and David jerked in response.

Grace resisted the urge to lunge forward, to help David, because the she moved all her muscles might give out completely. Ice-cold exhaustion flooded through her. The ground looked so inviting that it took all her strength to stay upright rather than dropping to the sand, curling up in a ball, and letting herself fall into the abyss of sleep.

JT shook David again. The choked sound that David grunted out snapped her out of her half sleep. She sucked in a couple deep breaths, swallowing enough oxygen to rouse her brain and body.

"The flash drive," JT said. "Or I snap his neck."

"It's not here, but I can tell you where to find it."

"Nice try." JT squeezed his astral hand and David gurgled from the increased pressure. "Like mother, like daughter. I'm not falling for that one again."

Pounding noises erupted from the upside-down SUV. Grace darted her eyes to look at the vehicle. Someone had kicked out the gummy, crackled sheet that had once been the windshield. A pair of legs hung out the opening.

Waldron slid out onto the sand. He looked disheveled, his face streaked with what might've been blood, and he also looked very, very angry.

Grace focused on JT again. "Don't you want my power? Isn't that what you really came for?"

A wild look came over his features. His grip on David loosened a little. She could tell because David's chest rose and fell as he drew in as much air as he could.

"You think you're stronger than me, right?" She spread her palms in an invitation. "So come and get it. Come and take my power."

Without letting go of David, JT turned the remainder of his psychic energy on her. She experienced it like a rip current dragging her mind down and down into a swirling emptiness. Gathering every iota of energy she had left, she clawed her way out of the invisible vortex. It hurt like hell. She gritted her teeth, clenched her hands, and gasped from the effort. Still she held on. Couldn't say how. Didn't know if she could keep it up for long.

David crumpled to the ground. Panting and wheezing, he pushed onto all fours.

JT had lost his grip.

The sucking sensation lessened, and she pulled her mind free of it.

The JT apparition bellowed. She squinted at him. He looked less solid now, though not quite transparent.

Over at the SUV, Battaglia had crawled out of the space where the windshield had been. He straightened and tried to walk, but staggered a few steps instead. His face was not merely streaked with blood, but virtually coated with it. As he stumbled away from the vehicle, falling to his knees in the sand, another figure rolled through the punched-out windshield.

It was JT. The real one.

The lantern flashlights cast a pallid glow on everyone, but JT looked so pale he could've doubled for Casper the ghost. He crawled away from the vehicle, and Waldron had to help him stand because Battaglia was having mobility problems of his own. Saddled with propping up his boss, Waldron could do little more than glare at Grace. JT was muttering to Waldron, and based on the look on the other man's face, she guessed JT was issuing orders that the bigger, stronger man did not want to follow. The duo trudged away from the SUV toward Grace, David, and Sean. The boy still lay unconscious on the ground.

The JT apparition stood motionless and dead.

His physical body went slack in Waldron's arms, forcing the other man to support the dead weight by hugging JT to him as he continued slogging through the sand.

The JT apparition came to life. He fixed a hateful scowl on Grace. Both of his faces, the real and the projected, shared the same deathly pallor.

"Why haven't you taken my power?" she asked with a scornful tone. "That's right, you're about as strong as a Pekingese that thinks it's a Great Dane."

He struck out at her psychically. She felt the hit like a blow to the gut—though not as strong a blow as she'd expected. Wincing, she shook her head.

"Is that all you got?" she said. "You're just a week little twerp with delusions of omnipotence."

He lashed out again, in a different way, falling back on the same trick he'd used in the tunnel. She saw herself pulling the gun out of her waistband, raising it in front of her to take aim at David, and finally pulling the trigger. Unlike the first time JT had tried this trick, the effect was like a ghost image rather than a vivid hallucination. While she watched the semitransparent vision of her hand perform the actions, she also saw her very solid and real hand remain at her side. Meanwhile, JT completely lost his grip on David, who'd sat back on his heels gasping. JT was getting weaker.

Waldron seemed to recognize what was happening. He halted, and his entire demeanor changed from annoyed and strained to something darker and far more determined. He let go of JT's limp, vacant body. JT crumpled to the ground.

Reaching inside his jacket, Waldron brought out his gun. He swung it up toward Grace.

David launched himself across the space between him and Waldron, at first running, then flinging his body through the air to tackle Waldron. Limbs flailed and grunts echoed.

Grace yanked the gun out of her waistband and took two steps toward the battling men.

Something smacked her in the chest with the force of a boot kick. It felt real, and it sent her staggering backward a few steps. Yet she knew the force that had struck her was psychic, not physical. JT's last gasp, in telekinetic terms. She kicked back at him with a force exponentially greater than what he'd lobbed at her. His apparition shattered and vanished.

His limp body, no longer vacant, stirred.

She had bigger problems.

Waldron had flipped David onto his stomach. Jamming one knee into David's spine, pinning him to the sand, Waldron settled the muzzle of his gun on the back of David's skull.

Grace curled her finger around the trigger of her own gun as she took aim at Waldron's back.

Arms clamped around her from behind, pinning her arms to her body and squeezing so hard she couldn't breathe. The gun tumbled from her grasp. The arms that restrained her lifted her up until only her tiptoes touched the ground. She gasped for air, flailing her legs at her assailant, but her ears began to ring and darkness began to close in around her.

"Quit fighting," Battaglia snarled into her ear, "and I'll let you breathe."

She really couldn't match his strength anyway. So she stopped fighting.

He loosened his grip enough to let her breathe. The ringing quieted and the darkness receded, giving her a clear view of David and Waldron.

"Now," Battaglia said, "you get to watch your boyfriend die."

Chapter Thirty

Grace looked around, searching for the other commandos. While some of them lay prone and unmoving where they'd landed, others had begun to stir. She really didn't need more problems. Now if she could just put them all to sleep the way David had done to her...

She didn't know how. And David couldn't help her. She sensed his diminished psychic energy. He looked awfully diminished on the physical level too.

Only one idea came to her. It was a bad one, she knew.

Waldron glanced over his shoulder to flash her an evil smile. Then he returned his attention to David and his body tensed, and she knew she was out of time.

So she did it.

A gust of hurricane strength blasted outward from a central point between her and Waldron. Battaglia flipped over backward, dragging her with him into a somersault. The momentum spun her out of Battaglia's grasp. She heard men screaming and bodies cracking as they hit the ground. Oh God, how many people had she killed?

No time to think about that. No time to think, period.

The instant she stopped rolling, she sprang to her feet and ran back toward where David and Waldron had been. They were gone. She spotted her gun, though, and snatched it up as she continued running.

Sean lay exactly where he had before. She stopped to crouch beside him and felt for a pulse in his neck. It surged under her fingers, strong and regular. She saw no blood or obvious injuries. There was nothing more she could do for him at the moment.

Rising, she turned in a circle to study her surroundings. The lantern flashlights had rolled and cast wedges of light in three different directions, leaving deep patches of darkness in between. She spotted a couple of the commandos, probably a hundred feet away, lying motionless on the ground. The wind blast must've thrown the other four even farther away, out of sight.

The screams. The crunching.

Her gorge rose in her throat. She gulped it down. Given the lighting conditions, the fact that she couldn't see the other commandos didn't mean the wind had flung them so far that they now lay in crumpled and broken heaps far in the distance.

Battaglia had come to rest a good fifty feet away, sprawled on his back, at the edge of one of the lantern beams.

She marched to the nearest lantern, plucked it off the ground, and swept the beam over the landscape.

There. She backtracked with the light. It flashed over a man-shaped lump on the sand. Not David. He'd been wearing a T-shirt and jeans. The man-lump was Waldron.

David and JT were nowhere in sight.

Too many bad guys, too many dangers. Dammit. If she had a way to disable Waldron and Battaglia, then at least she would have two less dangers to worry about.

Battaglia carried zip ties, which he used like handcuffs.

As much as she did not want to get within grappling distance of Battaglia, she sprinted across the distance to him and knelt beside the unconscious muscleman. He looked no less intimidating in this condition. Nevertheless, she rifled through his pockets until she discovered a clump of zip ties held together with a rubber band. She secured one of the ties around each of his ankles and connected the two with a third tie, forming a tight shackle. Next, she rolled him over onto his stomach and bound his hands behind his back with a single zip tie.

Satisfied that Battaglia couldn't chase after, she trotted over to Waldron and bound him in the same fashion. Tracking down every one of the six commandos so she could tie them up would take too much time. Besides, judging by the two she could see, the commandos seemed out of commission.

She had to find David. Traipsing through the darkness in search of him, even armed with a lantern light, left her more vulnerable than she liked. JT was out there too, after all. The last time she saw him he looked incapable of walking, much less attacking her—but she couldn't count on it. He might have another syringe in his pocket, chock-full of power-inducing drugs.

To find David remotely, she had one option. It left her vulnerable, possibly more so than marching off into the night. But she had no choice. It was the fastest method.

She launched her mind up into the crossroads, fast as a rocket. The void enveloped her, welcomed her. Two stars glimmered brighter than the rest. One was David—and the other, she knew, was JT. The stars hung close together.

Maybe that meant David and JT were close together in the physical world. She couldn't follow both paths, but try as she might, she couldn't feel which one led to David. Her mind was getting tired. She was getting tired. Her time was running out and she had to make a choice, albeit a blind one.

Down she went, plummeting faster and faster.

Then it stopped. She, her astral self, stood behind the overturned SUV. The indirect glow from the lantern light, the one she still held in her physical hand way over there, painted an eerie half light over the area. An arm's length from her, JT crouched under the rear tire with his back against the vehicle.

Wrong choice.

She wanted to fly out of there, to the crossroads, to take the other path and find David. Something tethered her here. The energy was draining out of her slowly but surely. How long she had, she didn't know. When her energy was gone, she would have no chance of finding David this way. And given how weak her body felt, finding him the old-fashioned way might not be an option anymore either.

JT moaned. His eyes were bloodshot. Deep shadows around his eyes gave them a sunken look. His hands trembled as he wiped a rivulet of sweat from his temple. He could neither see nor sense her. His hand fell to the ground, and then his entire body went limp. Though his lungs still pumped labored breaths, his eyes stared vacantly.

She started to leave, but the tether tugged at her again. No, not a tether. More like a beacon. A signal that pulsed in her soul. She followed it around the end of the vehicle—and froze.

David lay there, on his stomach, with one arm pinned beneath him and the other flung out to the side. He was facedown in the sand. A dark liquid dribbled from the back of his head.

No.

She raced toward him, falling to her knees at his side. When she stretched a hand out to touch him, it passed right through his flesh. This was no good. How could she make sure he was still alive when she couldn't touch him? How could she help him?

Dammit, she needed energy. And she needed it now. Right this second.

Was he breathing? She leaned close to his face, but through the pounding of her own heart she couldn't tell.

Now, now, now. She needed energy now.

Heat rushed through her. She felt woozy for a second as the world around her blurred and swirled. The motion stopped with a suddenness that shocked her. She knelt there for a few seconds, unable to think. Finally, she dropped her hands to her sides and curled her fingers into loose fists, scooping up handfuls of cool sand. Goose bumps prickled her arms in response to a breeze.

Her heart thudded. She looked down at her goose-bumpy flesh. Lifting her hands, she turned them so she could examine the fistfuls of sand contained in her palms. What the—

She dumped the sand and patted her arms, her hips, her thighs. They all felt real. Warm. Solid. Somehow, without even realizing it or meaning for it to happen, she had manifested. The question of how flitted through her mind, but she ignored it.

Slowly, she settled her hands on David's back. Contact. He felt warm and firm, yet soft, in a manlike way. When she pressed her fingers to his neck, a pulse throbbed against her skin. With great care, she palpated the wound on his head, parting the hair to get a better look. A scratch. It was just a scratch, one that bled profusely because of its location on the scalp. She let out the breath she'd been holding. He was alive and, unless he had another wound where she couldn't see it, he didn't appear badly hurt.

She laid a hand on his shoulder and shook it gently. He moaned. She took hold of him with both hands and, inch by inch, rolled him over onto his back. Sand clung to his face. She wiped it away. He made a little noise, halfway between a groan and a word.

Pain tore through her back. A scream lodged in her throat, choked off by the searing agony. Her back arched. Her muscles went rigid, and then gave out. She collapsed sideways.

A shadow draped over her as JT rose from his crouch behind her. He towered over her, his expression concealed by darkness, a bloody knife clutched in his hand.

He giggled with manic glee.

Pain. Hot and sharp and wet. It wasn't real. This body wasn't real.

It felt more real than any pain she'd ever felt before.

The mind is the body, David had said. *Whatever happens to your metaphysical body, also happens to your physical body.*

She had to get out of this body. Now.

JT raised the knife over his head. He plunged the blade down toward her chest.

Go, go, go. Her manifested body disintegrated with a pop. Like a hot air balloon cut loose from its moorings, she drifted upward. JT waved the knife through the air where she had been, his expression wild and confused. She floated ten feet above the scene.

And then she flew. At breakneck speed, she zipped through the crossroads and pitched downward to descend so quickly that the shift hit her like a physical force. Spinning. Falling. The pressure of speed wrung her like a wet towel. But it was nothing compared to the soul-crunching impact of returning to her own body.

Her knees buckled. She fell forward, throwing her hands out to brace herself. Although she recognized her surroundings, they lurched and twisted around her as if she stood on the deck of a fishing trawler during a category five hurricane. Nausea swelled inside her and she nearly vomited. Sweat ran down her face to dribble over her neck and chest, chilling her skin.

The spinning sensation decelerated. Bent over, held up by her trembling arms, she sucked in breath after breath and willed her senses to calm.

David. He was unconscious and alone with JT.

Who had a knife.

She felt a twinge in her back. It was nothing compared to what she'd felt the moment earlier, when JT stabbed her other self. But she had a horrible feeling that within moments the damage to her psychically generated body would catch up with her real body. She must help David before that happened.

A hard object lay beneath her right hand. She glanced down, felt a bitter smile curve her lips, and clenched her hand around the grip of her gun.

Through sheer force of will, David peeled his eyelids apart. It felt like a Herculean effort. Everything was blurry. He blinked until his vision cleared.

JT stood over him wielding a bloody knife.

David felt his body awakening, though not fast enough.

JT raised the knife high and thrust it downward.

A shot boomed.

JT jerked, dropped the knife, and toppled onto David. The knife plunged tip first into the sand inches from David's neck. JT's lifeless body lay draped over David's torso. A dark stain had spread outward from the gunshot wound in JT's back.

David shoved the dead man off himself. He scrambled to his knees, and then pushed up onto his feet. He spotted his savior twenty feet away, past the front bumper of the SUV. David smiled as Grace slowly lowered her gun.

Then she collapsed.

He bolted past the vehicle and straight to her. As he cradled her in his arms, he felt the warm wetness soaking into the back of her shirt. Shit.

Lifting her carefully, he carried her across the open expanse to where Sean lay unconscious. He settled Grace down on the ground beside the boy. Sean could heal her. If David could wake him. The boy was alive, he could tell that much.

David grasped Sean by the shoulders and shook. The boy's head lolled. David slapped Sean's face. The boy's eyelids fluttered, opened for a split second, and drifted shut again.

A sensation of static electricity washed over David. He recognized the feeling of psychic energy pulsing and crackling in the air. Letting go of Sean, he turned to Grace. The energy. The rising power.

It was coming from her.

Chapter Thirty-One

Everything around her seemed remote and detached, as if she sat inside a hermetically sealed capsule ten miles away, watching the scene through a telescope. As her eyelids drifted closed, she glimpsed David's anguished expression. It triggered no emotion in her. She couldn't feel anything, either physically or emotionally. She was a free-floating spirit.

She was dying. The realization came to her, but still she felt nothing.

Her mind, her spirit, floated through a multicolored mist. Without form. Without attachment. Without anything that had made her human, that had made her…her.

Something tugged at her. It held her in place, though she wanted to float higher and farther. A feeling pierced the numbness, pricking her like a needle. She tried to pull away from the tether, but it refused to let her go. *He* refused to let her go. David was speaking to her, and though she couldn't hear his words, she felt them tugging at her, felt him begging her not to leave. She couldn't do this. She couldn't go. As good as it felt to float away, she had to fight it.

Energy surged through her like a bone-jarring shiver. In its wake trailed a tingling warmth that scoured away the numbness. Pain struck her hard, convulsing every muscle in her body, and then it faded away. A new feeling coursed through her very essence, a sensation of clear and infinite knowledge. It burned bright for an instant, only to vanish as quickly as it had overcome her.

She opened her eyes.

David, kneeling beside her, stared down at her with an expression of unbridled awe. A few feet away, Sean had sat up and now gazed at her with an identical expression.

Grace pushed up onto her elbows. What the hell was wrong with them?

The back of her shirt felt wet and sticky. Blood, she realized, and her heart skipped a beat. Oh right, she'd been stabbed in the back, and not metaphorically. She felt fine now. Strong, actually. Healthy and right and—

David leaned forward, bracing himself with one hand. He ducked his head over her shoulder to peer down at her backside. Straightening, he gazed at her with a more subdued, but still awestruck, expression on his face.

"You healed yourself," he said in a breathless voice.

"Huh." It was all she could think of to say.

David glanced at Sean, who looked quite well now, and then swiveled his head to take in the panorama around them. As she pushed up into a sitting position, Grace followed his gaze. In the distance, the commandos had begun to rouse. They sat or crouched, scratching their heads and palpating formerly injured body parts.

Formerly injured. Why had she thought that? They couldn't have magically healed.

She had.

The truth sliced through her on a sharp chill.

David met her gaze and nodded. "That's right. You healed yourself and Sean and me. You healed everyone."

"Everyone?" The word came out as a squeaky whisper. She gathered up the tattered remnants of her composure, cleared her throat, and said, "How did I do that?"

David shrugged.

"I thought you knew everything about this psychic stuff," she said. "If you don't know, then I really don't have a clue."

His lips twisted into a partial frown. He looked at the ground.

He knew something—or thought he did. She slid closer to him, and her hand bumped into her gun, which lay on the ground beside her. Clambering onto her knees, she sat back on her heels. Their faces were inches apart.

"Tell me," she said.

He sighed and lifted his head to look at her. "You won't like it."

Planting her hands on her hips, she said, "Tell me anyway."

"I think you tapped into the Golden Power." She must've looked as startled as she felt, because his expression softened and he reached out to grasp her shoulders. "Think about it. How else could you have healed not only yourself but everyone in the vicinity? Sean can only heal others, not himself, and only when he's in intimate proximity to them." He smiled. "You healed everyone—including yourself."

She stretched out her hand to run it through his hair, feeling for the scratch that had bled so copiously moments earlier. It was gone.

Wow.

She brushed her fingers across his cheek and let them settle on his lips. She whispered, "Just don't ask me to do it again. I have no idea how I did it in the first place."

He smiled against her fingers.

She let her hand drop to her side.

"What did it feel like?" he asked. "Tapping into that power."

Clear and infinite knowledge. Oh yes, she remembered that feeling vividly. The certainty. The completeness. The power.

A cold rock settled in her gut. Whatever she'd tapped into had given her more than infinite knowledge. It had given her infinite power, at least temporarily. If JT had succeeded...

But he hadn't. And all of JT's research, contained on the flash drive, belonged to her now. She would destroy it as soon as she got home. The threat was over.

No.

She grabbed the gun, leaped to her feet, and fired twice.

Twenty feet away, Waldron had just raised his own weapon and taken aim at David. Instead of exacting his revenge, however, he collapsed onto the sand—dead. She'd shot him twice in the chest. He'd raised only his head and one arm to surreptitiously take aim. From her vantage point, David had completely blocked her view of Waldron. She hadn't seen him lifting his gun. She hadn't heard it either, because he made no sound. Some fragment of the infinite knowledge she'd touched had stayed with her, and warned her of Waldron's attack.

At least that was her theory.

She marched past David and straight to Waldron. His eyes were open and blank, devoid of life. A small pocket knife lay open on the ground beside his body. He had apparently managed to get it out of his pocket—his back pocket, she presumed—and cut himself free of the zip ties. She and David had been a little distracted by her almost dying and then healing herself and everyone in the vicinity. For all she knew, she'd inadvertently healed Waldron too, giving him the ability to make his attempt on David's life. If Waldron had succeeded, she had no doubt she would've been next.

I healed everyone.

A chill whispered over her neck, raising the hairs. She sprinted toward Battaglia. He was still bound, though he writhed on the ground in a vain effort to tear free of his restraints.

He spotted the gun in her hand. His face blanched. He stopped wriggling.

She tapped the gun against her thigh.

"Please," Battaglia whined. "Don't kill me. I was just doing my job."

She had no intention of killing a helpless man, but he clearly thought everyone was as nasty as he was. Given his current state of groveling, however, he possessed neither the ruthless determination of Xavier Waldron nor the maniacal drive of Jackson Tennant.

David came up beside her. He glanced at her gun and then at Battaglia.

The trussed-up commando whimpered.

Shaking his head, David said, "He's not worth a bullet. He's a coward underneath it all."

"I know." Grace tucked the gun inside her waistband. "We should go before his buddies snap out of their confusion and come for him."

"How do you suggest we get out of here?"

"In the car."

He stared at her. After a couple seconds, he slowly turned to look in the direction of the overturned SUV.

Except it wasn't overturned anymore.

The SUV sat upright, tires on the sand. The top was a little banged up, the windshield was missing, and the other windows were cracked. But she knew—she just *knew*—the vehicle would hold together long enough to get them out of here.

"You did that?" David asked, in a surprisingly calm tone.

She shrugged.

Though she didn't remember doing it and hadn't consciously known she'd done it, some part of her had known. When David asked how they would get out of here, the answer popped into her brain.

Without a word, David took her hand and led her to the SUV. Sean trailed along behind them. They had to crawl through the windshield to get inside the vehicle. Sean went first, wriggling between the front seats to get into the back. David took the driver's seat, leaving Grace as the passenger. When David saw there were no keys in the ignition, he started to ask a question. Grace cut him off with a wave of her hand, although she hadn't intended the gesture to silence him. Instead she had, without thinking about it, waved her hand in the direction of the car's engine.

The engine grumbled to life.

David said nothing. He simply shifted the car into drive, executed a U-turn, and headed up over the rim of the depression and onto the flat desert floor.

"Which way?" he asked.

She pointed, and he followed her direction without hesitation.

The lingering knowledge and energy from whatever source she'd tapped into was beginning to drain away. She felt it. Oh well. It had been borrowed power anyway. But even as the power boost faded, a fragment of knowledge stuck with her. It glistened like a diamond in her mind.

"Where should we go?" David asked.

"I know where my grandfather is," she answered. "We're going to get him."

Chapter Thirty-Two

The clunky, beat-up SUV somehow made it all the way back into town. They rented a nondescript sedan and headed out of town in the direction Grace indicated. David drove. Grace hunched in the passenger seat, stiff as a crash test dummy, fighting desperately to hold on to the knowledge of her grandfather's whereabouts. With each passing moment, she felt the information slipping away from her.

She leaned sideways to glance at the speedometer. It read sixty-five miles per hour.

"Drive faster," she hissed.

David floored the accelerator. The car lurched forward, and she watched the speedometer surge upward.

Without looking at David, she murmured, "Thank you."

"You're welcome."

She chanced a sideways look at him and caught his amused expression. "What's so funny?"

"Nothing."

"Hmm." Spotting a T intersection up ahead, she said, "Turn left."

David braked with caution and veered left onto a paved road with two narrow lanes and virtually no shoulder. They'd left Reston a couple hours earlier, abandoning civilization to drive deep into a wilderness populated with towering pine trees and little else. Though they passed the occasional overgrown two-track driveway, they saw no other signs of human occupation.

Still, David followed her instructions without question.

She relaxed her death grip on the edges of her seat. Glancing at David sideways, she asked, "Are you always going to do whatever I say?"

He chuckled. She supposed that substituted for a response. She supposed she knew the answer to the question anyway. Until today, David had done almost nothing that she told him to do. He was following her orders now because he recognized that she'd acquired some extraordinary, if temporary, knowledge that they needed right now. She shouldn't count on him bending to her will on an everyday basis. Not that she would really want him to. Life would get pretty boring if he always acquiesced to her.

The paved road petered out into gravel. Grace instructed David to make a couple more turns, onto two-track roads that got bumpier and bumpier. As she began to seriously consider duct taping her teeth to her jaw, the trees opened out into a little clearing. The two track dead-ended at a rough-looking cabin nestled amid the trees. The windows were boarded up. A generator hunkered alongside the cabin, apparently powered by a nearby propane tank.

David parked the car near the cabin's front door. After climbing out through the car's nonexistent windshield, Grace walked a few yards away and bent her head back to stare up at the trees. There, high above, a small satellite dish sat mounted to the top of a tree.

Inside the car, Sean started to climb into the front seat, heading toward the open windshield. David, halfway out of the car, leaned his head back in to whisper something to Sean. The boy nodded and climbed into backseat again. David strode toward Grace.

"Well?" he said.

"The windows and doors are electrified," she told him. "Do you know how to turn off a generator?"

"Yes. You're sure there's no backup power source?"

"Positive."

David marched toward the generator. Within a few minutes, he accomplished his task and returned to her side. The cabin looked the same. No lights had been visible before, thanks to the boarded-up windows.

"Guards?" David asked.

She shook her head. "A male nurse with a gun. He would've seen us coming, but I, um...convinced him otherwise."

David's eyebrows rose. "From a distance?"

She gave him a sheepish smile. "Uh-huh."

He looked impressed and a little mystified. She felt mystified too. When she'd manipulated someone's mind before, it had taken an enormous amount of concentration and willpower. Today, the same task had taken almost no effort and she accomplished it from quite a distance, without even thinking about it really. She simply knew it needed to be done and did it. Of course, the level of thought projection required was swiftly eroding the last of her enhanced power. Soon it would slip away from her completely—along with the vast, eerie knowledge she'd obtained.

David strode up to the front door, twisted the knob, and thrust it inward. A thirtyish man dressed in a flannel shirt and blue jeans leaped up from his chair. He didn't even think to reach for the gun strapped to his hip. Grace made sure of that. The final effort triggered a sharp, though not intense, pain behind her eyes.

Rushing forward, David grabbed the nurse's gun and forced the man to sit down again. The nurse glared at David with a mixture of confusion, anger, and fear. David stared back at the man with such intensity that the nurse squirmed in his seat. Then, as if someone had flipped a switch inside his brain, the nurse slumped against the wall and his eyelids drifted shut. He was asleep. And, Grace knew, someone *had* essentially flipped a switch in the man's brain. It hadn't been her, though. David had taken care of the task. He'd put the man to sleep, exactly like he'd done to her once.

Grace stepped across the threshold into the cabin. They stood inside a narrow entryway that dead-ended to the right, but to the left, it opened into a dimly lit room. She could see a sliver of the room beyond. David led the way, swinging rightward into the room. Grace walked a couple yards into the room and froze.

Nestled against the far wall, covered with a blanket, lay a human-shaped lump. The gray-haired man beneath the blanket sat up, yawned, and smiled at her.

"Grandpa," she whispered, afraid to say the word too loudly for fear she would wake up from the dream. But this wasn't a dream. She knew that with a certainty that came not from her brush with the Golden Power, but from her heart and soul.

Tears stung her eyes and rolled down her cheeks. Edward McLean looked relatively healthy, though a little disheveled and in need of a shave and haircut. David hurried over to Edward and helped the older man to his feet.

Grace ran toward the men. She flung her arms around her grandfather and hugged him fiercely. When she stepped back, dropping her arms to her sides, he reached out to pat her shoulder.

"I gather it's over," he said to her. "JT is—"

"Gone," Grace said.

"And the flash drive?"

"I mailed it to myself, to keep it away from JT and his goons. But once I get it, I'm going to destroy it."

David cleared his throat. "Maybe you shouldn't."

She glanced at him sideways. "Excuse me? People died for that damn thing. It needs to be thrown into an erupting volcano so no one else can get their hands on JT's research. It's too dangerous."

"David's right," her grandfather said. "You shouldn't destroy it. JT established multiple research sites around the world, which means he may have been holding more innocent people hostage."

"And there's Tesler," David said. "He escaped. Meaning he's free to torture those others."

"The information on the flash drive is our only means of finding them and Tesler." Sighing, Edward ran a hand through his hair. "It was our research—mine, Christine's, and Mark's—that helped JT find, capture, and terrorize these people. It's my responsibility to set things right."

Grace shook her head. "You didn't know what would happen. And you didn't willingly hand over your research to JT and his minions."

"It doesn't matter. I still have to fix this."

She bit her lip, and in a matter of two seconds, she made up her mind. A quick look at David told her he'd guessed what she was thinking and he agreed wholeheartedly.

"Okay then," she said, squaring her shoulders and lifting her chin. "David and I will help you. After all, you'll need a couple of psychic weirdos on your side."

"I prefer extrasensory perceptives," David said.

She made a face. "You made that up, didn't you?"

He smirked.

"Well," Edward said, "I'd prefer granddaughter and grandson-in-law."

He shoved a hand into his pants pocket and brought out a sparkly object, which he proffered to Grace. She took the object. It was a gold ring capped with a small diamond.

Her grandfather winked at her. "I've been holding onto that for you."

Grace closed her hand around the ring, shielding it inside her palm. "Can we get out of here please?"

David led them out of the murky room and down the short entryway. At the threshold, Grace hesitated. She looked back at the nurse slumped in his chair.

"What about him?" she asked.

"He'll wake up in a little while," David said. "When I was shutting down the generator, I saw his car parked out back. He'll be fine."

"Maybe we should call the cops and get these bastards arrested."

"We can't explain anything that happened. No one would believe it and we have no evidence to support our claims."

"The facility…"

"JT may be dead, but his company is still alive. Even if they didn't know what he was up to out in the desert, I'm sure they'll come up with a reasonable explanation for everything. Corporations love to obscure the truth and subvert the law."

She frowned. The pain behind her eyes was growing into a headache.

David took her hand and squeezed it. "We stopped a homicidal madman. I'd say that's a pretty good day's work." He nodded toward her grandfather, who now stood beside the car. "And we saved a very important life."

She felt the frown relaxing into a smile. He was right.

David led her toward the car. Halfway there, she tugged his hand to stop him.

He turned to face her, his brow furrowed.

She held the ring out to him. He took it, and bowing his head, muttered, "You don't want it anymore."

"No, that's not it." She grinned. "I love you too."

His head jerked up. He stared at her in shock for a few seconds, and then his lips parted in a grin that matched hers for giddiness.

She held out her left hand. He slipped the ring onto her finger.

A thread of fear pulled tight inside her. "What if I never get my memory back? I can't even remember how we met—"

"I can tell you anything you want to know." He touched her cheek. "And we can make new memories."

She opened her mouth to protest, but she didn't get the chance. He pulled her into his arms and kissed her with a passion and enthusiasm that burned out all her anxiety and melted away her headache.

They got in the car and drove away. In the rearview mirror, the forest swallowed up the little cabin. Everything it represented dwindled away along with it. The past receded into the distance as the road ahead became clearer, brighter, and smoother. She was no longer speeding headlong into darkness. Now, she rode into the light. Into the future. Into the unknown.

And for the first time in her life, that didn't bother her at all.